The Pepper in the Gumbo

By

Mary Jane Hathaway

Cover art provided by Steven Novak

Editing provided by Kathryn Frazier

Dedications

To Mrs. Gaskell, who wrote her books standing in the kitchen, while her five children ran through the house. Your romances captivated a generation. Your passion for social justice shaped my moral code. *North and South*, the story of a ruthless mill owner and a fiery minister's daughter, will live forever in the hearts of your readers.

To Elizabeth Barrett Browning, who wrote some very fine love poetry, but considered her life's work to be fighting child labor even though she lived in a time that didn't allow women a political voice. Virginia Woolf said it best when she said, "Elizabeth Barrett Browning rushed into the drawing room and declared that here, where we live and work, is the true place for the poet. The heroine's passionate interest in social questions, her conflict as artist and woman, her longing for knowledge and freedom, is the true heroine of her age."

Also to Christalee Scott May, who will never stop trying to bring me into the twenty-first century.

Chapter One

If we continue to develop our technology without wisdom or prudence,
our servant may prove to be our executioner.
—Omar N. Bradley

"Van Winkle, scoot. You're taking up half the desk."

Alice Augustine brushed aside piles of receipts and set down her steaming cup of coffee, but the sleeping gray cat didn't budge from his spot in the sun. Alice gently slid the kitty to the left and angled into her chair. She loved Mondays, loved the pale light of early morning illuminating her workspace, loved the way her little bookstore creaked and rustled like an old lady waking up from a long winter's nap. Or at least, she loved every Monday other than the last Monday of the month. Then it was sixteen kinds of terrible.

Balancing the accounts was becoming an unpleasant task. That far column of red numbers was growing at an alarming rate. She pulled her cardigan tighter against the unseasonable late-summer chill, and reminded herself that the store survived the last ten years of economic downturn and it wasn't going to fail now. Not on her watch. Not after Mr. Perrault kept it afloat for fifty years and made it one of the most famous bookstores in Louisiana.

Opening her laptop, she took a slow breath, letting gratitude for the place win over the nagging worries that fought for her attention. Her store was in the National Historic Landmark District, a local treasure at the very end of the thirty-three block stretch along Cane River. The rows of tidy shelves showcased the best in rare and vintage volumes. Customers traveled from around the state to spend the day in By the Book, sharing stories of the eccentric former owner, Mr. Perrault, and his wife, Angeline. Alice was proud to be the owner and so very grateful for every day she came to work. Usually.

Mr. Perrault. Alice paused, waiting for the ache in her chest to ebb. Mr. Perrault, the man who didn't snap at a surly teen girl who wandered into his bookshop and argued that Elizabeth Barrett Browning should not be placed next to her husband Robert just because they shared a name. He didn't laugh, even when she said Robert Browning was an overeducated blowhard whose collection should be used as a doorstop. No, Mr. Perrault spoke to her as if she were a poetry expert and a person. He took notes, offered her coffee, and asked her to come back to chat. Alice had spent so long being angry that she didn't even notice for the first six months of Saturday literary debates that she'd made a friend. She wasn't just the annoying little sister of four boys, all being raised by their grandmother and haunted by the accident that took their parents.

She could never get away from the pitying glances of the people of her small town. Natchitoches was one of the oldest communities in the south, and the people made it their duty to never forget anything, good or bad. Alice was not just Alice. She was "poor, sweet Alice, whose parents are dead." But not to Mr. Perrault and not to his wife. With them, Alice felt like she was someone apart from all of that, someone who had read more widely than anyone she knew. To them, she was a reader and a friend.

Mondays always made her pensive and she slipped the fragile chain out from her shirt, touching the two gold rings that hung there. Those simple, plain gold bands had once signified the marriage of her parents and the unity of her family.

"Darcy, come on down. You'll get all dusty," she said more from tradition than any real expectation that he would listen. Darcy didn't answer to anyone. The large black cat stayed high up, his perfect pink nose in the air. He came down to eat only after the other cats had wandered away. He was happy there, far above the fray, and there was no reason to coax him down. Her employees poked fun at Darcy's antisocial habits, but Alice felt a secret kinship with him.

A bright tinkle sounded from the little brass bell that hung from a faded red velvet ribbon on the door.

"Good morning," Alice called out. She added a wave although old Bix Beaulieu was so nearsighted he wouldn't know the difference. In fact, he shouldn't be driving himself to work. Somehow he kept passing his renewal test. Alice harbored a strong suspicion that had something to do with Bix's great niece working at the DMV. Like a moving landmark, it had been the cruel end of nativity scenes, award-winning rose bushes, and too many pink flamingos to count. The people of Natchitoches had learned to watch out for Bix and his bright green Cadillac of Doom.

"Mornin', *sha*," he called back. It made her smile to hear him use the endearment her Papa used. Alice was always "dear" to Bix. Stark white bristles sprouted from under his old straw hat, and his World War II, Navy-issue raincoat was buttoned to his chin. It hardly ever rained, but

Bix hated to be unprepared. "I thought I'd come in early and rearrange those bottom shelves of paperbacks."

"Would you like some coffee?" Alice could think of ten things more worthwhile than rearranging the paperback section. Customers sorted through them like folded T-shirts on sale at the mall. It was a waste of time to even put them on the shelves. She should just shovel them in mountains labeled *Romance*, *Thrillers*, and *Mysteries*, and not worry any more about it. But Bix did what he liked, when he liked. It could be aggravating, but Alice loved it a little bit, too.

"Thanks, but I got a cup at The Red Hen." Bix placed a paper bag on the desk and Alice inhaled the heavenly scent of fresh beignets. The Red Hen served hot Beau Monde coffee and the area's best bakery items. Bix's dark brown eyes crinkled at the edges, his face creased with a grin. "I figured you'd appreciate a little pick-me-up while you crunch the numbers."

Alice murmured her thanks as she opened the bag. She hated that Bix knew the bookstore was losing money. The man was pretty observant for being nearly blind.

"Louis asked after you," Bix said.

Alice took a large bite of still-warm beignet and chewed slowly. Louis Guillorie was balding, short-tempered, twice her age, and most definitely not Alice's idea of a romantic partner. The day she graduated high school, he'd asked her out by telling her he had a thing for green-eyed Creole girls. She'd almost cried, trying to let him down easy, afraid to bruise his ego. After nearly ten years of searching for the gentlest way to get through, she decided it wasn't her problem if he wouldn't face the facts. Now she just pretended the owner of The Red Hen didn't exist. It was a whole lot easier than feeling guilty about hurting his feelings.

"Wanted to know if you were still seeing that short Yankee with the horsey laugh."

"He's not short. He's three inches taller than I am." Eric was a perfectly nice guy who made great money as the area's only dentist. She didn't argue about him being a Yankee or the laugh. Eric didn't laugh much, so she could almost forget about his unfortunate affliction.

"I told him to bide his time. Horse boy won't last long. He don't even take you out. A girl's gotta get out of the house once in a while." Bix took off his straw hat and unbuttoned his coat, as if he weren't being rude in the slightest.

"He's lasted four months," Alice said. "And I'm a homebody. I don't mind." Eric was more than a little boring, but she was no rock star herself. Her *mamere* called her curvy, but that was just a nice way for her grandmother to say Alice loved beignets a little too much and didn't love exercise quite enough. Her hair was so curly it had a life of its own, her mouth was a little too wide, and she wouldn't ever be called anything more than pretty. Add in the fact that she owned too many cats and a bookstore that was hemorrhaging money, and Alice figured she wasn't one to point fingers.

"You've got to get out more, especially since you're up there all alone now. I felt better when that family was living in the other half. This is such a big old place. You could slip in that claw-foot tub, crack your head, and nobody would find you for days."

Alice tried to ignore the visual that popped into her mind. "A possibility, I suppose." If she fell and hit her head while getting in the tub, she certainly wouldn't want her neighbors to come rescue her. Then again, she couldn't think of a single person who would be really right for that job.

A short-haired tabby crossed the floor toward the back door, sending a glance at Bix that seemed to say she was highly offended but would suffer silently, as usual. "Jane Eyre wanted one of those maple-cured bacon slices you brought last time," Alice interpreted. "And Eric is a perfectly nice boy, whether or not he likes to go out."

"Boy. See? There's your problem. You need a man," Bix said, punctuating the phrase with a thump of the chest, his wrinkles magnified with a scowl. It would have been funny if he hadn't been so serious. "Louis wants to take you to the zydeco festival this weekend. He sure is sweet on you."

Alice loved zydeco music and the festival ranked as one of her favorite parties of the year. Her parents had met at a dance hall, her *mamere* sang in a juke band when she was young, and Alice had been listening to zydeco all her life. She could probably dance the crazy combination of swing and foxtrot in her sleep. But although Eric vowed he'd rather drill his own teeth than go, Alice wasn't about to accept Louis's invitation. "Yes, I'm aware. Well, we better get —"

"You could do worse than Louis, you know. He makes a mean croissant, and he's a morning person. My first wife was a bear in the morning. I love me some passion, and I gotta have a woman who puts a little pepper in the gumbo, but I didn't make that morning mistake twice. When she passed away and I was ready to look again, I said to myself, 'Bix, you get yourself a woman who won't bite your head off if you talk to her before noon.' Of course, Ruby is always real affectionate in the mornings so I had to adjust to—"

"Oh my, look at that dust!" Alice swiped a hand over the bookcase next to her. She cringed at the awkward interruption, but didn't want to hear any more about Ruby's morning affections. Every Sunday morning, nine o'clock, Ruby and Bix sat in front of Alice at the cathedral. If she heard any more, she would never be able to look the woman in the eye again.

"Dusty? That reminds me. My niece asked if you needed someone to come pass the mop once a week or so.

She started a cleaning business all by herself called *Nettie's Nettoyage*. She's got five employees and two big vans. Maybe you seen them," Bix said.

Alice glanced around. She would have died of embarrassment if anyone told her that By the Book was dirty, but apparently she'd just said as much herself and there wasn't any way to deny it. "I suppose. Maybe I don't even see it anymore. I'm thinking it's clean while the dirt is just staring me in the face. You can give her my cell phone number."

"I already did. She said you never answer. I explained how you're against modern inventions."

"I am not," Alice protested. "You can't possibly say that when I'm sitting in front of a laptop. I just believe all this technology has a place."

"And that place is not in your pocket, right?" Bix smiled. "Everything here is outdated. Just look at that radio. It's ancient."

Alice laid a protective hand on the faded red radio. "This is a 1955 Admiral. People pay a lot of money for these."

"Mm-hmm. And they pay more for something with stereo. My grandson has a little gizmo that holds fifteen hundred songs and fits in his pocket."

Technology was meant to be a tool, not a crutch. The entire world had become dependent on gadgets for entertainment and personal happiness. But it was silly to argue with a man who was wearing a raincoat he got in 1944. Instead, Alice pulled out a folded sheet of newspaper from under the stack of receipts. "I'm not against the digital age, I'm really not. See here?" She tapped the headline and several inches of column underneath. "There's some guy who's uploading rare books to digital e-book platforms. People are rediscovering the classics, poetry, old myths."

Bix cocked his head, the light reflecting off his thick glasses. "Those books have always been around. You go to any ol' tag sale and you'll find a bunch of old college textbooks."

"Right. At tag sales. Not when you need them and not in perfect condition. If they're copyrighted, they're usually in print. If not, they can be impossible to find. Anyway, this guy, he scans them, checks for formatting issues, writes a bit of a commentary, and puts them online." She leaned over the article and read aloud, "An e-book of lesser known works by the poet Gerard Manley Hopkins was published last month was received enthusiastically and shot to the top of the bestseller lists."

"Well, it seems like that's a fine thing to do, if you've got the time and the inclination. He must be an old guy like me with not much to do," Bix said.

Alice scanned the article again. "Not sure. He uses a pen name, Browning Wordsworth Keats." Alice smiled. She liked him already. "He also runs a website where people go to talk about their favorite authors and old books. Nobody really knows who he is. Which isn't unusual, is it? Technology has made us just a bunch of profile pictures we can grab from anywhere."

Bix shrugged. "Sounds like a smart move. He does this long enough and he's going to run into someone who's not happy about him making money off their great-great-grandpappy's poetry."

"Or great-great-grandmama's poetry. He also just put up a collection of the works of women poets. Christina Rosetti, St. Therese of Lisieux, Hildegard of Bingen. He definitely went past the Brontes."

"Sounds like one of those books with just the good stuff. You know, only the pieces you like in a five-inch anthology." Bix scratched his chin. "Maybe you should get one of those e-readers."

Alice had been thinking the same thing, but she slowly put the newspaper back on the desk. "I have a whole bookstore. I don't need to buy an e-reader for just one book." This is how it starts. One piece of seemingly harmless tech and the next thing you know, you can't go anywhere without it. You get lazy and just download a copy instead of finding the book on the shelf. And the finding is half the fun. Browsing on either side, above and below, that is the joy of it.

"You don't know until you try it. You could really be missing out. I'd get one, but I suppose I wouldn't be able to see the print on a screen any better than on a page." Alice felt her heart squeeze at the thought. Even large print was too small for Bix now. "I just figure, if I don't need it then I won't miss it." Alice tugged a few more receipts out from under Van Winkle's midsection and reopened the Excel page. "*Mais*, I better get started here."

"Me, too. I'm meeting Ruby for lunch. But where is Miss Elizabeth?" A few seconds later, a soft meow announced the arrival of the sleek calico. She stepped gracefully into view and Bix bent down, reaching out with both hands. "Up you go, *Mamzelle*. We have work to do."

Bix headed toward the back room, Elizabeth perched on his shoulder, staring at Alice with bright eyes that always seemed quietly amused. Bix talked as he worked, and Alice could hear the kitty answer back every now and then, as if in complete agreement. They were a pair, those two. Alice couldn't imagine one without the other, even though someday... She hurriedly grabbed a few receipts. She didn't have her head in the sand. People moved away, moved on. They died. She was perfectly aware that someday Bix would be gone and she would have to hire new help. But not now, not today.

A yowl made her jump in her chair and she turned to hush the Siamese cat who trotted after Bix. "Mrs. Bennet, stop your fussing." As long as Mrs. Bennet stuck close to Miss Elizabeth, she was fairly content, but the moment they were separated, headache-inducing protests began. The cat had the most annoying screech, but Alice couldn't bear to send her away. She knew the bookstore had a few more than normal. To be honest, quite a few more cats than anyplace she'd ever been to, but they were her family now.

When they discussed books, Mr. Perrault used the Louisiana French that she heard at home when she was little, never correcting her or becoming frustrated when she didn't know a word. Mrs. Perrault began to invite her upstairs to their apartment for dinner, then gradually extended the invitation to the hours before dinner, when all the cooking was being done. Alice watched at first, fascinated by the slow, methodical steps of Creole cooking. Within months, she could make jambalaya, gumbo, and Natchitoches meat pies by heart.

She didn't realize until years later that the books were secondary to all the other things she'd learned. The Perraults gave her what had been lost when her parents died. Alice straightened up and blinked back tears. It had been eight years since Mrs. Perrault had passed, and five years since Alice and Mr. Perrault last shared a cup of tea. No use crying over them now. He would never want that. He would want her to work hard and keep By the Book a success, like it had always been. No matter how many people turned to other entertainment, he'd been sure that bookstores would never become extinct. It was all that separated the civilized and sophisticated from the unwashed, ignorant hordes. As long as there were enlightened people in the world, the rising tide of frivolous technology would not prevail. He'd believed it with his whole heart.

As for Alice, she had a healthy streak of pessimism to remind her that surviving and thriving were two very different things. The last Monday of every month told her clearly the bookstore was not thriving. It became even more apparent when the renter in the second apartment above the store moved out. The historic district was the chic place to live and the hefty rent helped By the Book break even. Without it, she was in real trouble.

She opened the laptop and waited for it to warm up. Although she hated Excel with everything in her, the day she'd driven off with the ledger on top of the car and lost several years' worth of records, Alice had to concede that there might be a better way than pencil and paper.

She took a sip of coffee and squared her shoulders. No more dragging fanny. First, balance the books. Then, notify the realtor the apartment was available again. Better to get it done than to put it off. Her friends called her a "go getter," others called her "impulsive," but Alice considered herself a practical woman, simply doing what needed to be done. Reaching for the first receipt, her hand paused in mid-air, hovering like a Frisbee before descent, as she spied a large, black cat on the top of a bookshelf.

She brought up the accounting sheets as a long-haired tabby wandered across the store and settled at her feet. She reached down and gave him a scratch, whispering, "Mr. Rochester, everyone has it wrong. I'm not against all technology. I just prefer to keep things simple."

Mr. Rochester sat silent, as he always did. He wasn't much of a talker and his temper was legendary. He tolerated a pat or two, but if you rubbed him the wrong way, you'd feel his claws. The others cats walked out of their way rather than cross Mr. Rochester. But he did like the females. Before he became a resident of By the Book, he sat in the alleyway and yowled at all hours. His tattered left ear was a souvenir of those tomcat years. Alice felt a little guilty for luring him into a friendship when she fully intended to take away his masculinity, but when Mr. Rochester returned from the vet, he seemed calmer and happier. His shaggy fur even seemed a little more groomed and the wildness in his eyes faded. And Alice slept better, so the guilt didn't weigh too heavily.

She peeked at Bix to make sure he wasn't looking, then clicked onto the Internet. She needed to work, but she was curious. A quick search the Browning Wordsworth Keats blog. She expected to see book covers and links, but the site seemed designed as a meeting place for literature enthusiasts. Alice glanced at her desk clock. She'd give herself three minutes. Then, back to work.

Thirty minutes later, Alice closed the page. She'd registered an account, joined four different groups, left fifteen comments, and entered into two rather fierce debates over whether or not typewriters changed writing for the better. Sitting back in her chair, she let out a long breath. BWK, as she now thought of him, was brilliant. He knew books, loved books, and probably owned a bookstore. She'd wasted several minutes staring at his profile, but not because of the strong, stubbled jaw just visible under a lowered black fedora. There was an out-of-focus glimpse of his bookshelf. Alice zoomed in and tried to read the titles on the spines.

She had almost puzzled out the first row when the brass bell sounded and a short, teenaged girl burst through. "Miss Alice, I need you for a sec," she called.

"Hi Charlie," Alice said. "You're not scheduled until this afternoon." Charlene Soule wouldn't answer to anything except Charlie since she'd turned eighteen and decided it wasn't cool. When Alice or Bix spoke French to her, Charlie answered in English. It wasn't really worth making a fuss over, but it hurt a little bit.

"I know," she said, rushing up to the desk. "But you gotta see this." She was wearing black jeans and T-shirt with NERD written on it in bright pink.

Alice blinked up at her. "What, outside?" The teen's empty hands didn't give Alice any clues. Her face flushed with excitement as she moved back toward the door. "You know that lot at the corner where they've been buildin'?"

Alice stood up, wishing Charlie would just tell her what was so interesting. "Sure. I heard it was going to be a museum on the history of music, from the earliest zydeco to current artists. Or something more general for the city's three-hundredth anniversary celebrations, except the year's almost over. Eric said he thought it looked like a modern retail store, but that can't be right, because the parish would never approve something like that in the District."

She reached the glass door and stepped outside. She loved the smell of the river, the way the sun reflected off the water and threw shimmers of light into her store. The humidity had risen in the hour she'd been inside and the air felt thick and muggy. The middle of August was a great time for fishing tours, but not so great for the tourists who lightly populated the walkway along the length of her building, and wilted in the heat.

Charlie was speed walking, pointing toward the corner, her straight, blond hair bouncing behind her. "Nope. Somethin' much better."

Alice felt her stomach drop as they made their way down the sidewalk toward the construction site. Call it intuition, or blame it on the fact she hated change. Maybe it was because nothing had gone her way for the past six months. But whatever it was, all the little hairs on the back of her neck stood up. She felt as if she teetered on the edge of something. Whether good or bad, she couldn't tell.

Chapter Two

"Technology is a gift from God. After the gift of life, it is perhaps the greatest
of God's gifts. It is the mother of civilizations,
of arts and sciences."— Freeman Dyson

"Okay, I'm not getting it. You've got to explain this one to me."

"I've tried." Paul Olivier leveled a gaze at his best friend. "And it doesn't matter whether you get it. Construction started weeks ago." He tried to keep a poker face but couldn't help cracking a smile.

"Well, I'm still not understanding." Andy McBride perched on the edge of Paul's desk and waved a hand at the blueprints pinned to the wall. "Of all the places to open a flagship store, why your home town? I thought you hated that place."

"I never said that." Paul angled out from behind his desk and stood in front of the blueprints, arms crossed. "Natchitoches was a hard place to grow up as the only techno geek for hundreds of miles." He turned and flashed a smile. "But I won't be the only one now. Not anymore. Everyone has a computer, everybody uses the Internet--even the old folks. My great Aunt Sandrine has a Facebook page for her garden club."

Andy was quiet for a moment. "I thought you were nuts when you opened three stores in Atlanta in the same year, but it was the right move. I thought you'd lost your marbles when you partnered up with those reality TV stars at Comic-Con, but our profits doubled that year. Let's not even talk about that whole super-secret identity you have going on with the stolen books."

"It's not secret. I'm just using a pen name. And they're not stolen. They're all out from under copyright and it's fair use to upload." Paul tried to keep the irritation out of his voice. Andy was a genius at keeping the company on track, but the guy could get some serious tunnel vision. If it didn't have graphics and a soundtrack, he wasn't interested. In college, Andy had always nagged Paul to drop his double major and focus on computer science, but Paul wouldn't let go of his English degree. "I'm bringing classics of Western Literature to the masses. These are books that you'd have to hunt down in rare book stores, books that cost hundreds of dollars. People are thrilled to find them available so easily. They think I'm saving the world," he said. "I've got fan clubs."

"Nice. Fan clubs for your secret superhero identity which has no connection to the company and therefore won't give us any benefits," Andy said. "Anyway, I never argued with any of that, but I'm telling you as your business partner and your best friend, this Natchitoches store doesn't look like a good move, and not just because the town's name is unpronounceable."

"I hear what you're saying." Paul walked forward and stared at the property lines of the newest ScreenStop store. Even as they debated, the parking lot was being finished. Getting permission to build on that side of the river was usually a long and ugly process, involving mounds of paperwork and months of waiting. Getting permission to build in the National Historic Landmark District was unheard of. Paul had managed both in weeks. There were perks to being a famous billionaire after all.

"But it's a good place for a store. There's nothing like it for three hundred miles," Paul said. "We're filling a technology gap that reaches from New Orleans to Shreveport. It's a good move. I can feel it." He poked a finger at the maps. "This store will make money."

"And you get to come back home the conquering hero." Andy intoned. His lips were turned up in a smile but his dark eyes were somber. "I'm not saying you can't afford it. As your CTO, I'm perfectly okay with you throwing a store into the void if it makes you feel better. One store won't break this company. I just don't want you to disappear into the wilds of Louisiana when you said you'd never set foot there again."

Paul threw his head back and laughed. "The wilds?" He turned, clapping a hand on Andy's shoulder. "It's swampland. My friend, you're coming with me. It's time for a little Southern education."

He grimaced. "No, thanks. I went to that tech conference in Atlanta last year. That was as far south as I needed to go, and a weekend was more than enough."

"Sitting in a hotel for the weekend is not really getting to know the people, Andy." Paul sat back down in his chair and swiveled from side to side. He hated being still, especially when he had a new idea, and showing Andy a good time in Cane River was his best idea in a long time. "There's no reason to rush back here. You broke up with Reilly, right?"

Andy shot him a look. "Yeah. She said she thought our relationship had 'run its course,' and 'we should branch out,' whatever that means. I wasn't surprised. We all can't be billionaire playboys like you."

Paul smiled at Andy's dig because the guy wasn't far behind, himself. Tech industries did that, making normal programmers with great ideas into the wealthy elite. He'd always liked Andy, but watching the way he'd handled the rise in his fortunes made him trust him, too. The guy was solid. Paul wasn't sad to hear about Reilly. He wasn't convinced she liked Andy for anything more than how famous he was. He leaned forward, elbows on the desk. "Andy, let me tell you a little secret about women."

"I don't need your dating advice." He adjusted a shirt cuff and pretended to straighten his tie. "I'm an MIT grad. I go to the gym. I never eat red meat and drink only on holidays. I have a great relationship with my mother and I'm best friends with Paul Olivier, the boy genius who made technology so simple your granny can use it," he said. "Women love me."

"Sure they do." Paul tried not to smile. "But they'd love you more if you were Southern."

Andy let out a grunt. "Are you telling me to fake an accent?"

"Nope. When you're there for a while, it sort of just… happens. Women can't resist it."

"I don't see the magic happening for you. When was the last time you seriously dated anybody? A year ago?"

"I've been busy." Paul tried not to remember, but she popped into his head, unbidden. Holly was beautiful, smart, funny. He couldn't have been happier. But the more time they spent together, the more he realized that she was far more interested in when he planned to sell his stock and retire than in him. When she mentioned a pretty little chateau for sale on a lake in Italy, he knew that she wasn't interested in him at all. He'd decided then and there to focus on his job.

"Well, I did want to ask out Janine Land, that pretty girl who works for Dell," Andy said. "You know, the redhead? But every time I strike up a conversation, we get interrupted and she wanders away."

Paul shook his head. Andy was taller, better looking, and funnier than Paul. But when it came down to it, they were both geeks, through and through. No matter how expensive the suits or how tall the high-rise, they would never be the smoothest guys in the room.

"Let's make a bet," Paul said. "We'll go to Natchitoches for a month or two. I'll rent us a trendy little place in the historic district. Throw the big opening, bring in some famous people, maybe fly in a band or two. Then we'll spend the rest of the time at the old place on the river. I'll educate you in all things Southern. We'll go bream fishin', frog giggin', and crawfish trappin'. You'll eat hush puppies, mud pie, and collard greens. My aunts will feed you gumbo by the bowl and cornbread by the pan. By the end of the month, we'll see if Janine still wanders away while you're talking."

"You just want someone to run interference between you and all your crazy relatives," Andy said.

"Maybe a little of that, too." Paul stood up and held out his hand. "So, Mr. CTO, are you in?"

Andy gripped it. "Against my better judgment, boss. I guess we're headed Natchitoches, Louisiana."

Paul couldn't help the smile that spread over his face. "It's only a month. We'll go dazzle the townsfolk, get our Southern on, and then come right back to New York City. You won't regret it."

"I hope not," Andy said. He stepped to the door. "I'll ask your PA to make the reservations. Anything else? Should I go buy some bowties and seersucker?"

"Better not. Seersucker is for pros. We'll start you small. Maybe a backwards baseball cap or something." Paul snapped his fingers. "Hey, we'll get to go to the zydeco festival!"

"The what? Is that a seafood dish?"

"Music. It's got accordions and rub boards and..." Paul shook his head. "I guess that means nothing to you. Let me think… Oh, it's the background music in Sims Unleashed."

Andy stared at the ceiling for a second. "Okay, yeah. It's been a while since I played that game but I think I know what you mean. And there's a whole festival of it? Sounds like overkill."

"Nope. This isn't the game version. It's the real thing. Live, surrounded by people, all that energy just seeps into your bones. You start moving your feet." The more Paul thought about it, bringing Andy to Natchitoches was going to be the best part about going home.

"Okaaayyy," Andy grimaced, hand on the door handle. "I'm not sure if I want anything seeping into my bones."

Paul turned back to the map. The orange-red of the sunset tinted the blueprints. If he was really honest, he could have opened that store anywhere from the Gulf to Atlanta. It didn't have to be in the Creole region he'd left for the scholarship to MIT. But as famous as he'd become, and as much money as he'd made, a part of Paul Olivier was still that scrawny fifteen-year-old kid with the absent dad and the mom who cleaned rich folks' houses.

Paul walked to the window and stared at his own reflection. The people of Natchitoches might not even remember him. He'd grown another four inches and put on thirty pounds of muscle thanks to a fancy gym membership, a personal trainer, and a chef with history in the healthiest five-star restaurants. He'd traded his old jeans and faded T-shirts for custom suits. The buzz-cut his mama gave him every few months was replaced by a more fashionable style, trimmed every two weeks by a stylist that came to his office so he didn't have to deal with the traffic.

He frowned, dark brows drawing down, shading his eyes completely. Most people here thought he was Italian, with his dark skin and angular features. Even when he opened his mouth and they heard a hint of that slow Louisiana drawl, nobody thought to ask if he was Creole. When he conversed easily with the overseas team based in Paris, but struggled to understand the managers from Houston, people assumed he'd been educated overseas. They couldn't imagine that a quarter million Louisianans speak French at home, and Paul had been of them. To the rest of the United States, his people didn't even exist. For a while, that was perfectly fine with the awkward nerd from the wrong side of town. He was glad nobody knew anything about his past. But the older he got, the more he realized some things couldn't be erased. Not in ten years, not in a hundred.

It was time to go home. The question was whether Natchitoches would welcome him with open arms, or treat him like the outcast he once was.

Chapter Three

Men have become the tools of their tools. — Henry David Thoreau

"Come on," Charlie called. "Sitting down all day has made you soft." She threw back a teasing grin but Alice just smiled. She felt her own sagging spirits lift around Charlie. The girl never lacked enthusiasm, that was certain. She came to work every Monday and Wednesday as soon as she got out of her last class at the high school. Employing Charlie, a kid who had read every science fiction and fantasy novel going back to Jules Verne, was like having her very own reference librarian in that narrow field.

"I've always been soft. Nothing new about it." Alice glanced toward the elm trees rising from the grass near the river bank. Across the river, the development was booming. She wished the town would slow down. No more building. No more ugly concrete. But the Cane River region would lose its young people if it stayed a hundred years in the past. She was just glad the historic district didn't allow the kind of stores that sprouted up overnight. At least her little piece of Natchitoches would stay the same--sedate and sophisticated.

As they reached the corner, Alice hoped to see a *Coming Soon* sign with the name of the museum or a fancy restaurant. Instead, she saw a banner that read *ScreenStop* tied to a new chain-link fence perimeter. Heavy equipment rumbled off to the side, smoothing the area where parking would be. Most of the building was already completed and workmen swarmed the inside, carrying bales of wire and tools.

"ScreenStop?" Alice searched her memory. "What is it? A movie theater?" DVD rentals were a thing of the past, and they already had two theaters in the mall across the river.

"You've never heard of ScreenStop? They're like, the best game store ever." Charlie bounced on the toes of her red Converse sneakers, beside herself with glee.

"Games." That could be better than a theater. "It must have a lot of merchandise for a store that big. I'm betting they'll have more than Monopoly."

Charlie stared at her, eyes wide. "Monopoly? Nobody plays that. These are real games. *Battle of the Universe*, *Ninja Masters*, *Purple Penguin*."

"I've never heard of any of those." She turned back to the chain-link fence across the street. The banner was black with red flames forming the title, and what looked like a bunch of angel wings in the background. She felt a wave of unease. Even at the end of the row, a concrete and glass structure would be an eyesore. Alice took a deep breath and tried to think positively. She liked board games as much as the next person. Maybe it would be a good neighbor to have after all. Board games and books. The perfect pairing.

"Of course you haven't. You don't believe in this stuff. You don't even have a cell phone."

Alice would have been offended except that Charlie's tone was teasing. "I do have a cell phone. It's just—"

"Ancient. It doesn't even have data." She laughed outright.

"Why would it?" She couldn't help being a tiny bit defensive. "It's a phone. You talk on it." Except that she didn't, not really. That made twice this morning that she'd been gently rebuked for not being plugged in. "Anyway, have you been in one of these places before?"

"Sure. They've got a big one in New Orleans. Five stories of all glass and steel. Sixty-inch screens everywhere. Gaming systems. Walls and walls of games, plus areas to try them out." Her blue eyes glazed over. "Cell phones, tablets, e-readers, TVs. Everything you could possibly want. I got this cool patch." She pointed to her Converse high tops, where a matching logo shone back. Red flames on black, angel wings in the background.

Alice felt her mouth form a little 'o' as her brain caught up with Charlie's description. It sounded like nothing she would ever want and there wouldn't be any overflow from the customer base. Video game players weren't known for spending their time reading. People buying e-readers wouldn't come into her bookstore and buy a paper book when they could just download one at a touch. They were night and day, sun and moon. She turned back toward the shop. "Don't think I'm being a jealous cow because they're some fancy store. I just don't know who approved this. I'm on the historic district board and I never heard a thing about the plans. It's really too bad they're letting something like that into the area."

Charlie caught up to her in a few steps. She skipped along beside her, face glowing with excitement. "Too bad? It's fantastic! I can't wait to see it. I bet you ten bucks and a Frisbee that they have a huge opening day party with a boatload of prizes. The really big stores have celebrities come in and sign stuff. My friend Jake had his chest signed by Kim Kardashian's cousin."

Alice disliked this new store more and more with each passing minute. "I don't know who that is, but I hope it wasn't permanent. Anyway, I'm sure it would fit in really well across the river to the South. Maybe down near the hospital. The building isn't right. The whole," she waved her hands, "*clonkiness* of the structure just doesn't fit." She wasn't sure if clonkiness was a word but she could hardly express herself through her irritation.

"But why?" Charlie seemed honestly confused. "This is just what we need on this side of the river."

Alice blew out a breath. "No, it's not. What we need is more readers. We need more people willing to shut off the junk on TV and put away the phone and read a book. We need less technology and more paper. Nothing in that place is going to help keep my store running." She couldn't help the bitterness in her voice.

"You just haven't tried it. You'd love it. I can play for hours and hours." Charlie smiled, as if she hadn't heard half of what Alice had just said. "I made it to the fortieth level one night after I played Blue Penguin for six hours straight."

Alice shot her a look. "Fortieth level. And what did you get for that?"

"Well, nothing," Charlie admitted. "But it was a big achievement."

Achievement. Alice trudged beside Charlie, half listening to her detail all the games she was going to buy and all the blissful hours she was going to spend sitting in front of a screen, decapitating zombies or whatever people did when they played video games. Alice wanted to shake some sense into her, but Alice wasn't Charlie's mother. She couldn't believe this bright young girl was wasting her life on false achievements that meant nothing in real life.

"I hope they start hiring soon. I bet I could get a job there since I've been playing those games since I was little. I got my first Xbox for my twelfth birthday and I almost wore it out." Charlie had never looked so excited. "Would you write me a good recommendation, Miss Alice?"

Alice missed a step and stumbled to a stop. Her stomach curled up on itself. Alice hadn't really thought it through clearly, but now she realized she'd always thought of Charlie as someone she could rely on. Even though they were nothing alike, Alice felt Charlie was someone who believed in books as much as she did, someone who might be interested in helping manage the store someday. It was a blow to realize Charlie wasn't anything like Alice. In fact, she was almost the opposite. But she had always been a good employee. "Sure. Of course I would."

Alice felt her heart pounding as they neared the classically designed, hundred-year-old building that housed By the Book. Every building for miles around was in the same style, with ornate stonework around the arched windows. That store was an ugly surprise, destined to ruin the atmosphere of the district. One more thing to worry about, one more thing on her plate. She'd worked so hard, putting in the hours and the effort, but things just weren't going her way. Things hadn't gone her way in a long time.

Gripping the long brass handle of the front door, she let Charlie pass through first, still chattering. Alice turned back for one last look at the construction happening on the corner lot, and she made a decision. She was going to find out who approved it. The parish council sent out notices for everything else, even changing the street lamps. Nothing happened without a vote. Something was very wrong. This had been slipped by the people of Natchitoches and she wasn't going to let it pass without a fight.

She narrowed her eyes at the rumbling machinery. Mr. Perrault would have been appalled. This business threatened the health and welfare of the people she loved most but for more reasons than being an eyesore. It was contrary to everything about this place, the only town she'd ever loved and called home. Their Creole culture was being shoved to the side and buried as easily as the dirt on that lot.

Alice touched the rings hanging on the chain under her shirt. She wasn't about to roll over and let the owners of that abomination seduce the city's children with hours of meaningless, flashing images. This was personal. This was war.

****

"Mr. Olivier, your meeting starts in fifteen minutes." The personal assistant cut into Paul's thoughts. He hated the intercom system more than almost anything, but without it he never arrived anywhere on time.

He pressed a button and responded, "Thank you, Mrs. Connor."

There was a second of silence as if she were thinking of adding an extra warning, but then the connection was cut. Paul smiled. Mrs. Connor thought ScreenStop would go down in a fiery ball of disorganization if she didn't show up to work, and Paul was tempted to agree with her. The woman was inhumanly exact, annoyingly direct, and never failed to point out the flaws in any plan. In short, she was the best personal assistant Paul had ever had.

He turned back to the screen and groaned. His "super-secret superhero project," as Andy liked to call it, was growing out of control. Tens of thousands of visitors per day came to the place Browning Wordsworth Keats called his cyber home. The site was built to handle ten times that amount of traffic. They talked on the boards, argued over poets, and left long lists of books they needed in digital form but couldn't find anywhere. He had appointed a few regular visitors as administrators and they kept the ranting to a minimum, making sure the site stayed friendly and upbeat, while not losing the point of why they all came— to discuss good books. Paul dedicated several servers just for handling the blog, so none of that was an issue. No, it was the email. The site listed a contact address, and at first he kept up correspondence with many delighted (and sometimes disgruntled) readers. But now, it was out of control. Sometimes he'd receive a hundred emails in a day. Opening an email and reading it through, even without a response, took time. If he sent even a few lines back, it took longer. He hated to go to an automated reply system, but he couldn't see any other way around it. If he hired someone to sort his email, he would have to let them in on his secret. And there was no one he trusted enough besides Andy and Mrs. Connor.

Paul ran a hand through his hair and opened one more email. He needed to figure out how to handle the wave of correspondence or he'd have to become unreachable. His daily life couldn't support a five-hour website babysitting job.

Dear Mr. B. W. Keats,

I am an eighty-six year old retired librarian. My grandson gave me an e-reader last year but I never used it. I don't even have a computer. I think the Internet is a terrible waste of time. This machine stayed in its box on a shelf until my friend Rhonda told me about your project. I was curious, so I went to the library and looked you up.

Mr. Keats, I cannot tell you what a joy it was to see Mother Carey's Chickens *was available from your website. I called my son right away and he helped me set up my account. In seconds, the book was in my hands. This was my twin sister's favorite book and she knew most of it by heart. After she passed away, her children cleaned out her house and sold all her books. When I realized it was missing, I felt like I had lost her all over again. When I got it on the screen and read those familiar words, I heard them in her voice even though I'd forgotten what she sounded like. I heard her voice and I cried.*

Bless you, Mr. Keats, whoever you are. You have given an old lady tremendous joy.

Sincerely,

Beulah Ditzner

P.S. I'm going to send you another email with a list of books that you might consider adding. I know you must receive many recommendations and requests. I will understand if you choose other works. These are simply books that I remember enjoying in my childhood and would like to read again before I die.

Paul sat back in his office chair. This was why he started the Browning Wordsworth Keats project. This was how he'd meant the books to be used. Of course he'd dreamed of people debating the classics that had drifted into obscurity. He wanted to see folks discovering books that should be on every shelf but had been lost amid the glossy hardback Stephen Kings and James Pattersons. But most of all, he'd hoped to reunite old friends who'd been separated by time and space, lost amid the ever-growing greed of big publishing chasing the next best seller. He'd hated seeing vapid reality TV stars, scandal-plagued politicians and child beauty pageant queens given million-dollar book deals while great literature went out of print. So, he'd decided to do something about it, using the tools and technology he knew best.

Paul clicked the button to respond, rushing to type out a few lines. This sort of letter confirmed that he was doing the right thing. He wished he could use his own name but it was impossible. No matter how much he wanted to take credit for the project, it would always be attributed to Mr. B.W. Keats, not Paul Olivier. He covered his cyber tracks: connecting through proxy servers that changed IP addresses every few minutes, and using dummy accounts to send packets of information. He carefully chose only books that were no longer under copyright. Still, that wouldn't stop the lawsuits if publishers thought there was easy money to be made. So far, they seemed to think it was a waste of time to try and track down his alter ego. And that's the way he wanted it to stay.

"Mr. Olivier, your meeting is in ten minutes and it's down on the twenty-fifth floor, which leaves you approximately two minutes and thirty seconds before you need to get your jacket on and get in the elevator." Mrs. Connors kept her voice carefully neutral.

Paul glanced at the jacket on his chair. The woman was uncanny. "I'm done here, Mrs. Connors. Thank you."

She disconnected without responding and he sat for a moment, staring at the intercom. Maybe Mrs. Connors could take over the email sorting. She was professional, intelligent, and exact. But she also had enough to do as his assistant. Paul sighed and logged out, grabbing his suit coat. Folks liked to say money could buy everything, including happiness, but the only people who believed it were the ones who'd never had as much as he had. He knew the truth. Money bought a lot of shiny things, but when it came down to it, money couldn't buy loyalty, trust, or love. Or someone to keep your secrets. There would always be someone who would offer more, and you'd never know when that betrayal would come.

Punching the button to his private elevator, he stared into his own reflection. As a kid, he'd felt like he could only count on a few good friends and his family. Even though the world called him "tech genius" and "wunderkind," his face was on magazine covers, and journalists begged for interviews, Paul knew that he was still that geeky kid from the lowlands of Louisiana.

The doors slid open and he stepped inside. Andy said this project was his superhero identity, but he felt like he'd been living a double life for years. At least this one made him feel like he was doing some good.

Chapter Four

Technology… is a queer thing. It brings you great gifts with one hand,
and stabs you in the back with the other.—Carrie Snow

"A businessman from New York is needing a place to live while his company finishes some project here. He contacted me through the ad on the rentals site. Maybe you need some time to Hoover? I'd like to show him the apartment this afternoon, if that'll work for you." June LaTraye's nasal voice made this a statement, not a question.

"Of course. You have a key. And thank you for working on this so quickly." Alice couldn't help grinning. Natchitoches was a tourist town, not a place many wanted to come to live permanently. And if they did, they were usually looking to retire in a nice place on the river, not a walk-up apartment in the historic district. This was promising. Even a few months' rent would really help the book store's bottom line.

"You want to meet them first? If they seem like they're fixin' to sign a lease d'rectly, I mean."

Alice paused. June was a good realtor, but she also had a keen eye and great intuition. Her teased, blond hair and bright pink lipstick hid an uncanny ability to weed out unreliable renters. "You know, I think it's okay if you want to handle that part. I trust you. If they're interested, I'll run over and plug in the icebox." Plus, it was a really big building. They only shared a few walls and those were brick. If even this man held a few parties, it wasn't likely to disturb her peaceful evenings.

"Okay, hon. I'll ring you later and let you know how it went."

Alice hung up and whispered a prayer of thanks. She pulled the rings out of her shirt and kissed them, hoping her parents could see her happiness. Whenever she felt like things were falling apart, God sent her a sign that she hadn't been forgotten. She felt like a smile was permanently etched to her face. She filled the kitties' water dishes and poured herself one more mug of coffee, letting the promise of good news color her mood.

Padding back into her bedroom, she searched through her closet for the cheeriest sundress she could find. She had a whole closet of retro clothing but today she felt like celebrating the possibility of a new renter. Slipping on a fitted, red polka dot shirtdress and a little white sweater, Alice decided a simple ponytail would finish the look. Not that she ever did anything much with her hair, since it was untamable. She grabbed a pair of red patent heels and set them by the front door.

One more cup of coffee and she'd head downstairs. The black-and-white tile kitchen floor gleamed in the early morning sunlight. She lifted the double-hung window above the old porcelain kitchen sink, propped it with a chipped mug that was older than she was, and inhaled. The air smelled of the river a few hundred feet away, the sky was a brilliant blue, and the humidity was finally easing off. A feeling of intense satisfaction filled her. She led a charmed life, compared to most of the world. Even with her money worries, her existence was about as peaceful as anyone could ask for.

Looking across at the row of hardwood trees that edged the opposite bank of Cane River Lake, she remembered the moment she'd learned Mr. Perrault had left her the shop. She was a month from graduating with a degree in English Literature. She'd already enrolled in a master's of education program, assuming she would do what English majors did and teach. But Mr. Perrault's last will changed the trajectory of her life, spinning her out of the program and back to Natchitoches.

Her college friends did their best to warn her, even sitting her down in a sort of intervention, laying out all the reasons she shouldn't return to her tiny hometown. But what they didn't understand was that Alice liked her quiet life, her small town, her Cane River people. She had never yearned for the big city. She was content in this place and she felt no shame in choosing it. In fact, she was thrilled to come home. The first years after college her friends would travel from Atlanta or Miami or Seattle. They wanted to experience the food, the accents and the cypress groves without the commitment of trying to make a living in the tiny tourist town. Alice was happy to play tour director. As much as they encouraged her to travel to their cities, she just never found the time.

Alice turned, letting her gaze wander over her little kitchen and toward the bright living room where every wall was covered with full bookshelves and the furniture was more comfortable than stylish. Maybe she hadn't wanted to find the time. Maybe it had never been a question of money. This place was as much a part of her as her love of classic literature or her collection of cats.

When Cane River Lake flooded five years ago, she was out in the rain with everyone else, loading sandbags and praying for a miracle. When the grade school organized a bake sale to benefit the soccer team, she spent a whole weekend making pies, even though she'd never played soccer in her life. When the parish council wanted to impose an extra tax on little barbeque stands in the region, she picketed in front of city hall with her neighbors. She, Alice, who avoided crowds with the dedication of the truly introverted, had stood shoulder to shoulder with them and felt at home.

The smile that touched her lips at the memory, now slowly faded away. There was a new threat in town. It wasn't flooding or a lack of school supplies or exorbitant taxes. But it was just as insidious, just as damaging. Alice pulled in a long breath, as if steadying herself for an argument. That ScreenStop store was not what Natchitoches needed. Her people had a culture that was unique to Louisiana, unique in all of the South, and she wasn't about to let some entertainment giant kill it off with a steady diet of immorally violent games filled with bikini-clad warrior maidens. Mr. Perrault had given her countless lectures on the damaging effects of modern media and she was glad she'd listened. She kept her life simple and as low tech as possible. She ignored the fashion mags, didn't watch the talk shows, and refused to get sucked into the latest TV shows. Especially the TV. Really, it seemed like every Emmy winner was either sickeningly violent or extolled a shallow kind of lifestyle contrary to everything she held dear.

If she had to track down the council person that gave ScreenStop an okay without a vote, she would. She was going to stop the construction any way she could. If they moved it across the river toward the other big box stores, she might be able to live with it, but there was no way she was going to let that technological eyesore exist down the block from her building.

Alice picked up her mail and flipped through the stack. She needed to get going or she'd be late opening the store. She refused to be lazy about the store hours, even if there weren't many customers. She opened the first envelope without glancing at the return address and scanned the front page.

...Norma R. Green, hereafter known as the Testator, challenges the Last Will and Testament of Mr. Ronald B.

Perrault. The Testator, also an heir at law by blood relation, was named in the will of the decedent as inheritor of By the Book until 2009, when the current will was written to benefit Miss Alice Augustine. The Testator appeals to the court for a review of the unintentional exclusion of Mrs. Norma R. Green, in light of the possible unsound mind of Mr. Perrault or the possibility his actions were made under duress.

Alice snatched up the envelope and stared, heart racing. She forced herself to breathe, sat down, then took a glance at the page again. Mr. Perrault's will was being contested five years after he'd passed away? Maybe it was a mistake. She found the number of the lawyer's office, someplace in Houston, and punched it in.

A secretary answered and Alice explained what she'd received, hating the quiver in her voice. The secretary transferred her, a man answered the line, and seconds later she was hearing the sound of her life being turned upside down.

"I'm glad you called, Alice. My client would like to reach a fair and equitable resolution to this problem," Mr. Crocket said.

"I'm sorry. What problem? And how does your client know Mr. Perrault? He had no children or other relatives that I was aware of," Alice said.

"No, she's not a child. She's his niece, his sister's child. Mr. Perrault and his sister weren't close."

"But… the paper I got says that Norma was in the previous will? Is that correct?"

He sounded pleased. "Exactly. It must be an oversight. She was the heir to all the Perrault's property and assets until 2009, when a new will was drawn up, with you as the beneficiary. Since it doesn't exclude her specifically, we can only assume it's a simple oversight."

"The paper says he might have made the will when he wasn't of sound mind or that he was under duress. I can tell you he was perfectly sane and no one forced him to give me the store. I didn't even know he had until he'd passed away." She tried not to let her anger show at the suggestion of forcing Mr. Perrault to change his will.

"Well, I think it's best to let a court decide whether he meant to exclude his beloved niece, Norma." Mr. Crocket's voice had gone steely.

"Beloved? She didn't even know he was dead!"

"Miss Augustine, I suggest you retain a lawyer to present your case. You're aware of the petition to the court and if we can't come to an agreement about the property, then we'll have to let a higher authority decide."

"The property. It's just a store. And I live above it. I mean, there's another apartment but the rent money only offsets the amount the store is losing…" Alice couldn't help stuttering.

"The store may not be worth much, but the property has been appraised at seven hundred thousand dollars because of the parcel of property, the location, and the historic nature of the building. If you're willing to meet with us, my client is amenable to being bought out from her share of the property. A third of the appraised value would be sufficient."

Alice slumped against the chair. This woman and her lawyer wanted a quarter million dollars or they would take her to court to contest the will. "I don't have that kind of money."

"If the building is sold, then the profits could be split evenly between you," he suggested.

"I won't sell the bookstore. Mr. Perrault left it to me."

"Well, again, I'd advise you to hire a lawyer. Or you can take our offer. If the judge finds in favor of my client, then you could be left with nothing."

Alice felt as if she couldn't breathe, as if the walls were closing in on her. Black spots appeared in her vision.

"Goodbye, Mr. Crocket," she whispered and hung up. She leaned over, whispering prayers learned in childhood, the French words coming to her unbidden. God wouldn't let someone take her store, would He? She'd lived her life according to all His commandments, carefully guarding her eyes and her heart, making her store a place of refuge from the gritty ugliness of the modern world. Didn't that count for anything?

The sound of the phone ringing so close to her head made Alice jump. The lawyer might be calling her back to harass her into selling the store. Alice held her breath, not making a sound, as if the person on the other end might sense she was there.

The ringing stopped, and her own voice filled the room. Then there was a beep, followed by an extremely loud sigh.

"Alice, pick up the phone. I know you're there," Eric said.

She grimaced. Why couldn't he just leave a message like everyone else? Why did she have to talk to him at eight in the morning?

"Come on, Alice. I called last night and left a message. It's really your turn to call me, but here I am, talking into the void."

Ouch. That was right. She'd forgotten all about him.

"I hate your machine. I know you know that. Nobody uses them anymore. They cut you off just as you're—" Beeep!

Alice stood up, eyes wide, hand hovering over the receiver. Too late to pick up now, and probably not a good time to call back. He'd be irritated with her for not answering. She tried to tell herself that it was simply hard to pretend to be bright-eyed and bushy-tailed in the morning. Truthfully, she just didn't like to talk to Eric on the phone. He had one of those personalities that was better in person. Face to face, his rapid-fire speech and expressive voice was entertaining. On the phone, he seemed bossy and off-putting. She'd text him when she got downstairs and ask him to meet her for lunch. That would patch things up. Plus, she could really use some advice. Eric was a dentist, not a lawyer, but he might know what to do.

Alice took her mug of coffee and headed down the narrow, wooden stairs from her apartment to the back of the shop. It was Friday and Charlie would be in soon, because she had a half day of school on Friday. When she'd told Alice that she wanted to apply to work in ScreenStop, it had hit Alice hard, right in the heart. The lawyer's letter was a kick to the same spot. Alice knew she might be fighting a losing battle to keep her store, preserve their culture, and swim against the rising tide of technology, but she couldn't let any of it go. She was going to encourage Charlie in every way that being Creole was important. It was sacred. She'd speak French, even when Charlie answered in English. She'd remind Charlie to be proud of what she'd been given by birth. If only Charlie would give up the gaming and come back to what really mattered. Alice would explain it the way Mr. Perrault had explained to her. Charlie would understand how much was at stake. She had to.

***

"All ready?" Paul kept his voice as upbeat as possible.

"Huh." Andy responded with a grunt. In the background of the call, Paul could hear clanking and thuds. "With every item I pack, I ask myself again why we're doing this."

"Must be a short answer. Or you're not packing very quickly."

"I don't get any answer, so now I'm finished." He heard Andy pull a long zipper.

"You don't have to go," Paul said. He wanted Andy to come to Natchitoches, but he didn't want his friend to feel miserable, either. It might be better if the CTO just stayed in the big city.

"Nope. I'm in. Just questioning my own good judgment and your sanity. Did you get the apartment lined up?"

"We're seeing it this afternoon. Try not to look like a party animal," Paul said.

"I'll do my best 'working stiff' impression. And this place will be high tech, right? We're not going to be adjusting the rabbit ears to watch a game or playing on an old Atari or something?"

"It may not be now, but it will be when I'm done with it," Paul said, laughing a bit. He was sure the place had cable. Well, actually not very sure. But they could get a good gaming set up installed in a few hours. As soon as the lease was signed, he'd have everything overnighted. He'd managed to get the building permit shoved through faster than he'd ever dreamed possible. Surely he could get the manager to install cable Internet service. "I've got to pack. The car should be there to pick you up in about an hour. Meet you at the gate."

"You'd better. Paul and Andy's Excellent Creole Adventure is about to begin."

Paul disconnected, but instead of starting to pack, he walked to the floor-to-ceiling window. New York City teemed with bodies, noise, and choking exhaust fumes, but that was far, far below the glass walls of Paul's high rise bedroom. He stared out at the skyline and wondered if he should just cancel the entire Cane River project. He must be crazy to think of coming back to that backwater. Maybe Andy was right. Was he making a bad business decision just to satisfy his ego? He took a long moment to let the idea sit, and then he shook his head. No, Andy was only partly right.

Paul headed to the walk-in closet, where he pulled a suitcase from the back. It was true, he didn't need to spend two months in Natchitoches. He could open the store and fly in for the night, maybe two. His ego had everything to do with dropping out of his life in New York City to show off to the people who used to make him feel like trash. But he was certain it was a good business decision and the store would be successful. He wanted to cram his rags-to-riches story down a few throats, but he wasn't stupid enough to throw away a million dollars to do it.

Paul slid one of his favorite T-shirts into his suitcase and paused. It had been so long since he'd been home, he wasn't even sure what to wear. He grabbed another shirt, a black one with a favorite band logo on the front. He had a closet of nice suits he'd use for meetings and media events. The rest of the time, he wouldn't wear anything out of the usual. He knew better than anyone that putting on a nice suit didn't make you popular in Natchitoches. You had to really *be* someone. Of course, there were different levels of being "someone". It was always better to be born someone than to work your way up, but if you had enough money, sometimes you got a sort of honorary "someone" status. It wasn't always sincere, but you got to hang around with the old families and eat dinner at their long dinner tables, and date their daughters, just back from a few years in Europe or an Ivy League college. You were tolerated, if you were rich enough, no matter which side of the river your family came from in the beginning.

Tolerated. He clenched his jaw at the thought and slammed another worn out T-shirt on the pile. He wasn't the skinny geek anymore. He had money, power, and influence on his side. More than that, he was famous. Fame counted for everything these days.

He threw in socks, underwear, and his favorite jeans, and zipped the case closed. He'd hired Andy because he was the right guy for the job, but Andy was his best friend because the guy didn't care how many followers you had on Twitter or how many likes your business page had on Facebook. Andy understood the real measure of a man was wrapped up in faith, honor, and living above the standards of world. He knew that the rest was all show, just numbers and bits of data floating around in cyberspace, masquerading as reality.

Paul had learned to walk the fine line, to play the game. He played it so well, he'd become the master, making millions in stock off the sheer popularity of his name. When he wore a gray hoody, gray hoodies sold out. When he let himself be photographed with an iPad, sales went through the roof. Paul knew how to work the media, turning the Internet to his advantage, and he wasn't going to let that skill go to waste in Cane River.

Sliding into his desk chair, he brought up the ticket information again. Today he'd be voluntarily stepping back into the place that had nothing but a few good memories. His stomach dropped at the thought. Bringing up his email, he saw the realtor was ready to show the apartment. She'd sent him a few pictures of the inside. It wasn't anything close to his penthouse suite, but Paul was satisfied. He didn't want anything from this century. He wanted to stay in one of those historic homes with the twelve-foot ceilings adorned with vintage chandeliers, and living rooms with exposed brick walls and enormous fireplaces. It spoke of all the places he was denied when he was growing up. It was the kind of place he'd never even have been allowed to tour, before he created ScreenStop and made his fortune. And the historic district was perfect. Not because it was close to the new site, but because it was where everything important happened. Rich people lived, shopped, and hobnobbed there. The buildings were uniformly old and showy. Paul could have rented the graceful wooden river house with the wraparound porch for the whole two months, but he wanted this apartment. He needed it. He was going to come back to Natchitoches as if he'd born in high cotton, not dirt poor.

He leaned back and gazed at the photos of the enormous, sunny living room. He'd outfit the place with a sixty inch TV, the best gaming system around, and turn it into the techno bachelor pad he'd always dreamed of when he was fifteen. A wide smile spread over his face. They say the best revenge is success. Well, the wealthy snobs of Natchitoches better watch out. The day of reckoning was at hand. In a few hours, Paul Olivier was coming back to town and nobody was going to be able ignore him this time.

Or not. *Hope springs eternal in the human breast: Man never is, but always to be blest,* Paul whispered to himself. Alexander Pope said it, but he also had a lot to say about focusing on the good, instead of wasting energy on what couldn't be changed. Paul opened one of the cardboard boxes and searched through the contents. He had just enough time to scan in a small volume of old poetry if he was quick about it. As if in answer to his unspoken question, he saw a slim volume of Alexander Pope poetry and essays.

Removing a box cutter from his drawer, he carefully cut each fragile page from the rotting binding. As soon as he signed the lease, he'd have Mrs. Connors pack these up and send them on. He didn't want to neglect the community of readers who waited for the next out-of-print book to pop up in their notifications.

Paul paused, his hands full of paper. There was nothing better than the smell of old books. These poems reminded him of the miracle of words. They would have new life, in ten thousand different hands. Instead of molding in the basement of an apartment building, this book would be reincarnated in binary code, transferred in terabytes across the country, and read around the world. Alexander Pope's *Essay on Man* would live again in a way it hadn't lived before.

Chapter Five

Any sufficiently advanced technology is indistinguishable from magic. — Arthur C. Clarke

"Can I help you?" Alice approached the customer with a smile. It was rare to have anyone in so early on a Saturday. The twenty-something woman with short curly hair had the focused look of someone in search of a specific book. Alice held out a hand and introduced herself.

"Nice to meet you. I'm Karen." She glanced at the display of brand new hardbacks and then around the rest of the store, her gaze settling on Van Winkle at the desk. "Is that a cat or a really big paperweight?"

Alice had to smile. "Both, I'm afraid. He doesn't move much so on windy days I just tuck papers under his portly body."

Karen giggled but it was cut short when she noticed Darcy on the top of the range. "Oh, he gave me a start! He looks so…"

"Severe? Yes, he can be quite intimidating." Alice hoped the girl wouldn't notice any more cats. Maybe she was allergic. Alice did have a sign in the window warning people, but some might think the *resident attack cat* poster was a joke. She used a high-powered air filter and a top-notch vacuum to keep hairballs to a minimum.

"He's beautiful, even if he does look like he hates me," Karen said. "Anyway, this is the first time I've been in a book store in years. I usually order everything online 'cause I don't have to search for it and it's delivered right to my house."

Alice kept her smile in place. She heard some version of this a few times a week. Everyone told her what great deals they found on Amazon. She wanted to tell them that Amazon couldn't find your book when you didn't remember anything except the author's name started with a D and the cover had a seagull. But she could.

"Anyway, I read this great book and I wanted to find the rest of the author's stuff, but it's all…" Karen paused, as if searching for the right word. "Out of print, I guess. And you have to buy them from little bookstores, but I don't want to pay shipping and I thought…" Her voice trailed off and she looked around the store, as if wondering how she would ever find what she needed.

"I'd be happy to help," Alice said, doing her best to ooze reassurance. "Who's the author?"

"Um." Karen reached into her bag, grabbed a red, zippered notebook, and pulled out a tablet. She turned it on, scrolled through a few pages, and then turned the screen toward Alice. "Browning Wordsworth Keats", she announced. "No, wait. That's not right."

Here he was again, the mysterious BWK. Now he was actually bringing people into her store, bless him. Alice said, "I think that's the name of the man who's posting the book, not the author."

She frowned. "Right. I knew that, I think."

"Can I see the book?" Alice held out her hand, and the dark-eyed girl passed her the e-reader. The cover was bright and clear like a photograph, but before she could take it all in, Alice accidentally touched the screen and it was gone, replaced by a line of books. "I'm sorry. I think I did something and lost the page."

The girl took it back with a smile. "You've never used one of these before? But, I guess you wouldn't need one. You have a whole bookstore."

"Exactly," Alice said, nodding.

"My grandpapa just got a tablet for his birthday and we set it up to handle e-books. He didn't think he'd like it, but his eyesight has gotten so bad that he pretty much gave up reading. Even the large print wasn't enough. He'd tried books on tape and hated them. He said they all read so slowly."

"I would think reading on a screen is harder, not easier," Alice said.

"Oh, no." The girl touched a few buttons and the font on the page enlarged. "He's read more books in the last week than he's read in the last three years. He's so happy."

Alice stared down at the page. Bix's face popped into her mind. He'd just mentioned how much he missed reading. "I didn't know that they could do that," she said.

"Sure can," the girl said. She tapped it a few times and turned it back to Alice. "Here it is."

"*Beau Geste,* by P.C. Wren." Alice tried not to look surprised. "We have quite a few of his stories, including the sequels, *Beau Sabreur* and *Beau Ideal*. They made several movies out of this one. I think Gary Cooper played in one version." She motioned her toward the far aisle. "Let me show you."

As the woman followed her down the row, Alice had a sudden thought. "Have you ever been to the website run by Browning Wordsworth Keats?"

"Sure, but my friend May is on it a lot more. She loves old books. Her house is packed with them. Not just the romances, but everything, like this one called *Tom the Telephone Boy*, about a kid who runs the switchboard in his town." She laughed. "May keeps telling me to read it, but I don't think I'd understand half of it. Everything is so outdated."

Alice nodded, even though Karen couldn't see her face. "Even some of the kids' books from the sixties are sort of lost in translation." She motioned to another aisle.

"We have the reissued *Encyclopedia Brown* books and I loved those when I was little. But I had a lady come in, asking to return them. Her grandson said a lot of the mysteries didn't make sense anymore. With cell phones, people can be reached night and day. Plus, you can Google anything and there's no reason to have a boy detective at all."

Karen paused at the end of the aisle, reaching out to touch a book. "I know what she means. I was a French major and liked the title of *Beau Geste*, so I clicked on it, but the first chapter or so was a real struggle. It wasn't just the language, it was..." She stopped. "When they're puzzling out a murder and talking about breech-loading rifles and bayonets, I could understand that. But it was when I realized the whole book was wrapped around this idea of always doing what is right, even to the point of sacrificing yourself for your family honor, I thought it just wasn't the kind of book I wanted right then. Not exactly light reading." She turned, smiling. "But I didn't stop reading it. And now I'm looking for all the others."

Alice felt her smile widen in response. "If someone told you it was a book about three brothers joining the Foreign Legion, fighting terrible battles, and the main character dies in the end..."

"No way I'd ever read it," Karen laughed. "But I'd already picked up *Tess of the D'urbervilles* after I watched the movie, so I was looking on the list for something else and..." She shrugged. "It wasn't anything like *Tess,* but I'm glad I read it."

"Let's find those sequels, then." Alice started down the aisle and stopped near the end, pointing to the middle shelf. "You'll find all of Wren's work here, and some similar books. I'll let you browse for a bit."

"Thank you," Karen said, already scanning the titles.

Alice walked slowly back to her desk. Her mind had been caught up in the lawyer's letter and for a moment it was hard for her to see how one new customer could make a difference, but now she felt optimism rise in her. She wasn't one to fan-girl over anyone, except an author, but she just might make an exception for the mysterious BWK.

She opened her laptop, and in a few clicks she was back on his site. There were a hundred and fifty more comments on the thread she'd been reading a few days before, and another forty people had joined the group dedicated to Gothic romances. She clicked onto the About Me page and stared at his profile. She leaned closer, noting the way his hand casually reached to straighten his loose tie. It was a nice hand, with strong fingers and manicured nails. The slight beard stubble, his tan skin, and the way the collar of his shirt was perfectly pressed, made her think of an Italian mobster. But he was probably trying to channel someone cooler, like Hugh Jackman in that really long movie about Australia.

She leaned back, absent-mindedly fiddling with the rings on her necklace. Either it was a staged photo or the man had style and money. Money for the expensive shirt and tie, style to pull it all together with a sly smile. Or it wasn't even him. BWK could be anyone, anywhere.

Something about that thought gave her courage and she hovered the mouse over the contact button, and then finally clicked. There was an email address but any messages probably just got some automated response. Alice chewed her bottom lip and then quickly opened her email, pasting in the address. She didn't know what to write. She wasn't even sure why she was writing him. But she felt compelled to reach out, even knowing she must be one of literally hundreds of people wanting to make a connection to this person.

Dear Mr. (or Mrs.? Miss?) Keats,

I'm sure I'm one of thousands who feel the need to write and thank you for your hard work. I can't imagine the time and effort needed to create and maintain this website, unless you have a dedicated team of assistants. No one solely interested in monetary gain would give this much of his or her time.

Alice stared at the screen for a moment. That was enough. He didn't need to know anything about her and probably wouldn't read it anyway. But she found herself continuing.

I own a bookstore dedicated to rare and classic books. I just met one of your customers. She'd discovered Beau Geste *and was looking for more of P.C. Wren's work. I suppose you could say that I'm writing to thank you for the sales. My shop is suffering and has been for a long while, so this was a wonderful surprise on a usually quiet morning.*

I wish everyone had access to real books, but if that's not possible, I'm glad they get a chance to experience them on a screen.

If there's ever anything I can do for you, please don't hesitate to ask.

Sincerely,
Alice Augustine
By the Book
Natchitoches, Louisiana

Alice pushed *send* before she could change her mind. She really wasn't one to send fan letters, but this was more of a thank you note, really. Plus, nobody was on the other side of that email, probably.

"There you are." Eric's voice made her jump in her chair. "Did you get my message?"

Alice turned, feeling her face flush with guilt. She closed her laptop and stood up, catching her thigh painfully on the edge of the desk. "I'm so sorry! I forgot to call you back." She reached out to give him a big hug but he stepped back.

"I really feel like you're ignoring me, Alice. Maybe I should ask you to pencil in a few minutes on your calendar because just calling doesn't seem to be working. Maybe I should make an appointment." Eric's handsome face was devoid of any humor.

Alice felt, to her horror, a laugh welling up. The stress of the legal problem and the surprise of seeing him made her want to laugh. And she couldn't force back the realization that Eric sounded just like a girl she was friends with when she was little. Well, not really friends, because Lorinda nagged her incessantly so that their play times always went exactly as she wanted.

"You think this is funny? I'm not kidding." Now his arms were crossed and he was giving her a look of total outrage.

"I'm sorry. I'm—" Alice covered her face for a moment and tried to get control. Eric was a nice guy. She really shouldn't be laughing at his very understandable pique. "I had a shock this morning."

"Excuse me, I think I have everything I want." Karen's soft voice interrupted the tense moment and Alice stepped to the side.

"Come right over here to the register." She motioned toward the long counter where Charlie usually sat on a stool. Karen crossed the tile floor, glancing back at them.

"I'm sorry," Alice whispered, reaching up on tiptoes to give Eric a kiss. "Come back at lunch time and I'll leave Charlie in charge for a bit. We can go grab a sandwich at Babet's Café. I need your advice on something."

Eric shook his head and for a moment Alice thought he was going to walk away from her in anger. "Okay, but don't forget. I have a root canal scheduled for two this afternoon and I can't be late." He softened, leaning his blond head towards hers. "I'll meet you and we can walk over. It's such a beautiful day."

She gave him another quick kiss and whispered, "Promise."

As he went out the door, Alice wondered at the way he hadn't asked about what had shocked her, or what she needed to tell him. She thought of how many times she'd forgotten to call him. She liked Eric and enjoyed his company when she wasn't feeling guilty about forgetting him. But something was wrong, either with her heart or with him.

Chapter Six

If it keeps up, man will atrophy all his limbs but the push button finger.
—Frank Lloyd Wright

Paul settled back in the leather reclining seat and did his best to ignore the fact they were no longer in contact with the earth. He closed his eyes and let out long, slow breaths. His doctor had offered to prescribe a mild sedative but Paul didn't like the idea of taking a pill just because he couldn't handle his fears. His mama had asked him to get the jet blessed by a priest but he never had. Now he was wondering about the wisdom of that oversight. At least he'd been to confession recently. Flying was a good way to keep himself on the straight and narrow. He really didn't want to die in a state of sin. No matter how many times he got on a plane, he still felt the scrabble of panic in his throat as they made the slow climb into the clouds.

"You know, if you had a few beers before we got on the flight, you wouldn't have to do the Lamaze routine every time," Andy said.

"I don't like to self-medicate," Paul muttered. A beer was only a beer… until it wasn't. His mama once told him his absent father liked to drink too much, so he'd always been wary of needing a beer for anything, even flying. His mind flashed to his mama's face and he smiled. As soon as he'd been able, he'd moved her out of Natchitoches. Only a few hours from her sisters, she lived in a big farmhouse on the edge of a small lake. Swans drifted across the surface and when the sun set, it was like something from a calendar. He was proud of a lot of things, but being able to buy his mother her dream retirement property was one of his proudest moments. It would be nice to be closer than New York City, if only for a few months.

The plane seemed to level off a little and Paul opened his eyes. Andy was scanning reports from the marketing department, eyes narrowed, deep in thought. Andy called himself lazy, but everyone knew that was a lie. The guy never stopped working, something Paul appreciated in a business partner. He had a hard time going on vacation himself, so the two of them were well matched.

He flipped open his laptop and set it on the table in front of him. Some of the perks of having his own plane were not having to worry about losing his Internet connection, or fighting for space, or trying to tune out loud passengers. There was a theater room in the back but Paul hardly used it unless they had guests. He and Andy both usually worked through the flight. Paul wasn't sure if that made them dedicated or just boring.

He flipped through a few project overviews but couldn't focus. He felt like a kid on his first day of school, and that had never been a good thing. He logged onto Browning Wordsworth Keats and tried not to groan at the number of messages. But answering a few was better than nothing. He'd been trying to work from the bottom, but this time he clicked on the newest. A thank you note. Another thank you note. A complaint over the violence in a book on the African Safari. Another thank you… from Natchitoches?

Paul sat up with a snap. She owned a bookstore, offering him help. Interesting. He had people offer to send him boxes of old books, but he didn't want to sort through and then find a safe place for the vintage volumes if they weren't what he needed. But a book store… full of rare books. A slow smile spread over his face as he typed his answer.

Dear Mrs. (Miss? Ms.?) Augustine,

I'm glad your customer has discovered the glory of Beau Geste. *It was my favorite book when I was twelve. I didn't appreciate John's beau geste as well as I should have. I always thought he deserved to live and have a happy ending. Call me a romantic.*

Thank you for your offer. I do need assistance now and then. Some of these books are hard to track down, as I'm sure you understand. In fact, now that I think of it, would you have a copy of The Duke's Secret *for a fair price? If you do, I can arrange to have someone pick it up.*

Sincerely,

Browning Wordsworth Keats (Mr.)

He pushed *send* and went to the next email. Complaint. Request. Thank you. Thank you. Request. He paused, rubbing his eyes. Even as fast as he answered, his inbox filled faster. He wondered exactly how fast and hit *refresh*. Another message appeared. He refreshed again and watched the numbers climb. After a few minutes he figured it at a minimum of ten per hour. He shook his head, refreshing one more time.

The bookseller had responded and he leaned forward, mouse hovering. He hadn't thought to specify a price. Would she quote him an outrageous figure? Savvy businessmen always inflated the price when there was demand. Paul clicked on it.

Dear Mr. Keats,

I do happen to have a copy of The Duke's Secret. *The price is three dollars because the condition is somewhere between neglected and deplorable. It has a lovely cover and is still legible, though. I've put it behind the counter for you (or your friend).*

I'm sure you fend off many unwanted requests and demands but I was wondering if you could answer a personal question. Is that you in the fedora? If so, is that your bookshelf in the background? Forgive me for being a nosy parker but I believe you can tell a lot about a person by their bookshelves. Even (especially?) if they own a whole building full of them.

Alice Augustine (Miss)

Paul grinned. Three dollars. He flipped to the picture of himself on the website and squinted, trying to see which of his books appeared in the background. A sinking feeling filled his stomach. A few old textbooks, programming guides, *Watership Down*, *Brave New World*, a Ray Bradbury collection, the Steve Jobs biography, a Neil Gaiman book for children, *1984*, a favorite book of poetry so slender you couldn't read the title, *Dune*, a collection of Flannery O'Connor short stories, *Fahrenheit 451*, Wordsworth's poetry, a lot of Jules Verne, *Peter Pan in Kensington Gardens*. But at the end, a history book about the Creole people of Cane River and a fat video game programming manual were side by side. He'd written the manual with two other programmers and his name was clear as day on the spine. If anyone had any right to suspect that Browning Wordsworth Keats was Paul Olivier, video game programmer raised in Natchitoches, that was pretty strong evidence.

No one had asked Paul about the books in the picture before. Not the thousands of visitors who came for the message boards, not the hundreds who emailed. He frowned, considering, then decided it didn't matter much. No one had any reason to link him to the site. Paul Olivier was a man who spent his waking hours shaping the online gaming world. Browning Wordsworth Keats dedicated his life to giving new life to obscure classic literature. Not even Sherlock could piece that puzzle together.

Dear Miss Augustine,

Indeed, that is Browning Wordsworth Keats in the fedora and my books on the shelf. It must strike horror in you to see such disorganization. I wish I had kept all the books I've ever loved, but for some reason, there are only a few hundred that have followed me through college to my adult life. I only have three from my own childhood, and they were my grandfather's. Zane Gray had a baseball series and I have The Shortstop, The Redheaded Outfielder, *and* The Young Pitcher. *With dust jackets. Just holding them in my hands makes me happy.*

Your bookish friend

The air pressure made his ears ache and Paul reached for a pack of gum. After a few seconds of chewing, he felt his ears pop and he settled back in his chair. Andy was focused so intently on his work he didn't even glance up.

Paul opened a few more emails, sent a note back about Hardy Boys books being under copyright, and searched for a website for By the Book. There was nothing, not even a holding place for a website someday. Other mentions came up under her name, though. Pictures of fundraisers, a tax levy protest, a charity drive for the historical district. Paul blinked at the photos. Alice Augustine was about forty-five years younger than he'd figured. And pretty. Very pretty in that way that women are when they don't try to change too much about their hair and face. She looked slightly uncomfortable in most pictures, but there were a few that made him lean forward and look closely. In one, she was handing a sandbag to a pair of hands belonging to a person outside the frame. Her hair was pulled back, long curls flying around her face, rain soaking her jeans, both feet planted in several inches of mud. She looked intense, focused. He would not have pegged this woman for a bookstore owner. She looked like she would be more at home as a karate instructor. No, something outdoors. Landscaper? He could see her creating beauty and change from the boggy river land.

Paul caught himself at those last vague images and grimaced. He'd always been a sucker for the brainy girls. Especially the pretty, brainy girls. But he wasn't a kid anymore. He had enough on his plate without crushing on a bookstore owner. Plus, as part of the Natchitoches elite, she was one of those people that wouldn't have spared a glance for him or his mama, way back when. He closed the page and went back to his email. There was another message from Alice.

Dear Mr. Keats,

I don't come from a book-loving family so there are no special literary treasures from my grandparents, but I did inherit a whole store from my dearest friend Mr. Perrault. I stomped into his store, an angry teen know-it-all, and demanded he rearrange a whole section. He answered me with smile, gave me free reign to rearrange as I saw fit, and offered me a beanbag in a sunlit corner for as many hours as I needed.

When I was in college, I asked Mr. Perrault why he didn't tell me to get on out of his store. He said, "Anyone who is that passionate about books should be welcomed. I knew I had found a kindred spirit."

He was a wonderful man, Mr. Perrault.

Your friend,

Alice

P.S. I know what you're going to ask. What did I find so offensive about his poetry section? I'll just say… it's related to the leather volume of poetry between The Graveyard Book *(you know Gaiman wrote that as a modern day* Jungle Book*?) and the Flannery O'Connor stories (I've never understood her, I'm sorry, I've tried). I'm assuming the Browning in your name is not for the Mr., but rather the Mrs.*

P.P.S. We have a few book friends in common but your shelf is much heavier on the science fiction. Also, I'm confused by the video game programming manual. Do you share shelf space with another person? That would be the true test of a friendship. I wonder what that's like, to be able to intimately mix your books so casually. I find my shelves to be very personal property.

In two years, no one had come close to discovering anything about him. But in three short letters, Alice figured out more than his most dedicated fan club member.

The plane hummed along, the top of the clouds bright beyond the windows of the cabin. Andy was in the zone, not bothering to look up from his work. The steward sat reading at the entry to the cockpit. Paul looked around, unsure of whether to trust what he was reading. Could Alice have figured this out from a picture? Or she was someone he had once known in Natchitoches but didn't remember. Maybe she was teasing him, stringing him along. Maybe she wanted to draw him into a friendship with her tender tales of inheriting a bookstore from an old man, inviting confidences until she trapped him into exposing his identity to the world.

Paul raked his hands through his hair. Some days he hated his life. Everyone wanted money and power but it wasn't all it was cracked up to be. You never know whether you're making a friend or an enemy. He stared at the words on the screen, then flipped back to Alice's photo. She looked like a woman who didn't care about power. But pictures were deceiving. There was no way to find out whether someone was lying to you, not really. Online, his intuition was non-existent. Not that he was much better in real life. He'd been taken too many times, fallen for so many sob stories, and believed what turned out to be blatant lies, until finally, he'd learned. Be cautious. Slow down. Expect the worst.

The jet went through a large cloud and for a moment the sunlight in the cabin dimmed. Paul looked back at the screen. He didn't want to see everyone as a threat. He understood why Mr. Perrault had reacted that way. He wanted to believe there were kindred spirits waiting to stomp into his life and demand that he rearrange something he'd already figured out.

Dear Alice,

Mr. Perrault was very wise. Passionate readers are rare and we must stick together. (To be clear, I say we're different than "the bookful blockhead, ignorantly read with loads of learned lumber in his head" that Alexander Pope described.)

The books are all mine. I haven't met the right person to share shelf space with, I suppose. I agree that it's a very personal decision and it brings up a conundrum. If you've fallen in love with someone and decide to live out your lives in happily wedded bliss, but then realize your books can't coexist on a shelf, does that spell the end of your relationship? I think I would spring for separate book cases but I fear for those ardent readers with limited space and means. Perhaps the real cause of divorce is lack of shelf space? This needs to be studied at a higher level.

Yes to science fiction. I don't think I read outside the genre from the ages of ten to twenty-five. It has served me well. And I admit I'm disappointed in your lack of appreciation for Miss Flannery. Have you read any of her letters? Maybe some background into her daily life would help. The Graveyard Book *was the first new children's book I loved as an adult. There have been others since then, but that was the first.*

As for that book you spotted, The Seraphim and Other Poems *was the first collection she published under her own name but I have other reasons for liking it. Now I have to know how my Elizabeth Barrett Browning is tied to your youthful outrage in Mr. Perrault's poetry section.*

Your friend,

Browning Wordsworth Keats

Paul pushed *send*, set the laptop on the table and stood. He didn't mention the gaming manual and he wondered if she would notice. The six wings of the seraph in the logo of ScreenStop came from the title of that book she'd just pointed out. But nobody knew that except for him. Most people thought it was just a cool design, with two large wings crossed at the top, two to the side, and two crossed at the bottom. It made him nervous to dance around such a large clue, but Alice honestly seemed interested in the books, and not in his identity. He didn't mind letting slip the fact he wasn't married. She didn't seem the type to want an online romance. Just the opposite, really. She would be someone who would insist on face-to-face communication.

He watched the mist outside fade away as the jet slowly descended through the clouds. As soon as the jet landed, someone would spot the ScreenStop logo and the news would spread that he'd returned to his home town. He felt his stomach roll with nerves.

It had been a long time since he'd made a new friend. Well, not exactly. He made friends all the time. He had five thousand Facebook friends, ten million Twitter followers, and everywhere he went, people knew his name. But it never got around to books. His whole public life was gaming, the company, and the huge conventions that brought thousands of people together in cosplay. He never dressed up, but he never quite felt like himself, either.

Paul reached for a Coke in the cabin fridge and opened it with a crack. The soda tasted too sweet and he blinked against the burn of carbonation. Andy embraced the geek fandom with open arms, feeling like he had the best of both worlds. For years, Paul worked hard without a break, traveled without a real vacation, and tried to fit into the New York high-tech lifestyle. He'd succeeded beyond anything he could have imagined. But he didn't feel at home.

He wandered back to his seat on the couch and set down his drink. The laptop screen showed another message. Paul rolled his shoulders, feeling the tension in his muscles. Would she insist on asking about the video game programming book?

Clicking it open, he only saw a few sentences, and a .jpg attachment. She'd sent him a picture. Of herself? Of her store?

Dear BWK (that's how I think of you),

I'm conflicted on the subject of Mr. Pope. I agree with him when he says "an honest man's the noblest work of God," but then my hackles rise when I see that too-oft quoted "woman's at best a contradiction still." I'm not sure whether he had a sly sense of humor or if he really didn't like women much.

Also, I feel like I've been very rude. I'm sending this picture as a literary olive branch.

Your friend, Alice

P.S. I'll tell my story when you explain the gaming manual. I really am curious. It's not something I think is useful, good, or worthy. It's like seeing a bomb on your shelf, with the timer set and running.

Paul let out a bark of laughter. A bomb? His software manual was a weapon of mass destruction, set to take out everything around it?

Andy looked up, an expression of total surprise on his face. "What's so funny?"

He shook his head. "Sorry. I just got a shock. Wasn't expecting…"

Andy stretched and let out a wide yawn. "People are weird. Haven't you learned that by now?"

"I guess. Someone just compared designing games to building bombs." Paul paused. "I'm pretty sure that's what she meant."

“Who are you talking to?” Andy shot him a look. “I thought you were going to scan in a new book while we were hanging out up here in the sky.” His brows went up. “Wait. Did you meet someone new and I’m the last to know? Was she on one of those dating sites?”

“No, but thanks for implying I need one.” He read the line again. Yup, she had definitely just called him a bomb-maker. “She’s a reader from the classic book site. Well, a bookstore owner, actually.”

“Hold on, why are you talking about gaming? I thought you were doing your superhero secret identity thing. Is that over? Are you out?” Andy looked honestly alarmed. “You made sure those were all in the public domain, right? We could get the pants sued off us.” He held up a hand. “Sorry, *you* could get the pants sued off *you*. Remember to tell the lawyers I had nothing to do with it.”

Paul snorted. “Your loyalty is touching. I’m still anonymous. She just noticed the books on my shelf. You know, in my profile picture. She must have zoomed in and read the titles.”

“Buddy, you are playing a dangerous game with those people. They’re worse than gamers. They have no lives. Everything becomes about the online interaction. You talk to them enough and they feel like they own you.”

He had to agree, just a little. Watching the comment threads explode from one question about an obscure book to thousands of passionate arguments pro and con, he had to wonder if these people had jobs. Paul wasn’t willing to sacrifice hours of his time to argue about whether *Kidnapped* or *Treasure Island* was Robert Louis Stevenson’s best work and he was an above-average fan of the man.

“I’ll be careful. It’s just email,” Paul said. He pulled the laptop closer.

“Uh huh. That’s what they all say.”

"Who says? This isn't going to end up like Stephen King's *Misery*, with me tied to a bed by some crazed fan."

"I sure hope not. And I meant people who meet their spouses online. My cousin fell in love with this woman from New Zealand and he kept saying it was just a few emails. He lives on the other side of the planet now and they've got four kids."

"That's not happening here. She's a bookstore owner from Natchitoches." Paul shrugged. "I can't think of anybody less likely to be a candidate for my affections than someone who lives in that gator swamp."

Andy's mouth dropped open. "You're kidding me. Please tell me you're kidding. Your secret identity is corresponding with someone from your real-life home town?"

"It's nothing really. I only heard of the woman a few hours ago. It doesn't mean anything so keep your shirt on. I'm not planning a big Creole wedding so I can settle down in the bayou and leave you in charge of everything."

Andy didn't laugh. "If you say so." He looked as if he wanted to say more, but decided it wasn't worth the effort. He turned back to his reports.

Paul clicked on the attachment, already deciding not to respond to the picture. Whatever it was, it would have to wait, probably indefinitely.

The photo that popped up wasn't Alice or the store. It was a picture of a bookshelf. It wasn't the tidy organized line of leather bound volumes he was expecting. It was a very personal picture, as personal as it could get between bookish types. His face creased with a grin. She was letting him see what no one else saw: the jumble of best-loved books, side by side like adopted siblings. They had no connection, except for the fact the same person loved them all.

He leaned closer, cocking his head to read the titles. His smile widened. He never would have guessed, not in a million years. Alexander Pope essays next to Louisa May Alcott next to John Green next to Jane Austen's *Emma* next to some big science fiction tome with a dragon on the spine next to something called *Fat Vampire*. He let out a chuckle when he recognized Jane Eyre between *Freakonomics* and *The Big Book of Southern Cakes*. A whole row of Alan Bradley mysteries hogged the second shelf but they were sandwiched between a bookbinding manual and *The Letters of St. Teresa of Avila*.

"I really hope that goofy smile isn't for something she sent." Andy spoke into his papers, a scowl on his face.

Paul forced himself to sit back and look uninterested. "Just a picture of books. That's all."

Andy sent him a long look. "I find that hard to believe."

"Only the truth, my friend." Paul kept his tone offhand. He should close the picture and wait until later, but he might not get another chance anytime soon. They had meetings all afternoon. He tried to seem uninterested but it was hard to casually crane his neck to read the titles.

Then he felt his smile fade. A leather bound book, the gold lettering clearly visible, was almost lost between *The Wind in the Willows* and a picture book on the periodic table of elements. What were the chances Alice would have the same little book of poetry? He knew that first edition was rare, it had taken him ages to track it down. But not only did she have it, it was in a treasured spot on the messy shelf of most-beloved books.

He stood up and walked to the window. His mind was turning the possibilities over and over. She could have searched out a copy before contacting him and staged the picture. She was the one who asked about his shelf first, after all. She's the one who brought up Elizabeth Barrett Browning and implied that it led to the whole reason she owned the store. He paced up and down in front of the window, wishing he could be more suspicious, and then wished he could be more trusting because he truly wanted to believe in a world of such wonderful coincidences.

Paul turned back to the window, staring down at the fields below. Time was slipping away and all he'd done was flirt with someone he'd never met. He had a book to scan and real work to do. He should forget all about Alice and her books, never respond to another message. That would be the logical step, especially for a famous billionaire pursued by all kinds of unsavory people and who had that small issue of a secret online identity.

But he knew he wouldn't. Even as he considered it, he pushed it back out of his mind. Paul walked to his briefcase and pulled out the tidy pile of old pages that he'd cut from the Alexander Pope poetry book. Opening the portable scanner, he gently started to feed the pages through the machine. The red seraph logo on the side was the only thing that connected ScreenStop to his other life.

There was only one way to resolve the mystery of Alice. He would meet her face-to-face and see if she really was everything her bookshelf claimed to be. The only problem would be that she wouldn't know who he was. To her, he would be Paul Olivier, businessman.

Paul swallowed a lump of unease. This was more complicated than he thought it would be. But he couldn't think of any other way around the problem. He knew one thing for sure. He had to know if Alice Augustine, Natchitoches bookstore owner and swapper of intimate shelf portraits, was for real.

Chapter Seven

I force people to have coffee with me, just because I don't trust that
a friendship can be maintained with any other senses besides a computer
or a cell phone screen. — John Cusack

Alice sat down at her desk and stared at Van Winkle. It must be great to sleep one's life away in a patch of sunshine. She wished with all her might that the legal letter would disappear, along with "Norma the beloved niece." She rubbed her parents' wedding rings between her thumb and forefinger, trying to calm her thoughts. There was no use worrying about it right then. She couldn't do a thing until she found a lawyer.

She wandered the store, desperate for some distraction from her anxiety. She wanted to call this woman and ask what gave her the right to take something that wasn't hers. More than anything, she wished she could talk to Mr. Perrault.

Apart from the customer looking for books by BWK, no one else had opened the door. Alice had enjoyed talking to Karen, and had even exchanged phone numbers with her after the woman mentioned wanting to talk about the books she'd read with someone over coffee. Karen said the online forums were fun, but they could never replace a face-to-face book discussion over coffee. With that, Alice warmed to her completely. As different as they were, they were also very much alike. They both preferred friends to be of the breathing variety, rather than the cold screen and profile picture type.

Alice caught sight of her little shelf of personal books and grimaced. She should know better than to share private information with strangers. But he'd seemed so real, so much like herself. They even had the same small volume of poetry, The Seraphim and Other Poems. Except for the science fiction part. She couldn't see how reading that much sci-fi would serve anybody well in the real world.

With every new email, she'd been drawn in to the conversation, beginning to think of him as a new friend. After an hour passed with no response, Alice wished she could snatch back the picture and hide it away. She'd been flirting and was ashamed of herself. Maybe he hadn't read it that way, but she felt the way her heart rate quickened every time she'd seen a new message. Of all the traits she respected the most, loyalty was one of the highest and she hadn't shown Eric any loyalty this morning.

A lot of people would laugh at her scruples, but Alice saw it very clearly. She'd become momentarily infatuated with someone she'd never met and completely forgotten Eric. *Again.* He was coming to take her to lunch in less than an hour and he hadn't even crossed her mind.

Alice hung her head for a moment. Eric deserved better. He deserved honesty. Slumping into her chair, she caught her reflection in the long mirror across the room. She sat up straighter. Starting now, she'd be a better person, inside and out. She squinted. Maybe she'd neglected her outside a bit, too. Her normally tan skin reminded her of Dickens' description of Miss Havisham's wedding dress: "pale, like something shut up inside too long." The shock from this morning showed. She put her hands to her cheeks and rubbed them. Maybe she needed to get into the sun a little more. Her dark hair was going every which way, but that wasn't unusual and she didn't bother to redo her ponytail. Her brothers used to joke that she looked like Marge Simpson in the mornings, her hair a towering column of crazy curls. It wasn't quite that bad at the moment, but it was definitely not a smooth, professional look. She didn't really care. She had bigger problems.

She drew back her lips, showing off her best asset: straight, white teeth. The mirror was dusty and the glass wavered with age, but the image reflected wasn't too bad, considering. She turned her face to one side, and then the other, keeping her wide smile in place. Squinting, she lifted her chin and noted the softening of her jawline. Every year, she looked more and more like the old photos of her mother.

"It doesn't bother me. Doesn't bother me a single bit," she said into the quiet, but she heard the lie in her own voice.

She tossed her ponytail over one shoulder and flashed another smile. Her upper-eye area seemed puffy. She hadn't cried when she'd read the legal letter so maybe she was retaining water. She widened her eyes and smiled again, trying to reproduce the look of a girl ten years younger.

The barest echo made Alice's heart drop, along with her smile. She whirled in her chair, hoping it was just the mail falling through the slot, or Charlie coming in early so she could go to lunch. A man stood just outside the glass door, eyes fixed on her. He was young, tall, with straight black hair. His tailored button-up shirt and jeans said he was wealthy and on vacation. His expression was a cross between amusement and confusion.

Alice held his gaze, willing him to move on. Her mind flashed to the letter, but that lawyer had lived in Houston. This man was likely a customer, but she didn't care if he was looking to buy half her inventory, she wanted him to keep walking. He'd caught her preening at the mirror and she didn't think her ego could hold up under a whole conversation.

As if he knew what she was thinking, his mouth tugged up in a smile. Pushing the door open, he stepped into the dim interior as the tiny brass bell announced his arrival a few minutes too late. He walked confidently, as if he'd been born into privilege.

When customers came in, Alice usually hopped out of her chair and came to see if they needed any particular help. But this time she felt rooted to the seat, like a toad caught crossing the highway, frozen in the high beams of an old pick-up truck. She watched him saunter in, gaze locked on hers, until he stood directly in front of her. The corners of his eyes crinkled and Alice edged his age up a little further, closer to thirty than twenty.

He took in the snoozing Van Winkle, the piles of papers, her coffee mug steaming gently. He turned, slowly scanning the room. "A mirror," he said. His voice was deep and his accent was local, but muted, as if he hadn't been home in a long time.

"Excuse me?"

"I assumed you were having a conversation with someone you didn't care for, but you were simply menacing your own reflection."

Several responses flew through her mind but she didn't want to speak any of them aloud. She was a modern woman who treated herself kindly, including daily pep talks on body image and being good enough for any man who had the brains to look past bra size and her slight tendency to gain weight in the winter. If anyone had asked, she would have declared herself more confident and secure than the general female population.

"I looked pale," she muttered.

A dark brow arched upward. "Feeling okay?"

"Perfectly fine, thanks." Aside from an ebbing tide of residual embarrassment. "How can I help you?"

"I'm looking for old poetry. Specifically Alexander Pope and Robert Browning," he said.

He was fit but bulkier than a runner. She would have said businessman from the understated watch with the leather band, but his shoes were battered black Converse. He was looking at her, a smile tugging at his lips and she realized she'd been giving him the whole body scan.

She pushed back from her desk. "Our poetry section is small, but I have quite a few first editions."

"It doesn't matter which editions. Anything will be fine." He stepped aside to let her pass and she smelled something really good, a cross between a man and…old books. She led the way toward the front of the store and into the poetry section, but halfway down the narrow aisle she turned to face him.

"Are you a collector?" No, she already that knew that wasn't right. He would have specified an edition or a publisher.

"Not exactly." He smiled, but there was a tightness to his mouth. He glanced over her head. "Are they at the end? I can find them. No need to trouble yourself."

"Are you a bookseller?" She'd stepped forward without thinking. The sunlight was filtering through the range, hitting him in the chest, illuminating his neck and stubbled chin, putting his eyes into shadow. Something was wrong with this man who didn't care which editions he wanted but smelled like he'd rolled in a pile of old manuscripts.

"Kinda sorta," he said. He shrugged, as if pretending to be mysterious and a little bit flirtatious. but as he moved, the sun flashed across his face and Alice caught the hint of panic in his eyes. He didn't want to tell her what he was doing.

"You're not… You're not one of those people, are you? The ones who rip out pages from perfectly good books to make horrible art that ignorant folk hang on their walls so they can feel literary and bookish?" She dropped her hand to the shelf, steadying herself against the thought. She stepped forward, her nose almost touching his chest, and inhaled deeply. He held his hands up in surprise and she caught his wrist, pulling his palm towards her. He smelled wonderful, because on his skin was the unmistakable scent of dusty books.

She was filled with outrage. "You are. I can smell them on you. Murderer!"

He laughed--a deep, warm sound. "I assure you. I am no book murderer."

"Then tell me what you're going to do with them," Alice said, dropping his hand.

His gaze went over her head toward the leather bound books at the end of the row, like a hungry man who could smell gumbo simmering on the stove. He didn't answer.

"You can't have them." She crossed her arms. Everything about him spoke of privilege and wealth. He probably got his way in every bookstore he wandered into, especially with that laugh. Her bookstore was operating in the red but she'd rather die than let a book meet its end that way.

"But you run a bookstore. Are you telling me that you won't sell me any books?" His voice had dropped an octave and he spoke very deliberately.

"That's what I'm saying. They tell me you can find anything you need on the Internet so—"

"They tell you that, do they?" His lips turned up, but there was steel in his smile.

Alice ignored him. "I'm only prolonging the process a tiny bit but," she tossed her hair back and straightened her shoulders, "I'll be darned if I'm going to hand over a rare book to a… a book murderer."

"I said I wasn't--" He rubbed a hand over his face. He was really nice looking, in an offbeat sort of way. If life were like the movies, he'd always be cast as the not-too-handsome supporting actor, the kind that viewers naturally trusted and admired. But she knew better.

"People like you are the reason the world has given up reading," Alice said. "Everyone is stuck on their phones and their computers, never bothering to pick up a book unless they want to make some horrible art out of it, which they can post on Facebook for all their friends. But these," she touched the leather bound volumes, her voice rising, "are my friends. I only want them to go home with people who will treasure them."

His eyes narrowed. "That's a lot of persnickety proprietary nonsense. And that's also why you're not making any money."

She sucked in air. "Who said I wasn't making any money?"

"I did." He gestured to the center of the store. "No trinkets, no greeting cards. No board games or junior chemistry sets. No coffee mugs with inspiring quotations or T-shirts with Colin's Firth's face."

"I don't run a Hallmark store. I sell—"

"I know." He stepped closer. They were just inches apart now. "You sell books. There's no real money in books, you know. Especially if you work yourself into damp spot on the floor trying *not* to sell them, even to people who come in and ask for them ever so politely."

She blinked up, struggling to ignore that part of biology that convinces a woman that a handsome man means well, even when his words don't add up.

"Are you a book smuggler? Do you sell them on the black market? Just tell me what you're doing and let me decide whether to give you the books," she said.

"The black market? You mean eBay?" He seemed honestly confused by her question.

"Just tell me."

"I can't."

"It couldn't be worse than what I'm thinking. Anything that doesn't physically harm a book should be okay." She wasn't sure if what she was saying was exactly true. She preferred that books be read, of course. She'd sold a beautiful set of Thomas Hardy to a realtor from Atlanta, who then moved it from house to house as scene-setting décor, never to be read. That still bothered her and every now and then, late at night, she dreamed of stealing them back.

He shook his head, half-turning "You wouldn't believe me. And there's nothing I can say to convince you. I've met people like you before. Stuck in the past, refusing to move into the modern world. I could quote the greatest minds of the past century and you'd still believe technology was a curse."

Alice crossed her arms. "Give me one. And not a scientist. Give me a great mind, someone who wrote something I might actually have read."

"Alexander Pope. 'Be not the first by whom the new are tried, not yet the last to lay the old aside'." He gave her a look of triumph.

It was strange to hear that name just hours after seeing it in an email. Alice shrugged. "That's hardly a ringing endorsement. Sounds cautionary to me."

"I've met dozens of bookstore owners like you. I know how you think. Even if I did explain what I was doing, you wouldn't approve because these books should be treated like the rarest treasures. Nothing else matters and you'll do anything to inhibit progress."

Alice let that sink in. She wasn't sure what was offensive about his statement. She'd had her share of being overlooked, especially by handsome men. Maybe it was because it made her sound so common, so bland. Resisting the urge to order him from the store, she said, "I can't imagine that you know how I think. We're nothing alike. You're obviously some type of mid-level manager who wants a few pretty editions on your office shelf to impress the visitors." She paused. "Except you smell like you've been rolling in old books."

He stood motionless for a moment, a look of disbelief on his face. "Mid-level manager? Is that your best insult?"

"It's just a guess. But although you say you know everything about me, all you did was point out the fact my store doesn't sell trinkets. So, tell me what I am, if you've met dozens of me."

He blinked, as if not sure what to say. Then he shrugged. "Okay, I'll tell you." He turned and walked back down the aisle, headed for her desk. "You have a laptop, but I bet you only use it at work. You probably live close by in a little apartment that's stuck in the last century. You don't own a television. You might have a cell phone but you don't use it."

He ignored her little sound of objection and walked to her desk, standing over her workspace. He pointed to her fountain pen, her mint green rotary phone, and Van Winkle. "You still write letters, and only email when you have to. You think people who play computer games are wasting their lives and losing brain cells. You probably believe the world is going to hell in a hand basket because of technology. If you could jump back in time a hundred years, you would be perfectly at home in a world without any technology at all."

He was perfectly controlled, but Alice could see the anger flashing in his eyes. "You think it was more civilized, more humane, more genteel back then, and that people like you are the only reason the earth is still turning. You're proud you didn't drink the Kool-Aid like the rest of the deluded population. You're on a mission to turn back the clock. Only difference between you and the last ten booksellers I've met is that you're young and beautiful, but give it another forty years and a few more cats and —"

"Just hold on," Alice interrupted. A little bit of her was replaying the 'young and beautiful' part, but the rest of her didn't care what he thought would happen after another forty years. She crossed her arms over her chest. "I can't believe you march into a bookstore, insult the owner, and still expect to walk away with rare books."

He pinched the bridge of his nose and closed his eyes for a moment as if he were counting in his head. Alice hoped she was giving him a headache. She'd never been so put off by a customer in her life. Her brothers had been urging her to carry mace in case someone broke in and attacked her. If only she'd listened. Nothing would have been more satisfying than to wave the little canister in his face and ask him to repeat that part about the cats.

"They don't have to be rare. Just old." His voice was calm. He looked up and Alice knew he was waiting for her to ask him to explain again. She pressed her lips together. She hated riddles but she didn't want to be the one to give in. There were at a standoff.

There was a rustle from the stacks of paperbacks and Mrs. Gaskell walked between them, tail high, ears twitching.

"Oh, and I bet your cat is named Darcy," he said. "Book owners always name their pets after characters."

All the arguments she had been forming fled her brain and she felt her face go hot. "It's a she, actually." Darcy was perched not four feet above this man's head but she wasn't going to tell him that. But the cat had heard his name and for the first time in his life, decided to respond to it. He let out a low meow and jumped to the carpet between them.

The man shot a look at her as Darcy sauntered away.

"Jane Eyre?"

"No."

A whisper of sound made him turn his head, but Alice stood stock still. Maybe if she didn't move, Jane Eyre would go back into hiding. The next moment, the striped tabby stepped from between a row of books and put her nose to the man's pant leg. He cocked his head and a small smile touched his lips.

"Mr. Rochester? Everybody loves him. Crazy wife in the attic and all."

"No." She wanted to keep him from guessing but couldn't figure out whether to push him toward the poetry or out the door. A movement drew her gaze and Alice couldn't believe her eyes as Mr. Rochester took up a position at the end of the row. His tattered ear was even uglier in the bright sunlight, and he looked mangy and old. Something in her expression made the man turn around and his smile spread into a grin. Then he went back to guessing.

"Elizabeth? Mrs. Bennet?"

"No and no. We weren't talking about my cats. We were—"

"Just how many cats do you have?" He sounded simultaneously amused and alarmed as Miss Elizabeth padded over, her eyes bright with excitement, Mrs. Bennet following right behind her.

"Not that many," Alice exclaimed. Her cats had never once responded to her, even for breakfast. They came when they wanted, as if they owned the building and she was just living at their convenience. But they all seemed to know it was time to visit the obnoxious know-it-all customer today and prove how truly odd Alice was.

"It's from a romance. Definitely something made into a BBC movie. Let me think." He put a finger to his chin and pretended to consider it, but cracked an almost-suppressed smile. If she hadn't been so irritated, she would have let herself admire him a little more.

"It could be from a horror novel for all you know."

"You're a romantic," he said. "Look at the size of your poetry section."

She couldn't think of a word to say. She'd been called a lot of things. Odd, weird, reclusive, introverted, quiet. She'd even been called impossible to please by a few boyfriends. Just last week, Eric called her stubborn because she refused to trade in her perfectly nice car for something newer. But no one had ever called her a romantic. And she was, to her very core, a romantic.

Every relationship she'd ever had was doomed from the start because the men couldn't measure up to her book heroes. She wanted a Darcy, a Rochester, a Thornton, a Colonel Brandon, a Captain Wentworth. Alice couldn't change that fact, no matter how much she tried. This dark secret fueled her fear that she would never find true love, never marry. Now this stranger stood there describing her so perfectly, it felt like someone had peeled back a layer of her skin and exposed her very heart beating within her chest.

"Her name is Mrs. Gaskell," she whispered.

He snapped his fingers. "Right! The author of *North and South*. Richard Armitage as the cotton mill owner." He glanced at her face and the smile faded away. "Look, I didn't mean to offend you," he said, his voice no longer teasing.

Alice looked at her feet. The whole day had been a disaster and it wasn't even noon. She'd flirted ridiculously online, accused a customer of book abuse, been called the early version of a crazy cat lady, and now she was going to sell this man some books even though she really, really wished he'd just go away. She lifted her head to tell him to choose what he wanted, but she couldn't seem to get the words past the ache in her throat.

He seemed uncomfortable now. "About the books, they'll be read and enjoyed, I promise," he said. He cleared his throat, as if waiting for her to continue the argument. She stayed silent. There was something like tenderness in his eyes as he said, "They're not for me."

She nodded. "I'm sorry for being so suspicious. Some of these books have been in Cane River families for generations. They were passed down from father to son, from mother to daughter. These aren't just books. They're part of our city history, and I won't allow someone to destroy them. I know you think that's backwards and silly."

He dropped his head, leaving his face shadowed again. "I shouldn't have said that. I was just surprised by your questions."

Alice tried to pull herself together. "I don't know why you would be. You've met lots of people just like me before, right?" She pointed toward the poetry section. "Help yourself. I'm sorry I made this difficult for you." She heard the softness in her voice, the little waver at the end of her words, and hated it.

He paused, as if searching for something else to say, then shook his head. He walked away, leaving Alice alone.

She dropped into her chair and stared at the top of her desk, watching Van Winkle's chest rise and fall with every breath as he slept. She had always thought of herself as a complex, intricate person, woven together of all the complicated characters she'd ever read and re-read. She considered herself part Creole woman raised by an old woman who was too tired to really bother with an angry teen girl and part Mr. Perrault's living depository of book knowledge. Her past was bright college-girl freedom and her present was working-woman worries. She was a dedicated hometown girl and the historic district business owner who always felt as if she'd lucked into her life. But no matter what she'd always thought of herself, maybe she really was just someone who was afraid to join the real world. Her romantic nature seemed charming in this little place, but to the rest of the population, she was a nut job.

She rested her chin in both hands and thought about the picture she'd sent Browning Wordsworth Keats. How desperate she must have looked, sending him a picture of her shelf. He probably brushed it off. She was nobody to him and he certainly wouldn't give it a second glance.

It shouldn't matter, but it did, because Alice knew her own heart. She'd taken out the cell phone she never used, took her first mobile photo, sent it to herself on email and then on to him. That was a lot of trouble for a man who didn't even give out his real name. It was a whole lot more trouble than she took for the man she was actually dating.

As if called by her thoughts, there was a jingling at the door and Eric stepped through. Alice stood up, forcing a smile. It seemed impossible that she could have forgotten that they had a date, yet again.

As bad as this day was going, it was about to get worse. She had to tell him the truth. They weren't meant to be together. He was better off with someone who could remember he existed.

Chapter Eight

Technological society has succeeded in multiplying the opportunities for pleasure,
but it has great difficulty in generating joy. — Pope Paul VI

Paul stood with an old leather book in his hands, cracked open to a random page, his gaze unfocused on the words. He'd only planned to pop into the store long enough to take the measure of her and then go on to meet the realtor. He couldn't have predicted how his plan would go. The little book he'd scanned on the plane left enough book dust behind that she'd noticed. His mind flashed to the moment she'd stepped forward, put her face in his shirt, then grabbed his hand and smelled his palm. He choked back a laugh at the memory. He'd never been manhandled by a bookstore owner before and he had to admit he hadn't minded a bit. She must have superhuman olfactory senses along with those green eyes and perfect skin. But it wasn't just that she surprised him by asking what he was doing with the books, or even that she'd smelled it on him in the first place. It wasn't the uncannily astute questions or the whirlwind of the conversation, either. It was that she was ten times prettier than her pictures and a hundred times more captivating than any of those little notes.

He knew he'd been treading on thin ice this morning but now he was in genuine trouble. Of all the women he'd ever known, Paul had never been so instantly smitten. He wanted to know everything about her life here, ask her about those rings she wore on that necklace, ask her opinion on all his favorite books, and he especially wanted to impress the socks off her. Which would be pretty difficult now that he'd insulted her to her face.

Paul slammed the book closed and didn't bother to open the next. He'd acted like a complete jerk, implying she would die alone and surrounded by cats. He'd never been the smoothest guy in the room but this was a new low, even for him. Maybe his manners had sunk to that level without him noticing because most people cared more about his money and name, rather than whether or not he was decent human being. Andy would have told him to shut up if he'd been here, but Paul had sent him on an errand at the opposite end of the city so he could make this trip in secret. That was his first mistake.

Shame made his neck go hot. He needed to apologize. Whether or not they ever wrote each other again, whether or not she helped him find books he needed, whether or not they ever had another conversation. His conscience burned at the memory of the things he'd said. His mother hadn't raised him to speak like that to anyone, especially a woman.

He trudged down the aisle toward the little desk, forming his apology in his mind. He stopped short at the end of the range by the sight of Alice planting a kiss on a man's mouth. The man turned and gave him a look of surprise, which Paul was sure matched his own expression. He hadn't expected Alice to have a boyfriend although she'd never said she didn't. Paul swept a look from the man's blond head to his too-tight polo shirt to his tasseled loafers.

"Are you ready?" Alice came toward him, holding out her hand. Her cheeks looked pink but she didn't have the glow of a woman in love. She seemed under stress, anxious.

But of course she was. Paul was still in her store. She probably thought he was going to launch into another litany of insults. "Almost. I was wondering if you had a few more books I need."

The blond man let out a deep sigh. "Where's Charlie? You promised she'd be here and we'd go to lunch. I know I didn't imagine that." His voice was bordering on whiney and it grated on Paul's nerves.

Paul saw the little grimace Alice made, but she recovered quickly and turned back with a smile. "Sorry, Eric. She'll be here in a few minutes. I think you're early. We said noon, right?"

Eric shrugged. "Okay, but if we say noon for lunch, that means I come down here at eleven forty-five so we can get to the restaurant in time."

"Oh, did you make a reservation somewhere? How thoughtful." Alice's voice was a little too sweet. Her sarcasm said this guy wasn't the type to bother with making a reservation at a nice place on a Friday at noon, but he wasn't above whining when his plans got bumped.

She was half-turning back to Paul when Eric stumbled out a denial. "No, but I have patients waiting on me. You don't even have customers, usually. You could close and no one would even notice."

"I guess I would notice," Paul said. He shouldn't get involved but the man was talking as if Paul didn't exist, even though they stood less than five feet apart. Paul was trying hard to keep a straight face. This couple was in the last stages of a relationship. They'd probably been together for years and years, clinging to the comfort of old arguments. He glanced at Alice, saw surprise in her eyes. She deserved better than this too-tight-polo-and-loafer guy.

Eric gave him a once over, letting his eyes rest on Paul's favorite Converse shoes and then turned back to

Alice, as if Paul hadn't spoken. "Maybe you could call Charlie. I bet *she* answers her phone."

Ouch. The snide comment made Paul's offhand remark seem even more pointed. He saw Alice's face go red and he regretted ever having said those words. He stepped toward Alice, holding up the book. "I'm sorry to keep you. If you need to leave, I can come back later."

Alice bit her lip, glanced at the poetry books and then at Eric, as if mentally calculating how much it was worth to keep her boyfriend happy. "Well, maybe you should…"

"Or maybe I'll just buy these if you don't have the others I need," Paul said. "It would take just a second to check your inventory, right?"

Eric made another noise and walked to Alice's desk, slumping down in her chair. Alice kept her eyes straight ahead but her face went tight. Paul felt her frustration, being caught between the rudest customer she'd probably ever met and the boyfriend she apparently couldn't stand.

"What are you looking for exactly?" she asked. "I'm afraid we don't have much more poetry than what you saw in that section."

The weariness in her voice triggered something in Paul, and he made a decision without really thinking it through. "I'm looking for a present. This person is a collector, has almost everything. I need something really impressive. Doesn't matter what."

Alice frowned. "It should matter if they're a collector. Have you ever seen their shelves? Maybe you have some idea—"

"Nope. And don't worry, I won't come back and return it if he doesn't like it," Paul said. "But if you have something rare and valuable, I think that would be best."

"Eleven fifty-two," Eric intoned from the desk chair.

Alice closed her eyes briefly and Paul wondered if she was going to tell Eric to get out. Instead, she nodded. "I'll show you where we keep our most valuable editions," she said, and she led Paul toward the far side of the store, through a little doorway. There stood wall-to-wall cabinets, all climate-controlled. Paul peered into one case and was momentarily speechless. He didn't expect this little shop to have a treasure-trove of rare books that would put his own collection to shame. He thought back to the front of the store and wondered why she had no security system, no cameras, no alarms. She was asking to be robbed if she didn't take more precautions. But it all sort of fit with her refusal to join the modern world.

"*A Farewell to Arms*. Signed?" Paul didn't need a signed copy and he didn't really like Hemingway. But he knew how much that little book cost. He'd seen one in a bookstore in New York City for close to twenty thousand dollars. "*Cat's Cradle*. I don't think he has any Kurt Vonnegut."

He moved to the next cabinet without waiting for her to answer. "You have a lot of children's books," he said, almost to himself.

"The previous owner, Mr. Perrault, had always wanted children but he and his wife were never blessed with any. " Alice came to stand beside him and turned, eyes bright. "Would you like to see my favorite?" Paul nodded. If she had asked him to step off a cliff, he might have agreed. She took a small key from a bracelet around her wrist and opened a low display case.

She quickly tugged on a pair of white cotton gloves and brought out a cream-colored box. Inside was an artist's portfolio. Leaning over, the rings on her necklace swung forward and he could see they were plain gold bands in two different sizes. She untied the ribbons and moved close to him so he could see. "It's not really a book, but rather the pictures to a book. *Little White Bird*, by J.M. Barrie, was illustrated by—"

"Arthur Rackham," Paul breathed. He'd never seen anything so beautiful. Vellum gilt-edged pages, perfectly engraved plates of full-sized watercolors.

"Only twenty were signed even though the publisher had planned for hundreds. As far as we know, there are only twenty total." Alice sighed. "Probably money issues."

"I'll take this one," he said. "This will be perfect."

Alice opened her mouth, and then closed it again. She looked conflicted. "I hate to tell you this, but the price is more than a new car. It's a very rare portfolio."

"I'm sure it's fine," he said, smiling.

"It's almost sixty thousand dollars," she said, already moving to put the folio back in the box.

"I'll take it," he said. He wasn't trying to impress her with his wealth but he felt great satisfaction in knowing that buying this piece would make up for being a real jerk earlier. "I think my friend will really like it."

Her hand stilled on the papers. He wondered if she'd hoped to save it for her own children, but then he figured she would have put it aside. Unless she couldn't afford to put it aside for her future children when her store was suffering. Paul blew out a breath. He didn't know which way to go with this woman. It seemed whatever he did was wrong.

"Sorry, I probably seem like I don't want to sell you a single thing in this store," she said, rushing her words out. "I'm just surprised." She glanced at him, smiling a little. "Not many people can buy a first edition like this. Let me get this wrapped back up in its box back to the register."

"Thank you," he said, feeling his shoulders relax. Maybe meeting him wasn't a complete disaster on her side. Money didn't solve everything but it sure helped soften the blow. He glanced around the small room, unsure if they would get another chance to speak alone. He cleared his throat, feeling more nervous than he had in a long time. "And I wanted to say I'm sorry for the way I spoke to you earlier."

She looked up, meeting his gaze directly. "Don't be. You were right." Sadness touched her eyes. "Everything you said was right."

He let out a short laugh. "Not everything, surely."

She nodded. "Especially the part about—"

A teen girl with long blond hair came in at a trot, already talking before she was through the doorway. "Hey, Miss Alice! Why is Darcy down from his spot? Did you get the broom?"

"Darcy?" Paul asked. "I thought you didn't have a cat named Darcy."

"No, I said that *particular* cat wasn't named Darcy," Alice responded, her lips tugging up.

"You would have made a good lawyer," he said.

"Oh, my gosh," breathed the teenage girl. She came forward slowly, blue eyes wide. "Are you Paul Olivier?"

"Yes, I am." He smiled and held out his hand.

She grasped it, shaking it reverently. "Wow," she said. "Just… wow. I never thought I'd meet you. I'm Charlie Soule. I'm, like, your biggest fan ever."

Alice stared from one to the other. "Are you an actor? I'm sorry, maybe I should have recognized you. I don't watch TV."

He let Charlie's hand go and smiled. "I'm not on TV. And I should have introduced myself but I think we started off on the wrong foot."

"No, it was my fault." Alice put down the little box and took off her gloves. She held out her hand. "I'm Alice Augustine. Let's pretend we just met. I'll have better manners and you can buy anything in my store that you want."

He reached out and took her hand, feeling the softness of her palm against his. For just a moment, Paul forgot all about the portfolio and the argument and the teen girl watching them. And he forgot especially about the long-term boyfriend sitting at Alice's desk.

"Alice, are you coming or should I just go by myself?" Eric walked up, a scowl on his face. He took in the scene and his eyes narrowed.

Paul let go of Alice's hand. "We're just finishing up. I need to get going, too. I have to meet a realtor about an apartment."

"You're staying in town for a while?" Charlie asked breathlessly. Alice shot her a look.

"For a few weeks. I'm from this area but haven't been back in years. I thought visiting during the three-hundredth year anniversary would be a good time to come home for a while. Looking forward to things like the zydeco festival this weekend."

"I'm going to that, too," Charlie exclaimed. "I mean, my mom mentioned it and I thought it sounded kinda weird, but if you're going then I'm sure it's a good idea."

Paul moved toward the entryway, even though Eric was blocking the spot, face like thunder. "Plus, we want to make sure the store gets off to a smooth start so we're temporarily moving our home base here." At the last second, Eric turned and stomped toward the middle of the store.

"Which store is this?" Alice locked the case again and followed Paul out of the room. "Did you buy one of the local businesses? We'll be neighbors, then. I'm on the historic district board so if you need anything, I'd be glad to help if I can."

"The ScreenStop store," Charlie said, bouncing alongside of them. She looked thrilled to pieces. "This is Paul Olivier, the guy who invented the biggest online social platform *ever* while he was in college and sold it for like, a bazillion dollars. Then he started a company that designs some of the best games and got even richer! He has stores all over the country." She paused, her voice dropping shyly. "I'd love your autograph. I can't believe we're actually talking in real life."

Paul was used to awkward introductions but this was probably the most awkward, if only for Alice's expression. She'd stopped at the register, face blank with shock.

"It wasn't a bazillion," he muttered. "That's not a real number."

"ScreenStop?" Alice whispered.

"Excuse me," Eric called. He was only a few feet away but his voice was loud enough to reach the end of the store. "Are we going to lunch or not?"

Alice whirled toward him and said in a low voice, "No, Eric, we're not. I have a store to run. Whether you think this place is important or not, I do. I can't walk away from a customer just because you want to order at exactly noon so you can eat your lunch in exactly fifteen minutes, and have exactly ten minutes to walk back to your office so you'll have *exactly* eight minutes to flirt with your secretaries before patients arrive." She paused. "In fact, since we're having this conversation right now, I'd rather not have any more lunches with you again. Goodbye."

There was a beat of complete silence and then Eric sputtered something about not flirting with anybody, that she obviously she wasn't hungry, and he'd call her later. He turned around and left the bookstore, letting the door slam behind him.

Paul wanted to offer Alice a big high five but the fierce expression on her face told him that now was not the right time.

"I'm sorry about that," she said. Smoothing a hand over her hair, she sighed. "That was extremely unprofessional. It's just… I suppose it was long overdue."

"Not a problem, really. I completely understand." He shifted his feet. "You'd been together a long time?"

"Huh. Not even six months. Miss Alice is impossible to please." Charlie grinned, leaning against the counter. She was talking about Alice, but only had eyes for Paul. "In fact, she hates you, too."

"Charlie!" Alice glared at her.

Paul knew they'd gotten off to a rough start but thought hate was a rather extreme response. "Well, maybe we'll learn to appreciate our differences—" he started to say.

"Nope. Never gonna happen." Charlie jerked her head in Alice's direction. "I heard her on the phone yesterday, trying to track down who gave you that building permit. She wants to kick ScreenStop out of the historic district. She'd be happier than a clam if she could kick you all the way out of Natchitoches. She says people like you don't belong in a place like Cane River."

Paul turned to Alice, brows raised. *People like you.* She saw him as the poor kid he had once been, ignored unless he was being ridiculed, denied passage into the nicer parts of the city. No, Alice had never met that boy. She was looking at a rich businessman.

So she really did hate him before today. Then she hated him when he showed up in person. The only version of him she seemed to like was his fake identity. It was a triple ego-whammy. "We received the building permit in the usual way, going through all the regular channels."

Alice's face was pink but her voice was steady. "Impossible. Everything has to be passed by the board. I never saw any plans for that store."

"Not everything goes by the board. Believe me, my lawyers looked at the city bylaws very carefully." His gaze dropped to the portfolio she still held in her hands. "You're not going to sell me that, are you?"

Alice narrowed her eyes. "If I didn't, that would be spiteful," she said. "But will you think you've bought me off like everyone else in this city if I do? Because I don't have a price. Not even one this high," she said, holding up the Arthur Rackham illustrations.

He opened his mouth to respond, but she went on. "I do have a question, though."

"Go ahead." It couldn't get much worse. He had nothing to fear.

"The realtor you're meeting. Is she June LaTraye?"

He frowned. Maybe Alice was going to warn him off the woman. There were crooks in every city, every profession. "Yes. We're supposed to meet in about ten minutes. There's an apartment in the historic… district…" Paul's voice faded away.

They stared at each other for a moment. "Listen," Alice said, coming around the counter toward him. "You don't have to buy this portfolio. And you should probably find another place to rent while you're here. The Judge Porter House is a very nice bed and breakfast with full suites and it's right down the block. I wish you the best of luck."

Paul said nothing. The last few hours had been some of the strangest of his life, but he hadn't gotten where he was in the world by ignoring his intuition. Over and over he'd made decisions that weren't completely explainable, especially to his board of directors or to Andy. They'd learned to trust him and everything had always come out for the better. He didn't take her hand.

"I'd like to buy the portfolio. And I'd like to see the apartment," he said simply.

Relief, confusion, and something else flashed over her face. "If you're sure…"

"I am," he said. "I have no interest in trying to avoid a constant rotation of nosy tourists or sleeping in a canopy princess bed for a month."

"I won't promise to stop fighting your store."

"You should give me a chance to change your mind. Maybe you just haven't found your inner tech-loving geek. "

His chest tightened when she let out a soft laugh. She was more than pretty when she laughed. She was beautiful.

"I'm fairly certain I don't have one. Even if I didn't believe your company is changing society for the worse, your store just doesn't fit here, especially in the historic district."

Paul said nothing aloud. *Challenge accepted, Miss Alice Augustine.* Her words seemed to echo every time a resident of Natchitoches had told him that he was unwelcome, every single spoken and unspoken slight. He hadn't listened. He'd worked hard, devoted everything he had to proving them wrong.

"It's like I died and went to heaven. You're going to live upstairs? Right above the store? Are you going to have parties? Will they have cosplay?" Charlie put both hands to her face and let out a little shriek.

"Maybe." He couldn't help smiling at this girl's enthusiasm. He was just a guy who owned a gaming company and this sort of excitement never got old. He turned to Alice who had moved back around the counter and was wrapping up the portfolio in tissue, and placing it in a larger box.

Charlie leaned in, chewing her lip. "Listen, I know everybody must ask you stuff like this, but I've been on the new Ultimate Voyager game you created for, like, two weeks. I got that expansion pass and I got some awesome gear and weapons, but I can't get past the Planet of the Wolf Army. I'm just stuck in this forever cycle of injuries and recuperation, and I'm wasting all my time in that little canyon near the jump station. At this rate, I'm never gonna become Legend."

Paul wanted to laugh at Alice's expression. He was torn between outright laughter and wishing Charlie would leave this topic for another time. Alice's aversion to technology wouldn't lessen when people wandered around speaking the language of game culture. But he'd never been able to resist a gamer in trouble.

"There's a cheat. Use a broadsword on the first Wolf soldier. Nobody follows him if you do." He nodded at her protest. "It's true. If you'd tried every weapon, you'd have been able to get out." He held a finger to his lips. "And don't tell anyone I told you that or I'll deny everything."

Charlie was grinning hugely, bouncing on the toes of her shoes. "Man, this is awesome. Do you wanna play sometime? My name's UltimateStarCrossed. You can friend me and we can go on a raid sometime. I have a group I join every night for about three hours. They'd be so stoked if you dropped in." Her cheeks went pink.

Paul cleared his throat. He always hated this, when someone wanted to know his username. If he gave it out to everyone, then he'd never actually get to play. It would be all messages and friend requests. But he kept an alternate character in almost every game and that's the name he'd use if he ever played with Charlie. He'd always looked young and his love of T-shirts and jeans probably made him seem even younger. He was used to teen adulation at gaming expos and he was well aware that Charlie might not think he was too old for her, even though he was long out of college and sliding toward thirty.

"Sure, I'll friend you when I get set up here. I always like to meet new groups of players." He hoped his emphasis on "groups" would erase any assumptions on her part. He turned to Alice. "There are two apartments above this building, right? Is the other empty also? Maybe I could rent that side for my CTO who came with me. We're good friends but maybe he'd like his own space."

Alice looked up, her mouth open a bit. She seemed confused. "No, it's—"

"Miss Alice lives on that side. You guys are gonna see each other all the time," Charlie said gleefully.

"Oh," Paul said and tried to keep his face neutral. He should have known. He'd already said that she lived close by when he was being his jerky self earlier. And now he knew for certain the apartment was going to be as low tech as she could get away with and still be up to code. They would share a wall, this woman with the dark eyes and throaty laugh. The one who thought he was destroying society with his frivolous company. The one who had already grabbed his heart and squeezed it so hard he wasn't sure if he'd known her for a day or for a year.

Her gaze locked on his. A small smile touched her lips, as if she were daring him to back out now. It was silliness to think being next door neighbors would even matter. He desperately wanted to prove to her, and the rest of the Natchitoches elite, that he belonged here as much as she did. But staying within feet of each other might be last the drop of awkward to fill the bucket of bad feelings, spilling over into hate.

He held her gaze until she started wrapping up the box once more. As she reached for a larger box, he saw the bookshelf behind her. It was the picture she'd sent, with the colorful mysteries, the big science fiction with the dragon, the worn copy of Austen's *Emma* and the collector's edition of *Wind in the Willows*. And next to it was the little leather volume that he had on his own shelf. He felt the room tilt, as if the axis had shifted, and he looked back at this beautiful woman who sent personal bookshelf pictures to anonymous book-loving men. He thought of how the emails had made him laugh, made him feel as if he'd made a real connection with someone new for the first time in years.

It didn't matter if this apartment was a throwback to the Paleolithic era. He was going to take it.

"Nice to meet you, neighbor," he said and smiled.

Chapter Nine

Technological progress has merely provided us with more efficient means for going backwards. —Aldous Huxley

Alice let Charlie's excited chatter wash over her. She felt numb. She'd learned she might lose her store, made a fool of herself online, met the most infuriating man, broken up with her boyfriend, sold an incredibly expensive manuscript, met the man whom she was fighting to keep out of the historic district, and met her new renter. One person was responsible for almost all of those dramatic happenings. One clever, stubborn person.

She stared at the counter where he'd been standing minutes before. She'd never met anybody like him. She told herself that it was a very good thing her life had been devoid of anybody like Paul Olivier, but a little part of her disagreed. That little part was in no way connected to the logical, rational side of her, and had everything to do with the romantic she truly was.

"I wonder if his friend is just as cute." Charlie chattered. "I can't believe we're going to play together. He's so nice, too. The way he helped me out, I felt like my heart had like an extra layer of frosting on it or something. And sprinkles." She smiled dreamily at Alice. "And oh my gosh, he's so much hotter in person. The pictures I've seen are from some convention or whatever and there so many girls all over him that you can't really see him, but obviously the guy spends a lot of time in the gym. I mean, did you see his arms? They're like—"

"Charlie, I still need you to take over for an hour so I can get some lunch." Alice really didn't want to talk about Paul's gym habits and she seriously hoped he wasn't going to be hanging out with her barely eighteen-year-old employee.

"Sure! And so sorry about Eric." She paused, looking up at the ceiling. "Ok, not really. He was kind of a baby. Such a whiner."

"Yeah, he was. I hate to say it, but he was." She sighed. "He had his good points, though."

Charlie leaned over the counter. "Yeah? Like what?"

"Well, for one…" Alice paused, searching back to when they first met. "You know, aside from having a job and not being an ax murderer, I don't really know," she admitted, laughing.

Charlie giggled, covering her mouth. "I think Paul Olivier is hot. Like, really hot, not just geeky hot. And he's from around here so you guys will have so much in common."

The momentary sense of sisterhood evaporated. Alice rubbed the gold rings between her fingers and shook her head. "Nope. Nothing in common. Except we might actually have to see each other face-to-face a few times if he signs the lease." Then again, she wondered if he was just saying that. A billionaire couldn't possible want to live in her outdated apartment. At least, she sincerely hoped he wouldn't. Now that she'd sold that Rackham portfolio, it didn't matter if she left that apartment open indefinitely. It wasn't near enough to pay off Mr. Perrault's niece, but it would buy her some time.

The bell tinkled and Bix came in, the bright sun illuminating his old straw hat. "You'll never guess who I just saw," he called out.

"June LaTraye? She's showing the apartment upstairs," said Alice.

"Nope, I just saw Paul Olivier, the billionaire tech genius." He beamed at them. "I shook his hand. I told him I was his biggest fan."

"Me, too," crowed Charlie. "And we're gonna hang out together sometime."

"How do you know him?" Alice asked. "I mean, you don't even have a computer." The better question might be how someone with Bix's eyesight managed to recognize the man.

"How did you know it was him?" Charlie asked. "Was there a big crowd around him?"

Bix chuckled. "*Mais*, no. He was sitting on the bench outside and had the Arthur Rackham portfolio on his lap. I recognized the box. I been dusting the case around that thing for twenty years. I know it cost a pretty penny, so I stop to introduce myself. I tell him that he shouldn't open it in the sun and he should have some climate controls on the display case. He tells me his name and says he's having it shipped back to New York City today." He paused to wipe his forehead with a red kerchief. "That's when I thanked him on behalf of my sister Betsy and myself."

"Betsy?" Alice prompted.

"He invented this computer gizmo that keeps my sister able to live on her own, instead of in an old folks' home across the river." Bix took off his hat. "See, she could never remember when to take her pills and which pill to take. Lots of phones have alarms, but he made something that is an alarm and a picture together. The alarm goes off on her cell phone, she looks at the picture, finds the right pill, and stays on schedule. Genius!"

"I didn't know he'd invented more than games," she said, almost to herself. But one or two small inventions for the greater good couldn't erase the fact he was luring a whole generation into willful ignorance. She felt like the world was in love with Paul Olivier and she was the only sane person left.

"Miss Alice broke up with Eric while Paul Olivier was standing right there," Charlie said, pointing to an approximate spot near the counter.

"What on earth prompted that?" Bix asked. "I'm not saying you done wrong, *sha*. Not at all. Just curious timing if you ask me."

"It's a long story," Alice said, sighing. "Let's just say he got in the way of a sale."

Bix's smile grew wider and wider until he finally burst out in a belly laugh. "That boy don't have a lick of sense. If he had any brains, he would have been helping you run this place, not gettin' in the way."

"Well, it's over now and I need to grab some lunch." Alice shoved some papers into a drawer under the counter.

"Are you going to give them the tour of the apartment?" Charlie hopped down from her stool as if she thought she might be invited along.

"What tour?" asked Bix.

"No, I'm not," Alice said. She turned to Bix. "Paul Olivier wants to rent the other half of the upstairs. And I wish he would find some other place to live. I think he's doing that just to spite me."

"Spite you? Girl, he just bought the priciest manuscript we have and he's going to pay rent in your building when he could live anywhere." Bix shook his head. "If you call that spite, then I want to see your idea of a good deed."

"Well, I have a lot of ideas, but moving his ugly building out of our city would be a good start. I don't know why that's so hard to understand." With that, Alice turned and stomped out of the store, through the back door and up the small wooden staircase leading to her apartment. The long hallway was empty and she tried to pass silently by the door to the other apartment in case they were already inside.

As soon as she was safely behind the thick oak door, she kicked off her shoes, dropped her purse on the side table, and sank onto the little entryway rug. She pulled the rings out from under her shirt and clenched them tight in her fist. She wasn't a crier, but today had pushed her over the edge. She cried in a sad, pitiful way that felt good and annoyed her all at the same time. She knew she was being unreasonable about the apartment, but she had never been very good at conflict. How was she supposed to fight this man with everything she had when he was living under her roof?

She pressed the rings to her lips, wishing her parents were still alive. For the first time in a long time, Alice ached for a best friend. She'd never had any really good friends, unless she counted Mr. Perrault. She needed someone she could tell the whole story to and ask advice. But there was no one like that, not even close. She felt as if she were on the edge of losing everything she'd ever loved *again*, and there was no one for her to go to for help.

A light tap on the door jerked her upright. Maybe it was June Latraye needing her to sign the lease. She could leave it downstairs, if nobody was home.

"Miss Augustine? Are you there?" The deep voice outside made Alice stifle a groan.

She didn't answer, hoping Paul would just go away and leave her be. She couldn't possible have anything he needed.

He kept talking as if he knew she was there. "Miss Augustine, I'm afraid June forgot the key. She's gone back to her office to get it but we don't have much time. We have somewhere to be in thirty minutes. I hate to bother you."

Alice didn't breathe. He couldn't know she was there.

"I'm holding a first edition, signed portfolio of Arthur Rackham prints that cost more than a small house. If you don't have mercy on me and my schedule, think of me carrying them all over town, exposed to the sun and the humidity." She could hear the faint smile in his voice. "I'm appealing to the book lover in you."

She heaved herself off the floor and opened the door. At the sight of her face, Paul's smile froze and then disappeared altogether.

Alice dragged a sleeve over her eyes. "This has nothing to do with you," she said fiercely.

"Of course not. You've just broken up with your boyfriend. I'd expect any normal person to want to cry about it." He looked extremely uncomfortable.

"Oh, I did, didn't I?" Alice started to giggle and couldn't seem to stop. "Sorry. I'm not crazy, I promise."

He didn't look convinced.

"You see… I never remembered him. Not ever. It was like… he didn't exist," she said, laughing through her words.

"I can't see how you'd ever forget him. He's so annoying that I'd never get used to having him around."

"Oh, you should hear him laugh!" She paused, trying to get control over herself. "He sounds like a horse. Like this," she said, and did her best imitation of Eric's whinny, putting in a few snorts for good measure.

Paul's expression made her laugh even harder. She clutched the door frame with one hand and her stomach with the other.

"You must be a saint to ever have given him the time of day," he said.

"I'm no catch, myself." Alice wiped her face once more. "You can imagine that there aren't a lot of guys willing to take a chance on…" She looked up at him and gave a wry smile. "A technologically-backwards woman who runs a failing bookstore and owns too many cats."

He didn't laugh. "About that, I really didn't mean—"

She waved a hand. "Doesn't matter." Alice took a deep breath. "Look at me, telling you my boyfriend woes while you're politely waiting for a key." She turned and crossed the living room, her bare feet making soft sounds against the wood floor. Reaching up onto the carved mantel above the fireplace, she felt around for the spare key.

"Just so you know, I was kidding about the portfolio. I wouldn't haul it all over the city," Paul said.

"Good." Alice came back and handed him the key. She wondered if sixty thousand dollars even meant anything to a guy like Paul. "And just so you know, not all my cats are named after romances."

His neck went red. "That was rude of me."

"It's funny now, actually. But I wasn't angling for another apology." She pointed to the box. "The fat one who sleeps on my desk and never moves is named for a little-known picture Mr. Rackham drew of…" She smiled. "I shouldn't tell you. You'll have to figure it out."

Paul opened his mouth, then abruptly closed it again. "No, don't tell me. I'll have to look through these and maybe Google a bit. Give me some time and I'll figure it out."

They stood there smiling at each other until Alice remembered that she'd just been weeping out of frustration over this man and all the trouble he'd brought into her life. "I should probably make some lunch and get back downstairs. Go ahead and let yourselves in. Give the key back to June or leave it in my mail slot downstairs. Let me know if you need anything else."

He nodded and stepped out of the doorway. "Will do, Miss Augustine." Then he turned. "This is probably the wrong time to mention it, but…"

She waited. It would never be a good time, really.

"Can I ask what security measures you have on the building?"

"Oh, I see. Personal safety must be a real issue, as famous as you are." She didn't mention the wealth part. It was obvious he must deal with threats and stalkers fairly often. "Maybe we can add some extra locks or an outer door to the back side of the building, where the apartment stairs exit to the alley."

"No, actually, I meant for the bookstore." He looked down at his portfolio. "I was surprised to see such valuable manuscripts and no security. If you don't mind my saying, I think you should have a security system in place."

Alice wanted to say no, she really didn't need anything like that. It was for city folks who relied on electronics instead of their neighbors. But maybe it was foolish to leave the inventory unprotected. She wished she could ask Mr. Perrault for advice. The locks had been good enough for him and Mrs. Perrault. "Okay. I suppose I can look in the yellow pages and call around."

"I know a great company, actually. I think they have a store in Natchitoches, too. If you'd like, I can have them come do a walk through."

She nodded, but inside Alice wasn't sure she wanted to commit to an expensive alarm system she might not know how to turn on and off. And when the experts came in, of course they'd recommend the biggest, most elaborate set up. She sighed. Some days she felt as if she was in completely over her head, in every area.

"Have a good lunch." He seemed as if he wanted to say something else, but turned and walked down the hallway.

Alice closed the door more softly this time and leaned her ear against it, waiting until his footsteps faded away before she let out a long breath.

She could do this. It was only a matter of separating the man from the business. It wasn't personal. Successful business people did it all the time.

Alice closed her eyes and rested her forehead against the door. Unfortunately, she had never been very good at making any kind of decisions without her heart. Anybody looking at her group of stray cats would be able to see that. She would have to see Paul Olivier not as the handsome-but-slightly-awkward hometown boy who seemed to know her better than anyone else. She would have to see him as a corporate entity. And to do that, it was probably best if she didn't see him at all. From here on out, she would avoid Paul Olivier no matter the cost.

Chapter Ten

I just invent, then wait until man comes around to needing what I've invented.
—R Buckminster Fuller

Paul couldn't help grinning as he made his way down the hallway. He knew exactly which Rackham picture inspired that cat's name. Some might say the Cheshire Cat from *Alice in Wonderland*, but Paul immediately thought of Rackham's sketch of Rip Van Winkle. He wondered if Alice or the previous owner had named him. He paused, key in hand, trying to remember the man's name. The way Alice talked about him explained a lot about her devotion to the store. This place wasn't just a book store, it was her heart. But that was never a good way to run a business.

He turned the key in the brass lock and let the door swing open. The apartment was similar to Alice's, with pine floors and a grand fireplace in the large living room. The long brick wall that the two apartments shared was bare of anything, even shelves. He peeked into the large but outdated kitchen, then the two bedrooms. It would do, unless Andy really objected, which wasn't likely. He wasn't pretentious.

As soon as Andy arrived, he'd call for the luggage and the scanner to be brought from the plane. And then he'd have to give the place a tech overhaul.

His cell phone rang and he answered it without checking the screen. "Andy, are you even close? Maybe we should meet at the building site in ten minutes."

A girlish giggle sounded in his ear. "Sweetie, it's me. Holly."

Paul was momentarily speechless. If he'd had to pick the top one hundred people who might be on the other end of that phone call, his long-forgotten, ex-girlfriend wouldn't have been on the list. "Oh, hey. How are you? I'm not actually in town, so…" He left the rest of the sentence unfinished.

"I know. I just saw on Celebstalker site that you flew into your old hometown. And I thought it would be fun to see where the famous Paul Olivier came from."

He blinked. Holly had never shown any interest in his hometown. In fact, he didn't think she'd ever asked where he was from. She couldn't be suggesting that he invite her for a visit. It had been months since they'd even spoken. "I'll be working most of the time, actually. I don't know if—"

"An anonymous source said you were planning a huge opening bash with some really big celebrities. That doesn't sound like work. It sounds like fun!"

Paul sighed. The nightclub scene must be wearing thin in New York City. Personally, he'd rather clean out the lint trap in his dryer. It was more entertaining.

"I'll let you know when it is. Right now we don't even have a building."

"Oh, that doesn't matter. I can come down there anytime and keep you company. I'll help you plan everything. Plus, I know how lonely you get on the road." He could hear her smiling and it made him grit his teeth. When they were dating, he confessed how much he hated traveling, wishing he could just stay home for once. Days later, stories started circulating that he was agoraphobic and a recluse like Howard Hughes. A tabloid quoted an "anonymous source," claiming he sat around in his underwear, eating only candy bars and panicking at the thought of germs.

"I'll let you know as soon as any plans are made," he said and hung up before she could respond. He definitely had to be more careful about answering the phone.

Paul wandered to the built-in window seat and stared out at the river. This wasn't the view he'd had when he was growing up. He'd seen the factories across the tracks, belching smoke and disgorging exhausted workers in twelve-hour cycles. Turning his head from side to side, he tried to ease the tension in his neck. He'd only been here half a day and he was wound tighter than a two dollar watch. He smiled at the thought. His mama liked to say that and he could hear her voice in his head. She was coming to Natchitoches tomorrow for the zydeco festival and he couldn't wait to hug her tight. He was glad she was happy in her old farmhouse out of the city, but they were still Cane River Creole through and through. This would always be home in some way.

Paul checked the time and dropped onto the window seat. Andy had seven minutes to get to the apartment or he'd just decide for both of them. He tapped his foot, wondering why it seemed so quiet in this place. It was a long time since he'd sat in perfect silence. It was hard to hush his brain, shut off all the to-do lists and worries.

He touched the email app on his phone but didn't open any new messages. He went straight to Alice's note, and even though a quiet voice in his head told him to leave it be, he sent a quick reply.

Miss Augustine,

I believe Alexander Pope was a great genius, but his witty satire didn't win him many friends. He never took a walk without his Great Dane, and a pair of loaded pistols in his pockets. Whether this was due to his treatment of women, we can't be sure. He did seem to have a callous view of romance, saying, "they dream in courtship, but in wedlock wake." Maybe that's why he never married.

Thank you for the picture. It was the best part of my day. Actually, it was the best part of my week.

I'm traveling right now and I miss my bookshelves. I miss the familiar sight of all my favorites who have become like dear friends to me.

Yours,

BWK

He sent the message and sat staring at the screen. Maybe it was being back in his home town, or having made such a jerk of himself earlier, but he felt entirely off-kilter. He usually walked through life with the confidence of a man who had created a very successful company, even if he wasn't ever going to be a great public speaker, or be able to work a room like a pro. But today, all his confidence evaporated the moment he'd argued with Alice. He was left scrambling to make amends, to prove he wasn't the arrogant, wealthy, entitled guy she'd met today. And it seemed the best way to do that was to reach out to her with the only version of him she didn't hate: Browning Wordsworth Keats.

His phone buzzed and he saw a reply. Paul frowned, wondering if she had gone back down to the store already. That wasn't a very long lunch.

Dear BWK,

Please excuse any weird typos, I've just learned to use the email app on my phone.

A particularly unpleasant customer used Alexander Pope against me today and I like the poet even less now.

I'm glad you enjoyed the picture. I haven't traveled from my home town for almost five years. I'm happy with that state of affairs. My books are my friends, too. If I had to travel, I'd want to pack the whole store.

Alice

Paul closed his eyes for a moment. Sometimes when he was reading a particular poet or writer, they seemed to get into his head and everything seemed to be related. He would walk through his day, lines popping into his head that supported his current arguments. And he'd done the same with Alice. It was a bad habit he needed to end, before it caused him a bigger headache. He re-read the note and grinned. She was emailing on her phone for him. That had to count for something.

Dear Alice,

I'm sorry a customer was rude to you. Pope would say "never find fault with the absent," but I don't think that will bring our poet friend back into your good favors. Personally, I think anyone who would be unkind to a bookstore owner is clearly unhinged. This person must have succumbed to the urge to show off so "pride, the never-failing vice of fools" might fit well here. Anyway, "to err is human, to forgive divine." (You knew that was coming.)

Can I ask what happens when someone buys one of your favorite books? In a rare bookshop, you can't just order another. Do you give it a sending away party? Do you worry about its new home?

BWK

Ok, so he was technically fishing, but he was curious about the Rackham portfolio. She'd definitely been reluctant to let it go. Grateful, but also a little wary. And then when she'd found out who he was… He shrugged off the memory at the sound of another email hitting his inbox.

Dear BWK,

Fine! Mr. Pope knows best that "to be angry is to revenge the faults of others on ourselves." I'm only giving myself a headache by thinking about this person.

Funny you should ask about letting go of rare books. Today I waved goodbye to a very rare item I have loved from the first moment I stepped into the store. It was difficult, I won't lie. The buyer (that same customer who used Mr. Pope against me) assured me that the recipient of this gift will treat it well, but I can't shake that little whisper of worry. It's one of only twenty like it in the entire world. I feel an obligation to protect it from harm. I feel like my heart is wandering around in the world, closed up in a box. It will probably be set carelessly on a shelf, soon to be forgotten.

But denying books to people doesn't work, either.

I don't know the answer. Maybe I wasn't meant to own a bookstore after all.

Alice

He felt her words drop like stones into his heart. He knew exactly what had prompted her doubt.

Dear Alice,

On the other hand, "on wrongs swift vengeance waits." Perhaps your customer felt remorse soon after. I know that I often speak before thinking. It's my worst fault.

It must be a glorious and terrible moment, sending a beloved book out into the world. I don't have children but I wonder if it's like sending a half-grown child to college. My mother was cheerful and supportive when I went off to school, but recently she confessed that she cried every day. She was terrified that I would be treated badly, then come back to her damaged and disillusioned. She was brave outwardly and I never knew.

I think you are the best kind of bookstore owner.

Your BWK

He rubbed his forehead. It was weird to talk to her as if they'd never met. He stared off at the river, wondering if she was upstairs in the same spot, looking at the same view. Before he thought it through, he added another few lines.

P.S. I'll be in Natchitoches this weekend. I'm going to the Zydeco festival this Saturday. Perhaps we'll run into each other? "Those who move easiest have learned to dance."

He pushed send and then stood up, feeling a thrilling combination of anxiety and happiness surge through him. Was he really thinking of telling Alice his secret? Only Andy knew about his involvement but he was completely trustworthy and his best friend.

His pulse pounded in his temples. He must have lost his mind. She'd just vowed to do everything she could to keep his company from opening in her town.

On the other hand, this might help his case. He could prove he wasn't all bad, no matter how it looked from the outside. The phone dinged and he jabbed the icon.

Dear BWK,

I love the zydeco festival. I was intending to go, even though I don't like big, noisy crowds. I make an exception for our Creole music. (Your Pope quote is about learning to write well, but I like it anyway.)

When you said you'd have a friend come for your book, did you actually mean yourself? Is this an unexpected trip? Have you been to Natchitoches before?

I'm sorry to ask so many questions but I'm curious now. Most of all, aren't you supposed to keep that fedora on? If we meet, I'll know what you look like and I could splash your picture all over those rabid message boards.

You don't have to answer. Everyone loves a mystery. It probably draws people to your books. It's good marketing. Plus, Mr. Pope says, "And, after all, what is a lie? Tis but truth in masquerade."

Alice

He grinned. If he'd approached most any member of the fan boards and offered to meet them, they would have been thrilled. Alice didn't seem to harbor the same obsession with celebrities that most people did.

Dear Alice,

Yes, I'm supposed to be anonymous, but it's not so that I can bring in readers. I think the litigious types are less likely to file a suit if they can't find a legal name to attach to their complaint. The only thing I hide is my name and my profession.

As for running to the fan boards… It's true, you could.

But you wouldn't.

BWK

Seconds later her reply came and it was only one line. He read it twice, wondering if she was angry or just curious again.

How do you know?

He paced the length of the living room before responding. He'd claimed to know what kind of person she was only hours earlier, pointing out personal items and drawing his own conclusions about her life. And he'd hurt her. He didn't want to do that again.

He chose his words carefully.

Because you would have asked me where to meet you, instead of reminding me to keep my fedora on.

The door flew open and Andy ran through. "I'm here!" He looked disheveled and sweaty. His tie was askew and the front of his shirt was wrinkled. "This place doesn't really have any taxis, does it? I just jogged six blocks because all I saw was a horse-drawn carriage and a whole lotta tourists."

Paul waved a hand around the room. "This is it. Nice, right? Let's sign the lease and get stuff moved in."

He was already starting toward the door when Andy answered.

"Wait a sec. Does it have cable? Wi-Fi?" He stared around at the exposed brick walls and the carved fireplace mantel. "Looks like a museum. I can't believe you grew up like this."

He snorted. "Like this? My friend, in a few days I'll take you to the little shack where I spent my youth. We can play 'spot the cockroach' and 'watch those bedbugs' and 'no hot water for you today'. Unless they bulldozed it, of course."

"Oh, um, wow." Andy grimaced. "When you said you had a rough childhood, I thought you meant that you got teased for being a geek."

"That, too. The only thing worse than being a poor kid is a poor nerdy kid that everybody thinks is crazy because he spends all his time playing video games and pretending he's going to rule the world someday." Paul held the door open. "Run go look at the bedrooms and see if you can survive it here for a month or two. I think this is the best we're gonna get."

Andy crossed the room and stepped into the hallway, opening one door and then the other. "I can survive. I took that trip to the Himalayas last year, remember? As long as I don't have to eat eyeball soup, I'll be fine."

"Definitely no eyeball soup, but we do have a few regional dishes you might want to avoid." Paul shook his head. "I'd tell you but I'm afraid you'd get right back on the jet."

"Right. I don't want to know." Andy crossed through the front door and Paul followed, turning to lock the door again. "You bullied me into coming with you to this Cajun backwater and if I resist now, you'll just feed me to the gators."

Paul chuckled and was starting to reply when a woman's voice cut in. "Mr. Olivier, I'd prefer you find another way to dispose of your homesick friend. We wouldn't want our poor alligators to get indigestion."

Paul turned, wishing with all his might it was anyone other than Alice. He couldn't seem to avoid offending her, as hard as he tried. Her voice was light but she wasn't smiling.

Andy held out his hand, introducing himself. "Do you live across the hall? I guess that makes us neighbors."

Alice took his hand, her eyes still a little red from crying, and smiled sweetly. "No, it makes me your landlady."

"Ah. Even better," Andy said. "Then you're the one to okay the service order to install high speed cable." He gestured to Paul. "He's got party plans on the brain but we've got to rig up our gaming system first thing. It's a working vacation."

Paul elbowed Andy in the ribs hoping that he would get the hint as he turned to Alice. "Did you have enough time for lunch? I'm sorry that I interrupted," Paul said.

She slid a glance at him. "I did, thank you. A peanut butter and pickle sandwich hit the spot. It's a comfort-food kind of day."

He tried to think of something to say but his brain seemed to have stalled on the peanut butter and pickle.

Andy said, "We can call up the cable company, if you'd like. It would save you the hassle. Of course, they'd probably still need your okay since you own the building and they'll need to drill holes to run the cable."

Alice's eyes narrowed. "I'm not sure if this building can be updated like that. It's on the historic register. There are only so many changes we can make."

"Oh, I'm sure it'll be fine. Paul here got the board to agree to let us build our new store right in the middle of the historic district and a lot of people told us we couldn't do that, either," Andy said. "Ow!" He turned and glared at Paul, who had nudged him a little too hard that time.

"He did? That's strange since I'm on the board and I never approved that plan." Alice's voice was like steel. She seemed to be doing her best not to lose her cool. She closed her eyes for a moment. "I'll check into the cable issue and let you know. Nice to meet you, Andy."

And then she was gone, the red polka dot dress looking even better from behind, her high heels sounding on each step down the wooden stairs.

Paul sagged against the door frame. He kept his voice low. "Why did you have to bring that up right now?"

"What? If she's the landlady then she'd be the one to—"

"I know. It's just… we got off to a rough start," Paul said. "She's not really happy about the new store."

Andy peered down the stairs and then whispered, "Then win her over. Or give me the job. I thought landladies were supposed to be old, cranky, and have a hundred cats. She's gorgeous. Those eyes, that mouth, that—" he moved his hands in an hourglass shape and whistled.

"Well, she's got the cranky and the cats part down." Paul didn't want to discuss Alice's best features. "Look, we need to tread lightly here. She's one of those old guard types, protecting the city from ruinous newcomers."

"Then put on the charm. You're the local boy. Can't you impress her somehow?"

Paul gazed at the stairway Alice had just descended. He'd never been known for his charm and the Southern accent only worked on New Yorkers. Around here, it was standard fare. "I'm sure gonna try."

He could tell himself it was all about smoothing over the problem with the building plans, but Paul wanted Alice's approval in a way that had nothing to do with his business. The clever book store owner seemed to stand for everything he'd ever wanted in Cane River. He wanted her approval and her support. He just had to figure out how he was going to make that happen.

Chapter Eleven

The machine does not isolate man from the great problems of nature but plunges him more deeply in them. — Antoine de Saint Exupery

Saturday morning arrived after a full night of tossing and turning. The zydeco festival had kicked off the evening before and the party raged outside Alice's bedroom window until long past midnight. Even after all was quiet, her dreams were threaded through with images of legal papers and steel girders and stacks of Alexander Pope poetry. She'd dreamed of Paul's smile and missing books, then a full inbox and a man who wore a fedora who waltzed her across a dance floor. She crawled out of bed at dawn, grateful the night was over. After a long, hot shower, she slipped on a vintage shirtdress, hoping the bright green pattern would cheer her up. She pulled her hair back into a ponytail and swiped on a bit of mascara. She kissed the rings and tucked her necklace inside her shirt. Because of the festival, there could be scores of customers. Or it could be completely deserted. Either way, the day would be a long one.

On a normal Saturday, she made a simple breakfast, but Alice decided to take advantage of being up early. She pulled maple bacon, shredded a potato for hash browns, and fried it all up with a sunny-side-up egg. Beau Monde coffee brought it all together. She sat at her little kitchen table, looked out over the river, and reminded herself how very blessed she was. She heard the cat door. The kitties wandered in, one after another, as the scent of fresh bacon reached them. Well, everyone except Darcy, who expected her to deliver his slice, and Van Winkle, who didn't move for anything.

Grabbing a second cup of coffee, she tip-toed down the hallway, hoping that Paul and Andy weren't morning people. The shop was dark and quiet, the smell of old books like a balm to her anxious state. She settled at her desk, letting Van Winkle eat his bacon off a piece of paper on her desk. She didn't bother to turn on the little lamp. She held her mug in both hands, letting warmth seep into her fingers as the scent of the dark roast filled the little space.

A whisper-soft touch against her bare ankle made Alice pause. "I put your bacon in your bowl by the door." Darcy drifted out from under the desk and gave her a cold look before wandering toward the back door. He came and went as he pleased, and today was no different.

Darcy had been Mr. Perrault's favorite and Alice wondered if the cat was still mourning him. They all missed the man who spent most of his life in this little store, but managed to make friends with almost every person in Natchitoches. Alice closed her eyes. For a moment she could see his bright white mustache and clear blue eyes, could hear his measured tones and big belly laugh. Somehow she'd thought he'd live forever. Most days she still expected him to walk right back through the front door and sit down in his chair, the chair she occupied at the moment.

Tears burned her eyes and she felt them gather under her lids. Alice wished she could talk to him one more time. If he'd meant to include his niece, then Alice would honor his wishes. If not, then she had a legal fight on her hands and she hadn't even started looking for lawyers. She knew nothing about court battles except they cost lots of money.

The store had plenty of valuable inventory that could be used to fund a legal defense, but selling it was the problem. She had the Rackham sale in the bank account, but had no idea how fast the legal fees would mount up. Alice leaned forward, hunching against the pain of loneliness. She never really noticed how alone she was until moments like this. Her brothers were scattered all over the South, busy with their own families, her mamere gone before Mr. Perrault.

Turning, she reached for a little book that always gave her comfort. Her head had been stuffed with Alexander Pope the last few days but his wit was never soothing. He spoke truth but it didn't bring her comfort. *The Seraphim and Other Poems* was well loved and some pages were fragile and worn. Elizabeth Barrett Browning was Alice's own personal cheerleader. Maybe it was because she was mostly self -educated, or that she defied everyone's ideas of who she had to be and what she must do, but to Alice, her poetry felt like drinking espresso with just the right amount of sweetness.

She opened to a favorite spot and read aloud, letting the words wrap around her worries. "The Cry of the Children" was a terribly sad poem, but Alice didn't use it to wallow in her problems. It gave her courage, because Elizabeth had written it to condemn child labor in a time when all the great poets were writing about Greek tragedies. Alice loved her for it, this poet who declared that her own people, in her own cities, were worthy of her time, energy, and talent.

Alice took a deep breath and straightened her shoulders. She was going to do what she could in Natchitoches, for her people. Whatever she had to offer, she hoped it was enough to turn the city from the overwhelming tide of technology and industry that was swamping the Creole culture.

Feeling a little more centered, Alice opened the laptop to check her email. There was an email asking about a set of first edition Heinlein paperbacks they'd seen on a previous visit to the store, but hadn't bought. They wanted them now and requested shipping to their Florida address. Alice scribbled down the titles and headed for the science fiction section. This was when she missed Charlie. Alice had to hunt around for a little while. Charlie would have been able to find the books with her eyes closed. She brought the books back to the desk and replied, letting them know they were still here, and attached an invoice.

She allowed herself a small smile. Who said she couldn't use technology to run her store? She clicked back to her email and her heart dropped a little before she even realized she'd been looking forward to another note from BWK. But there was no reason for him to write again. He had asked if she wanted to meet, and although she hadn't said no, she certainly hadn't said yes.

She re-read the last message. *Because you would have asked me where to meet you, instead of reminding me to keep my fedora on.* A smile spread over her lips. BWK was interesting, but he was also astute. She sat back in her chair, chewing on her lip. She wasn't the type of person who enjoyed meeting new people, even when they didn't have a complicated secret identity issue. But BWK loved books with the same passion and fervor that she loved books. There were very few people in the world who understood what it really meant to be a bibliophile. The way he'd written about missing his friends on the shelf reminded her so much of how she treated her own books, whose words kept her company in the darkest times.

She hit the reply button and quickly typed out a response, before she could change her mind.

Dear BWK,

I'll be at the center stage area at eight this evening, when Step Rideau and the Zydeco Outlaws play. I'm not the best dancer, but it's impossible to sit still and listen. I'll be wearing red cowboy boots.

Alice,

who can't think of a single line of poetry that fits

Alice pressed send and then swallowed hard. This wasn't a great time to be starting a new— what? Friendship? She didn't even know if he was single. He could be married. He'd only said he didn't share any shelf space and didn't have any children. For her part, she'd flirted with him while Eric was still in the picture. She dropped her head in her hands at the thought of Eric. That had ended terribly, and right in front of Paul. He'd seemed sort of amused, really. He must think she was as country as a turnip green.

Alice stood up, smoothing back her ponytail, and went to flip on the lights in the main area. It didn't matter whether Paul Olivier thought she was sophisticated or not. And although her resolution of never speaking to him again had ended about five minutes later, this time it was for real. She was going to make a real effort to keep out of his way.

***

Paul rolled over and groaned as the sun hit his face. Didn't anybody believe in blackout curtains anymore? He flopped the other direction, pulling the pillow over his head for good measure, but some internal switch had been flipped, and his body refused to sink back into sleep. Throwing off the pillow, he sat up in bed, and rubbed a hand over his face. Last night had ended way too late, but not because of the Cajun party raging outside. He'd been using the mobile hotspot he'd brought to upload the files from the scanner to the website. The coverage was spotty and the upload would freeze mid-stream. He'd check the link in a few hours and see how his fans liked the new addition. The new equipment would be delivered sometime today so Andy could set up his workspace. To outsiders, it looked like play, but gaming was their livelihood. Their first game, *Mars Invasion*, a sci-fi fantasy, multiplayer online battle arena, made millions, because they'd treated it very seriously.

He inhaled the smell of dark roast coffee and country bacon. His stomach spoke up then, and he vaulted out of bed. It was good to be home. It was even better to know that a full Southern breakfast waited for him somewhere close by. There must be a little café already up and serving breakfast.

Paul didn't bother to knock on Andy's door. The guy had never been a morning person and Paul was positive that the promise of good country grits wouldn't lure him out of bed. He grabbed a towel and headed for the bathroom. The shower was hot in a matter of seconds, another difference from his years growing up. Their tiny trailer had warm water three days out of seven and never enough for two people to shower in a row. He stripped off his pajamas and jumped into the steaming water. Money could buy a lot of creature comforts, that was certain.

A few minutes later he threw on a pair of jeans, an old *Donkey Kong* T-Shirt, and his black Converse. He didn't have any meetings today. Expensive suits would come later, when the big shots of Natchitoches started circling like gators in the bayou. Before college, he'd spent months submitting for city scholarships and gotten nothing. He wasn't the right kind of kid, not from the right kind of family. Paul paused, his hand on his keys. No, he needed to think of them as partners, not the adversaries of his teen years. He swallowed back his bitterness and took a deep breath. That was all in the past. His full MIT scholarship had done what the city leaders hadn't—given him the shot he needed to make it.

He scribbled a quick note for Andy and headed out the door. Somewhere close was a hot Southern breakfast and he was going to find it.

***

The door opened with a familiar tinkle and Alice looked up with a smile. It faded from her face in the next moment.

"Hi, Eric." She tried to sound welcoming, but this wasn't how she'd imagined her first customer of the day. Dealing with the threat of a lawsuit was bad enough without boyfriend issues. Ex-boyfriend issues.

"Hey," he said, and cleared his throat. He looked like he'd put special effort into his appearance. An expensive button up shirt and nice slacks complemented a tailored suit jacket. "Am I picking you up tonight or were we just going to meet?"

Alice blinked. For a moment she wondered if they'd talked through their argument, forgiven each other, made a date and then she'd forgotten about him, like she always did. "Meet where? For what?"

"The zydeco festival. We made plans. Remember?" He leaned close, ducking his head a little.

"I don't remember." Alice thought he must be trying for a certain boyish charm but what she saw was a man who thought he could manipulate her. "In fact, I don't think we discussed the festival at all."

He straightened up. "Well, I'll just pick you up at seven. The main stage is twenty feet from your store. It won't hurt you to have some fun once in a while."

Alice stood. Eric was making her angry and didn't even know it. She would go to the festival, but not because it was right outside her door. Her family's history was intertwined with Creole music in a way that was hard to explain, but she would have tried, if Eric had ever asked, or even given her a chance to tell him about it. And in that moment, Alice realized how little Eric had ever cared about her. She knew everything about his daily stresses--the secretary who came in late every Monday, the billing system that took a genius to decode. She knew what his parents did for a living, that his sister traveled all over the world, that he hated hush puppies but loved cheese fries. She knew these things because she had cared.

"Eric, do you know what my favorite color is?"

“What?” He scanned the room. “How would I know that?”

“It’s red. Do you know my favorite poet? Do I like my coffee with sugar and milk? Am I a morning person? How many brothers do I have?” She was standing in front of him now, arms crossed. She didn’t expect him to answer any of these questions.

“Hold on, now. How could I know these things?” He looked panicked. “You like your coffee black,” he exclaimed, his gaze falling somewhere behind her.

Alice turned and spied her coffee cup on her desk. “With sugar,” she corrected him. “Elizabeth Barrett Browning. Not a morning person. Four brothers.”

He scowled, all his defenses were up now. “I just came in to ask you to the festival.”

She sighed. “Eric, you didn’t come to ask me to the festival. You came to *tell* me we were going.”

“Okay. Whatever. Are we going?”

Alice looked around the store, wishing there was some answer written on the walls. She knew in her heart that she was right but it was difficult to explain to someone who was being willfully ignorant. “No, we’re not. And I’m not sure how to say this, but we’re not going to anything else, ever again. I thought I made it clear the other day.”

His eyes narrowed. “Is it about that guy, Paul Olivier? You’re dumping me for him? If you think he’s going to look twice at someone like you, then you’re really deluded.”

For a moment it was hard for Alice to draw a breath. “Someone like me? What does that mean?” She held up a hand. “No, wait. I don’t want to know. I’ve always had the feeling that you didn’t think much of me, and now you’re proving me right.”

He stepped toward her. “You think you can do better? Try it. There aren’t many guys like me in this nasty little backwater.”

A deep voice cut into their conversation. "And what a good thing that is."

Alice jumped, seeing Paul standing there for the first time. She had been so focused on the argument that she hadn't heard the door or seen him approach. His hair was wet, as if he'd just stepped out of a shower and he was freshly shaved. Although his face was carefully neutral, Alice heard real anger pulsing under his words.

"Oh, you again. I knew this had something to do with you." Eric turned, a sneer curling his lip.

"Don't blame me for your bad behavior. I'm guessing your were digging this grave long before I showed up in town," Paul said. He was closer now, arms at his sides. Alice had the impression he was waiting for Eric to take a swing.

"We were happy before you got here," Eric said.

Paul shook his head, as if starting to realize that arguing with Eric was a complete waste of energy. "So, I managed to ruin your relationship all in one day? I came in, bought a book, rented her apartment, and everything fell to pieces?"

Eric swung around, glaring at Alice. "He's living up there with you? Oh, that explains a lot."

Alice felt her face go hot even before the words completely sunk in. Her hand went to the rings at her neck, as if to shield them from what Eric had just said. She was a secure, intelligent, professional woman. But his insinuation touched something deep inside, where old hurts and shame lurked. Fury coursed through her. "Get out," she whispered.

"Don't need to tell me twice. I don't like to share." He walked by Paul, smirking.

Alice didn't see the first swing, only saw Eric's head snap to the side and then he went down. Paul hooked a hand into Eric's belt, another under his collar and dragged-carried him to the door. He propped him up, opened the door, and tossed him out. Alice could see Eric through the glass door, stumbling to his feet, one hand over his cheekbone.

Paul walked back to the desk, face tight with anger. His brown eyes seemed black under dark brows. He was breathing heavily.

"That was completely unnecessary," Alice hissed. She peered behind Paul, watching Eric walk away, his expression furious. People on the sidewalk turned their heads to stare, a few pointing out the man who had clearly just lost a fight.

"I agree. But it felt great."

"You probably feel like you can do that sort of thing because you're..." Alice was having trouble finding words.

"Rich? Famous?"

"From out of town! But I have to live here. People talk." She put her hands to her face, feeling her cheeks burning. She felt sick at the thought of what Eric would tell people now.

He sighed, examining his knuckles. "I'm sorry. I didn't think it through."

"Obviously," she said, letting the word stretch into the space between them.

Paul shifted his feet, eyes downcast. He really did seem as if he regretted punching Eric and it certainly had happened faster than she could imagine. Maybe he was under as much stress as she was. She certainly wanted to punch Eric herself. Paul seemed calm and collected on the outside, but inside he might just be as hot-headed as she was.

Alice felt a laugh rise in her throat. She tried to keep her face straight, but the memory of Eric's expression as he went down to the floor had her giggling.

Paul looked up. "I'm afraid to ask."

Alice covered her mouth, snickering. "I'm not a violent person," she started to say.

"But you enjoyed that a little bit?"

She nodded, laughing. "Eric is one of those people who'd gripe with a ham under each arm. He is never happy." Then her smile faded away. For the second time in less than twenty-four hours, her resolution to avoid Paul Olivier had been broken. "Did you need something? Is everything all right with the apartment?"

"Fine, everything's fine," he said. "I always sleep to blaring zydeco music."

"Me, too. Must be a Natchitoches thing."

"As for why I'm standing in your shop, I woke up and smelled the most amazing breakfast somewhere very close. Maple bacon, eggs, maybe some hash browns. Definitely good coffee. So I went looking. I've been up and down the block and can't find the café. So, if you could just point me in the right direction, I'll be on my way."

"Oh," she said. "I'm afraid you just described my breakfast."

Paul gave her a quick scan from head to toe. "All of that? You must be a runner. Nobody can eat like that and stay so—"

Alice waited. It had been a long time since anyone complimented her appearance. She shouldn't have cared, but she really wanted to know what came after the "so."

His neck slowly turned redder and redder, and when the color reached his cheeks, she couldn't hold back a smile. "That's the nicest thing anybody has said about me for a long time."

"That you must be a runner?"

"No, that they got out of bed and looked all over the block for my cooking." She was teasing him and he knew it. The real compliment was the approving look and the longer pause. She thought of how Eric had never mentioned her appearance unless it was to suggest she straighten her hair or wear a little more make up because it fit his idea of a professional woman. Eric always talked about cholesterol, and salt intake, and how she should get a gym membership because working at a desk in a bookstore would shorten her lifespan.

"I didn't know the apartment came with olfactory torture."

"Wait until Monday. Gumbo simmers all day in a crock pot while I work. I can smell it through the vents."

"My mama always made gumbo on wash day, too," he said, his lips tugging up.

Alice nodded in surprise. Mrs. Perrault called Monday wash day, a tradition from back when the woman spent the day doing laundry and needed a meal that could simmer while they worked.

He grinned, and she stood there, thinking of how good it felt to share a joke with him.

His eyes dropped to her necklace. "Can I ask you something?"

She paused. Paul already knew more about her than most people. She nodded.

"What are the rings about?"

Alice quickly tucked her necklace back in place under her shirt. "My parents' wedding rings," she said. She drew in a shaky breath. Eric had never asked that. How had she been so blind? That relationship had gone on about six months too long. "Sorry. You asked about breakfast. Two blocks east is Babet's Cafe. Great pancakes, grits, and eggs. Biscuits are better before ten or after four when she makes another batch," she said.

He nodded, looking as if he wanted to ask another question. "Thanks. I'll head right over. And that's a great Heinlein series. *Starship Troopers* is my favorite."

Alice was grateful she didn't have to explain why her parents' rings were around her neck and not on their fingers. She picked up one of the books, looking at the mass market 1950's cover. "I've never read them. I'm not really into science fiction."

He'd turned toward the door, but came back and took the book from her hands. "These are in great condition, too. *Starship Troopers* was originally published as a serial called 'Starship Soldier' in *The Magazine of Fantasy and Science*. The interstellar war between the Terran Federation, which is Earth, and the Arachnids, which are called 'The Bugs,' was actually Heinlein's way of defending his views on production of nuclear weapons."

"Okay. I never knew that." Alice stared down at the stack of paperbacks. She wasn't really sure what an interstellar war had to do with the nuclear arms race. Probably one of those things that people read into a book when the author had no intention of ever having written it.

"There's a real famous soliloquy about violence that people think glorifies militarism, but I think has more to do with Heinlein's own views on moral philosophy, especially about how only veterans should be able to vote for a military intervention." He paused. "I think what I love about science fiction is how it's always just ahead of reality. Heinlein dreamed up this world of an all-volunteer, highly trained force in a time when our military was mostly conscripted."

Alice couldn't think of a single thing to say. She nodded instead.

He turned the book over in his hands, a smile touching his lips. "And the very best authors insert little nods to history, so even in this futuristic war, he's sprinkled in World War I and World War II references, which a lot of men in his time caught and appreciated. Like my Granddaddy. He loved Heinlein. Maybe not so many readers catch it now, since the study of military history isn't very popular."

Alice cleared her throat. She hadn't felt this out of her depth in a long time. Charlie nagged at her to read fantasy, but Alice had never seen a reason. But the way

Paul explained it, the stories were as relevant now as they were sixty years ago. Maybe more.

He seemed to notice that she had nothing to say and frowned, weighing the paperback in his hand. "It sounds kinda strange, doesn't it?" Then he snapped his fingers and said, "Well, it's just like *Beau Geste*, really, with the themes of personal responsibility, never leaving a man behind, and doing the right thing even when it involves tremendous personal sacrifice."

"Oh!" Alice saw all the details start to fall into place and she nodded. "I think I know what you're saying. And it's really odd you should mention that book. I've talked to more people about *Beau Geste* in the last few days than I have in ten years. It must be coming back into popularity."

He was silent for a moment, carefully placing the Heinlein back on the stack. "I'd better get some breakfast. Sorry again for—"

Bix burst through the door. "I was down at The Red Hen and Eric came in, caterwauling that you dumped him for that ScreenStop owner. But I told everybody it was impossible because you can't stand the guy." Bix seemed to see Paul at the same time he uttered the last words, right as he pulled up close to the desk. He turned, his straw hat askew and his green raincoat misbuttoned, and said, "Well, good mornin', Paul."

Alice rolled her eyes at the ceiling.

"Mornin', Mr. Beaulieu. Nice to see you again," Paul said.

"Call me Bix. So, the rumors are true?" Bix nudged his hat up and gave Paul a calculating look. "Let me tell ya, we keep a close eye on Miss Alice here. She don't have a lot of family. We're all she got. You think it's all sweet sugar now, but there will be rules and expectations. None of that bossin' her around, tellin' her which lipstick you like, and not to wear red, and how she needs to exercise."

Paul's lips were twitching. "I wouldn't ask her to change a thing. She's perfect just the way she is."

Alice was in the middle of forming a protest but the words died in her throat. He was placating Bix, that was all. But the words seemed to reverberate in her somewhere, like the ringing of a bell, sending out little ripples of surprise and happiness.

Bix continued, "And her store comes first. You get in between her and this shop, and it'll be the end of you."

An awkward silence fell and Alice stared at her feet. Everything Bix said was true. Especially the shop part. And that was the crux of the matter, wasn't it? Her shop and his store, her town and his business. They were at odds, no matter how many compliments Paul sent her way or how many bookish conversations they had.

"Duly noted, sir." Paul looked like he got the message. He nodded to Alice. "Thanks for the tip on breakfast. You two have a good day."

Seconds later he was gone, the tinkling of the bell like a post script to their conversation. Alice stood there, staring at the door. She'd felt more emotion in the past hour than in the past month. And it had been a pretty rough month.

Bix unbuttoned his coat and hung it behind the desk. "Well, I can't blame ya. I told you to find a man, not a boy. Even before the fisticuffs, I'd say he fit the bill. Not just because he runs that big company, either. You get the feeling he's worked hard to make it in the world and he doesn't walk around complaining. He gets the job done."

"Bix, you've got the wrong idea. We're not dating. He just came in at a bad time. He was looking for directions to a good diner. And I don't approve that kind of behavior, no matter what people will say."

"Not dating? You could have fooled me. I seen the way he looks at you. And if you're not, why'd he take out his aggression on Eric? The guy got it good, one side of his face was already swellin' up by the time he made it to The Red Hen."

She wondered why Eric decided to run down to The Red Hen. Any man who'd just been beaten in a fight should have slunk off home so no one saw a thing. Waving a hand, she turned toward her desk. "Doesn't matter. Something Eric said."

"And it had nothing to do with you?" Bix was honestly confused. "Paul doesn't seem like the kinda guy who cares if someone's tryin' to jerk a knot in his tail."

Alice cleared her throat and settled at her desk. She shuffled a few stacks of paper and gave Van Winkle a pat. The kitty raised his head and blinked, then went back to sleep. She could feel the heat rising in her cheeks. "Well, to be fair, it involved both of us… about Paul renting the apartment above the shop."

Bix let out a low whistle. "Just like that little snake to cast aspersions on your character because he's jealous."

She let a hand drop to the desk and said, "Jealous? It wasn't working between us and that had nothing to do with Paul."

"It sure wasn't," Bix said. He shot her a glance. "But *sha*, even though I got bad eyes, what I saw when I walked in here was enough. I wager Paul wouldn't say no to a chance at getting to know you better." He gave a wink, then called out, "Miss Elizabeth, where are you? We've got work to do." Miss Elizabeth trotted out and Bix picked her up, carrying her toward the back room where the paperbacks were stacked.

Alice couldn't find a thing to say to that. Of course Paul was handsome, funny, and seemed to have taken up permanent residence in her head. But the logical part of her could list ten reasons that Paul should be avoided at all costs. *She's perfect just the way she is.* Paul's words echoed back at her. The idea made her chest go tight. She'd never been one to take chances, in business or in love. And a relationship with Paul wasn't just risky, it was doomed.

She straightened her shoulders and shook off the swirling emotions. Who knew, maybe Paul was putting on the charm to distract her from her protesting his store. He knew she loved books, so he was trying to reach her that way. He was probably used to women falling all over him, begging for his attention.

Well, he was about to discover she was a lot harder to distract than he thought. Nothing came before her town and her people. Not even a man like Paul Olivier.

Chapter Twelve

In software systems, it is often the early bird
that makes the worm. — Alan Perlis

Paul walked toward the diner, dodging pedestrians and the occasional dog, his thoughts back in the little bookstore he'd just exited. That had been a stupid, sloppy mistake. He'd gotten caught up in convincing her that Heinlein was a genius and had referenced a book they'd already discussed. Unfortunately, he was Browning Wordsworth Keats when they'd discussed it. And now she was wondering why everyone in the world was discussing *Beau Geste* at the same time. He wanted to tell her, but not like that. Not out of the blue and right after punching her ex-boyfriend.

He trudged down the sidewalk, wondering if he was losing his sanity. His knuckles throbbed, reminding him of the moment he'd opened himself up for the mother of all lawsuits. More than that, an assault charge wasn't good PR, and PR was something he'd always been good at. When Andy heard the story, Paul was going to get an earful. Or maybe just a look of total disbelief. He couldn't believe it himself.

He crossed the street, barely hearing the honking of a slow-moving vehicle as it turned the corner. He'd never punched another person in his life. He wasn't a fighter. He'd had his share of battles against prejudicial people who only saw a quiet nerd from a tiny Southern town, but his battles had never gotten physical. Maybe Andy was right. Maybe this whole idea was doomed from the beginning. There was too much bad history in Cane River. If he'd wanted to open a store, he should have left the supervising to someone else. Nothing good could come from his returning to Natchitoches.

"Excuse me," a young man's voice broke into his thoughts. "Are you Paul Olivier? I heard a rumor you were in town, but I told my buddy he was full of it."

A gawky teenage boy grabbed his hand and shook it before Paul could even focus on the kid's wide-eyed expression. His T-shirt read 'Home is Where the WiFi Connects Automatically' and his red hair had outgrown a crew cut a few months ago.

"Yes, I'm just here for a little while."

"Dude," the kid whispered. "You're, like, the most epic game creator ever."

"Thank you." Paul glanced down the street. "We're opening a new store here. Be sure to come to the grand opening. We'll have some really good door prizes and—" His stomach was growling in earnest now. He glanced back and for just a moment, he saw himself. He'd spent years as the awkward teenager nobody really listened to, the kid everyone avoided because all he could talk about was gaming and always at the worst times. Paul looked the kid in the eye and gave him his undivided attention. "And what do like the most about our games?"

"You did such a great job with *War of the Universe*. People don't always get that it's not just the graphics. It's the *story*," the kid said. "The best part was the way Reena used the evil Commander Lorfan's secret past to bring him down. The dude woulda been totally invincible if he hadn't been obsessed with getting revenge."

Paul started to agree, when something else occurred to him. Flannery O'Conner once said that she wrote to discover what she knew. Paul wrote the script for *War of the Universe* while thinking about all the greatest morality tales--Greek myths and the tragedy of humanity. He'd never considered that he could turn into one of the bad guys, so focused on revenge and proving he was right that he doomed himself and everything he loved. He looked back at By the Book, and saw his violent actions in a whole new light.

"What's your name?" Paul asked.

"Tater Leaf, sir." The kid grinned hugely.

Paul blinked, trying to decipher why any parent would name their child Tater and pair it with the last name Leaf. He decided it most likely linked to some long history that would take ten minutes and a diagram of the kid's family tree to explain.

"Nice to meet you, Tater. I'll be in town for a while," Paul said. "If you're ever interested in joining our team of beta testers, we have a small group that runs through the very first versions of a game."

"Wow," Tater breathed. "The very first people to try it out?"

"Just to work out the bugs. Sometimes the final version is pretty different."

"Absolutely. Really. I would." Tater was nodding and grinning.

"Cool. Here's my card." Paul scribbled his cell phone on the back. "And now, I have to get some breakfast before I start eating my own hand."

"Sure," Tater said. He stepped out of the way, still grinning. "See you around."

Paul managed to make it the rest of the block without anyone else stopping him, although he did hear a few whispers and the quiet click of people taking pictures. Any other time, he'd have stopped, or at least flashed a smile. But he was focused on getting breakfast and getting back to the privacy of his apartment, where he could take a few minutes to process what he'd just realized about himself.

Babet's Diner was packed to the gills with hungry customers. Paul hovered near the door, breathing in the smell of bacon and eggs. The conversation ebbed for a moment when he walked in, but then picked back up to a respectable level. Although he felt more than a few pairs of eyes on him, he didn't feel as uncomfortable as he did walking around big tech conventions. You knew your fame had passed the comfort level when you needed a security detail to go to the bathroom.

He leaned against the wall and pulled out his phone, sending Andy a quick text. Looking around at the crowd, he wasn't sure takeout was an option. A lot of these old tourist places were sit down only. While he waited to see if Andy was awake, he clicked on the Browning Wordsworth Keats site, then to his email. Scrolling through the mail, his heart rate started to rise. He tried to tell himself it didn't matter, but as soon as he saw Alice's name, he almost stopped breathing.

It took several seconds to decide whether to open it. If she didn't want to meet him, this awkward double life would continue. Things were happening faster than he could predict and who knew what tomorrow would bring? He hoped not another fistfight. He took a steadying breath and opened the note. *Red boots.* He'd never been a great dancer, but he was more than willing to dance with Alice.

He hit reply and pecked out a short reply.

Dear Miss Alice,

I'll be there. Looking forward to hearing the story of EBB and your youthful outrage.

Your BWK

"Paul? Is that you?" A woman's voice cut into his thoughts.

He turned. "Mrs. Joubert?" He started laughing. He couldn't believe his eyes. "I haven't seen you since sixth grade."

She looked the same, except for the streaks of silver in her curly dark hair, and she looked thinner, more fragile.

Memories washed over him. He used to pepper Mrs. Joubert with questions that she couldn't answer during their science classes. She never got angry, and would return the next day with everything she'd discovered. Now she reached out, pulling him close, wrapping her arms around him. "Oh, Paul," she breathed. "Gimme a Yankee dime." She turned her cheek and he kissed her. He felt her shoulders shaking under his hands.

Were those tears in her eyes? "Mrs. Joubert, is everything okay?" He hadn't kept up on the local gossip. Maybe she was dying. Maybe she had lost a spouse. Or a child. The thought made his heart drop in his chest.

"Sorry, sorry, it's just a surprise seeing you," she said, wiping her eyes. She stepped back. "Look at you, so handsome. And I always knew you'd do real well just soon as you got turned loose. I knew it, Paul."

He nodded. He heard that kind of thing all the time. People who couldn't be bothered to give him the time of day when he was younger liked to tell him how they'd always been his most ardent supporters. But Mrs. Joubert was different. "I remember you telling me that. Sometimes more than once a day."

"You took a lot of convincing." She was still blinking back tears. She held onto his hands and leaned close. "Tell me the truth, son. Beyond all the money and the fame, are you doing well? Are you happy? When I see you in the news, I'm right worried about you. I want you to be happy, Paul."

Her words touched him deep inside, in a place he kept hidden from the rest of the world. Standing in an old diner, surrounded by chattering tourists enjoying their enormous platters of bacon and grits, Paul felt as if he were being asked to review the last ten years of his life. And he found it wanting.

"I'm doing fine. My mother has a nice farmhouse out of town. My company has branches in every major city and offers some of the best benefits around," he said. She cocked her head and said nothing. He went on, "I have a good friend. I'm not completely alone." He realized how pathetic it sounded.

She smiled. "One good friend is better than a hundred admirers."

"You've got that right," he said, not returning her smile.

"So what are you doing in here? Didn't you bring your own cook to make you grits? I know you have a jet. We all saw pictures of it on the front page of paper this morning."

"Nope, no cook. We just got in yesterday."

"Oh, not even enough time to get make groceries at the Piggly Wiggly. You and your friend come to dinner tomorrow after church. You still go to church, right?" She turned and gave him the eye.

Paul wanted to laugh but knew it was in his best interests to just nod. "Sure do."

"Good. I have another question maybe you could shed some light on. I hope you can forgive me for being nosy."

"Go ahead," he said. He couldn't imagine a nosier question than whether he was happy or if he was still attending church.

"I heard you're in town for a while. Now, my son lives in Atlanta and he said when a ScreenStop opened there, you came just for the day and then went back to the city."

"That's true," Paul said.

"Are you working on another project in these here parts?" She held up a hand. "You don't have to tell me if you don't want to, but I was hoping you'd heard about our problem and were coming to lend a hand." Her cheeks went pink. Paul realized that she wanted to ask him for a favor, but was worried he would be offended.

"Mrs. Joubert, anything you need. Please just ask. I'll do anything I can."

She swallowed. "We were tryin' to get a grant for a new computer lab for the elementary and middle school but it went to a bigger school in New Orleans. A lot of our kids don't have a computer at home. They think computer tech is all about getting on the Internet on their phones. They go on to the high school and the computer classes are so below standard that they're not worth a plugged nickel." Mrs. Joubert shook her head. "Our kids just can't compete, Paul. The ones who get into college are struggling from the moment they set foot on campus. They don't understand basic word processing, programming, web design, or graphic design."

"So the school needs help? Mrs. Joubert, whatever I can do, I'll be happy to pitch in." He felt the truth of it deep in his soul. She had believed in him when he was just a scrawny kid who carried a chip the size of a cinder block on his shoulder. "You made everything seem possible, if I worked hard enough."

She gripped his hand. "Yes! These kids could make the same sort of difference in science or technology in these here parts, if they got the chance. There are so many who need basic skills that they can only get with labs that are properly equipped. I had real hope that if we got the grant we could shore up the city, keep the young folks from movin' away, but…"

He understood. It was the age-old dilemma of a small town: stay or go. Those on the edge of technological innovation never got a choice. They always had to go. "Tell me what I can do. What do you need?"

She took a few deep breaths, as if struggling for control. "I knew you would help. I knew, if I just asked, you would…" Her voice trailed away as her dark eyes filled with tears.

"Can you get a copy of the grant application? We could work from there."

She nodded. "Sure can."

He reached for his wallet, getting out his business card. "My email address is there. Send the application to me and I'll find out where to go from there." He shifted uncomfortably as Mrs. Joubert wiped her cheeks with both hands. "I'm glad I can help. It's really nothing."

Shaking her head, Mrs. Joubert reached up and gave him a kiss on the cheek. "You were always such a good boy, Paul. You've grown into a wonderful man. Your mama must be so proud."

He patted her awkwardly on the arm and waved as she left the diner, still sniffing, although she was smiling.

The conversation in the diner had dropped while they were talking, and Paul looked up to see more than several pairs of curious eyes on him. He turned to the side, leaning against the wall, and took out his phone. He really didn't want anyone asking what that was all about. In fact, he wished he'd remembered to tell Mrs. Joubert not to say anything. Paul stared unseeing at his phone's screen, hoping the line would get significantly shorter in the next few minutes.

The door opened and Andy stepped through, glancing around the diner. His expression was a combination of determination and discomfort. "I'm guessing they're not going to have my favorite organic, free-trade, Honduran coffee beans here."

"Probably not." Paul was relieved to see Andy. He was showered, shaved, and had on jeans and a button-up shirt with a tie. The guy looked like he wasn't sure if he was on vacation or going to work. "I just ran into my sixth-grade teacher."

Andy let out a bark of laughter. "Did she say she always knew you'd make it big?" It was a joke between them. Andy knew exactly what it was like to excel in a field. Everyone and their cousin wanted to say they called it way back when, all the way to infancy.

He nodded. "Actually, she did." At Andy's look of disgust, Paul held up a hand. "And she's the only person who can say that honestly, besides my own mother."

"Well, I'm glad you got to see her, then." He shrugged, looking around the diner. "You're going to get a lot more where that came from, the longer we stay here."

"Yeah," Paul said. "Also, I may have promised to build them a technology center for the elementary, middle, and high schools. And pay for the teachers they hire."

Andy made a noise that was between a gasp and a cough. "Build a what? Where?" His face drained of color. "Oh, man. I knew letting you come back here was a mistake." He ran a hand through his hair, looking absolutely horrified.

"I didn't make that promise lightly."

"No, I'm sure you meant every word of it. And I'm sure you plan on following through." Andy blew out a breath. "This isn't how it works, Paul. You don't just start handing out money. The company should really set up a charity arm, and then you make sure the taxes are straight, and then you—"

"I know. It's going to be a long process. And I didn't just hand her a check." He stared out at the tables of tourists and locals, watched the faces, sure for the first time in a long while that he was doing the right thing.

A waitress appeared and greeted them, her blond ponytail swinging from side to side as she led them to a tiny table near the back. Her pink-check dress was a little too big, as if she'd borrowed someone else's uniform. She handed them menus. "I'm Jenny and I'll be your waitress today. I'll get you some water while you take a peek at the menus."

"I think we already know what we want," Paul said, smiling. He was going to die of starvation if he had to wait much longer. "We'll both have whatever special comes with hash browns, bacon and eggs."

She frowned, her pretty face scrunched up in confusion. "Sure, we can get you somethin' like that. There's the California special that starts with a braised romaine salad with fresh figs, or there's the Mediterranean smoked ribs with Texas caviar."

Paul took a moment to process those options. That didn't sound like the diner food he remembered from his childhood. "Anything with grits, bacon, hash browns, eggs?" he tried again.

She smiled brightly. "I'll just have the chef fix you some plates up, 'kay?"

"Thanks a lot." As she walked away, Paul shook his head. "Braised romaine with figs? Weird."

"Sounds good to me. And no weirder than you promising to build a few computer labs, complete with teachers," Andy said.

"About that… I had an epiphany," Paul said.

Andy's brows went up.

"See, I went into By The Book this morning and—"

"Oh, boy." Andy interrupted. "I knew it had to do with her. I saw the way you were looking at her yesterday. Isn't there a rule about getting involved with the landlady?"

"No, it really isn't about her. Just let me explain." Paul held up a hand. "I was looking for directions and then her ex-boyfriend came in and we got into a fight—"

"You what? Why?" Andy looked a little panicked.

"He insinuated something about Alice and my fist decided it didn't like his face." Paul held up one hand, looking at his swollen knuckles.

Andy closed his eyes for a second. "And this was your problem, how?"

He didn't have any answer to that question.

"I'll call the lawyers when we get back to the apartment. They'll need to know about this in case there's a lawsuit," Andy said almost to himself.

"So, after that, I was walking down here and this kid stopped me and talked about how Commander Lorfan was obsessed with revenge. I realized it sounded a lot like myself," Paul said.

"What? Wait, did you know Alice before you met her yesterday? Like back in high school or something?"

"No. She's the bookseller who wrote to the Browning Wordsworth Keats site yesterday, the one I was emailing on the plane. But that's unrelated."

Andy's eyes went wide. He said nothing now, just waited for the rest of the story.

"About Alice, I didn't know how everything would go. Really. And the realtor had just said the apartment was in the historic district so I had no idea that we'd be living upstairs with her." He paused as Jenny came by with ice water. She shot him a glance as she heard the last few words of his sentence.

As soon as she was gone, Andy spoke. "If I didn't know you better, I'd say this whole thing was a set up. It's too coincidental. What are the odds? Either you're the luckiest guy on the planet, or the unluckiest. I'm afraid to find out which it is." He shook his head. "Okay, your secret identity has been exchanging love letters with our landlady who hates you in real life."

"Not love letters," Paul protested. "Just book talk." And he wasn't convinced Alice hated him. Maybe intensely disliked him.

"I still don't know what this has to do with your sudden crisis," Andy said.

"Epiphany," Paul said. "This kid understood that the story was central to a good game. You know a lot of people think it's only the graphics that make a game successful, but you and I and every serious gamer knows the story is crucial," Paul said. He had Andy's attention now. Moving to Natchitoches for two months was a crazy idea and dragging Andy along was even crazier, but Paul knew who was the heart of ScreenStop. Andy believed that technology had to be as beautiful and distinct as possible, with the attention to detail only a consummate craftsman gave. And when they created a game, above all else, Andy believed in the story.

"Go on," Andy said.

"He was talking about how Reena took down Commander Lorfan with the trap that promised revenge, knowing he would take the bait." Paul shifted the water glass in his hands, watching the rings of condensation on the table overlap. "I realized that I am the Commander."

Andy made a noise in the back of his throat.

Paul hurried on. "I'm doomed if I don't get a handle on my need for revenge. I came here to show off to all these people who thought I wouldn't amount to anything. I wanted to rub my success in their faces, make sure they saw how rich I am, how I don't need them and their bigotry."

"And how's that going so far?" Andy gave him a sly look that was just short of a smirk.

"Pretty well. You know I got everything I wanted without even trying: the site, the building permit, everything."

"And that's a problem? I don't see why we have to try to fix what's not broken."

Paul leaned forward. "If it's for the wrong reason, then it could be a very big problem." He thought back to Tater, the way he described the Commander. "Right now, I'm the guy everybody loves. I'm invincible. But give it a few weeks and I could be knee deep in small-town politics because I'm obsessed with being right."

Andy nodded. "Okay, I can see it. So, you're over it? We're going home and just coming back for the opening?" He took a sip of his water. "I can't say I'm complaining. This humidity is unbearable. I feel like I just stepped out of the shower, all the time."

"No, my epiphany wasn't that I shouldn't care. It's that I need to put my bitterness to better use."

Andy raised an eyebrow. "Like building computer labs for all the schools."

"Right." Paul looked up, glancing around the crowded diner. He'd been walking around, his defenses up, waiting to run into people he used to hate and who had kept him from exceling. Now he looked to see if there was someone he used to know that needed help.

Andy sat back and let out a long breath. "I've always admired you, Paul. I admire your work ethic and your fire. You were determined to prove everybody wrong and it drove you to study the hardest, work eighteen-hour days, find a way around a problem when everyone said it couldn't be done. I could count on you to never give up even when our CEO left us in the lurch, and our first big launch was ruined by that massive bug."

"You think I've lost my fire? You think I'm going soft now?"

Andy shook his head. "No. Just the opposite. My dad worked two jobs to help put me through MIT. When I graduated I thought he'd be proud because I'd done what he never got to do, get a college degree. One night I asked him if he thought about those high school teachers who wouldn't help him apply for college. I was sure he'd say he pictured them every time he got four hours of sleep or worked the graveyard shift."

Paul could feel a pulse pounding in his head. He knew just what Andy's dad had said. Paul thought of all those people who'd stood in his way. Every time he was too tired to go through some code that wasn't working, he thought of them. And he gave it one more shot. Paul didn't want those people to win. Even now, he could bring up the memory of their names and faces at the merest suggestion.

Andy leaned forward. “He told me he never gave them a second thought. The only thing that got him out of bed in the middle of the night was the idea of me getting to go to college.”

The words sank deep, resonating with truth. Paul stared down at his glass.

“Bitterness can get you pretty far in life. But love always takes you farther,” Andy said.

“You’re a wise man, Andy.” Paul heard the roughness in his own voice and cleared his throat.

“One who’s proud to call you friend,” he said. He reached out a hand and gave Paul a fist bump. “And now that we’ve streamlined your new plan to take over the city, I hope the food is on its way. I’m going to start eating the napkins soon.”

Paul snorted. Neither of them enjoyed heart-to-heart talks. This was about as deep as they’d ever get. But it felt good to know Andy understood.

Paul thought of what was coming that evening, that he’d decided to tell Alice he was Browning Wordsworth Keats. It would be perfect. He was sorting things out, making a new start. He opened his mouth to tell Andy, but the waitress arrived, bearing plates of hot food.

The food derailed his thoughts. By the time he’d worked his way through half the sausage links and all the hash browns, Paul thought maybe he’d wait a little longer to drop that particular bomb on his friend. A guy could only handle so much drama in one day.

Chapter Thirteen

The march of science and technology does not imply growing intellectual complexity in the lives of most people. It often means the opposite.—Thomas Sewell

Alice pulled her hair back from her face and frowned at her reflection. The music was as loud in her bedroom as it was outside on the stage outside, with the first band starting off the night with a bang. She turned her head, squinting at her reflection. Mamere always said it was better to tame her curls than let them loose, but Alice felt as if her whole life had been spent trying to tame the untamable just because her grandmother had said so. She secured the top in a loose bun and let the rest fall around her shoulders. It wasn't a great style for dancing with the swing and jitterbug moves, but she didn't care. Not tonight.

Alice passed over the tube of beige lipstick and uncapped a bright red. Tonight was one of the few nights where she could really dress up, and it wasn't for the shop or for a date. This festival connected with the deepest parts of her family heritage and she honored it the only way she could. She would overcome her introverted self, head to that dance floor, and show the tourists how real zydeco dancing was done. Her childhood friend Julien Burel would be there, along with his four brothers, and probably every one of his cousins. Alice never longed to be the center of attention, but tonight she would step onto that stage and dance for every member of her family that couldn't.

She took a small photo from the front cover of her Bible and held it up. Mama and Papa smiled up from a porch swing, their arms wrapped around each other. Alice stared at their faces, letting their happiness ease the ache in her chest. They'd had a good life, surrounded by two of the largest Creole families in Cane River. Alice remembered family reunions that went on for days and days, with music and food to rival the festival that blared outside. She remembered her mama's green eyes and her papa's singing voice. She remembered how they whispered together in the kitchen and how her mama blushed when they got caught kissing. Alice wondered if they'd known how blessed they were, or if it was just normal life for them. Day by day, doing what came naturally, loving each other, loving their kids.

When they'd died in that accident, something had changed. Her mama's family had blamed her papa's people for letting him drink too much that night. Her papa's family had blamed her mama for saying she had to get home to her babies instead of staying the night with his folks.

Alice closed her eyes against the memory of the knock at her *mamere's* screen door. It had been almost morning, the pale light of dawn filtering through the sheer curtains. Her brothers always got to sleep on the roll-away cots upstairs while Alice got the divan in the living room. She was the littlest and didn't mind curling up tight so her feet didn't dangle off the end. The screen was locked, but the door was left open to the night breeze. Alice remembered the creak of the boards as she tiptoed to the door, then the sound of her bare feet as she took off running for *mamere* when she saw the policeman through the screen.

In time, her brothers were flung far and wide across the country, as if they'd sat down and decided to each take a corner. And by the year Alice turned seventeen, she was the only one left at home with a grandma too old to make sure she was being raised up right. Mr. Perrault and his wife became her family. The bookstore became her refuge. For an angry girl who felt invisible and forgotten, they became her saving grace.

Alice gently placed the picture back in her Bible and set it by her bed. She touched the rings at her neck, feeling the warmth of the gold under her fingers. She was a quiet woman who didn't like to leave her store, who preferred her kitties to people. But tonight was different. She would dance tonight for her mama, for her easy laugh and deep green eyes. She would dance for her papa, for his singing voice and how he had an easier time speaking with French tourists than his cousins from Georgia. She would dance for her brothers, who never came home, and for her mamere who knew she was sad but couldn't remember why. She would dance for the two families torn apart by a terrible decision. She would dance for what was left.

***

"Hey, you think this shirt is okay?" Paul smoothed down the white, Armani dress shirt and stood in front of Andy.

Andy looked up from his reading, confusion on his face. "You're picking out clothes for Monday's meeting? I thought you were scanning in that book of Christina Rossetti poetry."

"I already did. Maybe the blue striped Lauren? That one is tailored. And you think tucked or untucked?" Paul frowned down at himself. "I thought I'd wear jeans, but maybe I should get the Westwood suit. With a nice belt. And the Gucci shoes. Or maybe just the slacks and the vest?"

Andy put down his book. "I don't think I've ever heard you mention a clothing brand before."

"Maybe they don't all go together. Should the shoes be the same brand as the pants?" Paul felt himself starting to sweat. It didn't help that it was still at least eighty degrees and the humidity wrapped his skin like damp towel.

"What's going on? Are we getting visitors?" Andy tilted his head. "Not that girlfriend who giggled all the time. I'm convinced she must've had some sort of compulsive disorder."

"No, nobody's coming up here. I'm just headed out to the festival." Paul rubbed his hands together. His palms were sweating. He had no idea how he was going to dance with Alice without her noticing.

"And you're just going out there alone?" Andy crossed his arms.

Paul shrugged. "I won't be out late. I've got to be up for church in the morning. You already said you could hear it just fine inside."

He stood up and stretched. "That was before I knew you had some hot date. I'd never let a brother go into battle alone."

A grin crossed his face. He didn't want to seem immature, but it would be a lot easier to have Andy along. If Alice didn't show, he wouldn't look so silly sitting there by himself. Plus, Andy knew all the tricks to escaping the awkward situations that popped up when folks knew you had more money than the president. He was sure they'd be approached at least once tonight by someone who thought Paul gave out money like business cards. "You're just coming to watch me make a fool of myself dancing."

"That, too." Andy gave him a light punch on the arm and crossed the hallway. "Oh, and keep the jeans. This is some sort of hoedown right? Nobody will be impressed by your three-piece suit."

Paul nodded. "You're right. She said she was wearing boots, so I should keep it informal."

"Who is? Back up a second." He held up a hand. When Paul didn't say anything, Andy went on, "Or just start here and let me be all confused. That's fine. I suppose I'm confused about your social life most of the time and still manage to survive."

"I don't have a social life. Nothing exciting going on here." Paul threw it out with a laugh. But Andy just cocked his head and fixed him with a stare.

"I can't believe you've been here one day and you've already got a…" Andy's mouth formed an 'ohh,' as he guessed the woman in question. "I don't think that's a wise idea, Paul. I'm surprised she even agreed to meet you. She doesn't want our company here. Getting involved with her won't make that go away. It will probably make it much, much worse."

"Well, she doesn't know it's me," Paul said. "Not the real me. She thinks she's meeting Browning Wordsworth Keats."

Andy stood perfectly still, staring at him. Paul recognized that look. It was the look Andy had worn when they realized a million video games had been shipped to Canada with instructions only in Chinese. It was the same look he'd had when one of their top programmers had dropped out of sight, only to resurface in their competitor's company. "There's nothing I can say to convince you that this is a really bad idea?"

Paul straightened his cuffs and took a breath. "I think this will simplify everything, actually. I realized I was fighting battles on every side, when I don't need to. I'm going to tell Alice who I am, she'll realize I'm not out to destroy the world, and maybe we can open this store without any more drama."

"Or she'll feel betrayed by the way you've lied to her face, decide that you're worse than she thought, and do everything she can to destroy you."

Paul choked out a laugh. "Wait a minute. Alice just believes that our culture is dying and she wants to protect it." He paused. "And she has a little block against technology for some reason, but I think she's just not aware of how it can be used to her advantage."

Andy raked a hand through his hair. "I don't know if it's because she's Creole, like you, or because she's beautiful, but you're completely ignoring the problem here. Alice isn't your great auntie who needs a lesson on using the Internet. People like Alice already know what's out there and they're actively fighting it. She's not going to be impressed with a few flashy websites."

"No, but she *is* impressed by Browning Wordsworth Keats," Paul said. Except for the part where he ripped books apart. She would be livid when she discovered how the books get scanned and uploaded. But he didn't want to think about that right now. "Listen, Alice isn't a monster."

"No, she's a woman," Andy said.

Paul frowned. "I never knew you to be misogynistic. She must have really rubbed you the wrong way."

"My friend." Andy clapped him on the shoulder. "I'm trying to say that if *you* were a woman, it wouldn't be an issue."

"I don't follow."

His friend looked him straight in the eye. "Are you telling me that you don't have feelings for her? And you're positive she doesn't have any for you?"

Paul thought about the moment he'd opened her first email, of the picture she sent of her shelf, and of the time he saw her making faces at herself in the mirror. He thought of how he'd wanted her to dump the boyfriend, how his stomach dropped when he realized she was going to fight his new store, how he'd wanted to wrap her in his arms when he'd seen the tears on her face.

In the last two days he'd spent sixty thousand dollars on a book he didn't need and punched a man he didn't really know. In a few minutes he was going to reveal the secret he'd carefully kept for two years. It didn't make any sense. None of it did. He obviously wasn't thinking with his head, but his heart.

"I don't know what she feels," Paul said.

"Oh, boy," Andy said. "I knew the day would come when I'd watch you join the ranks of the love-struck zombies. I just didn't know it was going to happen here."

"I'm not--" Paul cleared his throat. He wasn't sure what he was. "I'm not a zombie. This is a calculated business move to help our new store."

"Uh huh. Well, let me go change and then we can see how this new business move goes." Andy stopped at the doorway to his bedroom. "But if I had to guess, I would say this is going to get a lot uglier before it gets better. If it gets better."

Paul walked to the window and looked out toward the stage. Maybe Alice was already there, looking for BWK. His stomach rolled. He hadn't been this nervous in years. Not when that actress took him to the Oscars. Not when he accepted the award for best Online Game Play of the Year before the Academy of Interactive Arts and Sciences. Not on his last date, that was for sure.

***

Alice turned and gave herself a long look. The tall, standing mirror showed the reflection of a young, pretty woman. She belted the waist of her teal, Western-style shirtdress with red embroidery on the hem and pockets, accentuating her hourglass figure. A scuffed pair of red cowboy boots replaced her usual vintage pumps. She tucked the rings into her shirt. The only thing left was a smile. Alice grinned at her reflection. There was nothing she could do about the lawsuit at that very minute, but it was hard not to worry. She leaned forward, examining her lashes and pressing her lips together. She wondered if she needed more makeup. Suddenly she remembered the first time she met Paul.

She sighed. She was excited to meet BWK and couldn't stop imagining this mysterious book lover. But at the same time, Paul crept into every thought. She wondered what he was doing tonight. Probably having a party. She'd never know because of the noise level of the festival right outside. Or maybe he was going out with friends. He was from Natchitoches and must have loads of friends here.

Alice glanced up, catching a glimpse of her reflection. "Green-eyed girl," she whispered. It was a mystery why she even cared. She hardly knew the guy. It wasn't like her to crush on a man just because he was handsome. Of course, he was smart and interesting and generous to his friends, too. But Charlie said Paul was a partier, that she'd seen pictures of women hanging all over him. Really, it made sense when she tried thinking logically about it. Famous people were famous for a reason. They were good at making strangers feel connected to them in a personal way.

She straightened her shoulders and flashed her brightest smile. She wasn't famous and she didn't have any fans. She would do what she did best, which was to be real. What people saw is what they got, no media spin required.

***

Alice looked around the crowd, examining every man under forty, looking for the jawline that appeared under the fedora in the picture. It was hard to see by the dim illumination of the stage lights. She could see the glimmer of the river in the distance. The warm summer air was still except for a small breeze every so often.

Dancers crowded the stage, milling around, looking for partners. There were women in jeans, dresses, shorts, and a few fantastical costumes that really had nothing to do with Creole culture but were certainly fun to see. The men stayed pretty close to boots, jeans, and T-shirts, but there were a few in fancy suits, mostly older folks who used any occasion to put on seersucker and a bowtie.

"*Allons danser!*" The lead singer of the zydeco band called out. The crowd answered with a wave of hollering and stomping that made the stage shake under Alice's feet. She felt a huge smile spread over her face. She belonged with these people.

"*Manzell, danser vous?*" She turned to find a teen holding out a hand. It was Julien Burel's little brother, Xavier. He had to be nearly ten years younger than her, and clearly nervous. He spoke the Creole of her mamere, not the European French that kids learn in school.

"*Mais, oui,*" she answered with a smile. As they moved to the center of the stage, she gave one last glance around. Her gaze caught a familiar face and her heart jumped into her throat.

Paul stood at the edge of the stage, Andy at his side. He was dressed in a light blue shirt and jeans. His gaze was fixed on her and her heart seemed to stop in her chest as their eyes met. He didn't smile, but simply lifted a hand in greeting.

Alice turned her head back to the band, swallowing back a wave of sudden nerves. It didn't matter if Paul was there, watching. Sure he was handsome, but he was just like any other tourist to the festival. People would stand and watch the dancers, tap their toes to the music, then go back home without ever thinking about it again until next year.

The accordion player took the spotlight and started with the song "I Done Got Over." A five-person band with just a few guitars, a drummer, and the singer, radiated energy. Her teen friend was a surprisingly good dancer, and Alice tried to put Paul out of her thoughts and focus on the complicated steps. Their hands were linked but their feet were moving at high speeds and Alice started to laugh. The dance brought everything back. Her family used to hold informal Saturday house dances in the summer, and the neighbors would come at dusk and stay until dawn. The women would bring biscuits and pots of gumbo to share. When it got late, Alice's mama would send her inside to lie down, but she would sneak out of bed to sit by the window and watch the dancing. Now, as her feet moved to the music, she felt the years slip away. Joy pulsed through her, unbidden, lifting her heart.

Before she knew it, the dance came to a ringing finish and she stood still, out of breath, with a huge smile on her face. "*Merci, misye*," she said, and shook Xavier's hand.

"*Merci, manzell*," he responded with a grin, and rejoined a group of teens near the edge of the floor. A few of the boys clapped him on the back in congratulations, and Alice wondered if she had been part of a good-natured dare.

The singer adjusted his cowboy hat and took a sip of water. "*Encore?*" he called out to the crowd and the dancers around her yelled back an enthusiastic response. Alice scanned the people around her, wondering if she should move off the stage to be more visible. BWK might be here, but outside the group, and not able to find her. Or maybe even approaching another woman with red cowboy boots. She frowned, wishing she'd been more specific.

"Evenin'." A man's low voice to her right made her catch her breath. She turned, wondering what BWK would look like without the fedora. Instead, it was the lead singer of one of the night's bands. For just a moment, she considered the possibility that BWK was also fronting a local zydeco group, but then she pushed the thought away. About as likely as him being the president, really.

"Good evenin'," she returned. "You play with Creole Kings, right?"

He nodded, his dark eyes reflecting the lights of the stage. He was the type that Charlie would admiringly describe as "tall, dark, and Creole." The man sang in front of hundreds of people and he looked perfectly at ease approaching a stranger. Alice admired that kind of extroverted personality. "My name's Alphonse DeCote, but everybody calls me Al." He held out his hands. "I was wonderin' if you'd like to dance."

She reached out. "I'm Alice Augustine and that's why I'm here."

The next song started and Alice let herself get lost in the music, focusing on Al's hands holding hers, and every now and then, his dark eyes. It was the one night of the year when she could enjoy being with a lot of people and not worry what anyone thought of her. The whole town was out dancing, whether they were locals or tourists, from across the river in the industrial wasteland or ten feet from a historic building.

As the song faded away, Al took her hand one more time. "I gotta go get ready, but I saw you, and you were so pretty, I just needed to have one dance."

Alice couldn't help the smile on her face. She didn't need anyone fawning over her, but it was nice to hear. After dating Eric, she'd forgotten what it felt like it be admired, instead of picked on.

Al took a card out of his back pocket and held it out it to her. "If you want, you can give me a call. I'm not far away in Shreveport. I'd be happy to drive down for lunch, or just to set a spell and talk."

She took the card. "Thanks, Al." She wasn't sure she'd ever call but she liked his ways, confident and polite. The farther she got away from her time with Eric, the more she realized that what she thought was Eric's self-confidence was actually arrogance.

Al grinned and left the stage, heading for the back of the bandstand. She watched him go, admiring the length of his stride and the easy grace of his steps.

There was the sound of a throat being cleared behind her and Alice knew who she'd see before she turned around. Paul stood there, dark eyes unsure, his hands at his sides as if he didn't know where to put them. She felt her mouth drop open in surprise. After what had happened that morning, she hadn't thought he would seek her out again and certainly not in public. She wanted to remind him of what a small town it was and how most of the locals were probably already discussing their relationship, but part of her really didn't want to talk about it right then.

"*Bonswe, misye*," she said with a smile.

And to her surprise, he answered back, "*Bonswe, manzell.*"

She was going to say that it was nice he'd learned a few phrases for the festival when he went on, as fluent as Mr. Perrault had ever been. "It's been a long time and I wasn't a good dancer to begin with, but …" He held out his hands. "Would you like to dance?"

Alice didn't move for a second as her brain processed his words. She looked up at the handsome man with dark hair and the soft accent, feeling her idea of him shift and tilt. Paul, who had left Natchitoches for New York City and never looked back, was as much a child of Cane River as she was, right down to the Louisiana Creole language that was dying out with every passing year. Alice reached out and took his hands.

Chapter Fourteen

The technology that threatens to kill off books as we know them - the 'physical book,' a new phrase in our language - is also making the physical book capable of being more beautiful than books have been since the middle ages.—Art Spiegelman

"I waved to Bix but he didn't respond. Did I do something to offend him?" Paul asked. He glanced over Alice's head toward the chairs set up in the grass for spectators.

Alice took a moment to process the words. She'd never really noticed what a wonderful voice Paul had. Sometimes she spoke Cajun French with tourists from other parts of Louisiana, and sometimes French with tourists from Europe. But it had been a long time since she'd spoken Creole with someone she didn't know very well. It felt strangely foreign and absurdly familiar all at the same time.

"Oh, he has terrible eye-sight. Both far and near. The only reason he spoke to you that day was because he recognized the portfolio when he passed you on the bench. He knows those books like his children. It's so hard for him to live without reading, but at least he can help in the store." She knew she was talking too much but he was still holding her hands and it was disconcerting. The band was playing a few chords, waiting for the singer to decide on a song.

"I see." He frowned. "He can't use an e-reader? Or a double screen?"

Alice shook her head. Paul said the words *e-reader* and *screen* in English. For a moment she wondered if their language had any words for current technology. She certainly didn't know. "He doesn't have one. And I'm not sure what a double screen is."

He opened his mouth to explain but the first few bars of the next song interrupted him. "We're gonna take requests for our next song. What do all y'all wanna hear?" the band leader called. The dancers responded with several suggestions and the band chose the song of a middle-aged lady near the front of the stage, wearing a red-check Western shirt.

Alice said, "Well, if you really can't dance, we'd better go over the basics, no?"

"I'll be your eager student," he said, and winked.

Alice felt heat flash through her and she dropped her gaze. Paul was good at making women like him, that was for sure. It was an undeniable fact. She jumped into rapid-fire directions to cover her confusion. "Step to the left and back, that's water and seasoning. Then step backwards and then forward, your left leg and my left leg. That's the meat and the roux."

They practiced a few times as the band warmed up and then she said, "Now we need the gumbo, so put your right hand around my waist, and keep holding my left hand. Let's try it all together." Alice focused only on the steps, not on the man in front of her. She tried to block out how close he was. He smelled wonderful, and he still carried the undeniable scent of old books.

"My mama made me practice these dances with her every Friday night. She was sure that it would help me when I found the right girl."

"Because women like dancing?"

"No, because she thought there was a girl for me out there, right then, being taught by her mama. She didn't want me to look bad in front of her future in-laws."

Alice couldn't help laughing. "Mothers are kind of all the same. They all want to do the choosing." She wanted to tell him how she loved to hear him speak Louisiana Creole. He sounded like her family, like everything she'd lost when she was young and then found again as a woman.

"And what did your mama think of Eric?" He gave the tiniest wink.

"If she were alive, I probably wouldn't have dated him. I think she probably would have set me straight before we got past the first date." She tried to say it lightly.

"I'm sorry." He looked pained. "And your papa?"

"Gone in the same accident. I was young." She looked around, wishing the band would start. This wasn't the conversation she wanted to have tonight.

"So that's why you have their rings." He reached out, slipping a finger under the chain against her neck, gently bringing forward until the rings dangled between them. He held them both, looking closely. "Your mama had tiny hands."

Nobody knew that except her family. In fact, nobody but Alice had touched those rings for years and years. She couldn't seem to tear her eyes from them now, held gently in Paul's fingers. She cleared her throat. "She really did. I have a pair of her gloves. They're just so little. I must take after my daddy's side because mine are huge." She held up a hand for inspection.

"You're right. Gigantic man hands."

"I mean, in comparison," Alice said. She turned her hand palm up and he dropped the rings into it. "What about your parents?"

"I was raised by my mama. Just her. We lived in a little shack outside the city limits. It's probably been condemned and burned by now." He smiled. "Here's to surviving childhood, eh?"

She had to grin. "Yes. I think we should both get a medal." It felt so strange to talk about her parents and not feel sad or awkward. Most of the time she felt like people either asked too many questions or acted like they'd never existed.

A few more dancers arrived and there was a lot of quick practicing around the floor. The band seemed to be arguing about the choice of a song. Alice knew the zydeco festival was serious business and she loved how the musicians wanted to get it just right.

"Aren't you sad to let go of your culture?" she asked.

"What? You mean because I live in New York City?"

She nodded. "I think you just can't raise Creole kids outside of the area. It's hard enough keeping the traditions alive with everybody plugged into cable and their iPods and everything." She felt her cheeks go pink. "Not that I have kids, but you know..."

Paul laughed. "Just because I live in New York doesn't mean I've rejected my roots." His expression turned serious. "I've been thinking about it a lot recently. I know we can't have everything, all at the same time. Choices have to be made. I do understand that."

Alice didn't know what to say. She hadn't meant to start such a serious conversation out there on the dance floor but she and Paul didn't seem to be able to keep the topics light.

The band finally launched into a waltzy number and the singer stepped to the microphone, the words coming too fast for her to understand. She remembered the song, "Zydeco Gris Gris," from when she was younger. Her mama had loved this song but she'd never learned it. Paul took a moment, then matched her step for step. He sang along as easily as if he still went to house dances every Saturday night.

Alice swallowed back her surprise a second time in just a few minutes. He really could dance, no matter what he'd just claimed. He was better than she was, effortlessly bringing her close and swinging her around, then bringing her close again. The sound of his voice in her ear made a shiver go up her spine, and for a moment she forgot they were on opposite sides of a fight. She wasn't Alice the bookstore owner and he wasn't Paul the video game mogul. She was a woman and he was a man, simply enjoying the late summer night, moving to a music that was deep in their blood.

For the first time in a long while, Alice didn't worry about what was going to happen tomorrow, or the next day, or the day after that. She felt like everything was right with the world. More than all right. It was perfect.

Zydeco music isn't known for its short, easy tunes. Jazz musicians borrowed their idea of long, complicated riffs on a repeating melody. Blues singers borrowed the melancholy words and some of the beats. And the dances are meant to give as much pleasure, for as long as possible, until the dancers are worn down and tuckered out. Alice was glad it was only the third dance of the night because Paul moved with an energy that was hard to match. This wasn't the dancing of an awkward teen boy. He was confident and smooth, as if he'd had years of practice like she had, in backyard barbeques and summer festivals.

When the last notes finally faded away and the dancers all came to a stop, Paul didn't let go of her hand. He looked happier than she'd ever seen him, but there was something like worry in his eyes.

"Can I talk to you for a minute?" he asked. He looked around. "Maybe over here," he said, pointing with one hand toward nearest edge of the temporary dance floor, away from Andy.

"Okay," Alice said. She was supposed to be watching for BWK, but it would probably only take a moment. He led her to the little row of trees at the side of the stage and they stepped off into the grass. It was much quieter now that they weren't directly in front of the speakers. The twinkle lights wrapped in the tree branches gave everything a festive, cheerful feeling.

"I wanted to tell you something the day I came into your shop." Paul looked down at their hands linked together.

Alice tried to ignore the way her heart was beating in her ears. She watched his face, saying nothing. He'd said a lot of things that day and she couldn't imagine what else he'd missed. It wasn't a conversation she wanted to revisit.

"I know it seems as if we're really different, but we're not."

Her eyebrows went up. To be fair, before tonight she would have said they were night and day. Now she could see they had their Creole culture in common so maybe they were more like daybreak and twilight.

"You think I'm some rich New York City businessman who's come here to Natchitoches to show off his big, flashy store." His face was tight.

"And you're not? Because seems a pretty fair description to me, although it left out being arrogant and running roughshod over the entire city." She knew following him to this little private spot under the trees was a mistake. A few lines of Louisiana Creole and one perfect dance couldn't erase the facts. Alice shook her head and started to pull away. "Paul, maybe I should go. Thank you for the dance."

He held on to her hand, gently bringing her back. "I don't know how to explain, but we're alike, you and me."

She could have tugged herself free and kept walking but she stopped, feeling the truth of his words. She knew he was right, but wasn't sure how. "Because we're Creole? Because you come from here?" She heard the disbelief in her own voice and hated it. If she had to name something that made a person "like her," being Creole would certainly be one. But loving this place with an undying passion would be another, and that is where they were different. Paul may have come from Natchitoches, but he didn't love it the way she did. She was willing to fight to preserve the culture in her little town, all the way up to and including engaging in a legal battle against the man who stood before her.

"Books," he said, almost desperately. "We both love books."

Alice searched his face. "So we're similar because you like to read? Or because you bought your friend a rare portfolio?" She sighed. "Paul, I do love books. And I like to read. But the way I love books is hard to explain—"

"They're like your friends." He spoke quickly. "You re-read favorite passages and even though you've read the words a hundred times before, it's all new again. Walking by and touching the covers is like reaching out and shaking hands. You wouldn't travel without your favorites. You read a great book and you get this weird missionary zeal, where you have to tell everybody about it until they all agree to read it, too. You want to keep your books safe, protect them from slipping into oblivion. You wonder how you'll ever share shelf space with another person." He took a deep breath. "You feel them beat underneath your pillow, in the morning's dark, an hour before the sun will let you read."

Alice stood still, eyes fixed on his. Had he just quoted a line from Elizabeth Barrett Browning's poem *Aurora Leigh*? That stanza hung in a little gilt frame near her bed, right above her towering pile of books. It was one of the last things she saw at night, and one of the first things she saw in the morning.

"Yes," she whispered. "It's just like that."

"Now, do you understand?" he asked. He stepped closer, his expression intent.

She nodded. They weren't so different after all. Everything she had felt for him, from the first moment he'd walked into her shop, made a little more sense.

"Thank God," he said. In the next moment, he put an arm around her waist and pulled her in close. Her right hand was tight against his chest and she could feel his heart pumping under his shirt. She didn't look up, just closed her eyes and breathed in, letting the moment stretch between them. His arm tightened and he shifted, bringing his lips to her ear.

The next song burst into the moment and the dancers on the stage began to whirl and step to the beat. Paul didn't move a muscle, as if he hadn't heard a sound, his arm strong against her waist. They were perfectly still, just the two of them, like the eye of a hurricane in the middle of the festival. She never wanted to move from that spot, tucked against his chest, held tight against the world. It had been so, so long since she had felt like there was anyone to hold on to, anyone who truly understood her.

"Alice," he whispered. "I meant to tell you the truth before." His voice was rough.

Slowly his words filtered through the swirl of emotion and Alice felt a shadow cross her heart. Loving books wasn't exactly a terrible secret. She said she understood, but maybe there was more to this than she was catching. She moved back, trying to gather her thoughts enough to form a question.

"As soon as I met you, I knew you were special," he said. Then he lowered his head, pausing once, as if to see if she was going to object.

A few minutes ago she'd been pondering a question about his family, wondering where he'd learned to speak so fluently and dance so well. Her thoughts were tangled up in his words, trying to catch up with his meaning. He'd meant to tell her something before now but those questions disappeared like mist in the sunshine.

Paul was going to kiss her, something she'd been wanting since she first saw him just days ago. It didn't matter where they were or who saw them. She didn't care about her reputation or her store. There was no other thought in her head except the anticipation. Her eyes fell closed and she met him halfway, glorying in the pressure of his mouth, the heat of his skin, that delirious scent of man and old books. Her arms went up around his neck and she threaded her fingers through his hair. He made a low noise in his throat and he pressed her closer.

Alice had no idea how long they stood there, wrapped up in themselves, oblivious to all her friends and neighbors just feet away. It wasn't the kind of kiss she was used to from Eric. Or anyone. Suddenly, Paul lifted his head and she struggled to catch her breath. She looked up, feeling her heart pounding in her chest. Her eyes finally focused on his face and her body went cold. His eyes were filled with shock and surprise, and his gaze was focused somewhere behind her.

"Hi there, Alice," Andy said, his voice barely cutting through the noise of the music and the boots hitting the stage. He stood behind her, hands in his pockets. Andy shrugged a little, as if in apology.

Alice stepped back, her knees shaking. She put a hand to her mouth. Andy must have seen what was happening and made his way through the dancers to rescue his friend.

"I'm sorry to interrupt, but I need Paul… over here… for a second." Andy looked incredibly uncomfortable. He pointed to the side of the stage where a dark-haired, middle-aged woman was standing. She was wearing a flowered top, fashionable jeans, and a leather tote purse. Her fists were planted on her hips and her expression was a mix of amusement and disapproval. Mostly disapproval.

"Oh, wow." Paul's hand dropped from around Alice's waist. "Would you like to come meet my mother?"

A bolt of white hot embarrassment went through Alice. She'd never been one of those girls that kissed guys in public, in the dark, under the trees. Her face felt like it was on fire. She pressed her hands to her cheeks for a moment, willing herself to get control.

"No! No, I can't. I was actually looking for someone else before you showed up." She cringed inwardly at the last sentence. The words were tumbling out of her mouth.

Paul caught her hand. "Please. We can talk. And I'd like you to meet my mom." He glanced at Andy and then back to Alice, as if his friend might be able to convince her to stay.

She shook her head, fighting to put on a bright smile. "This has been fun, but I'm not like this. I don't just—." She motioned between them. "I need to go." And she turned on her heel, practically running from under the trees, past the stage, and toward the boardwalk.

Alice dodged couples, trying her best to ignore the laughter and whispered comments that followed her. Her heart was pounding but she kept walking until she reached the safety of her front door. There she turned, looking back for one brief moment. She had come to the festival with such high hopes. She was going to meet BWK, a real friend who understood her like no one else seemed to understand her.

Instead, she'd let herself be distracted. More than distracted. She'd made out with the man she'd vowed to fight, the man she'd been determined to avoid. Alice took out her key. Her hands shook so badly she thought she would have to give up and go around to the back door until she could calm down. Finally, she got the key in the lock and tumbled inside, closing the door against the music and the noise of the party outside.

She walked toward her desk without bothering to turn on the lights. Her eyes burned with hot tears and she choked back several gasping sobs. For the second time in as many days, she was crying over Paul Olivier. The first time he'd made her so angry she trembled with rage. The second time, it felt as if he'd reached inside and touched her heart with his bare hands.

Alice slumped into her chair, clutched the rings to her chest and let herself cry. Van Winkle lifted his head and made worried sounds but Alice couldn't stop. A terrible fear was growing inside. Maybe something was wrong with her. The stress of the inheritance lawsuit and running the store was becoming too much. Grief and anxiety could cause a mental breakdown, she knew that for a fact. And her behavior was completely out of the norm.

Sure, she was shy, but it was more than that. When she went out on a date, she wanted to keep a little distance. Eric had put in two weeks and three dates before he got a kiss, and it had been just a second or two. She wasn't cold, just cautious. It was always better to be safe than sorry. A girl needed to trust a guy before she could give up her heart. People weren't always what they seemed and not everyone had the best intentions. It was just better to take it slow. But tonight she had thrown away everything she thought she believed about first dates.

Alice sucked in a breath, half-laughing through her tears. Forget about first dates. This was a random dance-floor hook-up. He'd said a few words in Louisiana Creole, swung her through a song from her childhood, and she'd been all his. Who knows what would have happened if Andy hadn't shown up… with Paul's *mother*.

She groaned and dropped her head into her hands. There was no way she could go back out there. The night was ruined. She grabbed her cell phone off her desk and opened her email. Maybe he was out there, waiting. BWK deserved to know that she wasn't coming.

Dear BWK,

I'm so sorry. Something has come up. I won't be able to meet you tonight. You're always welcome to come by my store on Monday.

Your friend,

Alice.

She wrapped her arms around herself. Maybe it was some sort of mid-life crisis, about twenty years too early. Maybe she needed to take a vacation and give herself a break. As soon as Monday came, she would start looking at weekend packages. Maybe a nice bed and breakfast somewhere. She would leave the phone at home and spend the whole time blissfully unaware of the world.

Alice stood up and headed for the back stairs. She would sneak into her place now before Paul and Andy returned. It might be possible to avoid an awkward meeting tonight. But the next time she saw him, she knew she wouldn't be able to think of anything except those moments under the twinkling lights.

Chapter Fifteen

Getting information off the internet is like taking a drink from a fire hydrant.—Mitchell Kapor

"What on earth happened over there?" Andy whispered loudly.

Paul took a moment to step around a dancing little girl with pigtails. "I told her I was Browning Wordsworth Keats." He'd successfully merged his alter ego and his real life, and she hadn't been angry at all. It wasn't anything that he'd been expecting but he couldn't say he was unhappy. Just the opposite. He felt like he was walking on air, his heart still beating out of his chest. The end was a little awkward, when she almost ran from the scene, but he was sure they could sort it all out.

"And that was her response?" Andy asked, his eyes wide. He glanced towards Paul's mom as they closed the last couple of feet between them. "Now I'm sad that I don't have a super-secret identity, too."

"Who has a super-secret identity?" Paul's mother reached forward and gave her son and hug with a big kiss on the cheek. "And where did that gal scamper off to? You didn't bring her over to meet me and I find that a bit hurtful."

"Mama, I'm really sorry. She had to go." Paul searched for a place to sit. "Let's get some meat pies and watch the dancing."

"Oh, I was watchin' already. I was right proud of you. All that practice sure paid off." She stopped, giving Paul a serious look. "Maybe paid off a little too good, now that I think on it."

"Mrs. Olivier, I'll go get the food. Just point me in the right direction," Andy said.

Paul picked a stand farther down the sidewalk and Andy headed down the packed walkway. Paul didn't blame him at all for trying to get out of this conversation. He'd get out of it too, if he could.

"I just met her." He stopped. That really wasn't the way to get his mother to like Alice. "Come on, let's sit down and I'll explain."

They walked for a bit and found a free table. Paul could see Andy in line at the meat pie stand, chatting with a girl in jeans and a cowboy hat. He smiled. Whatever Andy may think about this trip, he couldn't deny he was being entertained. Their last business trip involved hours and hours at a hotel bar, watching most of their colleagues slowly get drunk.

"So, tell me about this gal." Mrs. Olivier peered toward the bookstore. "Why did she high-tail it out of here like that?"

Paul paused, trying to think of how to explain Alice.

"Honey, the look on your face…" She started to laugh. He'd always loved the way his mama laughed, full-throated with her head thrown back. She looked so much younger than her years.

"It's complicated, Mama," he said. He hated that phrase, but it didn't seem as if a better term was available.

"Your cousin Jimmy says that every time he gets a new girlfriend and he don't want us to harass her." She glanced at the bookstore again. "Does she live there in that fancy place?"

"Above her shop. It's a rare book store."

"Oh, honey, I bet you just love her for that!" His mama reached over and grabbed his hand. "Is that how you met? Looking for old books? Did you tell her about your collection? You've always been such a reader, just like your granddaddy."

"Sort of. We're renting the apartment next to hers and…" He stopped at the look on his mama's face. "I know what you're going to say."

"Do you, now?" She sighed. "You're a big boy, Paul. I won't be telling you how to live your life. But I know how hard it is to live right when the world is living all wrong." She squeezed his hand. "Listen to me. All worried 'cause you'll be living next door to that pretty girl when you've been on your own in New York City for years."

Paul wanted to remind her he wasn't staying long, that Andy was his roommate, and that she was looking miles down a path he didn't even know if he was walking.

"Who are her people?"

"Her family name is Augustine. She said her parents died in an accident." He watched realization dawn on his mama's face.

"I remember it. That was a bad one." She looked down at the table, picking at a little hole in the plastic top. "Drunk driving, they said. His family blamed the wife and her family blamed him. Kids got caught in the middle. Shipped off to the grandma's house and the grandma wasn't as sane as she shoulda been."

Paul shook his head. He couldn't imagine that kind of change. His childhood had been ugly, but it hadn't varied in its ugliness. "I've never met anyone like her, Mama."

She nodded, waiting for him to go on.

"We're both real shy. I mean, she can sure let you know when you've done wrong. The first day we met, we got into it over some old books. She's tough as nails and twice as sharp." He smiled at the memory. Paul could hear the way his speech was shifting from New York to Louisiana. Being with his mama always did that.

"Watch out for that, son. The drama is exciting for a while but it wears a body down. And some folks raised in it sometimes don't ever know how to live in peace."

"I know. And it's not the arguing. I would love to never argue with her again. I just want to be near her. She's like the antidote to all those years of cocktail party chatter. When she talks to me, I feel like she cuts to the heart of it all. Oh, and she speaks Creole about as well as anybody I've ever met. It's like we're just the same, deep down."

"Except for the part where she hates your guts," Andy said, dropping into a chair. He laid out the little paper containers of meat pies and removed bottled Cokes from under his arm.

"She doesn't hate me. Not exactly," Paul said hastily. "Just the company. And the new store. And what we do for a living."

Mrs. Olivier had been in the process of picking up a meat pie, but she paused, the pie halfway to her mouth. "But she likes something about you well enough to be kissin' you under the trees in front of the whole town."

Paul grinned. "Yup, apparently so."

His phone dinged and he reached for it automatically. An email showed on the screen and he tapped it, feeling his heart rate double at the sight of Alice's name. *Won't be able to meet tonight.* He read the note twice, three times. Hadn't she understood when he quoted Elizabeth Barrett Browning? He thought she'd kissed him because he was BWK.

He leaned back, running a hand over his face. Alice had kissed him as Paul, the man she couldn't stand. That news rocked him to his core. She must feel just as strongly for him if she could forget everything else that was happening, everything she'd vowed to fight. She didn't seem to be the kind of woman who picked a fight for nothing. Or took a kiss lightly, either.

"Uh oh. That's not a good look." Andy was chewing slowly, watching Paul.

"No, everything's fine. Just… took a step backwards when I thought we were going forwards." Paul tossed the phone onto the table and picked up a Coke. "But I'm not going to worry about it now. Tonight," he said, raising the bottle, "tonight we're going to enjoy ourselves. Here's to the new Natchitoches, Louisiana branch of the biggest and best company in gaming."

His mama and Andy raised their Cokes in unison. They clicked the glass bottles together and drank, smiling.

Paul picked up his meat pie, letting Andy take over the conversation for a moment. Andy asked his mama about hiring someone to come cook for them. He smiled as his mama seemed to take it as her personal responsibility to find a good local chef to make them a few meals a day. She took that sort of thing very seriously.

He let the smile fade from his face as he thought of Alice's note. He wasn't going to give up. Now, more than ever, he needed to tell her the truth. Their online connection had been strong enough for him to seek her out in the real world. Their connection in person had overshadowed all of that.

Paul took a long draught of Coke and stared at the dancers on the stage. At this point, he could still walk away. He could find another place to rent, avoid any contact with her, and let that kiss live in his memory as one perfect moment.

He thought those words to himself but knew it was a lie. He was going to walk this road to the end, for good or bad. And he hoped with everything in him, it was going to be for good.

***

Alice trotted up the steps to the cathedral just as the bells started to toll. She was never late. Ever. Except for today. She'd tried on ten dresses and none of them looked right. Maybe Eric was right and she needed to take up running. She'd finally picked a pretty pink top with a black skirt. She probably looked like a waitress from one of the cafés . And her hair… there was no taming it. After thirty minutes of fixing, she'd given up. By the time she'd stopped trying to accomplish the impossible, she'd realized it was now or never. Well, now or take the car. She hated to drive just a few blocks. It was wasteful and finding a good parking spot was a bear.

She had just not been able to get herself in gear. It wasn't just that she kept checking her email, wondering why BWK had not written her back. She hoped he wasn't angry. But there wasn't any reason for him to be upset with her. They'd barely gotten to know each other. Just a few notes. Nothing real. Except that it felt a lot more real than her relationship with Eric.

Maybe she'd had trouble this morning because she'd slept so badly and then she dreaded trying to get down the hallway without running into Paul or Andy. She sighed. There was no way to come back from last night. The only option was complete avoidance. Then again, she'd said that before and it hadn't worked out.

"Hey there, sweetie. Find yourself a spot real quick-like." Helen Delassixe gave her a kiss on the cheek and tugged her toward the aisle. Alice felt the angst of the morning slowly fade away at the touch of Helen's papery skin, a little cloud of baby powder accompanying the kiss. The elderly woman had been part of Alice's Sunday morning since she was a child, before the cathedral was named a minor basilica, and before Alice had become a respected bookstore owner.

The organ was just reaching its usual roar when Alice slipped into a pew and reached for a hymnal. She knew most of the songs by heart, but if the organist decided to go for that fourth verse, she'd have to get out the songbook anyway. She sung familiar words and felt the muscles in her shoulders start to relax. Sunday morning was her favorite time of the week, bar none.

Or it had been until a movement caught her eye. She glanced to her left in time to see Paul and his mother coming up the side aisle. Alice felt her mouth drop open and her hands went numb. He wore a nice suit and tie, looked freshly shaved but about as tired as Alice felt. She wondered how long he'd stayed at the festival. She slouched down, hoping they would pass by and head for the front pews. Surely he'd want to be seen by the congregation, especially if he was trying to win support for his store.

Instead, his mother turned her head and caught Alice's eye. She smiled, then tugged Paul to a stop. He was staring down at his feet and seemed to follow where she was leading without looking up.

His mother wouldn't… she couldn't… but she did. Alice watched in growing horror as his mother stopped at Alice's pew, stepped to the side and motioned for Paul to go first. He genuflected, then looked at Alice for the first time.

She wished she could have seen her own face, because she figured they wore the same expression. Surprise, shock, dread. There was nothing like seeing your make out partner from last night in church the next day.

"Hey," he whispered as he side-stepped into the pew.

"Hey," she whispered back, and scooted down several feet. She looked longingly at the far end and wished she was bold enough to just keep going until she hit the next aisle. Or even slip away and come back at a later service. But her manners wouldn't allow her to be so obvious.

The organist decided three verses was enough and let the last few chords fade away. Alice mumbled the opening greeting and hoped her face was set in a smile. Of course, he couldn't see her expression since they were shoulder-to-shoulder. He smelled wonderful, as usual, except he lacked the old book smell this time. She let her eyes slide to the left, taking in his charcoal-gray suit and nice dress shoes. She'd figured he spent all his time in T-shirts and jeans, but of course he would be wearing a suit every now and then. Even when the whole world thought you were the cat's meow, you still had to dress up for church.

After a few minutes, the congregation settled into the pews for the first Bible reading. As she sat, Alice snuck a look at Paul's mom. Her dark hair was pulled back and she had just a hint of makeup on her face. She seemed perfectly at ease. Alice would have liked to believe his mom was trying to bring them together. But it was much more likely his mom was trying to give a little nudge in that special way that moms always have. Guilt was always a great way to get the message across, just in case Alice thought she could get caught kissing Paul and get away with it.

The words all seemed to blend together and Alice clenched her fists, letting her nails dig into her palms, forcing herself to concentrate. As the lector finished the first reading, Alice shifted uncomfortably. She never could have imagined the torture of sitting just feet away from the man she'd kissed, then run away from, *and his mother* whom she'd refused to meet. At the announcement of the Gospel, the congregation moved to stand and Alice shot a glance at Paul. He looked calm enough, but his jaw was tight and the line of his mouth didn't speak of happy Sunday vibes. Well, if he thought he was uncomfortable, it was nothing compared to what Alice felt.

***

The last hymn finally faded away and Paul dropped the hymnal into the pew pocket. He cleared his throat, leaned closer, and whispered, "Sorry. I never would have decided to sit in the same—"

"Paul!" His mama had ahold of his elbow. "Why don't we have your friend over for lunch?"

He saw the look on Alice's face and it would have been funny if he hadn't felt just the same.

"Mrs. Olivier, thank you so much but I really should get back," Alice said, a hint of panic in her voice. She was edging out of the pew, looking around her.

"You keep the store open on Sundays?" His mama narrowed her eyes. "Or do you have another date?" The *another* seemed to reverberate in the air between them all.

"No. And well, no…" Her face turned bright pink. She shot Paul a look and seemed to be asking something, but he shook his head.

"Please come to lunch, Alice." He gave a little shrug as he said the words. She met his eyes and at first he thought she was going to argue, but then he added, "please".

Her lips turned up at the corners. "That would be lovely," she said. "I walked here today but I can go home to get my car and meet you wherever you're going."

"Wonderful," his mama said. "I was just fixin' to make a little something at Paul's new place. So, I guess we're going the same direction." They walked in silence down the steps and he tried to catch Alice's eye, but she resolutely faced forward.

"Paul, why don't you go get the car while we wait for you in front?" his mama asked. Paul nodded, feeling his stomach drop into his shoes. Leaving his mother alone with Alice was the worst case scenario but he didn't know how to avoid it.

With a sigh, he trudged off to the parking lot, hands stuffed in his pockets. He loved his mama but she wasn't known for being demure and quiet. She spoke her mind, especially when she felt her son was on the wrong track.

It seemed most of the congregation was skipping the doughnuts and heading for breakfast. There was already a line of cars backed up at the parking lot exit, waiting for a chance to get onto the road. Paul wondered if Andy would be awake. Maybe he could run interference between the two of them and Alice wouldn't have to suffer through the third degree. That was assuming she wasn't getting an earful right that minute. At the thought, Paul doubled his pace, beeping the remote unlock button, slipping off his jacket and angling into the seat.

He'd acted without thinking last night and he couldn't believe how the situation had gotten more and more complicated. She probably hated him enough as it was, without having to deal with an angry mother bear. Alice was as far from a seductress as could be, but Paul knew how mothers thought. They always believed their child was a saint. His mama was going to give Alice the what for, and make sure she understood that Paul was a good, Catholic boy.

He slid the car out and took a place in the long line of cars waiting to exit the lot. Well, it was a proven fact he was far from perfect. Alice shouldn't have to pay the price for that. If he could just get over there quickly enough, he could keep that from happening.

Chapter Sixteen

Soon, silence will have passed into legend. Man has turned his back on silence. Day after day he creates machines that increase noise and distract humanity from the essence of life, contemplation, meditation. — Jean Arp

Parishioners streamed out of the double doors and after greeting Father Carl, a few headed to the hall for doughnuts and strong coffee. As much as Alice didn't want to face Paul, watching him walk away had filled her with panic. She stood off to the side of the cathedral, arms wrapped around her middle, Mrs. Olivier waiting quietly next to her. The silence between them felt like an accusation. Alice searched through the crowd, hoping someone would come over and rescue her, but there were only a few waves and one fly-by kiss from old Mrs. Gerbier, her second-grade teacher.

As the crowd thinned, Alice waited for Mrs. Olivier to say something. Shame mixed with frustration, and she repressed a sigh. Of course Paul's mother was curious and wanted to get to know her. She couldn't blame the woman for wanting to poke her nose into the situation.

Mrs. Olivier tucked her hand into Alice's elbow and smiled, her eyes the same dark brown shade as her son's, but the wrinkles around them spoke of years of sun and laughter. "My goodness! There were so many people you couldn't stir 'em with a stick. We never came to this church when Paul was little. It was too big for us. It still feels a bit fancy for the likes of little ol' me. I should have dressed up better."

"I think you look real nice." Alice knew when one woman mentioned her looks, the other should offer a compliment. It wasn't hard to do. It was clear where Paul got his good looks.

She patted her hair. "Oh, my beauty operator made me look like Betty Boop this week. I don't know why I bother except I've been goin' to her for years. I can't just stop. That would be downright rude."

Alice smiled. She could see her dilemma.

"You like to cook?" Mrs. Olivier asked, as if the topics were related.

"I— I do, actually."

"What do you make? Desserts? My sister has the best peach pie recipe. It's got a secret ingredient." She leaned close. "If you're real nice, I might tuck it in your Christmas card."

Alice blinked. No words occurred to her. This wasn't what she was expecting.

"Paul told me your breakfast got him out of bed one day. He says he wandered up and down the block looking for bacon and hash browns."

"He's got a good nose," she said, her lips tugging up. She wondered if Paul had mentioned punching her ex-boyfriend that day, too. Probably not. She turned a little, facing Mrs. Olivier. "He speaks Creole really well. Did he learn it from you?"

"*Oui*," she said, pronouncing it "way," and letting it stretch for a few syllables. "Myself and my family. He wasn't always real proud of where he came from, but in the last few years, that's changed a bit."

Alice couldn't imagine wanting to walk away from this place and pretend to be something she wasn't, but she could see how a person could want to come home. "Maybe New York City isn't everything he thought it would be."

"Maybe so." Mrs. Olivier looked up at the sky. "I hope Paul hurries. It looks to be comin' up a cloud."

Alice looked up at the sky, watching the thunder clouds building on the horizon. "We'll be getting a good storm this afternoon, I'm guessing."

"Love and thunder. They always go together." Mrs. Olivier winked at her.

"I've never heard that phrase." Alice refused to take the bait. Paul's mother was going to be nosy after all. She was just easing up to it.

"No? My Papa used to say that. He'd rock on the porch and watch the afternoon storm, and every time he'd say 'love and thunder always go together.' He knew a lot about love, bein' married to my mama for sixty years."

Alice rubbed her arms and wished Paul would get there already.

"He said he could tell a man in love at fifty paces. Didn't matter the age or the circumstances. It was something in the way he acted." She tipped her head to the side. "I think I might have inherited that gift. At least where my boy is concerned."

Alice almost swallowed her tongue in surprise. "Oh, no. It's not like that." Alice held up a hand. "We just met."

"That's no account. Love doesn't care how long you been knowin' each other. But are you saying you don't have feelings for my boy? Maybe you were expecting something else when you kissed him t'other night?"

Awkward. Alice would have been offended except that Mrs. Olivier's tone was light. There was no condemnation, just a big dose of sass and a hint of teasing. But she still didn't want to talk about it. Not on the steps of her church with all her neighbors milling around. "Mrs. Olivier—" she started.

"Call me Rosie," she interrupted.

"Okay, Rosie, I know Paul is wonderful." Alice let out a sigh. "He's charming and really handsome and everyone loves him. Apparently, he's also some sort of genius, too."

This time, Mrs. Olivier waited patiently for her to finish.

"But there are so many differences between us."

"He's Creole like you. That should cover a lot of differences," Mrs. Olivier said.

Alice bit her lip. "Yes, fine. He's Creole and a great dancer and a good Catholic guy and protective and generous and everything I've ever looked for. I'm sure he'll make a wonderful husband and a really great dad and—"

She broke off suddenly. Mrs. Olivier was looking somewhere behind her and Alice had a terrible suspicion that she wasn't looking at Paul pulling up to the curb.

Alice turned slowly, afraid to see what she already knew. Paul stood right behind her, his expression a mix of total surprise and something else she couldn't quite read.

He cleared his throat. "I tried to get your attention but you all seemed to be having such a good chat."

Alice closed her eyes for a moment. He'd heard all of that and probably thought she was sending out wedding invitations. She couldn't imagine how many women had tried the same thing. One kiss and then they're picking bridesmaids. Well, not her. She certainly wasn't looking for someone who lived in New York City and was constructing the ugliest building the historic district had ever seen, while seducing the nation's young people with mindless video games that contributed nothing to their development. But that wasn't anything she could say in front of the man's mother. Even Alice had her limits.

"Thank you," she said, smiling her sweetest smile, and following his direction toward the car. She could almost feel Paul and his mother exchanging looks behind her back. There was nothing she could do about it now, but as soon as possible, she'd excuse herself back to her own apartment. Nothing good could come from this. Especially since she'd resolved that Monday was the day she would file a complaint with the city over the construction of

Paul's new store. If she could get them to stop construction, even for a few weeks, he might just decide it was better to take his business to some other town.

***

Paul flopped backward onto his bed, arm over his eyes. The lunch had gone well, surprisingly. His mother and Alice seemed to get along just fine. They spent most of their time in the kitchen talking about food and avoiding him. Well, his mother kept trying to drag him into the conversation, but he stayed out in the living room with Andy.

Right before they had sat down to eat, a thunderstorm hit and the power flickered. Alice didn't seem to think anything of it, but Paul wondered how old the electrical system was. He hadn't wanted to ask her right then, but outdated electrical could be downright dangerous. The storm passed, Alice left for her own apartment, his mama left with a promise to come back in a few days, and Andy passed out on the couch in a food coma. Paul was left to his own thoughts. He paced the living room and watched the storm pass outside.

Everything I've ever looked for, I'm sure he'll make a wonderful husband and a really great dad. Alice's words kept echoing around in his head. Of course that sentence was going to continue with a *but* that included every detail she absolutely hated about him. Despite that, those words settled somewhere in his heart and he couldn't shake them loose. He got a lot of compliments from women, but none of them had been particularly interested in whether he was a good person or if he'd make a solid partner and father. It seemed as if Alice didn't care at all that he owned a huge company and had more money than almost everyone in the country.

Now hours later, he sat up and rubbed his face. It had been a long time since anyone thought those things didn't matter. A few days ago he would have been outraged. He'd worked years to build his company, missing out on vacations and birthdays, putting in the long nights and most weekends. His fortune represented the entire decade of his twenties. But if he stripped away the company and the money, who was he? And that was why he sat on his bed in a darkened room at two in the morning, unable to sleep. He didn't want to be that guy who didn't have much to offer the world. He wanted to be the kind of person Alice saw when she looked at him.

He stared down at his bare feet. He'd considered it a victory to get permission to build in the historic district, right in the middle of all the fancy buildings. It was his way of sticking it to everyone who looked down on him in high school, every person who ignored his mother when she went into one of those old stores, clearly not the kind of person who could shop there every week.

Paul stood and walked to the window, looking out at the river. The moonlight shone in the ripples of the water and the trees were like dark sentries, unmoving and ominous. He'd told Andy that his epiphany was about revenge and how it would eat him up from the inside, making him weak and doomed to failure. But maybe there was more to it. He needed to let go of the need for revenge, put his energy into helping the city, and then further. Not just in this town, but everywhere. Christmas donations to the Red Cross were fine, but throwing money at a charity corporation once a year didn't mean he was making a real difference.

A plan began to take shape in the back of his mind and he opened his laptop, searching out contact information from several sites. As he clicked into his email, he saw another message from Alice. Paul forced himself to send the short note to the recipients he'd chosen before he opened her letter.

Dear BWK,

I hope you had a good Sunday. I spent the day thinking of that line of poetry from Gerard Manley Hopkins:

I have asked to be
where no storms come,
where the green swell
is in the havens dumb
and out of the swing of the sea.

Do you ever feel this way? As if you need a place "out of the swing of the sea"? I never have until now.

Did you enjoy the zydeco festival? I'm sorry again that we weren't able to meet. I hope you practice Alexander Pope's ninth beatitude. It's the safest way to live.

I'd like to be peaceful, I think I'm doomed to follow Louisa May Alcott's path of resolving "to take Fate by the throat and shake a living out of her".

Your friend,
Alice

Paul let out a chuckle. But his heart dropped as he read the note again and let the poetry sink in deep. Alice felt like she was being tossed around, a piece of flotsam on the ocean of life.

Dear Alice,

I enjoy imagining you with your hands at Fate's throat. She has been kind to me, overall, but I've heard she can be an uncompromising, vengeful slacker, reluctant to give what is due. I whole-heartedly approve of your current plan of action.

The zydeco festival was pure excitement, from start to finish. I didn't stay long. I'm afraid Pope's ninth beatitude of expecting nothing and never being disappointed didn't apply to me, though.

I, too, long for a place out of the swing of the sea, but... Do you know how Walt Whitman said that we should let our soul stand cool and composed before a million universes? I've never been that type. On the outside, perhaps. But inside I've never been able to stand unmoved before any beauty or deep emotion. And so we end up like Goethe, who said the soul who sees beauty may sometimes walk alone. Or live out in the swing of the sea, in our case.

Your friend,

BWK

Paul sent the email and closed the laptop, setting it on his desk. He crossed to the bed and dropped onto the covers, staring up at the ceiling. That probably made no sense at all. He was exhausted and his brain seemed to be tied up in knots. He wished he could shelter Alice, give her the peaceful life she wanted.

He leaned back against his pillows and shut his eyes. Maybe this was all he would ever get, late night email with poetry sprinkled over it like bitter chocolate shavings. He should just accept that reality.

His phone dinged and he rolled over, picking it up from his nightstand. A touch of the screen and Alice's response popped up.

Dear BWK,

Are you back home now? You must live on the West Coast. It's very late here. I can't sleep. There are so many worries tonight that I didn't have a week ago. Some are personal, some have to do with my store. All of them (except one) are probably silly in comparison to most problems. Like the fact that I need to get an alarm system installed and I don't know anything about them. I hate high tech things and I'm afraid I'm going to lock myself out of my own house.

As for the one problem that's not so silly, you know that I inherited this bookstore. Well, the previous owner's niece has filed a lawsuit against me, in hopes of receiving half the estate.

Paul bolted upright in bed. Alice was being sued?

We both know you can't split a bookstore. (I don't even share shelf space.) If Mr. Perrault had wanted to give her the store, I think he would have. But he's not here so he can't tell them that. There's nothing to be done, really. Just waiting and wondering if the judge will decide this stranger deserves half of the store she's never seen.

I'm trying to be "like barley bending in low fields by the sea" as Sara Teasdale wrote, but I'm afraid I've never learned how. It's always served me better to be unyielding, hard as stone. But under all this pressure, I feel as if I'm flint, ready to splinter into a thousand sharp blades.

Your friend,
Alice

Paul sat still, resisting the urge to slip on his shoes and walk down the hallway to Alice's apartment. He knew she was awake and he knew she would answer. But unfortunately, Alice hadn't told Paul about the lawsuit. She told BWK. So, even though he felt close to her, she had chosen to share this trial with someone she'd never met.

He pulled out his e-reader and opened a book he'd uploaded a few weeks ago. In moments, he found what he was looking for.

Dear Alice,

When you get your alarm system, remember two things: choose the one you think is the simplest because if you're not comfortable with it, you won't use it. And when you get the system installed, use it every time. That's all the wisdom I have on that.

As for the once-lost-now-found niece, perhaps you should stop trying to bend.

An emerald is as green as grass,
A ruby red as blood;
A sapphire shines as blue as heaven;
A flint lies in the mud.

A diamond is a brilliant stone,
To catch the world's desire;
An opal holds a fiery spark;
But a flint holds fire.

I think you should ignore Sara Teasdale (she's a bit of a moper, to be honest.).

Take Christina Rossetti's advice and be fire.

Your friend,
BWK, who is still in Natchitoches

Paul sent the message and then stood up, walking to the long window and staring out at the river. The apartment was quiet, the city was hushed. It seemed like the whole world was asleep, except for two lonely people.

He heard the ding of his phone from where he stood but didn't reach for it. He couldn't guess her response. Would she ask him to meet her? Would she ask where he was staying? For some reason, his stomach was twisting with nerves.

Picking up his phone, he held it in his hand, feeling the cool metal against his fingertips. If she asked him to meet her, then he'd go through all the emotion and anxiety he'd felt before the dance. And even though he knew it was selfish, Paul didn't know if he had enough bravery to try and tell her twice in one weekend.

He touched the screen and her response popped up.

Dear BWK,

Yes, be fire!

Tomorrow, I'll spark the flame.

Thank you.

Your friend,
Alice

Paul felt the huge grin spread over his face. *That's my girl*, he thought. And moments later, tried to erase the idea. She wasn't his girl. She was a lot of things to him but she wasn't *his*.

He shut off the phone and fell into bed, a smile still touching his lips. He fell into sleep like falling under water, all at once. He dreamed of bright sparks and her kiss and piles of old books. He tried to keep them apart, knowing even in his dream that it would be a disaster, but in the end, it all merged together into a towering flame.

Chapter Seventeen

We live in a society exquisitely dependent on science and technology, in which hardly anyone knows anything about science and technology. —Carl Sagan

Alice gave herself a silent pep talk. She was about to do something she could never have imagined just weeks ago. She was going to sue Paul Olivier and her beloved city of Natchitoches. She had only one friend who might be crazy enough to file that kind of paper for her and she quickly looked up his number. A few minutes later, she set the phone back down, her heart pounding in her chest. Randy Rittenberg, an old high school friend who lived in LaFayette, asked her more than once if she was sure she wanted to go ahead with it. Once she'd convinced him she wasn't backing down, he agreed. By noon, he would fax the papers to city hall. She would have to go down there, sign and file them.

Alice picked up the old rotary phone and dialed again, letting the loud ringing in her right ear act as a sort of wake up call. Two cups of coffee weren't enough to get her sluggish brain moving after a night of worry. After BWK had given her a pep talk, she'd finally been able to rest, but that had only been a few hours before dawn.

"Mayor Cointreau speaking," said a gravelly voice.

"Hello, mayor. It's Alice Augustine, from By the Book. I was hoping we could meet sometime today and talk about that new store that's going up in the historic district."

There was a long silence at the other end and Alice could imagine Mayor Cointreau straightening his tie. It was a nervous tic, like other people cleared their throats. "I suppose you can come by, if you like, but everything's already been approved. I can hear them working on it from here."

Alice took a deep breath. "I've decided to file a petition seeking a temporary injunction with the city to block the construction of ScreenStop in the historical district. And I'm going to sue to seek the enforcement of the zoning laws."

There was another long silence and this time she couldn't imagine what he was doing. Finally he said, "I don't think you could win that case, Alice."

"I'm claiming undue hardship, since that store will bring down my property prices." Alice hadn't been sure what sort of claim she could make but Randy had given her several options, the best of which was that By the Book would suffer.

"I would suggest you rethink that course of action. We went to a lot of trouble to make sure ScreenStop could build quickly and without issues. Whatever has happened between you is no cause for that kind of behavior."

"What?" She nearly choked on her words. "Nothing has happened. I mean, it's not what you're thinking. I decided this before—"

"If you do find someone to file this, I'll have to come out and say that I'm against your actions and that the city supports Mr. Olivier." His tone was cold.

That was pretty clear and nothing that she hadn't expected, but it was still hard to hear. "I understand," she said and hung up the phone.

If Alice had ever wondered how Paul had gotten that building permit without it going through the board, she knew now. The application hadn't followed the city bylaws. No matter what Paul had said, or what he'd been told, that store was being constructed without being properly approved.

The knowledge made her furious and hopeful at the same time. If she could prove it, she could stop it. Alice wiped her hands on her linen skirt and took a deep breath. She didn't mind tangling with city hall. Authority figures had never bothered her. It was the thought of facing Paul after he discovered what she'd done.

Be fire. Alice held on to those words, repeating them to herself as she slipped out from behind her desk and paced the small front room. She needed to let her anger spark itself into something that would create change, not just let it smolder inside, growing hotter and more painful.

Jane Eyre came out from around a range and jumped into her lap. Alice buried her face in the short-haired tabby's fur and tried not to cry. The kitty was quiet, loving, and kept to herself, but she had a sort of sixth sense for when Alice was upset.

"Thanks for the womanly commiseration," she whispered. Alice took a tissue from her desk and wiped her eyes. She was sure what she was doing was the right thing, but her emotions were still a mess. But that was what happened when you fell for the man you'd promised to fight.

***

Alice walked out of city hall without feeling the joy she thought she would. She was taking action and not allowing some big corporation take over her beautiful city. She was standing up for a simpler way, an educated life of books and conversation, rather than mindless flashing TV screens. But even though she knew she was right, her stomach rolled with the realization of what she'd done. As much as wanted to believe she could separate Paul from his business, she couldn't. She felt as if she'd just attacked a friend.

***

Alice looked up to see a blond man in a business suit and two technicians walking through her store's front door. She felt sweat instantly appear on her forehead. Paul said he would call someone, but she hadn't expected it so soon.

And here she just returned from throwing a wrench into his building plans. She felt more than a twinge of guilt. She stood, brushing papers to the side and startling Van Winkle.

"Miss Alice Augustine? I'm Larson McGee. I own Cane River Home Security." He held out a hand and Alice took it, hoping her palms weren't sweaty.

"Paul said you needed a consultation. We were working down the street and I said I'd stop in on the way back. Did you want to set up a time to go over what we could offer you in terms of security for your business and home?"

Alice cleared her throat. *Be fire.* She needed to make decisions as quickly as possible so she wasn't spending the whole night awake. "I'm free right now, if you are."

Larson smiled. "Works for me. Why don't you show us around and then we can talk about different packages."

She stepped around Mr. Rochester who was giving the intruders a cold stare, and headed for the rare book room. "Let's start here."

***

Paul pushed open the door to By the Book and felt his mouth go dry at the sight of Alice. She stood up from her desk and turned, her dark eyes fixed on him. He took a second to admire her red silk top and pencil skirt, and then he forced his eyes upward.

Her expression wasn't just surprise but dread. Paul paused halfway across the floor. Maybe she thought he'd become a stalker. They'd spent most of the day together yesterday and then emailed in the middle of the night. He certainly was showing up every time she turned around. "Hi, Alice. I'm sorry I didn't call but I have something for Bix."

"For Bix?" she asked. Her dark eyes flickered down to the small box he held in his hand.

A tall black cat leaped from the top of the range, landing gracefully in front of him. Paul managed not to jump out of his skin. "That's Darcy, isn't it?"

"Yes." She frowned down at the cat who had taken up a position in front of her, green eyes unblinking. "He doesn't usually come down here. Either he really likes you or he really doesn't."

He continued towards her and Darcy didn't twitch a muscle. The two of them stood like soldiers at a guard station. "How will I know which it is?" He stopped a few feet away.

"You won't." Alice put a fist to one hip and winked. "We're good Southerners. We know how to be hospitable."

Maybe it was the saucy wink that got him but Paul stepped forward. "Mm-hmm," he said, letting his voice drop to a level that was just between them. "I think I can tell the difference. Not always, but every now and then it's pretty clear."

Her face went pink and he couldn't help a little smile. Man, she was beautiful. "Will he be in today?"

"Who?" Alice asked.

He lifted the e-reader box. "Bix. I'd like to show him how this operates."

"Oh, right. Actually," she looked at her watch, "he should be here any moment. He and Charlie both come in on Monday afternoons. If you want to just…" She looked around the small space and the few comfortable chairs in corners of the bookstore.

"I'll just sit over here, then." He turned toward one of the chairs near the front.

"Oh, and thank you for calling the alarm company. They came this morning."

"And how did it go? Did you feel comfortable with the package you chose? They're usually pretty easy to operate. You won't lock yourself out." He tried to look reassuring.

She cocked her head. "Yes, I think it will work out. And do I look like the type to lock myself out of my house?"

"Well, no, but you—" He started to laugh, and then caught himself. She'd written those words herself not twelve hours ago, but that was to BWK. "I'm glad it will work out. Your inventory needs to be protected. I'm just going to sit over here and wait for Bix."

He made his way to the overstuffed chair and settled in, shaking his head at one more stupid mistake. The best course of action was to just keep his thoughts to himself until Bix got here. The chair was near the window and the sunlight had warmed the red corduroy fabric. He put the box on his lap and stretched out. If only the apartment upstairs had this chair. It was perfect for gaming. He could feel himself sinking into it, body relaxing, anxiety easing away.

Alice stood for a moment, watching him, then went back to her desk. There was a short display between them and as soon as she sat down, she was hidden from view. Paul felt his phone buzz in his pocket but he didn't feel like checking it. He leaned his head back and took in the long rows of shelves, the smell of old books and good coffee, the bright sun shining through and hitting the tiled floor.

He could hear her moving papers around on her desk. Even though they were thirty feet apart, he felt like they were sitting next to each other. And it felt good. He thought of how she said she'd loved a certain corner of the store and he wondered which one. The idea of a teenage Alice reading in a bright spot of sunlight for hours after school made him smile.

A long-haired cat wandered out from another room and he squinted at it. Was that Mrs. Gaskell? He couldn't keep them all straight. It gave him a short glance and continued toward the desk. The store was so quiet, Paul could hear Alice whisper a few words to the cat. There wasn't any of the usual beeps, buzzing, and background noise. Somewhere far away a clock ticked. He looked up at the pendant lights, absent of the usual annoying buzz of fluorescent lighting. The cars passed outside in a muted, almost soothing way, like waves gently hitting the shore.

He closed his eyes for a moment. Getting only a few hours of sleep didn't bother him too much in college, but he wasn't nineteen any more. He was going to need some coffee before he toured the construction site that afternoon. There was a coffee pot somewhere near, he could smell it. It was a dark Louisiana roast, probably Beau Monde. He should just get up and get himself a cup, just as soon as he relaxed a few more minutes in this amazingly comfortable chair.

Chapter Eighteen

Adding sound to movies would be like putting lipstick on the Venus De Milo. — Mary Pickford

Alice tried to read the papers in front of her but all she could think about was the man sitting just across the store. Paul must have some sort of meeting because he was wearing navy slacks, a blue button-up shirt, and nice leather shoes with thick soles. He was freshly shaved and looked well-rested. Nothing like what Alice felt, and what was confirmed when she looked into the mirror across from her desk. She looked old and haggard, with dark circles under her eyes.

She took a sip of coffee and grimaced. Cold. But she didn't want to get up and rewarm it. Plus, she should have offered Paul some as soon as he came in the store. After they'd invited her over for lunch, she couldn't even seem to remember to offer him a beverage. She had been so sure he was there because of the papers she'd filed, but he didn't seem to know yet.

What would he say when he found out? She tried to take a deep breath and almost choked. After a few loud coughs, she managed to get control. She sat lower in her chair. This was torture. She felt as if every movement was magnified, echoing through the small space. What if she sneezed? Or worse? She could feel her facc get hot just thinking about it.

Mrs. Gaskell crossed to her desk and wrapped herself around Alice's feet. "Did you come to keep me company?" she whispered, lifting the kitty to her lap. Van Winkle wasn't much of a cuddler and Alice appreciated visits from the more affectionate kitties.

Van Winkle didn't even bat an ear when Mrs. Gaskell stepped off Alice's lap and onto the desk, where she nosed around the papers. It was fine. Alice wasn't getting any work done anyway. All she could do was sit here and pray Bix arrived within the next few minutes. As it was, it felt like two warring countries in a ceasefire.

Alice closed her eyes. She had no idea why she thought it was a good idea to flirt, even a little bit, with Paul. She wasn't the type of girl who could pull off that sort of sassy comment. And he'd turned it right back on her, leaving her red-faced and humiliated. *I think I can tell the difference. Not always, but every now and then it's pretty clear.* Well, not humiliated. More like… shyly reliving everything that was wonderful about that moment and hoping there would be another round somewhere in her near future.

Mrs. Gaskell jumped from the desk to the floor with a light thump. Alice wondered what Paul was doing. She hadn't seen him pick out a book. Maybe he was reading on that machine or checking his phone. She desperately wanted to peer over the little bookshelf and check. He seemed so quiet. She sat back in her chair, considering. It was rare to find a person who could sit in silence. Most people needed their technology. They couldn't face themselves, alone, and see what might surface. It was a lost art to be at peace in the middle of the hustle and bustle of the day. She had to admire him for that.

She reached for her cup and remembered the coffee was cold. Maybe she should offer him a cup now. She sat up straight, lifting her head until she could almost see over the short shelve between them. Then she slumped down again. That would look horrible if he caught her peeking at him. She should just stand up and walk to the coffee pot, then turn and ask if he wanted a cup, almost as an afterthought.

Alice swallowed hard. Her knees felt shaky and she wiped sweat from her forehead. It wasn't so hard. Just get up. *Get up!* She forced herself to her feet, stepped out from behind her desk and headed for the coffee pot. She could almost feel his eyes on her. She wondered if her skirt was wrinkled in the back and how out of control her hair looked. Resisting the urge to smooth it back, she made it to the coffee pot and poured a cup, accidentally splashing the hot liquid onto the hand that held the mug.

Grabbing a napkin and pressing it to her burning skin, she tried not to hiss in frustration and pain. If she poured him a mug and brought it over, she just might trip and spill it on him, the luck she was having. But if she carried her mug back to her desk, he might think she was rude. Alice stood there, debating for what seemed like hours, all the while feeling Paul's gaze on her.

Taking a breath, she fixed a smile to her face and turned around. "Would you like—" She broke off as she caught a glimpse of him in the chair. His head was leaned all the way back, eyes closed, hands resting in his lap. He was completely motionless. Alice frowned, wondering if he was meditating. Was he okay? She crept forward, intent on his face. When she got to less than a foot away, she could see his chest rising and falling. A faint sound issued from his throat.

Alice stood still, holding the mug in both hands, smiling. She couldn't imagine falling asleep anywhere but her bed. She wasn't the kind of person who could nap, even while traveling. Forget about sleeping in public, where anybody could see you, where you were completely vulnerable. She couldn't fathom having that particular talent.

It occurred to her that she'd been agonizing over him while he slept peacefully. One more confirmation that Paul Olivier wasn't like her. He was an extrovert that dealt with fans, crowds, and legions of interested females. She, meanwhile, lost a night of sleep over one kiss.

Now that he was asleep, she could finally get a good look at him without feeling awkward. She could see his mother's features, but also the strong jaw and nose that must have come from his father. His dark, angled, brows made him look a little angry, even though he was completely at rest. It made her realize that some of his expressions might be less irritated than she'd perceived. His lashes were thick and full, true to the Creole genes. She'd thought his hair was straight but now she could see it curling a little at the temples. His legs were stretched out and she thought of how tall he was, at least six feet, but his mother was more Alice's height. She wondered if Paul had any contact with his father.

A sound outside the glass door caught her attention and she looked up. Bix was coming through the door. She barely had time to step away from Paul as the little brass bell rang.

"Hello, Miss Alice," Bix said. It sounded like a shout in the quiet room.

She waved him closer and pointed to Paul, who hadn't moved a muscle. "He's asleep," she whispered.

Bix stepped close and leaned forward until he was just inches away. Alice covered her eyes with one hand, knowing Paul would wake up and have the scare of his life finding Bix at close range. "That he is, Miss Alice, that he is. How did you manage it?"

"I didn't manage anything. I just offered him a seat." She could feel her face flaming. "He was waiting for you."

"For me?" Bix rubbed his chin. "Well, what do we do now? Looks like the poor fella needs his rest, wouldn't you say?"

Alice said nothing. She didn't know anybody who slept that deeply. Maybe he was faking it. Maybe it was a joke and they were being filmed as a prank. She glanced around nervously.

"Hi, guys!" Charlie burst through the door and almost fell flat when she saw Paul in the chair, head back, and eyes closed. "What on earth did you do?" She had on a black T-shirt that read 'I Could Be Gaining Levels Right Now' in bright yellow. Her blue eyes, ringed with heavy eyeliner, opened wide at the scene in front of her.

"Shhh," Alice said. She needed to get away from the area before anyone else came in and decided to join in on the store's new spectator sport. "And why do y'all think I did something? Do you both think I'm so crazy I'm just going to run around drugging people?"

Neither of them answered, but they both gave a "well, you know" expression.

"Fine," Alice hissed. "I may be a little bit crazy but I would never hurt anyone. He sat down and fell asleep, I promise." She frowned. "But he hasn't moved at all."

"You should wake him up. I gots to know why he wanted to talk to me." Bix took off his hat and started unbuttoning his coat.

"Why me?" Alice lifted the mug in her hand. "I can't. I'm holding—"

"Here." Charlie took the mug from her hand and stepped back. "Now you can."

Alice shot her a look and then leaned over Paul. "Hey," she said softly. There was no response.

Charlie giggled and took a sip of the coffee.

"This isn't funny," Alice whispered. She crouched down next to the chair while Bix hovered on one side and Charlie lurked on the other. For just a moment, she saw how silly the situation was, and a laugh bubbled up inside. She forced it back down, trying to keep her face straight. A second later, the laugh emerged as a guffaw. Alice clapped a hand over her mouth but the dam had been breached. After just a few seconds, her shoulders were shaking and tears blurred her vision.

Charlie started to laugh just as hard, mouth open wide, one arm around her middle. It was contagious.

Alice turned to ask Bix for help, but he was shaking his head, chuckling. "Now you done it," he said. "Once you start a-laughin' at a time like this, it's like the church chuckles. You just can't stop."

Church chuckles. Bix's description of the infectious, unstoppable laughter that happened in the pew made Alice laugh even harder. She braced herself against the chair, letting one hand fall on Paul's knee. She wasn't even making much sound anymore, just a slight wheezing with each spasm.

Paul bolted upright. "Are you okay?" He gripped Alice's shoulders and pulled her forward, looking into her face. Tears streamed down her cheeks and she waved a hand, still unable to talk.

"You want some coffee?" Charlie managed to get out some words, most of it lost in giggles.

Paul looked from Charlie, to Bix, to Alice and cocked his head. "You drew something on my face, didn't you?"

Alice took a second to digest that comment and collapsed against the chair, shaking her head, her smile stretched in a silent rictus of laughter.

"I had a roommate in college that did that every single time I fell asleep." Paul sounded a little irritated, but mostly amused. "He shaved my eyebrows, wrote words on my forehead with a Sharpie, took pictures of me drooling. I started thinking it would be safer to sleep in the local bus terminal."

"No… no, we didn't touch you." She took several breaths that ended in giggles but the worst was over. "We would never do that. You fell asleep and I was trying to wake you up, and it just struck me as funny how we're all crowded around you and what a shock it would be when you woke up surrounded by this group." She looked up and met his eyes. He was grinning now.

"Well, you should have taken your chance while you had it. I'm a deep sleeper. I always have been. I grew up in a house about forty feet from the train tracks. I learned to tune it all out." He stretched his hands over his head. "Sorry about the impromptu nap, but at least y'all got some entertainment out of it."

Alice stood up, wiping the tears from her cheeks. "I don't know how you can sleep like that in public. I'd be afraid to ever shut my eyes."

He stood, holding the box in one hand. "I don't usually. It was just so peaceful in here and this chair is heavenly." He smiled. "I was up late talking to a friend."

As soon as the words left his mouth, Alice felt a sharp stab of jealousy. She turned to hide her expression as the words registered. It didn't matter who he was talking to, friend or girlfriend. She shouldn't even care.

"Bix, let Paul show you what he brought." She kept her voice carefully cheery.

As Paul opened the box and turned on the e-reader, Alice went back to her desk. She felt totally exhausted, as if she'd run several miles. The conversation in the store barely reached her as she dropped into her chair. She'd just laughed until she cried, but now all she wanted to do was cry. Whether from stress or lack of sleep, her emotions were too close to the surface.

She reached up to cradle her parents' rings in her hand, but didn't find them. She felt her body go cold. She stood up, reaching around her neck, frantically feeling for the chain. It was gone.

She jumped from behind the desk and crouched down, peering at the area underneath. It had to be here somewhere. She leaped up, turning in a circle, scouring the store for a hint of gold.

"Just press here to adjust the font and—" Paul broke off as she paced the floor. "Alice?"

It was just her name but she felt her control start to slip at the concern in his voice. "My rings," she said, her voice shaking. "They're gone."

He walked toward her, leaving Bix holding the e-reader. "Did you leave them in your apartment?"

"I never take them off. Ever." Her eyes were swimming in tears. If it had been anything less important, she would have been embarrassed and wondered what he thought, but she didn't care. Her entire focus narrowed to the only thing she'd inherited from her parents.

"Where did you go today? Just the store? They have to be here." He put his hands on her shoulders as if to keep her calm.

Bix crossed the store, e-reader forgotten. "It won't take us long to search down here. Can you remember which rooms you went into? Maybe they rolled under the ranges."

"I bet they're in your bed," Charlie said. "I lost a necklace and looked for a week before I found it under my pillow."

Alice looked up into Paul's face. "I did leave the bookstore. I walked down to city hall today."

"And you had it this morning?" Paul wrapped an arm around her shoulders. His voice was confident but he looked as worried as she felt.

She nodded. "I remember seeing them when I got dressed."

"Oh, boy. That's at least a mile along the river walk." Bix rubbed a hand over his white crew cut. "What were ya doin' down there?"

Alice didn't want to say, wanted to have Paul find out some other way. She didn't want to be there to see his reaction. She took a shuddery breath. "I was filing legal papers to stop construction on the new ScreenStop store."

She felt him freeze beside her and then he stepped back, eyebrows raised. A long silence stretched between them all.

The lines of his mouth had gone tight. He inhaled slowly. "Okay, so we'll search all the way from here to there." He looked around. "Bix, why don't we-- No, actually, Alice could use you better here. Charlie, do you want to walk with me to city hall? We'll look along the boardwalk while y'all search the store."

"Sure!" Charlie jumped at the chance, her face lit up with eagerness.

"I have a meeting at four," Paul said, turning to Alice. "But we'll search as long as we can and then we'll regroup back here."

Alice nodded, a feeling of disbelief washing over her. That wasn't the reaction she was expecting. Not a single comment about the papers. Maybe he was so confident that he didn't feel threatened at all, but his expression said differently.

"Thank you," she whispered.

Paul nodded. "Come on, Charlie," he said. They walked out of the store, scanning the ground as they went. Or Paul scanned the ground while Charlie walked next to him, clearly in awe of getting to walk around town with her hero.

There was a minute of silence and then Bix cleared his throat. "That's a good man, right there. I know you two have your troubles."

Alice nodded, her throat closing around the words she wanted to say. Maybe she'd made a mistake. Maybe Paul wasn't an arrogant, ruthless, business man trying to take over the city. But then again, sometimes people were personally very nice while running cut-throat companies. Except he was more than very nice. He was patient, kind, and faithful. Everything he had done showed his character to be noble, just like the heroes in all her favorite books.

Bix seemed to understand she couldn't even begin to discuss what was happening with Paul. "Well, let's start at this end of the store and then work our way upstairs." Bix gripped the counter and slowly lowered himself to a kneeling position on the hard tile.

"Oh, don't get on the ground, Bix." Alice rushed forward to heave him up, but he waved a hand.

"*Sha*, you know my eyesight. I'll have to go inch by inch. And don't you think twice about it. I know how much those rings mean to you." He was already sweeping his hands back and forth, creeping toward the desk.

Alice choked back a sudden wave of emotion. She didn't deserve any of these people. She was petty and stubborn. She'd rather alienate someone who had made only a positive difference in their lives than admit she was wrong. *Lord, I've gone so far down this path I don't know how to turn around.*

She got to her knees, feeling the cold bite of the tile against her skin. She skimmed her palms along the floor, blinking back tears, just as blind as Bix.

Chapter Nineteen

Tweeting is like sending out cool telegrams to your friends once a week.—Tom Hanks

"I can't believe Miss Alice is trying to stop your store from opening. It's totally unfair," Charlie said. Her arms were crossed over her chest and her face was like thunder. "I just want you to know that even though I work there, I don't agree with her at all. She's totally obsessed with keeping technology away, like her lifestyle is more pure, or something."

Paul stopped walking and scanned the sidewalk. When Alice lost her necklace, it would have fallen inside her shirt, and then down, maybe bouncing off her leg as she walked. Or maybe it was outside her shirt and it fell directly to the sidewalk. He clenched his fists in frustration. How could two people find something so small in all this space? Charlie's words filtered into his thoughts and he raised his head.

"Don't be too harsh on her. I get her point, in a way," he said.

"What? But you know that computers are the best thing ever!"

"No, not really." He turned, scanning the other direction. He could use a metal detector for the grassy areas. And more people. If Alice didn't find it in the store, there would only be four of them out here looking. Bix's eyesight was too poor, but he could get Andy to help. And his mother. Maybe they could put up flyers and offer a reward. "Computers aren't the best thing ever. They're a tool. And games are simply entertainment."

She made a sound of pure disbelief.

"Listen," he said, turning to face her. "I spent five hours a day playing Atari at my friend's house when I was a teenager. I played more than that every day when I went to college. I was such a techno geek I worked three jobs so I could get the latest controllers and games and equipment. My dream vacation is a big comfy couch with a giant screen and a couple hot new releases of some game I didn't design because knowing the cheats isn't everything it's cracked up to be." He paused for breath. Pedestrians wandered by, sending curious glances at the two of them. "But technology is a tool and this stuff is just entertainment. What I do isn't saving the world. Having a few million Twitter followers doesn't really mean anybody likes me."

"But we do!" Charlie shook her head. "You're the very coolest guy ever!"

"I mean," he said, trying to find a way through to the teen girl, "you like who you *think* I am. You like what is presented to you, what you've been given as marketing."

She frowned at him. "So, you're not like that at all? Going to Comic-Cons and cosplaying with fans and everything?"

"I am." He sighed. "It's just… complicated. I guess I want to say I agree more with Alice than you might think I do. She understands that real life is more important than any game. People can take it all too seriously. I've heard about players dying because they won't stop the game to get a drink of water or sleep. I hear about parents abusing their kids because they want more uninterrupted game time…. I get desperate tweets from people offering me all sorts of things they shouldn't, just to get what their character needs." He held up a hand. "Wait a minute."

Charlie looked around at the busy boardwalk. "What?"

"Even if the building doesn't open on time, we can still have the release day party for the new game in two weeks."

"Okay," she obviously didn't know how it was all connected. "You don't think Alice can really stop the store from opening, do you?"

"No, not really." He shook his head. "But I was thinking. What if we make a scavenger hunt? There would be only one item, Alice's rings. And the prize would be some sort of advanced pass for the new game."

"Like the passport? I bought that last time."

"No, like the rare-spawn that show up only every hundred times through the area. I've seen guys go through the same sequence a thousand times to see if they can catch the gear they wanted, but it never showed up." Paul knew why. He designed the thing.

Charlie gaped at him, eyes wide. "Wait! Back this train up and pick up some passengers you left behind, like Mr. What the Heck and Mrs. Why?" She leaned forward. "Not that I'm trying to talk you out of it."

He knew how much time and effort went into catching those one in a hundred bonus gifts. The person who had them all was treated like the president in the groups. Everyone wanted to friend them and go on raids together. They became as famous as any actor on TV, or more in the gaming world. "I'm sure we could create it so this person would catch them every time, no repeating the raids just to get what they wanted, hoping it would show up right when they passed by."

Charlie grabbed his arm. "Does that apply right now? I mean, if I find the rings right now would I get that?"

For a moment, he wanted to remind Charlie that Alice was her friend and employer and that she should want to find the rings just to make her happy. But he also realized in that moment why his idea was a good one.

There were thousands of people just like Charlie, who would be motivated by that prize. "Yeah, it sure does."

He looked at his watch. "We only have about an hour. Keep looking."

Charlie stopped talking and tied her hair back. She hunkered down and started walking slowly forward, her expression one of complete focus.

Moving to the other side of the sidewalk, Paul searched for the tiniest glint of gold. He didn't want to think of Alice watching him sleep, or the way his heart stopped when she laughed. When she'd realized her rings were missing, he had never seen anyone so devastated. And when she told him why she'd been at city hall, her expression was filled with sadness, fear, and regret. He was starting to understand why people wrote complicated poetry about love. He was so frustrated and angry, but at the same time he wanted to gather her close and tell her it was all going to be okay.

He couldn't be a business man right now, or BWK, or a game designer. He shut it all out and focused, praying for St. Anthony's intercession as the patron saint of lost items. "And for us, too. Me and Alice," he whispered. Whatever they had, it was surely lost now. You can't ask out the girl who is suing you. No matter how much chemistry they had, or how they connected over email, it would never work. It would take a miracle to bring them together.

***

Alice stood at the bathroom mirror, motionless. Outwardly, she looked just the same. Dark eyes, curly hair, maybe a little paler than usual, but nothing out of the ordinary. Only she knew that part of her was missing, lost somewhere on her mission to stop Paul Olivier and his company.

She bent her head and willed herself not to cry. There were people who didn't have food or shelter. She didn't need to weep over a pair of rings. But they were all she had, even though she knew that they were just gold, just a shiny metal. That cold metal was once worn with love, warmed by her living parents, back in a time when they were happy and all together. The rings were more than sentimental, they were symbolic. Standing for everything she once had, and now everything she'd lost, the loss of those two rings had gutted her in a way that the lawsuit couldn't.

She looked up, into her own eyes. Today, she was going to be fire, like BWK had said. But it wasn't to wage a campaign against Paul's store. It was to simply get through the day.

***

"Hey, what's up with you?" Andy dropped into the overstuffed chair across from Paul. The living room was bright with late summer sunshine and the windows were open to the river breeze.

"Nothing." Paul straightened up. He'd been hunched over, staring at his shoes. Caught in mope mode.

"Listen, Alice isn't going to win. That injunction is plain stupid. The building is nearly finished. Just the minor cosmetics and it will be ready for opening day."

"I know." Paul hadn't talked to her since yesterday, when he swung back by the store to tell her that he and Charlie hadn't been able to find her necklace. The look on her face haunted him.

"Then why the sparkly vampire impression?" At Paul's look of confusion Andy said, "You know, dead guy wants live girl, they can't be together and so he exiles himself away from humanity."

Paul stood up. "I'm not in exile. I just get tired of being stopped everywhere I go and harassed."

"You didn't mind it so much until she filed those papers." Andy stretched out in the chair, hanging one leg over the arm.

He shot him a look. "It just brought it home, that's all. She's serious about fighting the store even though I thought she might be softening up toward it."

"No, buddy. She was softening up toward *you*. Big difference," Andy said. "You have to hand it to her. She stands by her convictions. Any of the other girls you've dated would have given up whatever hang-ups they had way before now."

Paul walked to the window and looked out at the river. "We're not dating."

"Whatever it is. And please don't call it hooking up."

"No worries. Not saying anything."

"Okay, you're not a bad roommate, but I've got to get some gear in here." Andy heaved a sigh. "I feel like I'm being forced into the life of a Luddite hermit, only with Southern food and a cranky hutmate."

"The cable's being hooked up today." He couldn't resist a smile at Andy's description. He wasn't a social butterfly but he was a far cry from a hermit. They still had their laptops running from a mobile hotspot, but Andy needed his bandwidth. You just couldn't run the big raids on a spotty connection.

"Thank you," Andy said, lifting his hands in the air. "I was about to book tickets home.
I'd go commercial just to get somewhere that supports streaming bit torrents. Don't worry, I'd come back for the opening."

Paul came back to the chair and said, "About the opening…"

Sitting up, Andy fixed him with a look. "Oh, I don't like that expression. Are you thinking of canceling all of this? Can your Chief Technical Officer remind you of how much we've invested in this project?"

"No, don't worry." Paul frowned. He wouldn't say it hadn't occurred to him, but he still had a little bit of logic left in his brain. “I was thinking of a new strategy for the opening. A sort of scavenger hunt.”

“Sure, okay. I’ve seen those before. People usually start a week ahead and go everywhere on the list, and then at the opening they show the pictures of themselves at the site, or bring something, and then get a special prize.” He grinned. “I actually like this idea. You’ve got all sorts of inside knowledge. You could send these people into some pretty weird places, like frog gigging, or whatever you were threatening me with.”

“Right.” He cleared his throat. Those plans he’d made back in New York City seemed a lifetime away. “But I have an idea for the big granddaddy treasure.”

“Catch a catfish with your bare hands?”

“No, but that’s a good one. I was thinking of Alice’s necklace being the last on the list.”

Andy sat back. He didn’t say anything for a moment. “The one she lost? How would that work?”

“Look, we know that it’s somewhere between here and city hall. Think of all the people we could get looking for it. We went up and down the boardwalk a few times, but think of the hundreds of gamers that come to the opening.” Paul knew it sounded ridiculous.

“Why not just offer money? We could offer a reward and half the town would be out there.”

“No.” Paul remembered Charlie’s change of attitude. “Money is a good way to get attention, but to find this thing, we’re going to need some real detail-oriented people. We need them to show up, armed with treasure-hunting gear.”

“All for a bonus pack and a free passport to the outer worlds? I can’t see that happening.” Unless you’re going to fly in bigger celebrities, which will be hard to get, last minute.”

“I was thinking of offering an early-access pass to all the bonus prizes. The player wouldn’t have to repeat any raids because the rare-spawn would just drop right out of the wall. Any special gear or power, automatic."

His words dropped into the middle of the room like stones down a mine shaft. He watched Andy's face go from amusement to incredulity and then worry. "You're serious."

"Yeah."

"Wow." Andy slumped into the chair. "Wow."

"I know it's a crazy idea but—"

"No, it's a good idea. I bet it would work."

"So, you agree?"

Andy looked over at him. "If I said not to, you wouldn't listen to me."

"I would." Paul fought the disappointment. He'd wanted Andy to be on board.

"No, you wouldn't. You're a goner. This girl has…" He shook his head. "I don't know what she did but you're sunk. Nothing I can say would change that."

"I just want to help her find her necklace."

"Why? What's so important about it?" Andy burst out. "You can't fix the entire world, Paul. People lose things. It happens. What about the time I left my favorite watch in that London hotel room and I never got it back. You didn't offer an early-access pass for that."

"Her parents' wedding rings were on the necklace."

"They divorced?"

"They died in an accident when she was little."

Andy dropped his head into his hands. He let out a low sound.

"If I can help, I want to. It won't change anything between her and me. I'm not doing this so she'll…" Paul didn't know how to finish sentence. Love him? Stop fighting him? Give him a chance?

Andy grabbed his laptop and logged in. "Let's get it started."

He grinned. "You're sure?"

"Hey, just remember who came up with the idea when it all goes bad." Andy shook his head. "I have to give you points for originality, though. Most guys just bring flowers."

"Funny," Paul said. He rummaged for a pen and started preparing to do what they did best, causing a firestorm in the gaming world. This time, it wasn't just for profit. It was to bring back something that was lost, something precious. He didn't want to think too closely about why he was going to this much trouble for a woman he'd just met, but he knew with everything in him that it was the right move to make.

***

Alice looked up at the sound of the brass bell and blinked at the sight of Alphonse DeCote. He wasn't wearing a cowboy hat today but his jean shirt was nicely pressed. He wore a wide smile and greeted her with a hug. Alice wasn't a touchy person but she leaned into him, not able to keep the smile from her face.

"Hey, there. I'm surprised to see you," she said.

"How's that? I made you a promise." Al gave her a wink. "I came down to see my brother, T-Bear. I thought maybe we could go to lunch, if y'all aren't too busy here." He looked around at the empty store.

"I'd love to, but I'm the only one here right now." Alice smoothed back her hair. She did like the idea of a lunch with someone completely unconnected to the drama of the past week. It didn't seem like there was a person in the whole city who hadn't heard about the new store or the handsome tech billionaire. "But I've got someone coming in about ten minutes."

"Well, I s'pose I could sit a spell until you're ready." He smiled and Alice noted two perfect dimples. He really was the most handsome Creole man she'd met in a long time. Paul was handsome, but in a boy-next-door way. Or maybe he was more like the nontraditionally handsome guys, like Tom Hanks, that sneak up on a woman. Alice pushed back the thought and tried to focus on Al.

The door opened and she looked up, thinking Bix was in a few minutes early. She caught her breath at the sight of Paul.

Paul walked forward, taking in the two of them standing there. He held out a hand to Al. "You played at the zydeco festival, right?"

"I sure did," Al said, grinning. "Name's Al DeCote. And I managed a little dancin' before our set, too. I live in Lafayette but I got myself back here to see if my pretty partner would allow me to take her for hushpuppies or somethin'." He gave Alice a wink.

Paul looked as if he didn't know what to say. "Oh, well, sorry to get in the way, but I wanted to remind Alice about the cable crew coming today."

"Do you know what time? I was hoping…" She glanced at Al, then Paul. Awkward.

"I'd be glad to supervise, if you trust me with it," Paul said.

"Of course I do." She tried to keep her voice light. "As long as they don't wire up my apartment with some big screen and a lot of gadgets."

Darcy jumped down from the top of the nearest range and Al clapped a hand to his heart. "Why's there a big black cat in here?"

"Oh, sorry, he's harmless, really. He's just curious." Alice stepped forward, trying to shoo Darcy away but he gave her an icy stare and walked between them.

"He crossed my path," Al said in a strangled tone.

"Depends on which way you're going." Paul pointed toward the door. "If you go now, I don't think your paths would technically be crossing. No telling what would happen if you stayed."

Alice shot Paul a look. If she didn't know better, she'd say he was jealous. "About those cable guys, I'm okay with you handling that."

He nodded, not smiling. "Well, have a good time. Nice seeing you again, Al." He turned and left without another word.

Alice tried to shake off the feeling that she was caught doing something wrong. Sure, they'd shared a very unplanned kiss, but they both knew there couldn't be anything real between them. It was impossible, considering he wasn't even going to be around very long. Of course, Al lived in LaFayette, which wasn't exactly next door, either.

"That a friend of yours?" Al jerked his head toward Paul.

"I rent out the apartment upstairs to him. Just let me sort a few papers before Bix gets here," she said. "You're welcome to pick out a book and have a seat."

"Oh, I'm not much of a reader." Al shrugged. "I think I read half of some book called *Grapes of Wrath* in high school. Made me depressed. I prefer music."

Alice forced a smile. "I'll be right back." She angled behind her desk and pulled a few papers out from under Van Winkle's furry body. She pretended to study them until Al wandered toward the chair.

She reached up for her parents' rings and felt the shock of their loss all over again. Maybe she would never get used to it. She closed her eyes for a moment. It was odd how quickly a person could become attached to a situation and how long it took to relearn it. A week ago, she would have loved to go out to lunch with Al. Even now, it sounded like a pretty good idea. But the reality was that since Paul had taken up residence in her head, she couldn't help comparing every other guy to him.

Stacking the papers with a little more force than necessary, Alice straightened her shoulders. She would go to lunch and have a wonderful time. The best way to get

Paul out of her head was to give herself some space from the store, from the building, and from Paul.

***

Chapter Twenty

The internet is a telephone system that's gotten uppity. — Clifford Stoll

"We need to be wired for several routers," Paul said.

The cable guy pushed his cap back on his head. "Sure, we can get ya set up, but we're gonna have to make some holes. We'll bring it up the side of the building and drill right about here." He pointed to an area near the windows that faced the river.

Paul glanced around. The exposed-brick living room wall wasn't going to make setting up their gaming gear very easy but it had to be done. They'd been here almost a week and had been limping along with tablets and 4G hotspots. Even getting into his email was painfully slow unless he used his phone. "Do what you need to do. It had to be updated sometime, I guess."

The man nodded and went downstairs to start the rest of the crew on the outside work. Paul wondered if Alice had considered having her apartment wired at the same time. It would be silly to have them come back. But he didn't have a key so it wasn't going to happen right now. He supposed he could try to call her cell phone but he was pretty sure it wasn't anywhere near her, especially as she was out on lunch date.

Paul walked to the window and looked out. There wasn't any reason that Alice couldn't date someone else. They'd never even gotten close to that conversation. Al looked like just the kind of guy Alice would choose.

Besides being pretty good looking, he was local, clearly steeped in Creole tradition and played in a band. Wasn't playing in a band like some sort of super power? Women just loved that, more than a secret book seller.

He rubbed a hand over his face. That wasn't really fair to Alice. She obviously loved books, too. He turned and paced the living room. Being jealous wasn't a great feeling and it had been a long time since he'd been jealous over something other than another company's graphics.

The cable guy came through the front door, barking into his walkie talkie. "Yer gonna have to drill it!" He looked up. "These old places are a pain and a half. We was gonna run the cable right up the front but I remembered Miss Alice said she don't want it seen from the banquet." The man clarified. "Ya know, from the sidewalk. So now we gotta go 'round the side. Takes a lot more time and manpower. But nobody wants to pay the extra fees. Everybody's got champagne tastes on a beer pocketbook."

"I'll cover any extra time and equipment. We just need to get some decent speeds in here," Paul said.

"Gotcha. And what about the inside? Where's your flat screen gonna go?" He walked to the fireplace. "It would look real nice right up here."

Paul considered the room. They hadn't bothered to set up the couch or chairs in any particular way, but the man was right. "Sure. Let's do that. We might have another screen over on this side, but we can get a stand for it." He pulled out his phone. "I've got them waiting in a warehouse near here. I'll have them come and deliver the equipment now so we can get everything hooked up and working."

"I'll go down and get my tools. I hope the bricks aren't real crumbly. Sometimes the drill don't make much of a punch, but then the bricks start to fall apart. We might have to put in some spacers," he said, walking through the front door.

Paul looked around at the apartment. He didn't want to have piles of wires and cables hanging out in the open but this place wasn't his New York City apartment, with the temperature, lights, and security controlled from any room, by voice.

Andy walked through the door and dropped his laptop on the couch. "Please tell me the cable guys are here to bring this place into the twenty-first century."

Perching on the arm of a chair, Paul opened his arms to indicate the whole room. "Soon to be ScreenStop gaming central. No more ten-inch screens and dropped connections and music sounding like it's coming from a toilet paper tube. The gear should be here anytime."

"That's a relief. I was about to join the Amish because it at this point it wouldn't even be a hardship."

"I've always wanted to live in one of these old places but I would have to make some serious renovations," Paul said.

"Well, we'll get ya started today." The cable guy had come back through the door. "So, tell me how we're gonna do this. All rooms? Or just the one?"

"All," said Paul and Andy at the same time, then both laughed.

"Man, I miss watching TV in bed," Andy said.

"Each room could function like a private office while we've got games running out here." Paul glanced around. "This would make a great office building. Lots of character. They'd probably tear out the dividing wall and keep one kitchen, just updated as a break room."

There was a knock at the door and two delivery men stood there, black uniforms pressed and clean, the ScreenStop seraph clear on the breast pocket. "We've got equipment for Mr. Paul Olivier?"

Paul came forward and signed the clipboard. "That was fast. The warehouse is fifteen minutes away."

The shorter of the two cleared his throat and said, "We might have broken the speed limit just a bit. Mr. Olivier, I just want to say what a huge fan I am. I've got every game you guys have ever designed and I'll be at the grand opening. I'm gonna camp out in line a few days before to make sure I get in." His blue eyes shifted from Paul to Andy and back. "You guys rock. Seriously."

Paul smiled and took two cards out of his wallet. He scribbled something on the back of each and handed them over. "Show this at the door and get in without waiting in line. For you, plus a guest."

They both looked stunned. "Thank you so much," the shorter one whispered.

"The best thanks would be everything making it up the stairs without getting dropped," Andy called over. He tried to look serious but he'd never been able to pull it off. "And have a good time at the opening. I think we're going to have hush puppies and gumbo and fried catfish."

"Really?" The other delivery guy finally spoke.

Paul shot a look at Andy. He had no idea about the food. He didn't handle that part personally. He supposed it would be the usual opening fare, catered by someone local and everything tasting like it came out of a box. And, always, non-spill drinks only.

"Maybe. It's still under discussion."

"Speaking of food, I'm starving." Andy wandered to the kitchen. "I thought we were hiring a cook."

"They're starting next week. I thought we could live on sandwiches for a while." Paul frowned. "Except I never went to the store."

"Does anybody deliver?" Andy pulled out his phone. "Maybe there's a Thai place. I'm craving Thai."

The cable guy straightened up. "Not sure about that, but my Aunt Glynna runs the Round'emup Café two blocks down. You can get it to go. Pretty good food. A little spicy for my wife's taste but the ribs are famous."

"Ribs?" Andy looked down at his shirt, then at Paul. "You run down there and get us some while I'll go change into something I can throw away."

Paul snorted. "It's a lot easier to eat ribs with your fingers than to use chopsticks." He looked around. "Keep an eye on everything, okay? Alice left me in charge and if this installation goes south, it's my neck on the chopping block."

"Aye, aye," Andy said. "And see if they have any biscuits like at the breakfast place. Those were great."

"Gotcha," Paul said and walked out the door. Halfway down the hallway, he pulled out his phone. A few hours earlier he'd called his legal team and asked them to find papers naming Alice Augustine, or anything mentioning By the Book. They got right back to him with the name of a lawyer in Houston.

He dialed the number and seconds later was transferred to his lawyer's line.

"Mr. Kimmel, I'd like to talk to you about settling a case that was filed against a friend of mine. Her name is Alice Augustine and the claimant is named Norma Green."

***

"Bix, I'm sorry it took me so long," Alice said, rushing toward the desk.

"Not a problem. We had two customers. Both looking for something from that website you like." Bix hadn't even looked up from his e-reader.

"Browning Wordsworth Keats?" Alice set her purse down and smoothed back her hair.

"Yep." He still hadn't looked up.

"What are you reading?" Alice looked over his shoulder and almost giggled at how large the font appeared. Every word took almost half a page.

"Clive Cussler. I loved his books. Haven't read them in years." Bix touched the screen and showed her a row of book covers. "Now I got them all."

"They look so bright." Alice could never get over the covers. Just like the customer who showed her the first one, it seemed almost clearer than real life.

"Paul got me the fancy one that shows all the colors. It even connects to the Internet. Me and Ruby watched *Breakfast at Tiffany's* last night when we shoulda been sleepin' but we don't regret it for a minute."

Buying one of those was probably like tossing a penny on the sidewalk for Paul, but Alice couldn't help being a little impressed. "You'll be just as addicted as Charlie. All the time you used to spend doing other things, you'll be attached to that screen."

Bix stood up and stretched. "What other things, Miss Alice? I couldn't see to read. I never knew I could watch those movies on the Internet. Ruby wants to watch *Casablanca* tonight." He flipped the cover closed. "I feel like this little contraption gave me back a lot of my old friends. I don't know how to thank Paul. I really don't."

Alice stood by as he got up from the desk. Her cheeks burned at the quiet rebuke in his words.

The front door opened and a man walked through, carrying a roll of cable over one shoulder. "We're about done up there, Miss Augustine."

"Thank you. Did everything go okay? You didn't run into any problems?"

"Naw. Just the usual in these old places. This is gonna make a real nice office building."

Alice took a moment to digest the words. "Excuse me?"

"Well, Mr. Olivier said he'd be pulling down the wall between the apartments and the bedrooms would be offices." He frowned. "We just hooked up the two bedrooms on the one side today."

"Pull down…?" Alice shook her head. "No, you must have misunderstood. Mr. Olivier is just here for a few weeks."

"Huh. Well, if we'd known that we wouldn't have drilled so many holes. We have portable signals he coulda used for the TVs." He shrugged.

So many holes. Just the way he said those words struck fear in Alice. "Thank you. The first bill will come in the mail or do I have to go down to the office to pay it?"

"Mr. Olivier already took care of it," he said as he headed out the door. "Evenin', Miss Alice."

She stood there, thoughts spinning. Did Paul think he could buy off everyone in town? Is that how he got his building permits? *This is gonna make a real nice office building.* Maybe Paul thought she was going to sell the building sometime soon. Alice closed her eyes for just a moment, her stomach twisting in on itself. Well, he would just have to get in line because Norma Green thought she deserved the store, too.

No, that didn't make a lot of sense. He said he was only here for a few weeks. It had to be a misunderstanding. Alice brushed it off and refocused.

"Well, I'm headed home for the night." Bix gave her a kiss on the check. "Don't fret so much Miss Alice. Everythin's gonna work out."

She nodded, trying to smile. Bix wouldn't say that if he knew everything. She watched him walk out of the store, her chest growing tight. Bix had been part of her life for as long as she'd owned the store. She couldn't imagine telling him that she was closing it down. She could only pray that she would never have to.

***

The smell of warm ribs made Paul's stomach rumble. The Round'emup Café was packed, even in the middle of the week. He hoped that meant good things. His mama had called a few minutes before and said she would meet them at the apartment for dinner. He'd placed his order and waited for his number to be called. Andy texted a few minutes later that the cable guys were done and gone.

The evening was shaping up pretty nicely. Good Louisiana barbecue, high-speed Internet, his mama over for dinner, and a very productive conversation with his lawyer about Alice's legal situation.

Paul opened his email and stared at the screen. He should wait for Alice to write him first, but he missed her. Ridiculous, but there it was.

Dear Alice,

I thought of you today. I imagined you as "fire answering fire," the way Shakespeare wrote it. Did you triumph? Or perhaps it was just the promise of good things like Gerard Manley Hopkins wrote "as kingfishers draw fire and dragonflies draw flame." I hope your spark brought you closer to success.

Your friend,
BWK

Paul sat back and waited. She would have closed up the shop by now and gone upstairs. He grinned at the thought of her making one of those peanut butter and pickle sandwiches. You could never say Alice was boring, that was for certain.

A familiar voice cut into his thoughts. "When we get married, she'll have to sell the place. It's probably not up to code and we'll need someplace safe to raise a family. That is, if we stay in Natchitoches."

Paul swiveled his head to the right and saw Eric, both hands covered in sauce. He had a white napkin tucked into his collar. One cheekbone sported a large purple bruise. He chewed, bits of rib on full display. He was talking to an older, balding man.

"But I can't loan you money on the promise of a sale sometime in the future. It don't work that way, boy." The man's voice carried the sharp twang of a man right out of Tennessee. "And I sure can't loan you money without her signin' the building over as collateral."

Paul edged closer. Eric must be some player to have moved on so quickly from Alice. Apparently, he was also a player with money issues.

"See, here's the problem," Eric said. He took a moment to wipe his fingers. "Alice has this old aunt, and she promised the old aunt that she wouldn't sell the store, ever. Now, if Alice signs something and the aunt finds out, then it would cause a rift in the family. You see? So, she can say it, but she can't put her signature on a piece of paper."

Paul wanted to rewind that conversation and listen to it again. It sounded like Eric was bartering Alice's building.

The other man shook his head. "I dunno. My bosses don't work like that." He looked down, putting a hand in his pocket. He pulled out a phone and tapped the screen. "I gotta take this. Be right back."

The older man scraped back his chair and headed for the door. As he passed, Eric met Paul's eyes. His expression went from shock to fear and then defiance.

Paul walked to the table and sat down, pushing the other man's plate away.

"I could have you arrested for what you did the other day." Eric glanced around, looking a little panicked.

Paul said nothing. These were the moments when he wished he had been blessed with being able to think of just the right thing. As it was, all his words were lost in rage.

"You think you can intimidate me. You think because you've got a lot of money that you're better than me." Eric had started to sweat. His forehead glistened in the dim overhead light.

Paul put his elbows on the table, not breaking eye contact. He didn't know where to start arguing. He wasn't anywhere near close to punching Eric, but the guy leaned back quickly.

Eric's eyes started to water, making the light blue almost gray. "You don't understand. I have dental school bills to pay. And even if Alice thinks we're done, I know I can convince her to give me another chance."

Paul shifted in his chair and Eric flinched. "Fine," Eric said, his voice high and strained. "She'll never give me the time of day again, now that she's got you. The least you can do is compensate me for my loss. You stole her right out from under me."

Letting the words sink in, Paul's hand curled into a fist. If he had ten more minutes he could come up with something really frightening to say. Eric watched him with wide eyes, his whole body vibrating with anxiety.

"If you ever involve Alice or her store in any of your schemes, I will know." He leaned forward. "If I hear that you so much as mentioned her name in relation to your bad business deals, I will come looking for you."

Eric nodded. "Okay, okay."

"Now get up and go home."

Scooting back his chair, Eric dropped some cash on the table and ran out the door. Paul stood up, feeling anger blazing a path of destruction through his insides. Some people would do anything for money, even stealing from a sweet girl like Alice. Eric obviously never cared for her. He'd only wanted her store.

Paul took up his place near the door and tried to get his heart rate back under control. He knew what it was like to be a target, to have people drop your name in their business deals, to be involved in frivolous lawsuits, to learn you were used as bait or collateral. He also knew what it was like to find out a kiss wasn't just a kiss, but a carefully thought-out strategy to entrap a person. He could understand how his wealth attracted those negatives, but Alice had been barely scraping by. It made him sick that

Alice had to deal with people like Eric and Norma, when she was simply trying to earn a living.

His phone dinged and he pulled it out of his pocket. He swiped the screen, his heart still thudding in his chest.

Dear BWK,

I'm not sure if I was fire today, but I tried. Maybe everything will work out "so long as fire outlives the parent spark", like Shelley says.

I thought you might come by the store today. I have your copy of The Duke's Secret *behind the counter. I'd like to meet my new friend face-to-face. But if not, I'm still thankful for this, these words. Like our Elizabeth Barrett Browning, I've been feeling "a little sunburnt by the glare of life", and your notes are like a cool shade.*

If you give me your P.O. box address, I'll send the book along so you can add it to the site. I believe in your project, but I also have my own ulterior motive. You seem to be driving customers to my doorstep.

Your friend,

Alice

Paul smiled at the "our Elizabeth Barrett Browning" part. *Our.* And he was like cool shade for her. He felt his heart lifting. Looking ahead was only making things more complicated. He should just be the kind of friend she needed, the only way he could be, as BWK. Being with Alice in real life was preferable, but it somehow always ended in misunderstandings or embarrassing clinches. She needed a friend right now, especially a friend with money and power. Pursuing her romantically wouldn't help either one of them.

Dear Alice,

I'm glad customers are coming to find more of what I'm adding to the site. I started this project on a whim but it's become a passion.

As for this city, it's "a slow sort of country," like the Queen says in Alice in Wonderland. *I arrived not a week ago and feel like I've been here for years. Even those I've just met seem almost like family to me now.*

My P.O. box address is below.

Your friend,

BWK

Paul sent the email just as his name was called from the register. A pretty young waitress handed him his bill and smiled nervously as he handed her his card.

"I'm Tiffany and I hope you enjoy your dinner, sir." She handed him his bags and took a breath. "You come back now, Mr. Olivier."

Paul nodded. "Thanks, I'm sure I will." He took the bags with a smile and headed out the door. It was nice to have such polite service. In New York City getting takeout could be a nightmare if you crossed a grumpy shop keeper. It didn't matter who you were. If someone decided you shouldn't get service, you wouldn't.

In a few minutes he was back at By the Book. He saw a new set of stickers in the window, notifying visitors of an alarm system with remote cameras. Looking around, he saw the tiny camera above the door and resisted waving. He already knew which package she'd chosen because the bill had been sent to him. Or to BWK. She would get a note about it from the alarm company.

Paul paused, a bag of hot, barbecued ribs in each hand. He wondered if Alice would be suspicious of BWK paying for the system. It hadn't occurred to him that she would be. They were friends. At least, he had thought so. Well, time would tell if she would be irritated or pleased. Maybe he was overstepping, but since he was anonymous, it removed the burden of repayment or feeling indebted. He smiled to himself. Just like when she heard from Norma Green's lawyer.

He turned to the back of the building and went up the narrow stairs. He hesitated for a moment at his door. Looking down the hallway, he fought to control the urge to walk down there, knock on her door, and invite her for dinner.

But BWK was more useful to Alice. She wouldn't accept Paul's help like she might accept BWK's, so it was better if he just stayed away. He turned the handle and went inside, his heart sinking at the thought.

"Finally," Andy exclaimed. "I was ready to eat my hand."

"Here, sweetie," his mama said. "Let me help you." She reached for the bags and opened them. "Mmmm, Round'emup has the best ribs." She opened the other bag. "And you got some slaw, beans and biscuits. That's my boy."

"Look, I even changed." Andy showed off his T-shirt, all black with the seraph logo in deep red. "If I drop barbecue sauce on it, it won't even show."

"Funny," Paul said, dropping onto a stool in the kitchen. He fiddled with the knob on the kitchen drawer. It was always loose. Maybe he could find a screwdriver.

"Uh oh." His mama paused in the act of putting some ribs on a plate. "*Mais*, what happened?"

"Nothing. Why?" Paul straightened up.

"You have that sparkly vampire thing going on again." Andy pulled an exaggerated sad face.

"Everything is fine." He looked at the plates. "Probably just hungry. And I ran into Alice's old boyfriend in the café."

"The guy you punched in the face?" Andy asked.

"The who you did what to?" His mama looked from Paul to Andy, half-smiling. She looked as if she expected them to start laughing and explain that no, Paul hadn't ever punched anyone in the face.

"It's a long story." Paul shot Andy a look that said he should be afraid to sleep because he was going to pay for that comment. Andy responded with an apologetic grimace.

"Alice is the gal we met at church, right? The one you were… dancing with?" She'd completely forgotten about the ribs now. "The one who supposedly hates you?"

Paul sighed. "Yes. The one who just filed a petition with the city to stop our store from opening. The one who is suing for personal hardship because my ugly building will cause her property values to drop."

His mama put down the bag and headed for the door, her mouth a thin line.

"Wait! What are you doing? Don't go over there and yell at her." Paul jumped off the stool and tried to beat her to the door.

"Oh, honey, I would never do that." His mama stepped into the hallway. "I'm fixin' to invite her for dinner."

Chapter Twenty-One

The 'Net is a waste of time and that's exactly what's right about it. — William Gibson

She set off, heels clacking down the hallway. Paul stood there, immobilized.

"Well, this should be interesting," said Andy. He dragged a bag closer and looked inside. "I'll just get a biscuit while we wait."

Paul shook his head. "I don't want her to… It's not about…"

"You're not even forming complete sentences," Andy said through a mouthful.

Paul looked down at himself and smoothed the wrinkles in his shirt. He didn't shave that morning and his five-o'clock shadow was closer to an eighteen-hour one. Ducking into his bedroom, he stripped off his shirt, applied fresh deodorant, and grabbed something with a collar. Slipping it on, he buttoned it up as fast as he could. There was nothing he could do about shaving, but he ducked into the bathroom, splashed water on his face, brushed his teeth and combed his hair in record time.

Paul turned to leave and nearly jumped out of his skin. Andy was standing in the doorway, shaking his head.

"This is bad news. I don't see this ending well."

Paul ignored him, brushing past and heading for the kitchen. His mama wasn't back yet, and she might not even be able to convince Alice to come, but at least he was presentable.

"Buddy, are you hearing me? Whatever is going on, it needs to stop. *Romeo and Juliet* isn't everything it's cracked up to be." Andy perched on a stool and bit into another biscuit. "Why can't you chase supermodels like all the other billionaires?"

Paul paced the kitchen, feeling his palms sweat. "Shut up."

Andy grinned. "That's more like it."

The sound of voices came down the hallway and they both froze, watching the open door. Seconds later, Mrs. Olivier appeared, leading Alice into the living room. "Come on in and make yourself comfortable. We're just going to warm up the ribs."

Alice looked nervous and a little wary, but she smiled brightly. She lifted a hand. "Hi, Andy. Hey, Paul." Her cheeks were pinker than usual, but maybe that was because his mother had just pulled her from her apartment and down the hall to dinner. She'd already changed from her work clothes, now in a comfortable-looking pink T-shirt and jeans.

Paul tried to lean against the counter in a nonchalant way and put his elbow squarely onto a plate of ribs. He jerked it back, grabbing a napkin to wipe off the sauce now covering his shirt. Andy started to laugh and choked on his biscuit, almost tumbling off the stool.

"Don't mind them." Mrs. Olivier gave them both a stern look.

"Hmmm." Alice responded. She looked half-amused but as she scanned the living room, her smile faded away. She walked to the window and stared at the hole the cable men had cut into the floor.

"What— What happened here?" Her voice was high and tight.

Andy coughed. “Cable. For Internet.” He was still struggling to remove the biscuit from his windpipe.

She turned to Paul, her eyes wide with shock. “You didn’t say he’d be cutting holes in the floor.”

He walked forward, looking for the first time at the cable work. He hadn’t actually been in the room when it had been installed. Fat orange cable wound up from the floor and followed along the wall to the fireplace.

Alice traced it with her steps, walking toward the fireplace where the sixty-inch flat screen was mounted. “How is that staying up there? And the speakers? And those… boxes?” She pointed to all of the equipment. Stepping closer, she peered underneath the screen.

“I guess they’re held on with brackets.” Paul had a very bad feeling that they had done something wrong. He hadn’t thought about the bricks. He should have known better. A stand for the screen would have been better, not screwing brackets into the wall. “Definitely not very elegant, but since it’s temporary there’s no way to hide the cables.”

Standing on tiptoe she looked onto the top of the mantel and sucked in a breath. “You let them put holes in the fireplace?”

Paul stepped up beside her and saw the orange cable stapled up the side of the fireplace mantel, then all along the top. “I guess I should have made sure they used the wireless set up, with the connector plugged in to the TV. Then the cables…” He stopped talking as he met her eyes. They were filled with tears.

“The floor is wide plank, hand-hewn, quartered oak from a grove north of here,” she said, her words spilling out in anger. “The bricks were made by one of the biggest Creole businesses of the day, and we know the names of the men who laid the bricks for this wall. This is a two-hundred-and-twenty year old, cherry wood mantel, imported from France. It was brought here by boat and survived a hurricane on the way. I know it just looks like wood. I know it seemed like none of these things matter because you can just buy another, but they're important. They can't be replaced. They're part of this building's history. You can't just," she hauled in a breath, "cut holes and pound staples in something without asking."

"I'm sorry." Paul knew as he said the words it wouldn't make any difference. He had failed her. She'd asked him to watch the workers. She'd trusted him. He felt sick to his stomach. The damage to the mantel could be fixed, but only in the way that items were fixed as long as no one looked too closely. The floor could be patched but it could never be whole.

He saw her reach for her necklace, and the wave of anguish on her face urged him forward. He desperately wanted to wrap her in his arms. But he was sure that any move like that would be an insult after what he'd just done. The silence in the room was deafening and he couldn't even look toward the others, knowing his mama's expression would be utter disappointment in him.

"I'm sorry," he said again. He rubbed a hand over his face. There was no way to make up for what he'd done and for once, all the money he had didn't make a difference. What she said hit home, hard. His answer to everything was to throw money or favors at it. But sometimes someone just needed you to pay attention.

He didn't mind so much that Alice hated his company or his games. He was proud of what he'd accomplished. But now, watching her stand there, trying not to cry, was almost more than he could take. This wasn't some philosophical disagreement over technology's role in society. She was really hurt and it was his fault.

***

Alice fought back tears. She shouldn't have left to go to lunch with Al. She should have stayed and supervised. One bad decision and the cable men had done damage that couldn't be fixed. Not really, anyway. She was sure she could find someone to fill the holes and patch the wood. But it was one more way she had let down Mr. Perrault's memory lately.

Sure, Paul was the one who should have been watching, but ultimately, the responsibility was hers. She'd agreed to let him put in cable, just like she'd agreed to the alarm system. Was she making these changes for her, or just because she had a weak spot where Paul was concerned? The previous tenants had mentioned cable and she'd told them it wasn't possible. They'd lived in the building for two years but Paul and Andy would only be here a few weeks. Obviously, Alice was making decisions without thinking them through. And the Perrault's beautiful building was suffering as a result.

What was done was done. She needed to shake it off and be a gracious guest. She looked up at Paul and her eyes went wide. He stood there, head down, and hands in his pockets. He looked as if he had run over someone's kitty. Of all the times they'd argued, he'd never looked upset. Defiant or amused or exasperated. Never like this.

"Hey," she said, reaching out. She touched his sleeve. "It's not…" She almost said it wasn't a big deal, but that wasn't true. "It's not the end of the world. These things happen."

"Do they?" He seemed angry. "Seems like you took care of this place pretty well before I got ahold of it."

"Well, you don't really have ahold of it," she said, smiling. "A month lease isn't forever."

"Yeah, who knows what else I'll do before we bug out of here." His shoulders slumped.

It was funny. When Eric pouted, Alice wanted to smack him. When Paul did the same thing, Alice wanted to cheer him up. Maybe it was because Eric was always pouting over something Alice had done, but Paul was upset with himself. Alice slid a hand down to his wrist.

"Come on. Let's go eat. It might not be so bad after we've had some ribs." She tugged him toward the kitchen and he pulled his hand out of his pocket, their hands twining together easily. They walked to the counter and sat down on the stools.

Andy cleared his throat. "I think I need to say something. Paul said he always wanted to live in an old place like this. He never would have let them do that. He left me in charge. This is my fault."

She glanced at Paul. He'd never said that he loved the building that much. But he also shouldn't have let Andy take over. She sighed. "It's okay, Andy. It's done. It happened. I'm over it. Let's eat."

Mrs. Olivier had said nothing until now but she came around the counter and wrapped Alice in her arms. "I'm so sorry. And I just knew you were a special girl."

Alice didn't want to let go of Paul's hand but since his mother was hugging her, she thought she'd better participate. When Mrs. Olivier stepped back, Alice was grinning. "Because I'd rather eat ribs than argue?"

Paul snorted. "Nothin' special there," he teased. "That applies to most of Natchitoches."

Mrs. Olivier turned to the oven. "Funny, you two. I better warm these up real fast. Have a biscuit and some beans and slaw, y'all."

They took turns dishing out the food and Paul asked the blessing. Alice smiled at the Louisiana Creole words, so familiar and yet still so strange coming from him.

Alice took a biscuit and then turned the bag for a closer look and cocked her head. "Who's Tiffany?"

"Who?" Andy got up and peered over her shoulder.

"It says 'call me, I can show you around. Tiffany'," Alice said. She looked from one to the other and noticed Paul's face had gone red.

"I think that was the waitress," he said, clearing his throat. "You want slaw with that?"

"Poor Paul. He can't go anywhere without girls throwing themselves at him," Mrs. Olivier said. "It's just not right. These girls don't have any raisin', the way they carry on."

"You should be at some of these game-release parties, Mrs. Olivier. The last one, he was trying to make a speech and the whole front row was flashing him. He could hardly remember what he was trying to say," Andy said, chuckling. "I just wish I hadn't been in the row behind them. But that's the perk of being the CEO, I guess."

Alice paused mid-bite. The idea of Paul surrounded by beautiful young women willing to do anything to get his attention made her stomach go sour.

"Andy," Paul spoke quietly, but something in his voice must have told Andy that now was not the time to reminisce on the good times they shared at those parties.

Alice searched for something to say that wasn't related to how many women loved Paul. Andy's T-shirt caught her gaze. "Your company logo is a seraph, isn't it? At first I thought it was just an angel, but then I saw the other sets of wings. With the red and black, it's really striking. I heard companies pay a lot of money for just the right design."

Looking down at his chest, Andy nodded. "True. But Paul came up with this. It's from some book he likes."

"Oh, one of the Heinlein books?" Alice asked.

"No, just… Some old thing." Paul stood up and went to the sink to wash his hands.

"He's got all sorts of weird little names registered around. All of our games are officially trademarked under Fifty Wim—"

"Andy," Paul interrupted, voice urgent. "Let's not talk about the company right now. Okay?"

He shrugged. "Okay. It's not like I was teaching her how to code. We're just being sociable."

Alice poked at her coleslaw. She didn't think for a moment that Paul was shielding her from shop talk. Andy was going to say something she wouldn't like, and Paul was telling him to keep a lid on it. Maybe there was something worse than the game store opening. If so, she couldn't imagine what it was.

"I'm real glad you could come to dinner. Paul probably wished I wouldn't be such a busybody. I know you young people like to hang out without all of us old people listening in to your business," Mrs. Olivier said. She was smiling but something in her dark eyes seemed not as friendly as they had been the other day. She'd probably heard about Alice filing the petition to stop construction by now. Maybe Mrs. Olivier wondered why Alice was suing her boyfriend because Mrs. Olivier assumed they were dating.

Alice swallowed a bite of coleslaw and nodded. "Thank you for inviting me. It's true, I don't usually spend a lot of time with my boyfriends' parents." She choked on the last word. "No, that's not what I meant to say. I meant to say *friends'* parents." Alice had no idea why her mouth had decided to betray her. She studiously avoided looking at Paul, her face burning.

Mrs. Olivier paused, a cookie sheet filled with barbecue ribs in her hands. She looked from Alice to Paul and back. Then she opened the door and slid in the ribs. "And how many boyfriends have you had, Alice?"

"Mama," Paul growled under his breath. "Let the girl eat."

"Can you pass the biscuits?" Andy said. "These are great. So tasty. Fluffy. Just the right amount of…" He frowned at the one in his hand, "…dough."

"It's okay," Alice said. She loved those two for trying to run interference, but she knew Creole mamas. They found out the truth, whether you wanted them to or not. “I haven’t dated that many. I like running my store. I’d like to have a family someday but I’m not lonely.”

“Plus, you don’t know anybody willing to take on that many cats,” Paul said. He winked and Alice had to laugh. He was the only person in the room who knew how accurate that was.

“So, then,” Andy started to say. He looked innocent to Alice but something in his expression must have tipped off Paul.

“Hey, pass back those biscuits,” Paul interrupted, a little too loudly.

Andy ignored him. “What would Alice Augustine look for in a boyfriend?”

“Current residency,” Alice said.

Andy guffawed in surprise.

“Temporary or permanent?” asked Paul.

Alice smiled. He’d known what she meant. “Permanent.”

“I guess Al’s out, then. Didn’t he say he lived in Lafayette?” Paul sounded a little smug.

“I s’pose you’re right.” She pretended to be disappointed. “Or he can just drive over here every so often.”

“And some people can fly over here every so often in their personal jet,” Paul said.

“Now, hold on.” Mrs. Olivier stood there, arms crossed. “Let’s just get to the meat of the matter here.”

Alice felt her smile fade away. She obviously deserved the truth talk because she’d just been flirting with the woman’s son, but she still knew that it wasn’t going to feel very good.

“How is it that you can be fixin’ to sue Paul and want to step out with him at the same time?”

“I’m not—”

“She’s isn’t—”

"Oh, y'all are givin' me a head ache. I thought we could get some things straightened out here but we're goin' in circles for the umpty-umpth time." Mrs. Olivier threw her hands up in the air.

"It's not personal, Mama," Paul said. He seemed chastised.

"Well, it should be." She glared from one to the other. "If I expect anything from you, it's to keep things personal. Only big city folk act like business ain't personal." She turned. "And that goes for you, too, Andy."

"Yes, Mrs. Olivier," he said. And there wasn't a hint of a smirk.

Alice stared at her plate. Paul's mom was right. Pretending that there wasn't a person behind ScreenStop wasn't right. But she didn't know how to separate this man from the building down the street. He'd acquired a construction permit despite the zoning bylaws and she couldn't just ignore it, either.

She took a biscuit and cracked it open. She still didn't agree with the way Andy and Paul made a living. Games were a colossal waste of time. But she was beginning to understand how ignoring technology wasn't the answer, either. It had introduced so many people to the old books that were once almost forgotten, and the e-reader gave Bix back the ability to enjoy books again.

She caught Paul's eye and looked away. She'd been so sure she was right. Now she just didn't know what to think.

***

"I'll walk you back," Paul said, getting up. They were stuffed full of ribs and all the fixin's, happy and fed. But it was getting late and Alice looked tired. A little sad, too.

Mrs. Olivier reached out and gave Alice a quick hug. "Don't be a stranger. And pray about that petition you filed."

"Mama," Paul groaned. That was the Christian way of saying "I know you're wrong but you won't take my word for it, so God will have to explain it to you."

"Take care, Alice," Andy said, waving from his chair. He was stretched out, one leg over the arm. His T-shirt had sauce on it but you could hardly tell. "I'm sorry again about the holes."

Paul could tell Andy felt bad, but he was also sure he didn't really understand why it mattered.

"It's forgiven," Alice said, smiling. "But who knows? Maybe I'll sue *you* next."

Paul snickered. It was weird that they could talk about it like it almost didn't matter. But legal papers were no laughing matter, especially when the opening had been scheduled for months.

"You don't have to walk me back. I live down the hall." She smiled up at him.

"My mama didn't raise me like that," Paul said, opening the door.

"Actually, your mama has some sense, and would say, 'She lives twenty feet away,' but suit yourself," Mrs. Olivier said.

Paul pretended not to hear her comment or Andy's laughter. He followed Alice into the hallway, closing the door. They walked to her apartment in silence. He wanted to say something, now that they were finally alone, but nothing occurred to him. He wanted to reach out and take her hand again, but for some reason he couldn't find the courage.

"Your mama is a good woman. I like her," Alice said as they reached her door.

He nodded. "She's worked hard and she expects a lot from me. But she also… it's hard to explain. She's got a generous spirit."

"Real giving, like you? I know Bix sure appreciates his e-reader." Her eyes were greener than he remembered, probably from the golden light of the hallway fixtures.

"No, she reminds me of a Gerard Manley Hopkins line: 'I say that we are wound with mercy round and round as if with air'." He paused, unsure if he should have brought up poetry at all. "She's merciful. When someone disappoints her, she wraps them in mercy. I know everybody loves their own mother, but to me, she embodies grace when it seems the world only values revenge." His need for revenge had brought him all the way back to Natchitoches.

Alice's lips turned up in a soft smile "She's wonderful. And my friend Mr. Perrault loved that Manley Hopkins. He liked his line about 'a man living with a few strong instincts and a few plain rules, that he seemed of cheerful yesterdays and confident tomorrows'." Her smile faded. "It sounds nice, doesn't it? So simple. A recipe for the perfect life."

"But it's hard to tell which rules to make your 'few', right?" He understood. Some people said it was just the Golden Rule, or just some little catchphrase, but there were always more. You start asking questions and the rules added up until you couldn't keep track of them all.

"And which instincts do we follow?" she said, her eyes fixed on his. "Is it the instinct to stand up for what's right? Or the instinct to protect what's been passed down?" She bit her lip. "Or the instinct to love a man who seems to be in opposition to both of those?"

Paul felt her words slip under his rib cage and lodge somewhere near his heart. "Maybe that man isn't really in opposition at all," he said. He couldn't convince her that he wasn't trying to destroy the historic district. He couldn't even prove that he cared about her building.

She stepped toward him. "I want to believe that. I really do," she whispered.

Paul slipped an arm around her waist and pulled her close. Their first kiss had been slow and hesitant. This one was the almost the opposite, with both of them rushing together, as if afraid they would be interrupted at any moment. If Paul had ever wondered if Alice thought about him when he wasn't around, he knew the answer now. This wasn't a casual kiss, the kind that happened as a matter of fact at the end of a date. It was the kind of kiss that built for days and finally came to fruition almost like a miracle.

When she drew back from him, her eyes were bright with some unnamed emotion. For a woman who described herself as flint, she was warm and soft, yielding to his touch. She let out a shaky breath, her sigh feathering against his jaw. "I should go," she said, her words barely more than air. Her arms were around his neck and one hand slid down, tenderly cupping his face, then dropped to her side.

He nodded, trying to focus on something other than her lips. There were so many things he wanted to tell her, but the words just wouldn't arrange themselves in his brain and come out his mouth.

She gently untangled herself from him and stepped back, searching her pocket for her key. He stood there while she put it in the lock, smiling a little at how long it took her to get the door open. He would have offered to help except he wouldn't have been any better. He felt completely undone.

She slipped inside and started to close the door, smiling at him through the crack until it met the door jamb and he heard a click. Paul stood there for another minute, still feeling his heart pound in his chest, seeing Alice's bright green eyes, feeling her touch.

He walked back down the hallway, barely noticing his surroundings. Andy had said this was a bad idea. He said Paul and Alice were like Romeo and Juliet. Paul had never liked that play, thinking of it as beautiful words for an ugly story and a horror movie ending. But for the first time, Paul understood Romeo. Even if they really were doomed to be in eternal opposition, he didn't really care. He wanted to be with Alice, no matter the cost. And he had never felt that way about any woman, ever before.

Chapter Twenty-Two

A satellite has no conscience. —Edward R. Murrow

For Alice, Friday morning was starting off all wrong. Last night's kiss was still humming through her veins and it was hard to concentrate long enough to make breakfast. The second time she burned her toast, she gave up and headed downstairs. As she walked through the back door, she accidentally set off the alarm and it took her what seemed like hours to remember the code. Completely rattled, she turned and tripped over a cat dish, showering Darcy with water. He let out a hiss of anger and retreated somewhere in the store to sulk and repair his pride.

She really just needed some coffee. Her dreams had been fractured with vivid flashes of city hall, her lost necklace, and Paul's kiss. Alice set the pot and stood there, trying to center herself. The coffee machine burbled quietly and she felt herself gradually relax. A smile touched her lips at the memory of how she'd been so nervous about Paul in her store, only to find him sound asleep. He'd looked much younger there, passed out in the overstuffed red chair. She turned, smiling at the memory, reliving that moment. The coffee machine finished its cycle and Alice reached for the pot… only to see she'd forgotten to add the grounds and had brewed a piping hot pot of water. She groaned in frustration and quickly started over.

She smoothed back her hair and straightened her wrap dress. When she was especially out of sorts, she liked to wear something with lots of color. The bright pink-and-purple pattern usually lifted her spirits. But it wasn't working today. She addressed the front of the envelope and tried not to sigh. She had hoped to meet BWK in person, but it was never meant to be. Still, she couldn't help wondering what it would be like to have a conversation with someone who loved these old books as much as she did. That was something she hadn't known since Mr. Perrault, and she missed it.

The phone rang and Alice reached over the desk to lift the receiver.

"Alice Augustine? This is Peter Chatham from city hall. I wanted to let you know that your petition for an emergency injunction was approved by the court. Construction has been halted on the ScreenStop store."

"Oh. Thank you for letting me know." Alice cleared her throat. She should sound happier. Or not. It was clearly a complicated situation.

"I've already notified the owners that they won't be able to complete work on the premises until the injunction is lifted. The court date for review is December first."

"December? That's three months away."

The man let out a sigh. "Yes, both sides usually like to have plenty of time to gather evidence. You've sued to prove the zoning laws were bypassed and you want them to be enforced. They will need to be able to produce the necessary applications and when they were approved and by whom. These cases usually take years to be decided."

"Thank you," Alice said slowly, and put the phone down. When she'd filed the petition she hadn't been thinking of years of this battle. She'd wanted the store to somehow magically move somewhere else. But now the store may just sit there empty for months and months. It might be more of an eyesore now than if it were actually finished.

Bix came through the front door, whistling something jaunty and upbeat. "Hello, *sha*!"

"Mornin', Bix. How was *Casablanca*?"

"Oh, it was just the way we remembered it. So romantic. It put Ruby right in the mood and it wasn't even morning time."

Alice pretended she hadn't heard that last part. "I'm just sending a book to the man who runs the Browning Wordsworth Keats site. Just think, *The Duke's Secret* will be rediscovered by thousands."

"Well, that is a mighty fine thing." He took off his hat and started to unbutton his coat. "I'll be able to download it as soon as it's up."

"But don't go crazy with all these downloads. Even ninety-nine cents adds up when you buy a few hundred books."

Bix pulled the e-reader out of his pocket. "I've already got fifteen hundred."

Alice put her hand to her mouth. Bix was on a fixed income and Ruby didn't come from money, either. "Just in the past few days?"

"Well, some are free. But Paul told me he linked it to his account, so anything I buy comes out of his pocket. He said to get whatever I wanted." He slipped off his coat and hung it on the hook.

Alice crossed her arms over her chest. "And so you did."

Bix looked up, surprised. "Of course I did. The man has more money than he knows what to do with. If he wants to help feed my reading habit, I won't argue."

She said nothing for a moment. It was true that Paul had plenty of money, but that didn't seem right. "Are you sure that's what he wanted?"

"I tried to refuse but he said it was already set up." Bix flipped open the case and touched the screen. "He'd already downloaded a bunch of different things for me. He said he didn't know what I'd like but thought it would get me started. Some of 'em look like those books from the

Browning site you keep talking about. *Beau Geste* is on here. And there's a lot of old science fiction I used to read when I was a lot younger. But there's James Patterson and Louis L'Amour, too."

Alice peeked over his shoulder. It did look pretty nice, the way the books moved across the screen like they were on some sort of literary carousel. The covers were bright and clear. She reached out, tapping one called *The Story of San Michel* by Axel Munthe.

"I read that one already. Fascinatin' stuff. Some old doctor wrote about his life on a tiny island in the Mediterranean at the turn of the century." Bix looked up. "Sounds duller than dirt but I'm tellin' you, I could hardly turn it off."

Alice smiled. "I'm so glad you get to read again."

"I don't know how to thank him. He's given me back somethin' I never thought I could have again." Bix's brown eyes filled with tears. He shook his head. "Look at me. A crazy old man cryin' over some stories."

Alice's throat closed around the words she wanted to say. She'd thought people like BWK were rare, but maybe in his own way, Paul was a little like him. "I understand," she said, squeezing his hand, feeling the warmth of his papery skin under her fingers. He'd brought joy to Bix in a way that she couldn't, and she was so grateful.

"This might not be the right time, but I don't know what is." He sighed. "I don't want to be tellin' you how to run your life."

"But you're going to." Alice braced herself. She respected Bix. Beneath all the offbeat habits and the marital TMI, he was a man who had the wisdom of having lived much longer than her.

"I know you think you're doin' the right thing, but I don't see how fightin' Paul makes sense," Bix said. "City hall did what you wanted but nobody's happy. Charlie said she wasn't gonna work here anymore if you stopped the construction."

Alice froze. "She said that?"

"Yep, these kids take their technology very seriously. She feels like you're keeping the city in the Dark Ages."

"And where did you hear that it was approved? I just got the phone call."

"Everybody knows." He shrugged. "Small town, *sha*."

"I just don't think it belongs here. Is that so bad? They didn't follow the zoning bylaws and nobody even got to vote." She heard the frustration in her own voice.

"I know. But it's done now. The store will bring in a lot of business to the boardwalk." Bix held up his e-reader. "I don't see how selling these is so different than what we do."

"That's not what the store is about," Alice said. "It's games and gadgets and… junk that people don't need. We're becoming a nation of mindless screen-gazers. Nobody ever talks to each other anymore. It's all Facebook and Twitter and email."

"I would try to change your mind, but I don't think a thing I say will convince you otherwise. Once you're set on somethin', you follow it all the way to the very bitter end," Bix said. "And that's not always a bad thing, Miss Alice. Lots of folks can't stay a course to save their lives. You're stubborn, and I like that about you. I just hope you're ready for gettin' your way." When she stayed silent Bix reached down for the bright-eyed tabby that had come to wind a path around his ankles. "Come on Miss Elizabeth, we've got sorting to do." He put her over one shoulder and turned for the back room.

Alice plopped into her desk chair and stared at Van Winkle's sleeping body. She needed to forget about Paul and his store for a minute and do some work. Flipping open the laptop a little more forcefully than necessary, she gritted her teeth as it connected to the Internet.

She checked her email first and felt a smile touch her lips. BWK had written her even though he didn't seem interested in being friends in person.

Dear Alice,

I've taken the liberty of contacting Mr. Crocket. Please forgive me if I've overstepped the boundaries of friendship but I don't believe anyone should be forced to share shelf space, especially with greedy, neglectful nieces.

Your BWK

P.S.

We walked too straight for Fortune's end,
We loved too true to keep a friend;
At least we're tired, my heart and I.
Elizabeth Barrett Browning

Alice read the note twice, three times. He hadn't said 'your friend', just 'your'. She couldn't understand how BWK knew Mr. Crocket or how he could have contacted him. The verse was a sad post script, and her stomach rolled every time she read it.

She clicked the reply button and typed out a quick response.

Dear BWK,

I don't understand. I know I'll have to call Mr. Crocket to get all of the details but let me say that I would rather battle this horrid niece for years than lose your friendship.

That verse sounds suspiciously like a goodbye.

Your friend always,

Alice

Alice stood up and paced the floor, returning to refresh her inbox several times. There was no response. She felt tears prick her eyes. She hadn't known him very long, but he was a friend, and she had very few friends.

Sitting back down in her chair, she took a deep breath and dialed Mr. Crocket's number.

"Yep, Miss Augustine, I was expecting your call." He sounded extremely cheerful.

"I'm not sure exactly what happened here. Could you give me the details?"

There was a short silence. "It appears you have a wealthy benefactor. He wishes to remain anonymous but he's compensated my client for the oversight in the will."

Alice choked back a response about how it was clearly no oversight. "Compensated? What does that mean?"

"I'm not at liberty to give a figure but your friend has offered a sum of money, and we have accepted, that she feels accurately satisfied her suit."

She couldn't respond. She slowly replaced the receiver in the cradle and stared around the store. BWK had paid off Norma Green and the store was completely hers, as it had always been.

Alice knew she should take a few minutes, or a few hours, before she responded. Instead, she pulled up her email and started to type.

Dear BWK,

I understand now. When one party is so completely in the debt of another, can a friendship survive? It's true, you 'loved too true to keep a friend' but I'll always be grateful.

I'm sad. I can't help it. I will miss our conversations.

I keep thinking of those George Meredith lines:

Not until the fire is dying in the grate
Look we for any kinship in the stars.

Thank you.

Your Alice

P.S. I'm sending The Duke's Secret *today. I look forward to seeing it on the site.*

Alice sat back and wiped a hand across her eyes. It was silly. She hadn't even known him that long. She stared up at the ceiling, thinking of how fast life changed. One day someone is trying to wrest your treasure away, the next someone is giving it back. Along with the news about the injunction, it was a probably the best day she'd had in weeks.

Except that she didn't feel particularly happy. In fact, she was wiping tears from her face with both hands now, small sobs escaping. She buried her face in her arms and cried. She'd gotten what she wanted and but it didn't feel the way she'd thought it would. It felt like she'd ruined everything.

***

After he heard the petition had been approved, Paul retreated to his room. Andy knew better than to bother him. Paul had been worried that Alice would be crushed when her petition was denied. He should have been worried about his company. Along with BWK's *beau geste* that rescued her store, but doomed the balance of their friendship, Paul had never felt so low.

The hours crept by and it was time for bed. He tossed and turned, finally getting out of bed and spending hours on the Browning Wordsworth Keats site, responding to fans and catching up on email. It made him feel just a little better.

When the sun rose, Paul slipped down the stairs and trudged down the block to Babet's. Even the smell of maple-cured bacon and hot grits didn't lift his mood. He ate without really tasting it, then carried an order of biscuits and sausage home for Andy. The air seemed colder, wafting off the river and across the sidewalk, sending a chill through his T-shirt. Paul zipped up his sweatshirt and thought of New York City. He loved the bustle and the smell of Autumn in the city. He'd never thought of it as home, exactly, but he really didn't belong here, either.

The hallway was quiet as Paul opened the door and slipped inside. He didn't want to see Alice right now. They'd laughed together the night before, joking about lawsuits and legal maneuvers. It wasn't funny now.

Andy's eyes lit up when he looked in the bag. "Biscuits? You're a real friend. Or you're trying to make me fat so you get all the girls." He looked up. "Sorry. That came out wrong. I know you're... you've got problems..."

Paul shrugged. "No big deal." He dropped onto the couch wishing he'd had at least a few hours of sleep. Watching the Saturday-morning financial reports wasn't the way Paul liked to start the day. The overly-somber reporters and the dire projections irritated him.

He sat up as the next segment opened. Pictures of the Natchitoches historic district flashed across the screen, tall historic buildings lining the river. A news anchor intoned, "A temporary stay was approved today against ScreenStop, the billion-dollar tech company, and its newest flagship store." The picture changed to one of the distinctive brick roads in Natchitoches and a horse drawn carriage frequented by tourists. "Local residents objected to the construction of the modern building in the historic district of Natchitoches, saying it illegally bypassed zoning laws. The grand opening of the store was scheduled for the twentieth of this month, with Jared Darren scheduled to perform."

The picture cut to a crowd of people outside another ScreenStop store. A spotty-faced boy with shaggy hair spoke into the camera. "I've been waiting for this release for months. Then I read about the scavenger hunt and the prize so I emptied my college account to pay for tickets down there. Now it's canceled. I hope they're gonna refund me all my money."

The picture flashed to the Natchitoches ScreenStop store, abandoned and silent. Several dirt movers sat idle where the parking lot should be. "The company spokesperson declined to comment at this time. Though ScreenStop stock is expected to dip in response to the current troubles, long-term predictions for the company are still strong. However, time will tell whether they will be able to hold onto their fan base after this disappointment."

"It wasn't residents. It was only *one resident*. This is bad. This is really bad." Andy stared at the screen, both hands clutching his head.

The reporter continued on with the rest of the news and Paul muted it. "We need to make sure this opening happens." He grabbed a laptop and logged onto the official ScreenStop site. The red seraph glowed brightly against the black background. Paul paused, thinking of Alice's copy of *Seraphim and Other Stories*. That symbol once had meaning just for him, a blend of his favorite poetry and his gaming passion. Now it was intertwined with Alice, just like everything else in his life. Everywhere he looked, he was reminded of her. He couldn't understand how in just a few weeks she had become so much a part of his life. Or maybe she always had been, her life mirroring his from the beginning. Maybe they had walked around the world for years, unaware of each other as their lives flew forward on a trajectory that would finally collide right here in this tiny town.

"Need help, sparkly vampire?" Andy was watching him, a worried look on his face.

"Funny. And no, I got this." Paul shrugged off his thoughts. "We'll have to make sure the warehouse is up to code for that kind of crowd. We'll fly down Tom Wallace and Nancy Sandoz. They handled the Houston opening on a tight timeline."

"I really didn't think she'd get it approved," Andy said. "You've got to hand it to her. On the outside she's so sweet and pretty, but inside she's ruthless. She's not afraid to crush anybody in her way." He grimaced as he reconsidered his words. "Sorry."

"I'm not crushed." He focused on the screen. "Just surprised. I wasn't thinking this would happen, either."

Andy didn't say anything for a moment. "She sort of reminds me of you, actually."

"Oh, no. Ruthless?" Paul sat forward, trying to type and talk at the same time. "Nothing like me."

"Sure she is. Maybe it's the Southern charm. She's soft-spoken— wait, until we poke holes in her mantel piece."

"She didn't even yell." Paul flinched inwardly at the memory. She'd forgiven him but he still felt bad.

"True. But I guess it's more about how she's so concerned for how things should be, like she's from a hundred years ago. People don't act like that now. I get the feeling she really didn't want to sue, but she was doing it for some kind of ideal, the greater good." Andy seemed like he was just warming up. "She's making a sacrifice. Everyone's going to be angry, but she went ahead with it because she believes she's right. Even if she suffers for it."

"*Beau geste*," Paul mumbled.

"What?"

"It's from a book. Here, should I say, 'inconsequential lawsuit,' or 'minor legal speed bump'?"

"The second one," Andy said.

"Okay, almost done." He wanted Andy to stop trying to figure out Alice's motivations and how she was working against herself. His sleep-deprived mind couldn't tangle with the problem anymore. He had a company to drag out of the internet gossip sites.

Chapter Twenty-Three

"Once a new part of technology rolls over you, if you're not part of the steamroller, you're part of the road."— Stewart Brand

Alice ran her hand over Van Winkle's sleeping body and tried to sense the usual peace of a Saturday morning spent in By the Book. The bright, fall sun shone through the side windows, and the familiar scent of old books and good coffee filled the air. It should have been the most perfect of mornings, but all she felt was a knot in her stomach and an ache behind her eyes.

She hadn't slept well. She hadn't heard anything from Paul, hadn't even glimpsed him in the hallway. Of course he wouldn't want to talk to her, but somewhere inside there had been a tiny spark of hope that he could separate this lawsuit from the two of them. It had been foolish to expect that kind of charity. Her whole body felt heavy and sluggish with the knowledge.

She'd paired a dark blue silk top with delicate pearl buttons, and a fitted skirt. It usually made her feel pretty and feminine. Today, nothing could shift her mood. The only thing she had to look forward to was Charlie coming in for the day.

Alice treasured their weekend girl time, with no interruptions from Bix and his unintentionally embarrassing remarks. They would sort inventory, or pore over catalogues, chatting like only two book-lovers could. Charlie would try to convince Alice to read something with a dragon or a broadsword on the cover, while Alice would try to convince Charlie to read something else, anything else. When they closed, Alice treated Charlie to dinner at

Babet's Diner. Charlie reminded Alice so much of herself at that age. Charlie's family was happy and intact, but something about Charlie's teenage worries reminded Alice of the girl she'd been, raised by a mamere in a house full of older brothers. Sometimes, a girl needed to talk to someone who wasn't related, and Alice was happy to be that person. Not that she had a lot of life experience, but she tried her best.

"Miss Alice," Charlie said, already talking as she came through the door. "I won't be helping you today. Or any other day. I can't believe you kept ScreenStop from opening." She was panting with anger.

Alice stood up, struggling to switch between the idea of a normal Saturday in the store with Charlie, and the angry girl who stood before her. "Okay, come sit down and let's talk. Let me explain why I—"

"No!" Charlie crossed her arms over her chest. "I always thought you were cool, bein' a girl and havin' your own store. But that's not really important, is it? It's about how we treat each other."

"But I had a reason for the lawsuit. It's not what you—"

"You can't explain it. Not in any way that changes what you did. I just can't believe you'd do this to Paul, especially after how he offered that grand prize for the scavenger hunt. You just don't get it and you never will." Charlie turned back toward the door, blond hair flying out behind her.

Alice stood there, shock coursing through her. She reached for her necklace, and realized for the hundredth time that her parents' rings weren't there. Their loss made every situation worse, like a second wave of pain.

Paul had won over everyone in town in just a few weeks. He'd given Bix an e-reader and suddenly Bix was on Paul's side. Charlie had been sucked into the promise of a party with some kind of big prize. She tried to think clearly, but anger spiked inside. Paul thought he could buy off the world. Maybe that's why he'd bought the Arthur Rackham portfolio the very first day. For just one horrible moment she wondered if his interest in her was part of a plan, if his kisses had an ulterior motive. She brushed the thought away. Paul would have to be a sociopath to appear so generous and noble, but be so scheming in real life.

The little bell on the door jingled and Mrs. Olivier walked through. She carried a large leather tote and was dressed in a pale-blue linen pantsuit. Alice stood up, but didn't speak, feeling like a frog on the highway in the headlights of an oncoming truck. Last night, Mrs. Olivier had been polite, if a bit blunt. This morning might be a completely different matter.

"Mornin' Alice," she said.

Alice nodded. She adjusted the front of her blouse and smoothed her skirt over her hips.

"You look lovely. Are you going out?" Mrs. Olivier might have just been asking an innocent question but Alice was almost positive she suspected Alice had a lunch date lined up.

"No, I just thought it was…" She looked down.

"Pretty? But you always look pretty." Mrs. Olivier smiled. "Now, I'm sure you know why I'm here. You hear that?"

Alice shook her head.

"It's the perfect silence of a building not being constructed."

"Oh, yes. The petition." She felt her cheeks go warm. She never should have gone over to dinner. Now it felt as if she were repaying their hospitality with a stab in the back.

Mrs. Olivier reached out and took her hand. "Alice, dear, I understand you love this neighborhood, but so does Paul. He would never hurt it in any way."

"It just doesn't fit here, Mrs. Olivier. I'm sorry." Alice straightened her spine. Paul couldn't love this place as much as she did.

Mrs. Olivier took her hand back. "He's heard that a lot in his life, you know. That he doesn't fit somewhere. He doesn't belong. I think that was his plan, in the beginning, to come back and prove that he really did belong."

Alice wanted to clarify that she'd said the *store* didn't fit, but really, Paul and his store were linked. She tried to imagine Paul being denied entry anywhere, and she couldn't. To her, he seemed to own the world. "I can imagine it was a shock to learn he couldn't just smile his way into this historic district. Well, he did for a while. But there is a reason we have these laws. A store like his doesn't fit here."

"I want to be honest with you." Mrs. Olivier seemed to be choosing her words carefully. "But first I want to say how much I like you. On any other day, in any other season, I would be forcin' you two together. I woulda hand-picked you out of a crowd of pretty girls."

Alice felt her face go warm.

"You think that stopping his store will save Natchitoches. You think it will keep our people speaking Creole, keep our kids from movin' away. But it doesn't work that way, honey. The more you fight to keep 'em, the faster they run away."

"I can't just give up and forget everything my family had," Alice said. "I owe it to them to carry on our traditions."

"I know, Alice. But that has nothin' to do with Paul's company." She sighed. "Let me put it another way. What are you doing to help keep our ways alive?"

Alice blew out a breath in frustration. She'd always thought she was a mentor to Charlie, but that hadn't really worked out. She was running a bookstore and wasn't that enough? But that didn't have much to do with Creole culture. And that was the heart of Alice's gripe with technology. It was smoothing out all the edges of her people, blending them until they weren't any different than any other.

Mrs. Olivier went on. "Paul thinks we need to keep people here, if we want Natchitoches to stay Creole. The kids leave for the city and never come back. The schools here just don't have the equipment. Our kids are leavin' school without the basics they need. Paul met up with an old teacher and now he's fixin' to fund a grant for the schools, for computer and science labs." She held up a hand at Alice's look. "You think I'm just braggin' on my boy, but I'm tryin' to explain. You can't waste all your energy on petitions and lawsuits. You got to do some good."

Alice clamped her mouth closed. Mrs. Olivier made it sound as if Alice was litigious and petty, while Paul was out educating children of Natchitoches.

"So, we've got that outta the way." Mrs. Olivier took a deep breath. "Now, this part isn't real nice, either, but it needs to be said. I know my boy, inside and out. He's a good man. And you know I like you. But he deserves a woman who will commit to him and support him in everythin' he does."

"I— I agree."

"Well, then. You can see why I'd be here askin' you to stay away." Something in Alice's expression must have touched Mrs. Olivier because she leaned close again and gripped her hand. "I can see why Paul loves you. But this isn't good for him. It's tearin' him up inside."

I can see why Paul loves you. The words echoed around Alice's brain. She wanted to object but she couldn't seem to get back on track.

"So, I'd like you to give him some space." She let go of Alice's hand and smiled. "Maybe after this has all blown over, we can go out to coffee and chat. I met your mama and daddy a few times. They were real good people and they'd be right proud of you. I'd like us to be friends, Alice. But not right now. Not while you're standin' in the way of all the good things my boy is trying to accomplish here."

She turned around and left, the little brass bell jingling one more time. Alice lowered herself into her desk chair and tried to catch her breath. Did she just get dumped by the mother of her not-really-boyfriend? That was a first.

She reached out and ran her fingers through Van Winkle's fur. Mrs. Olivier mentioned a grant for the schools and Alice wished she could dismiss it as crazy mama bragging, but knew it was true. It was just like something Paul would do. He was generous and kind. If he knew the schools were struggling in the sciences, then he would help any way he could. The kids might know how to post to Facebook on a smart phone, but they wouldn't know anything really useful, like Excel, or go even further into real programming.

She rubbed her forehead. She'd been so focused on the mindless entertainment but it all went hand-in-hand. She wanted to ban one, without the other, and it didn't work that way. It might end up sending Cane River back to the Dark Ages like Charlie had said.

She'd gotten what she'd wanted. Paul hadn't seemed like he was going to hate her for it, if that kiss from the other night was any indication. But somehow, she hadn't thought about all the other people involved. His mother, Bix, Charlie, the whole town. She'd won and there was no turning back now.

****

"We're making an official statement later today. That's all I have to say right now." Paul tried to zip up his sweatshirt and wave the camera out of his face at the same time. Reporters crowded in, shouting questions as he power-walked down the sidewalk. He'd gone to Babet's for a little breakfast and the reporters met him as he came out the front door. He hadn't expected the news of Alice's injunction to cause such a media circus.

"Is it true the lawsuit comes from an ex-girlfriend?"

"Is it true she's your high school sweetheart?"

"Are you still living with her?"

"Who's the other woman?"

"Did you promise to marry her?"

"Is there a baby on the way?"

Paul stopped short and turned so fast the woman tripped over the back of his feet. "This wasn't personal. I do know the petitioner. It has nothing to do with us as a… as friends. Now, that's all. You'll have to wait for the official statement."

He walked the block to By the Book, doing his best to ignore more and more absurd questions. Then he paused, undecided, a few feet from the front door. If he walked around the back, they'd camp out in the alleyway. He'd have to get a few of the security guards from the warehouse down there to guard the entrance to the apartments or they'd have reporters lurking in the stairwell. Going through the front, they might assume he was just visiting another store. He stepped forward, putting his hand on the knob, and then stopped.

Looking through the glass door, he saw Alice in the middle of the room. Her expression was one of shock and horror as she took in the madhouse just feet away. Her gaze locked on his. Paul saw clearly, for the first time, what his arrival in Natchitoches meant to Alice. Her life had been wrapped in peace and beautiful words, cushioned and protected from the ugliness of the world. It was a utopia and one he had never clearly seen, until now.

Paul dropped his hand from the knob, sourness rising in his throat. Involving Alice in his life had been a mistake. She had tried to tell him, tried to fight what he was bringing to her town. He hadn't listened, just barreled through like he always did, so sure he was right.

He turned his back, pushing through the crush of reporters until he made it to the sidewalk. Pulling out his phone, he dialed Andy.

"We've got a problem."

"Another one? Where are you? And what's all that noise?"

"Reporters. You've got the rental car and I need to get out of here."

"Okay, it'll be a few minutes. You can't get into the apartment?" He could barely hear Andy but there were thumps and rustling as if he were packing up his briefcase in the middle of the meeting. His voice was muffled, as he covered the phone. "Sorry, everyone. We'll reschedule for this afternoon."

"Long story. We may have to find another place."

There was a silence. "Alice kicked us out?"

"No!" Paul nearly trampled a reporter trying to get his microphone near enough to Paul's cell to hear the other side of the conversation. "I'll explain later."

"On my way." Andy disconnected. Paul put in his earbuds, went to the music on his phone and cranked up the volume. He'd loop around the boardwalk until he saw Andy. Flipping up the hood of his sweatshirt, he could almost pretend he wasn't being chased by paparazzi. It didn't do anything to soothe the vicious ache in his heart. He'd been wrong to come here and Alice had tried to tell him. Now he understood.

****

Alice stumbled back to her desk as the reporters chased Paul down the sidewalk. She had done this to him. She had returned lawsuits for kisses, curses for blessings.

When he looked through the glass door, his face had borne such a look of regret. His dark hair was disheveled and he had circles under his eyes. He wore a simple black hoodie and jeans. When he'd first arrived she'd thought he was arrogant and showy, but the man on the other side of the door wasn't much different than she was. He wanted to work, have friends, live in peace. Paul Olivier didn't deserve that kind of treatment just for trying to open a store.

Alice wanted to protect the historic district and thought his store would hurt the people of Cane River, but she'd only seen good things come from it. The only person who'd been hurt was Paul. She'd been wrong. If she hadn't been sure before, she was now. Her hands shook as she dialed the rotary phone, willing her heart to stop racing. Randy answered on the first ring.

"I've got to cancel the injunction," she blurted.

"But our petition was approved," Randy said slowly. "It's natural to have second thoughts. Especially if you've had some negative reactions from friends and neighbors. But if you're serious about this lawsuit, you can't let them affect you."

"No, I was wrong. I need you to— to take it back."

"I can unsuit the petition, if that's what you really want. But I can't do it until Monday."

Alice let out a breath. "Okay. I can wait until then."

"As long as you're sure. You can't file again. I mean, I guess we could, but you probably wouldn't get the petition granted twice."

"I'm sure. I thought I was doing the right thing. But I was wrong."

"I'll file it Monday. And if you change your mind before then, let me know." Randy sounded as if he fully expected her to call him tomorrow and tell him she'd changed her mind— again.

"Thank you, Randy. Thank you so much." Alice hung up. She'd spent a lot of money, wasted a lot of energy, and irritated a lot of people for nothing. Well, not nothing. She wouldn't have been able to see the situation as clearly before. She had to reach the end before she realized she'd been going in the wrong direction the whole time.

Alice stood up, her muscles easing. She hadn't realized how cramped she'd been, curled up against the worry and the pain. Mr. Rochester wandered by and she almost reached out to grab him up. She wanted to hug someone, right then, and tell them all about it but there was no one to tell.

Well, there was just one person and they weren't even really speaking to each other. Alice chewed her nail for a moment and then sat back down, clicking open her email.

Dear BWK,

I know we sort of said goodbye, but I don't have anyone else to tell this to and I'm going to burst with it. You know EBB's verse:

God answers sharp and sudden on some prayers,
And thrusts the thing we have prayed
For in our face,
A gauntlet with a gift in it. –

That happened to me. I prayed that I was doing the right thing, but only in the way that people do when they won't take no for an answer.

Can the Holy Spirit face-palm? If so- doing it right now in my direction. I don't think I'll get a second chance with the people I hurt, but I'm fixing what I ruined as best I can. And I finally feel 'out of the swing of the sea'.

Your Alice

She sat there, staring at her email, waiting for a response. Nothing came. After a few minutes, Alice stood up and paced the store. Darcy peered down at her from the top of a range, tracking her path with unblinking green eyes.

"What do you think Darcy? Should I try to talk to Paul?" She nibbled her nails for a moment. "No, you're right. When Elizabeth refused that first proposal, he didn't go running back, did he?" She paced some more. "But he did send that letter explaining himself."

Mrs. Gaskell wandered out at the sound of Alice's voice. She scanned the room, as if wondering who else was there. Alice reached down and picked her up, not caring if she got cat hair all over her silk shirt. "And when Margaret refused Mr. Thornton, he didn't run back to her the next day. He went on with his life." She scratched Mrs. Gaskell behind the ears. Jane Eyre crept in, sitting near the desk in a small shaft of sunlight. "And you. When you found out about the crazy wife in the attic, you didn't stay. You were no caged bird."

Alice gently set Mrs. Gaskell on the ground. "All of you are telling me to keep myself safely at home and let Paul get on with his life. I get it."

She dropped into her desk chair and stared glumly at her papers. This wasn't where she wanted to be. She raised her eyes to the screen and saw there was another message from BWK.

Dear Alice,

I remember I kinda sorta said to ignore mopey Sara Teasdale but she wrote:

Spend all you have for loveliness
Buy it, and never count the cost;
For one white singing hour of peace
Count many a year of strife as lost.

I wish you well with making amends and I pray the people you've hurt will respond with grace.

Your BWK

Alice grinned at the screen. All the greatest romantic novelists of the nineteenth century said that she shouldn't try to talk to Paul, but BWK disagreed. She read the note again, cocking her head at the *kinda sorta.* Paul said that the first day they'd met, when she'd accused him of murdering books. That day seemed years ago, a lifetime away.

Closing the laptop, Alice stood up and crossed the room to the poetry section. If she was going to try and make amends, she should come bearing gifts. And she knew just the book to bring.

Chapter Twenty-Four

"Despite our ever-connective technology, neither Skype nor Facebook- not even a telephone call- can come close to the joy of being with loved ones in person."— Marlo Thomas

"No sign of reporters downstairs. They're camped across the street but the guards are doing a good job keeping them away from the door." Andy dropped a package into Paul's lap. "You had something overnighted? I hope it's pair of leggy models for the opening. I still don't have a date."

Paul glanced over and then logged out of the raid he was running with a team. The dungeon was boring him anyway.

"Hey, no need for that." Andy frowned at his bad manners. A guy didn't just drop a game and leave his buddies in the lurch.

"I'll say it was a bad connection," Paul said and reached for the package. "It's a book I needed for the site. Alice sent it to the P.O. box."

"Why? Couldn't you just pick it up downstairs?"

Paul shot him a look.

"Oh, right. She doesn't know your secret identity." Andy unzipped his sweatshirt and tossed it on a chair. "So, Meg Ryan just sent Tom Hanks a book but…"

"No, Meg Ryan just sent NY152 a book, which was then overnighted to Tom Hanks, who lives above Meg Ryan and knows she's Shopgirl, while she has no idea he's NY152."

"I'm a little disturbed you know that movie so well."

"It was actually a remake of a 1937 play called *Parfumerie* by Miklós László." Paul blew out a breath. "And it's really not as fun as they made it sound."

"But hey, at least you can say you've got mail," Andy said, chuckling.

"You're hilarious," Paul said. He peeled the package open and *The Duke's Secret* dropped into his hand. Alice had been right. The binding was broken, there were water spots on the cover, but all the pages were there. It was the perfect candidate for a Browning Wordsworth Keats upload. He might just make it through the day if he had another project.

"Are you leaving the apartment today or should I call your mom to help stage an intervention?"

"You want me to set up shop down at the Starbucks and see if I get anything done?" Paul walked to the table and picked up his X-ACTO knife.

Andy followed him. "Listen, I don't care if you go into hibernation mode until the party. It would probably add to your mystique. But we've got some big meetings coming up. I need to make you sure you're going to be at the top of your game. You seem… like you've been gutted by an orc and left on a pike at the city gates."

Paul turned around, knife in hand. "Am I really giving that impression?"

Andy held up his hands. "Watch where you wave that thing. I'm just looking out for you."

He went back to slicing pages out of the book. "I'm good. You know me."

"Yeah, I do know you." Andy's voice was quiet. He didn't say any more, moving toward the couch and picking up the controls.

Paul worked quickly, and soon *The Duke's Secret* was stacked carefully, free of its binding and ready for the scanner. He examined every page for spots and tears but it was in remarkably good condition. And it only cost him a million dollars. He smiled at his own joke. Buying off Norma Green was one of the most satisfying things he'd done all year and he had no regrets.

He stacked the pages into the feeder and turned on the machine. The ScreenStop logo sticker had gotten scratched somehow during delivery and he smoothed back one of the angel's wings. Alice's letter to BWK still made him wonder. He wished he could walk down the hallway and ask her.

His cell phone rang and he answered it, frowning at the local number.

"Mr. Olivier? This is Peter Chatham from city hall."

"Hi. How can I help you?" Paul punched a few buttons on the scanner and adjusted the papers, holding the phone between his ear and shoulder.

"I wanted to let you know that Alice Augustine dropped the lawsuit against your company this morning. The injunction has been lifted and construction can resume on your building."

Paul lifted his head and the phone fell to the floor with a crash. It bounced under the table and Paul stood motionless for a moment before he dropped to his knees and grabbed it. "I'm sorry. Can you say that again?"

"The injunction. She asked her lawyer to unsuit it, or cancel the petition for a temporary stay." He was speaking slowly now, as if he didn't think Paul was very bright.

"Thank you for telling me. Is there anything we need to do?"

"No, not on this end. If you had your lawyers preparing a defense then you can tell them they can let it go."

Paul thanked him again and disconnected. He stood there, watching the pages of *The Duke's Secret* slide into the scanner, disappear for a few minutes, then emerge out the other side.

"What was that about?" Andy called over, his gaze fixed on the screen as he fought his way through an army of white orcs.

"Alice dropped her suit." Paul's voice sounded odd to his own ears.

"What? It sounded like you said—"

Paul turned around. "I did. She did. And we have a store to open."

Andy stared at him for a moment. Then he logged out of the game and stood up. "Let's get this party started."

"You just razzed me for dropping out of a game like that," Paul said, laughing.

"Yeah, well, you did it for a piece of mail. This is serious." Andy grabbed a laptop and pulled up the ScreenStop official page. "People are going to start getting real confused if we keep changing the venue."

"I don't think we're going to have a problem." Paul sat next to him, watching the seraph logo pop up on the screen and feeling an enormous sense of relief wash over him. The opening was happening. Fans wouldn't be disappointed. And for some reason, he and Alice were no longer legal adversaries. Her letter to BWK was making more and more sense.

"Whoever said Mondays sucked never had a Monday like this one," Paul said.

"Agreed. That girl could have done some damage. Forget selling gossip to TMZ. I'm just glad she didn't decide to drop your dox onto one of those crazy fan boards. Someone got ahold of Steve Job's info once. The next day, fifty pizzas and three tow trucks showed up at his house."

Paul shook his head. "She never would have done that."

"The girl sued you. I don't think a pizza prank would be below her." Andy typed a quick celebratory update and published it on the blog. He refreshed the page and watched the page views start climbing. He reached out and gave Paul a high five. "We're in business again, my friend."

***

Alice stirred the gumbo and inhaled the spicy scent. Monday meant washday gumbo. She smiled at the thought, remembering how Mrs. Perrault would sing as she cooked. Alice had always been in such a hurry when she was a teenager. If she'd tried to speed things up, Mrs. Perrault would say, "Slow down, honey! You try to stir too many pots and you'll end up putting vinegar in the pudding and vanilla extract in the turnip greens."

When Alice told Bix what she had planned, he'd shooed her upstairs. "Nobody likes to eat at bedtime, *sha*," he said. He'd refused to let her work that afternoon, declaring that she was taking a sick day, or a cooking day. It was for a good cause. She figured that if Paul didn't want to open the door for her, he just might if he knew there was gumbo for dinner.

Alice took a taste of the rice and frowned. It needed a bit more pep. She grabbed the Louisiana hot sauce and gave the gumbo a few more dashes. She wasn't a very convincing speaker, but a pot of hot gumbo and a book of good poetry might go a long way toward making amends. Rochester wandered through the kitchen and gave her a solemn look. He usually preferred to stay in the dim corners of the room and watch, but he stopped near the stove. His one tattered ear and scarred forehead looked startling in the harsh light.

"Wish me luck, Rochester." Alice leaned down and fed him a bit of shrimp. She could only hope Paul would as merciful as Jane Eyre, but nothing was for certain.

She changed into a deep green, sleeveless shirtdress with a white cardigan. Staring at her reflection, she realized she looked like a 1950's housewife. All she needed was a kerchief and some horn-rimmed glasses. Alice sighed, stripped it all off and started over. Her closet was packed with cute clothes, but for some reason she couldn't find anything to wear.

Twenty minutes later, she put the green dress back on and muttered to herself, "He's not going to notice your dress. You're bringing gumbo." She slipped on some heels and, tucking the little book of poetry under her arm, and picking up the pot of gumbo, she made her way to the door. It took a little bit of balancing but she got the door shut behind her and started down the hallway. Her heart was pounding out of her chest and she focused on breathing slowly.

At the door, she poked the doorbell and listened to the old-fashioned jangle inside. She wondered if Paul and Andy thought it was ugly. They were probably used to a video intercom or something. She wasn't really sure how the New York apartments were. Probably a lot nicer than this place.

There wasn't any answer. Alice felt her throat go tight. What if they knew she was here and just didn't want to answer? Her stomach curled in on itself. She reached out and hit the bell again, letting it ring a little longer. After a few seconds, she put her ear to the door. She couldn't hear anything from inside. Their rental car was out front, but maybe they'd walked down to dinner at one of the cafés.

Alice looked at her little blue pot of gumbo. She should have called, but she was afraid she wouldn't get the words out. Showing up in person with a big pot of steaming dinner sounded like a good idea at the time. She sighed, leaned forward, and rang the bell one more time. After a few seconds, she felt the vibration of footsteps and straightened up.

The door swung open. "Did you forget your key or—" Paul said. He stopped short when he saw her. He clutched a tiny towel around his waist. Soap bubbles clung to his chest. “I thought you were Andy.” He blinked at the pot. His hair was plastered to his head and water was dripping down his face. A small puddle formed at his feet.

Alice didn’t know where to look. She held out the gumbo a little then realized he couldn’t take it. “I made some gumbo for you. Because of the, you know, reporters.” She stared up at the ceiling.

He didn’t say anything, just stood there silently. The only sound in the room was water drops hitting the floor.

“I’ll just go.” Alice backed away.

“Thank you,” he said suddenly. “I wish I…” He shrugged, both hands still holding his towel.

“No, I understand.” Alice turned and walked back down the hallway, hearing the door of his apartment close with a thud. She made it back into her apartment and set the pot on the counter. Miss Elizabeth wandered over, tail twitching.

Reconciliation fail. She flopped onto the couch and threw an arm over her face. A note would have been fine. She must look like some kind of nut case. She groaned, grabbing a pillow and tossing it across the room. After a few minutes of jaw clenching and eye rolling, Alice sat up. Okay, that hadn’t gone well but it was a minor setback. At least he hadn’t called security and had her thrown out of his doorway.

There was a knock at her door and Alice froze. Looking around, she saw piles of books and cushions strewn over the floor, Mrs. Gaskell napping on the coffee table, cat toys, Jane Eyre lounging on the end of the couch, papers, and the dishes she’d left on the table. There was no way she could clean it all and still make it to the door before he turned around and left.

Alice opened the door and peeked out. “That was fast.”

He grinned. He hadn't shaved and his hair was still wet but he had on a Tshirt and jeans. No shoes. The shirt was black and the image of an old Atari system on it. It read "Classically Trained."

"The power of gumbo," he said. "Sorry about that. For some reason the towels that got delivered are really…" He moved his hands close together. "I would have invited you in, but all I could think of was the fact I couldn't really turn around."

A guffaw burst out of her and Alice slapped a hand over her mouth.

"If I didn't know better I'd think it was one of Andy's pranks. But he's stuck using them, too, so it was probably just a glitch in the order." Paul stuck his hands in his pockets. "Any chance that dinner is still on offer?"

"Of course! But," Alice glanced behind her. "I didn't think I'd have guests and my place is a bit of a mess."

He peeked over her head. "It looks perfect to me, but we can go back to my place if you want."

"Let me just grab everything." Alice dashed back to the counter. In seconds she was back at the door and Paul snapped to attention, pretending he hadn't just been checking out her living room.

"Floor-to-ceiling bookshelves and lots of cats. I never would have guessed."

Alice grinned. She liked that he was curious about her life, and if she'd had five minutes to tidy up, she'd invite him to stay.

They walked down the hallway in silence and Alice snuck a glance at him. He seemed totally at ease. But, of course, he wasn't the one trying to make up for filing a legal injunction.

Once they were in his kitchen, Paul hurried to the living room, straightening papers and closing a few laptops. He stood near what looked like a copier for a few seconds, stacking small sheets together and then carefully tucking them into an envelope.

As soon as he was back in the kitchen, Alice took off the lid. "Gumbo." She took the book out from under her arm. "And a book of poetry I thought you might like."

Paul stared down at the copy of *The Seraphim and Other Poems*. His mouth was open slightly and he seemed confused.

Alice rushed on. "The first day we met, you asked for a book of old poetry, remember?"

He nodded, slowly reaching for the little volume, running a finger over the letters on the cover.

"I have one just like it. This is the first time Elizabeth Barrett Browning published under her own name, so it's really special. She was announcing herself to the world. No more pen names." Alice swallowed. He heart was in her throat. "And I remembered what you said at the zydeco festival. You quoted *Aurora Leigh* so I thought you might like Elizabeth Barrett Browning poetry."

He still hadn't said anything.

"Do you have bowls? We should dish this up while it's hot. Do you know when Andy'll be back?" She knew she was jabbering but she couldn't help it. He had the oddest look on his face, as if she'd given him one of her cats.

He reached out as she started toward the cabinets, his hand wrapping around her wrist. She looked down, surprised.

"*Merci*," he said, his voice rough, the language of her childhood reaching out and grabbing her heart. "I can't believe that after everything I've done to your life here, you still think you're at fault."

She watched the emotions flash over his face, feeling as if she was missing something very important. She started to speak, but he pulled her close. The stubble on his chin rasped against her skin as he pressed a kiss to her lips, then her cheeks, then her eyes.

"I'm sorry," she whispered back to him in Creole, forcing the words out. "I never meant to bring all of this trouble on you."

He held her face in his hands, switching to English. "And each man stands with his face in the light of his own drawn sword, ready to do what a hero can."

Alice smiled. "So, you do like Elizabeth Barrett Browning. And I guess that means you accept my apology."

Paul leaned forward as if he was going to kiss her again, and then seemed to decide against it. He dropped his hands to her shoulders. "I need to tell you something."

"Okay." She took a deep breath. Then another. "You hardly touched the book and you smell like you've been handling dusty books all day. It's really strange." She glanced up, laughing. "Not that I'm complaining. The combination of Paul-plus-old-books is really fabulous."

He wasn't smiling. His gaze slid toward a piece of equipment in the living room and back to her. "I tried to tell you before. At the festival." He waved a hand toward the machine and then said nothing. He acted like she should understand what he was trying to say.

Alice followed his gaze to what looked like a fancy printer. It had a decal on the side, the seraph logo of Paul's company. On the table was the cover of a book stripped of its pages. She walked toward it, tendrils of shock creeping up her scalp. She reached out to pick it up, turning it over in her hands, unable to comprehend how *The Duke's Secret* ended up back in Natchitoches when she'd sent it to New York City. Piece by piece, all the small details fell together. And then just as quickly, her life was tumbling away around her, leaving her teetering on a ledge.

The smell on his hands the first day, the seraph logo, the poetry, *Beau Geste*. Alice closed her eyes tight at her own blindness. She'd never met another person who quoted poetry in real life. She'd willfully ignored all the signs. How stupid she'd been.

She turned slowly, still holding the cover in her hands. She could see BWK now, the strong jaw, the stubble, the curve of his mouth. All he needed was a fedora tipped low over his face and a shelf of books behind him.

BWK. Her *friend.* Alice's heart squeezed in her chest. He'd come to the zydeco festival after all. He'd been in Natchitoches the whole time. He'd also known about Norma Green and how her store had been threatened. *After everything I've done to your life here.*

"You've always wanted a building like this one," she said, almost to herself.

"What?" Of all the things Paul had thought she would say, apparently this wasn't one of them.

"You want to turn it into an office building. The cable guys told me. That's why you wanted a good security system installed, too." Alice rubbed her eyes. She refused to cry now. "I've been so blind. All of these little signs I tried to ignore. Nobody is that generous without a motive. I kept telling myself that you weren't trying to buy us all off. I tried and tried to make myself believe you were just that nice."

He stepped toward her. "Alice, it's true. I paid off Norma Green but—"

"You're so clever, really. I would never have agreed to it if I'd known it was you. But as BWK you could walk in here, scope out the place, get set up, and make your move. They call that a hostile take-over, right?"

"I don't own this building. The security system was a good idea, to keep you and your books safe. Everything is still in your name." Paul said, frustration coloring his words.

"Your mom came to my store and asked me to leave you alone. I thought that was so sweet." For some reason the thought of Mrs. Olivier hurt more than almost anything else. "I really liked her, you know. Maybe she was more worried about me than about you. She already knew, didn't she? About how you bought the building?"

"Alice! I didn't buy your building and she doesn't know anything about BWK." Paul ran a hand through his hair, tension in every line of his body.

"Sorry, but I just don't believe you. It's hard to trust someone who has lied to your face every day you've known them." Alice looked down at the cover of *The Duke's Secret*. "Ironic, really," she whispered to herself.

She turned toward the door, stopping to ask one more question. "You didn't really buy those Arthur Rackham prints for a friend, did you?"

He looked pained. "I admit it. That was a lie. I just wanted to make up for being such a jerk."

"No, Paul. That's called buying people off." She picked up the Browning book. "You have one of these, right? Unless you already stripped the pages out of it and fed it through your machine."

"Alice, wait—" Paul said but the rest of his sentence was lost when she slammed the door.

She arrived at her apartment, not having seen a single step of the way, tears running down her cheeks. She should have trusted her first instinct and known that Paul was busy buying off the town. Nobody was that generous, that thoughtful. Everyone wanted money and power. It was part of the human condition.

She stood in the middle of her living room, weeping and clutching *The Seraphim and Other Poems* to her chest. After losing her parents and Mr. Perrault, watching her grandmother slide into dementia, and then having her brothers drift away into their own busy lives, Alice thought the world couldn't break her. She thought she was stronger than anything life could throw at her. She certainly thought she was safe from someone she'd only met a few weeks ago.

Everything she'd known about herself was shifting, changing. She wasn't invincible. Her comfortable life had been completely open to anyone who wished to plunder it, and she hadn't even known.

Chapter Twenty-Five

Everything is fraught with danger. I love technology and I love science. It's just always all in the way you use it. You can't really blame anything on the technology. It's just the way people use it, and it always has been.—Steve Martin

"We've got cosplayers on the sidewalk with broadswords and metal detectors," Andy said. He was staring out the front window.

Paul heaved himself off the couch and stood next to Andy. Tuesday had started with the undeniable influx of out-of-towners searching for Alice's rings, hoping to win the grand prize at the opening.

"They're scaring the locals. We should ask them to leave off the body armor until the party." Paul went back to the couch and slouched into the cushions, reopening his book. The sun streamed through the window and it would have been ideal if he hadn't been in such a foul mood.

"And the chainmail bikinis. Not that I really object," Andy said.

Paul grunted and turned a page.

"Hey, Sparkly Vampire, life is still worth living." He came and sat on the coffee table across from him. "Did her gumbo not taste like your mom's? That stuff was spicy. I felt like my mouth was melting."

"Gumbo's fine."

"Did you tell her you've never really wanted to live with twenty cats?"

"I like cats."

"Wait, did she decide you're too rich and famous to date?"

Paul said nothing.

Andy said, "I had this roommate in my freshman year of college whose girlfriend broke up with him and he decided to take it out on me. First, he just stopped talking. Then, he stopped showering and emptying the trash. Finally, he decided it was all my fault and one day, when I left my laptop unattended, he decided to download a vicious cocktail of viruses and I had to nuke the hard drive from orbit."

"Have you checked your computer today?" Paul asked without looking up.

"Funny. But I'm just a little worried about you."

"Don't be. I'm fine."

"And you are a terrible liar."

Paul heaved a sigh and slammed the book closed. A tiny puff of dust appeared in the sunlight, and the sight of it made his chest ache.

"I did something I probably shouldn't have, even though I thought it was a good idea at the time, but it actually makes me look like a terrible person."

"You've just described every bad decision I ever made," Andy said.

"And she'll find out pretty soon that I'm not a terrible person. Not the way she thinks I am," Paul said.

"Which is good, right?"

He stared at the ceiling. "How many times can someone say they're sorry, and you accept that apology, before the hurt feelings don't go away? Eventually, there are too many misunderstandings and apologies. They start to build up."

Andy shook his head. "My parents have been married forty-eight years. I don't think there's a limit on it if you really love someone."

"Not if you've already decided you're in it for the long haul," Paul said slowly. "But when you're just starting out…" He didn't finish his sentence. He wanted that long, long future with Alice, where they would weather the petty arguments and bumps in the road and probably a few major failures on each side. But when those things came too soon, before real trust was built, the relationship didn't have a chance.

Paul stood up. "I don't even know why I'm thinking about this anymore. Romeo and Juliet, remember?"

"I suppose," Andy said, but he didn't seem as sure as he had been before.

Paul's cell phone rang and he pulled it out of his pocket. "Hello?"

"I'm here!" A high pitched squeal formed the last part of the word.

"Holly?" Paul swiveled and made eye contact with Andy. He'd forgotten to mention she threatened a visit. Andy's lip curled up in an expression of extreme loathing.

"I'm in Natch- ih- toechez," she crowed. "I want to stay in a mansion. Where are the mansions?"

"Where are you now?" Paul asked. He hoped she wouldn't say on the boardwalk somewhere.

"Right outside your door, sweetie! I tried to get up there but you've got some big, burly security boys who just won't let me by." Her voice had gone high and girlish.

"Be right down." Paul disconnected. "We've got trouble."

"She's not staying here," Andy said. Then he raised his hands at Paul's expression. "I mean, obviously."

He rubbed his face and then touched an icon on his phone. "Mama? How fast can you make it to town?"

***

"I've always wanted this collection." Karen turned over the little poetry book and smiled. "I remember reading one of her poems in high school. Didn't she marry a poet, too?"

"Robert Browning." Alice handed Karen the receipt and mustered a smile. "Enjoy. The *Sonnets from The Portuguese* is probably one of the most quoted set of poems. How do I love thee and all that."

Karen tucked the receipt in her purse. She looked up, a frown line appearing between her brows. "Are you okay? I don't mean to be nosy, but you seem… sad."

Alice straightened up. "No, no. Just tired. I didn't sleep well."

"Oh, I know. All the people coming in for the ScreenStop opening. I ran into a big crowd of them in Babet's Café and they were painted blue. I think they were supposed to be some character in the game that's coming out. I don't really play video games but I can't wait for the opening!" She bounced on her toes. "I've been dying to get a new iPad and if you buy one there before midnight, you get a hundred dollar gift card."

Stacking a few papers to the right of the register, Alice kept her expression neutral. "Well, have fun and let me know how it goes."

"I will, and thanks again," Karen said, heading to the door. "You should really go. It's going to be amazing."

Alice waved without answering. As soon as the door swung closed again, she sank onto the stool behind the counter. She reached up for her parents' rings and realized they were gone, again. She closed her eyes for a second, imagining the weight of the gold in her hand. They had always been like a quiet, reassuring touch from her parents. No one else knew what they were, no one ever touched them. Except for Paul. The image of him holding the rings in his hand flashed through her mind and she pushed it away. Just like everything else, he had somehow weaseled his way right into the middle, seeking out all her secrets, finding all her weak spots.

Alice took a breath, redirecting her seething anger into trying to decide on her next step. All she could hope for was that the week would pass quickly. She'd called Mr. Crocket, the lawyer. Although he'd insisted that he couldn't reveal who had paid off Norma Green, Alice asked him to fax all the information to her as soon as possible.

She picked up the phone, and then set it down again. She hated to bother Randy any more than she had, but she desperately needed to know whether the building was hers or not. Surely the land title would have to be signed over before the building could legally change hands. Alice rubbed her eyes. She just didn't know what to do next. Logic told her that she'd been tricked, and Mr. Perrault's gift to her was going to disappear the same way as everything else she'd ever loved. But a small spark of hope still lived inside. It snuck up on her when she wasn't looking, bursting into a full fire of wishful thinking before Alice tamped it back down. Smothering that bit of hope was the kindest thing she could do for herself.

The bell tinkled again as another customer stepped through. Alice took one look and knew this woman didn't come from Natchitoches. If the black leather minidress and the sky-high heels didn't scream out-of-towner, the sheer number of gold bangles and necklaces would have. Her blond hair was stick straight and impossibly long. She wobbled into the shop, having trouble getting through the door with her large, leather tote and rolling luggage.

"Oh, this is darling!" Her voice was high and breathy. She headed straight for Alice. "I saw the cutest display on Pinterest that had a stack of old books made into a table lamp."

"A lamp set on a base of books?" Alice asked. That pretty much described her entire decorating theme.

"No, they glued them all together and drilled a hole right down the center for the cord." The girl stared around.

"Ooooh, with all these, I could have a bunch made for my friends."

Alice tried to keep her voice level. "I don't think these are the books you're looking for."

She pouted. "I suppose. I dunno." Pulling her suitcase closer, she sighed. "Those guards around Paul's apartment are so mean. I told them I'm his girlfriend but they just wouldn't even call him."

Alice froze. "His girlfriend?"

"Well, it's complicated." She tossed her hair over one shoulder. "But he invited me down here for the opening and everything so I just need to reach him."

"I have a phone if you need—"

"Oh, no, I just called him. He's on his way." She stared around the store. "I hope he takes me to stay in a Southern mansion. Did you know they filmed *Twelve Years a Slave* around here? That black actress--what's her name? Lupita something--she is so pretty. Too bad about her hair. Maybe she can get extensions like me." She shook her head so that her hair fell in a curtain around her face.

Alice opened her mouth but didn't know what to say so she closed it again. She'd never figured Paul for the kind who went for beauty over brains, but Alice obviously wasn't the best judge of his character.

The door swung open and Mrs. Olivier walked through, her lips set in a thin line. She had on a casual top with nice slacks, but her expression said she was ready for business. Alice eased back toward the counter. She didn't want to get involved in some weird love triangle. This woman could have Paul. She was welcome to him.

"Holly, how good to see you again," Mrs. Olivier said. She held out both hands. Holly hesitated to let herself be kissed on the cheek. "It's been a long time. Two years, right?"

"Hi, Rosie. Time flies when you're…" Holly paused. She looked confused.

"…having fun." The way Mrs. Olivier said it made it sound as if Holly had been neglectful in contacting her. "Well, it's always nice to see Paul's friends. I've got the perfect room reserved for you, down at the Violet Hill Bed and Breakfast."

"Oh, no, I'm sure Paul has something in mind." Holly flipped her hair and peered past Mrs. Olivier. "He'll be right down."

"He's pretty busy, dear. He asked me to help you get settled. He wants you to be comfortable so I'll take you right down the boardwalk to this pretty little place." Mrs. Olivier was already reaching for Holly's rolling luggage.

"No!" Holly gripped the handle hard and Alice thought for a moment they were going to tussle over it. "I mean, he said he would be here."

"He'll see you in a few hours. Why don't we get you settled in and then when you're all freshened up, you two can have some dinner?" Mrs. Olivier managed to wrestle the luggage away from Holly, and headed for the door.

She sighed. "I suppose. I do feel a little grimy from the plane. Business class was just packed. There were people on either side of me. Can you believe it?"

"I can, honey. I can." Mrs. Olivier waved Holly through the door first. She turned back and nodded to Alice. Her expression wasn't anything like what Alice expected. In fact, she winked as if they were co-conspirators in a plot. Alice mustered a smile, unsure what exactly had just happened.

When they were gone, she stood up, walked to the door, and peeked at the boardwalk. It was worse than it had been the other day, or even just that morning. The sidewalk was packed with people, most of them focusing on the grass or the pavement. A group of four men walked past, side-by-side, all dressed in green armor, slowly sweeping metal detectors with fierce concentration. A girl followed them on her knees, parting the grass as she made her way toward the end of the block.

Alice shook her head and went back to her desk. It made her slightly sick to see adults reduced to crawling around on their knees to win a contest. Even if it hadn't been Paul's idea, it left a bad taste in her mouth to see it right in front of her door. But Charlie said it was all his idea and that made it worse, somehow. He was manipulating people, watching them debase themselves for his games.

Darcy jumped down from the top of a range and stalked over to her. "I wish I could be like you, Darcy." Alice reached down and tried to pet him, but he dodged her hand and continued to the back of the store. She straightened up and wrapped her arms around herself. If she could just stay out of the fray, happy to be by herself, not needing anyone else, then she would be safe. Even though Alice thought she had been cocooned in her quiet life, she hadn't been safe at all. Paul had walked right in, with his shy smile, and his poetry, and his smooth Creole words. He'd walked right in and broken her heart. And it was all her own fault.

Chapter Twenty-Six

If the human race wants to go to hell in a hand basket, technology can help it get there by jet.— Charles Mengel Allen

Paul's phone rang and he didn't move to answer it.

"You can't ignore her forever," Andy said. He didn't lift his eyes from the screen where he was working.

"Says who?" Paul muttered. Holly had been calling nonstop since she arrived the day before. His mother had managed to get her settled into one of the old-time bed and breakfasts, but Holly was convinced they would be spending lots of time together. Her voicemails included detailed descriptions of the canopy bed and the antiques in the bathroom. Paul was waiting for the ugly moment she realized he wasn't going to be joining her. He gritted his teeth. None of this was his fault. He'd never given Holly any kind of encouragement, but here she was anyway.

"After this is all over, maybe we can take her on our bream fishing trip. Or the frog gigging. You did promise some frog gigging, if I remember correctly. That would scare her away." Andy said.

"Oh, man. I'm sorry." Paul dragged a hand through his hair. "I've been so wrapped up in these—"

"Girl problems," Andy said.

"*Business* issues," Paul said, "that I completely forgot I was supposed to be making a Southerner out of you."

"Well, maybe I better find another mentor. Maybe you're not the right guy for the job. In fact, I think you just might be a Yankee in disguise," Andy said, pretending to be disgusted.

"Huh. I'm so Southern, I'm related to myself," Paul said. "Just because I can pass in two cultures, doesn't make me a traitor."

"Seriously, though. We should take an afternoon and get out of here."

Paul nodded. "I think you're right. Nothing like a Tuesday afternoon spent on the river." He didn't know if he could take running into Alice right now. Every day, every hour, he went through the same cycle of emotions: anger, sadness, acceptance, hope. No matter how it started, it always came back to hope, even though there was no chance it would work out for them.

"Let's do it, then." Andy pulled out his phone. "I'll move the meeting we had this afternoon and let's just go hang out in a leaky boat somewhere."

"Sounds like a plan." He stopped, thinking hard. "But I don't know where a good spot is. I suppose we could hire a river boat or book one of those fishing tours."

"Doesn't sound like we'd have much privacy." Andy knew what it was like sometimes. Anything they said could and would be held against them, if someone was offered the right price. It got old when they had to watch every word.

"Well, there might be someone…" Paul hauled out the phone book. After a few minutes he dialed the number. "Mr. Beaulieu? It's Paul Olivier. I was wondering if you knew any good fishing spots."

Paul flashed Andy a thumbs up. "Great! And would you like to join us? We can meet you in about thirty minutes. I'll stop for night crawlers at the shack down on Bayou Pierre Cutoff Road." He beamed at the response. "See you there."

After he hung up, Andy asked, "Who's that?"

"Bix. From Alice's shop." Paul started to shut down his laptop, feeling lighter than he had in days.

"Is that a good idea? I mean…"

"Why? It's not like we're divorcing and we have to split up the friends." Paul shrugged. "I only met the guy a few times. Seems real nice. I don't think Alice cares what the old guy does on his own time."

"Well, I sure hope you're right." Andy closed his computer and stood up. "I'll go change into my overalls and plaid shirt."

"You'd be better off with a life jacket. The skimmers are feisty, but some of these older bream can grow to fifteen pounds." He looked up at Andy's expression. "Don't worry. I won't let you get dragged down to the bottom."

Andy wandered away, muttering under his breath about a conspiracy to get a new CTO. Paul tried not to laugh as he cleared up the table, gathering packets and papers. He picked up an envelope and, as he touched it, he remembered the book he'd scanned. Paul stood there, staring down into the loose pages of *The Duke's Secret* and wishing he'd never responded to Alice's message. It would have been a lot better for everyone. It certainly would have saved him a lot of heartache.

***

Alice was just setting the alarm when she looked out the front window and saw Bix pull up neatly in front of the shop. But it couldn't have been Bix driving the bright green Caddy, because he didn't drive along the curb for twenty feet until he saw the big sign in the front of her building. The sun reflected on the windshield, but she could see several people in the car. Ruby didn't drive. Alice was already out the door, heart hammering in her chest, before she thought of any other people who could be in the driver's seat.

She arrived at the car, worry giving her speed, just as the engine switched off. Alice crouched down. She spoke to a man in a hat through the cracked driver's side window. "Is Bix okay? Did he crash?" She turned as Andy pulled up behind them in the rental car. A moment later, she realized her mistake and stepped back.

Paul opened the door and angled out. "Bix is fine. I just thought it would be better if I drove back from the fishing spot." He stepped closer and whispered, "People kept running to get out of the way when they saw us coming. He's blind as a bat and shouldn't be driving."

"He's fine," Alice hissed back. It was true Bix was unfit to drive, but she didn't want Paul to be the one to make that decision.

Paul frowned down at her. He wore a wide-brimmed straw hat like her uncle used to wear when he spent the day out on the boat. He wore jeans and a T-shirt with Pac-Man on the front. There was a smear of dirt on one shoulder and he smelled like the river. Alice thought of how well he seemed to fit in here, and what an illusion it all was. Paul reached up and swiped the hat from his head, but said nothing more.

"Oooh, the fish are bedding 'cause it's near the full moon. The shellcracker and bluegill were there, too. Three cane poles, a can of wigglers, and we got us a whole bucket of sunfish." Bix made his way up to her on the sidewalk. He reached over and kissed her cheek. "I had a great afternoon, *sha.* I haven't been fishing since my cousin Petey passed on. Just not as fun by myself."

Alice managed a smile. It was if Bix thought she was going to be mad that he was out fishing with Paul. Well, she wasn't happy. Paul was obviously focused on damage control. But she hadn't told Bix anything about Paul buying her building. Now she wished she had. "I'm glad. I know how much you love fishing." Just like he loved reading. Two things Paul had done for Bix that she couldn't. He was good at finding a person's weak spot.

Andy came up behind them. "Hi, Alice." He sounded cautious, as if she might bite his head off.

Alice smiled sweetly at him. "Hey, Andy. How've you been? Probably nice to have the place to yourself."

He frowned, looking from her to Paul and back again.

"I mean, since Paul's staying with Holly." That woman was a terror. She and Paul fit well together. Crazy and crazy made a good team.

"Oh, no." Paul shifted his feet. "She's not… I didn't invite her here."

"I'm sure you didn't. But girlfriends have a habit of showing up at the worst times." Alice turned to Bix. "I'm going to go lock up. I'm glad you had a good afternoon."

Bix tipped his hat up on his head. "See ya tomorrow." He seemed amused. It was probably pretty funny from the outside. But from Alice's perspective, love triangles were rotten no matter which angle you occupied.

Seconds later she was safely in her store and all her anger slowly evaporated. Even though Paul had schemed and lied, seeing him still made her heart feel as if it was stuck in a vise.

***

"Don't say anything," Paul muttered as Alice walked back into By the Book.

"Bust-ed," Andy said, drawing the word out in a long whisper.

"I heard Louis talking down at The Red Hen this morning. Your girlfriend has made quite a stir in town. Alice is right to be jealous," Bix said.

"No, Holly and I aren't—" Paul started.

"Oh, I figured that. I ain't seen you two together and when a man's in love with a woman, he ends up in her general vicinity whether he wants to be or not." Bix winked.

Paul stared down at his shoes. He'd done his best to get out of town for a while and it wasn't his fault she'd run out to see what happened to Bix. But he couldn't argue there was some truth to Bix's statement. He had found himself talking to Alice over and over in the past few weeks, and usually directly after deciding he should stay away.

Paul sighed. They'd managed to get through a whole afternoon of fishing without approaching the topic of Alice and her misunderstanding.

Bix went on. "Now, sir. Alice just has the wrong end of the stick. As soon as she comes around, you'll see how sweet she can be,"

"I don't know. I don't think it should be this hard."

Andy put his hands in his pockets and leaned against the green Caddy. The expression on his face said it all. Nothing good came from a start like this. No matter how much Paul wanted it to be otherwise.

"You know Ruby is my second wife? My first one passed away ten years ago. Took me a long time to get over her," Bix said.

Paul nodded that he understood, but inside he was thinking that nothing Bix could say would touch what was happening in Paul's life.

"What you probably don't know, is that my Ruby is my first wife's sister."

"Whoa," Andy said quietly.

"Yep. We had thirty years of Thanksgiving dinners all together, with her husband and my wife. He was a good buddy of mine, too, God rest his soul." Bix sighed, brown eyes misting over for a moment. "You can imagine the ruckus that got kicked up when we announced we was fixin' to get married. Her kids worried she'd lost her marbles and my son was convinced she'd seduced me. It was a right mess."

Paul couldn't hold back a laugh. He'd thought Bix was going to tell him some story about being late on a first date. The smile faded from his face. "But you knew you wanted to be together. We can't even get to that point."

Bix clapped a hand to his shoulder. "Don't give up, son. I've known Alice a long time. There's not another woman like her. People like Alice, we say they put the pepper in the gumbo. Life just ain't the same without them. Whatever you have to do to untangle this mess, she's worth it." He walked to the Caddy, opened the door, handed Andy a bucket full of fish, and got behind the wheel. Andy jumped away from the car as he started driving, tires squealing alongside the curb until the end of the block.

They stood there, watching him go. Andy spoke first. "Well, that was pretty powerful stuff. Too bad you never take advice."

Paul shot him a look. "Come on. We've got fish to fry."

It was true, Bix's words had touched him, making him rethink what he saw as a hopeless case. *The pepper in the gumbo.* He hadn't noticed his life needed anything until she came along, but now he couldn't imagine it without her. The thought of going back to New York City and his old life seemed bland and cold.

But there was one problem with smoothing things over. Alice was the one who was going to have to eat crow. And she didn't seem like the type of woman to do that more than once.

***

Alice opened her eyes, then closed them again. Friday morning had never looked so bleak. She lay still, listening to the low thump of bass music from down the block. The grand opening of ScreenStop would be going on all day, culminating in a release party at midnight for the newest game. Alice sat up, prying her eyes back open. She'd kicked her quilt onto the floor in her sleep. Mrs. Gaskell and Rochester were curled at the end of the bed. "Don't let Jane Eyre see you," she said, and scratched them both behind the ears.

A long, hot shower did nothing to improve her mood. She leaned into the spray, wishing she could turn back the clock. She hadn't seen Paul since Tuesday when he'd pulled up in Bix's green Cadillac. Mr. Crocket still hadn't faxed her any papers, which just solidified every terrible doubt she had. And soon, Paul would be gone back to New York City and she'd have to fight him long distance. Alice turned around, letting the searing hot water pound against the base of her neck and shoulders. Paul was leaving and the phrase 'mixed emotions' couldn't even begin to describe what was going on inside of her.

She shut off the water and grabbed a towel. A few minutes later, she realized she'd been standing in front of her closet without even seeing her clothes. *Snap out of it*, she muttered to herself. *You're a stuck duck in a dry pond and no use moping about it*. Nothing she could do would reverse what had already happened.

She threw on a pair of black slacks and a green silk top. Breakfast didn't appeal, so she headed downstairs, peeking out into the hallway to make sure it was empty. Down in the store, she fed the kitties, counting paws and tails, giving each one an extra pat of love. Not Darcy, of course. As she dumped coffee grounds into the machine, she heard the sound of the fax machine starting up.

Her stomach lurched. The store Mr. Perrault had lovingly maintained— the building that had been home to her since she was a teenager— was going to be in someone else's hands. Now was the moment it would all be confirmed.

Alice walked toward the machine, her legs numb and her pulse pounding in her ears. Papers spewed from the slot. She watched them, sourness in the back of her throat. When the machine went still, she forced herself to reach out a hand and pull the stack from the tray. It was almost too hot to touch. Her fingers trembled as she flipped the pages over.

Scanning the words, Alice's eyes went wide. The price Paul had paid Norma was three times the price of the building. She shook her head. He must have known that if he offered her the same money, and let her pay off Norma Green, she would have refused. She wouldn't have sold for any price.

The second page contained so much legalese she had to read it three times. *Jurisdiction remains with the current owner, Alice Millicent Augustine, as stated on the property title. The plaintiff, Norma Greene, agrees that she has no further claim to the property...*

Alice sat down on the stool behind the counter, reading the paper one more time. Paul had been telling the truth. Her face felt tight with unshed tears. Her first urge was to run upstairs and throw herself in his arms, begging him for forgiveness. But there were some slights that were too large for a simple apology. Accusing someone of stealing your home was one of them.

Darcy jumped down from his spot and stalked across the floor toward the counter. Alice watched him, her body numb, mind turning in on itself, over and over again. She couldn't grasp how she had been so wrong, so many times. Darcy came around the counter and sat in front of her, green eyes steady.

"What's wrong with me, Darcy?" Alice whispered, her voice choked with tears. "How can I receive so many good things, and turn them into ashes? Why do I push everybody away?"

Darcy stepped toward her and rubbed his head against her leg.

"I was just trying to do the right thing. I wanted Charlie to be proud of her culture. I wanted the kids of Cane River to keep reading. I feel like I ruined everything." Her breath hitched on the last word and she raised a hand to wipe a tear from the corner of her eye. "But the harder I held on, the faster everything slipped away."

She reached down and picked up Darcy, cuddling him close. "When you realized you were wrong, you paid off Wickham and saved Lydia's reputation. But there's no *beau geste* for me, is there?"

She buried her face in Darcy's fur. She used to be so sure of everything. Her way was right, everyone else's was wrong. It was simple, really. Until one man walked into her life and she realized that might not really be the case. And between that meeting and the realization was a whole lot of bad behavior on her part.

She'd been petty, jealous, and small-minded. Mr. Perrault would never have treated Paul that way, even though he felt technology was a dangerous tool that was more likely to be abused than to make the world better. Alice had let her personal opinions stand in the way of seeing him as a person.

The little brass bell at the door jingled. Darcy wiggled out of her arms and Alice let him drop to the ground. She quickly wiped her eyes and turned to greet the new customer.

Charlie stood there, hands in her pockets. She was dressed in her usual T-shirt, jeans and red Converse. Her black T-shirt had the ScreenStop seraph in bright red, and her blond hair was dyed blue at the ends. "Hey, Miss Alice."

Alice came around the counter and walked toward her. They'd never been the hugging type but she was so glad to see Charlie, she didn't even ask. She gathered her close and squeezed her tight. "I missed you."

"I missed you, too" Charlie said, her voice soft. "I'm sorry what I said to you."

Alice pulled back. "No, you were right. I've been a real…"

"McJudgy-pants jerkwad?"

"Um, okay." Alice laughed. "Not the words I would have used, but I suppose that will work."

"Because that's what I feel like I've been, too," Charlie said, gaze down. "I really put this whole store opening before anything else. You've been my friend for a long time and I was gonna quit just so I could get discounts on games." She looked up. "My mom said that was pretty rude and I didn't think she was right. But I had some time to think about it."

Alice hugged her tight. "I'm so glad you came in."

Charlie smiled. "When I heard someone found your rings, I wanted to tell you I was happy for you."

She felt the air stop in her lungs. "What?"

"The scavenger hunt. Someone found your rings and they won the big prize."

Alice stepped back. "I don't understand."

"I told you. The day I left, remember?"

"No, I don't know what you're talking about."

Charlie stared at her for a second, then shook her head. "Wow. I thought you and Paul were really close. Maybe it was supposed to be a surprise. Or maybe he just didn't want to get your hopes up. But that's why everybody's been crawling up and down the board walk. Of course, the guy who found it had a metal detector. That made it easier. But all they knew was it was a necklace with two gold rings somewhere between here and city hall."

Alice looked over Charlie's shoulder toward the sidewalk. There were plenty of strange people walking around. A man with a leather facemask and a studded breastplate held hands with a woman in a long, purple dress. Two women passed by wearing tiny shorts and knee high boots, their leather corsets laced up tight. But none of them were searching through the grass anymore on their hands and knees.

"What was the prize?" Alice's voice sounded muffled to her own ears.

"Early access to the newest game, some bonus equipment and a map to where all the rare-spawn items are." Charlie went on when she saw Alice's expression. "Like flying dragons and special gear and... It's hard to explain. People go crazy looking for that stuff. And if you have it, you're totally famous. Everybody wants to know where you found it. You can't buy them. You just have to play and hope you get lucky."

You can't buy them. The words echoed in Alice's heart. She'd accused Paul of trying to buy everyone around him, of using his money to make people like him. He could have offered a reward for her rings, but instead he used what he knew would bring more attention.

"Are you going to the opening?" Alice asked.

"Sure," she said. "I think everybody is. Well, except you, probably. I've been working on my costume all week."

Alice swallowed hard. "What if I wanted to go? Would you help me fix up a costume?"

Charlie's eyes went wide and then she laughed out loud. "I sure would, Miss Alice, but we better get started right away."

"Let me just lock up," Alice said, moving toward the front door.

"Right in the middle of a Friday?"

She flipped the welcome sign and turned the lock on the front door. "It's the ScreenStop grand opening. I don't think I should miss it."

Alice barely heard Charlie's chatter as she rushed to the stairs, hoping there was something in Alice's closet they could use. She followed behind, thinking of how she was acting on faith that Paul would even want to see her.

She used to roll her eyes when people would say they received some kind of divine message from God. She was a believer, no doubt about that, but she thought people sometimes looked for signs where there weren't any. But maybe it was like that famous quote and you "knew it when you saw it." Well, Alice knew it. She got it. These past weeks had shined a light on the dark places in her soul. And as selfish and petty as she'd been, there was only one thing to do: ask forgiveness and vow to do better.

Whatever happened between her and Paul tonight, Alice knew she had a chance to change for the better. And that was something money couldn't buy.

Chapter Twenty-Seven

Technology is the knack of so arranging the world that we don't have to experience it.—Max Frisch

The bass thump of the techno music seemed to be burrowing deep into Paul's brain. He massaged one temple and tried to smile as he passed a group of screaming gamers lined up at the door. "Mr. Olivier! Mr. Olivier! Paul!" He reached out and shook a few hands, feeling the unnerving tug of many hands grabbing him closer.

Andy played bad cop and pulled him toward the door, not sparing a glance for the disappointed fans who waved posters and games.

"Popular as ever," Andy said as they got through the front door.

Paul shrugged. He'd never loved this part of the opening. He liked a party, but much smaller and a lot less noise. "Everything's on schedule. Jared Darren flew in a few hours ago. He should walk on to perform right at midnight. We'll open the doors in ten minutes."

They'd been at the store all day, meeting with performers and directing the setup of the stage and displays. They had a great team in place, plus the two they'd flown in from Houston. But both he and Andy liked to be hands-on before the openings. *If you want it done right, do it yourself* they said. Usually the excitement was like a quadruple espresso shot, keeping him awake through the night.

Andy put a hand on his shoulder. "Let's get this done and then we'll get out of here. Straight to the jet."

Paul nodded. "Sounds good to me." The words didn't set well and his stomach twisted with thc lie. No part of that sounded good, but he didn't really have any reason to stay in Natchitoches. He'd teased Andy about spending a month on the river and making a Southern boy out of him, but he couldn't imagine running into Alice again and again. He didn't want to go back to New York City and live as if he'd never met her, never fallen in love with her, but he didn't have a lot of choice.

***

"Alice?"

She turned at the sound of her name and saw Mrs. Olivier walking down the sidewalk. Paul's mother gave her a long look, then turned to Charlie. "You must be Aalyea, the dragon queen."

Charlie flipped her blond braid over her shoulder and beamed. "Yes! It took me all week to sew this dress." The shimmery silver gown crossed in front and then tied around the back, the skirt falling straight to the ground. Alice thought she looked more like a Greek goddess than a dragon queen, but then again, she'd never seen either one.

"And who are you cosplaying, Alice?"

She cleared her throat. "Elizabeth Barrett Browning." She smoothed down the brown folds of her gown and straightened her lace cuffs. Charlie had borrowed a black velvet coat with lots of small, brass buttons from a friend who'd been the Headless Horseman one Halloween. It was snug on her, but over the brown dress, she did look quite a bit like a nineteenth century poetess. It took a while to get the hairdo right, parted in the middle, combed flat, and falling in ringlets. It wasn't particularly flattering, but Alice thought it had to be better than an orc costume.

Charlie rolled her eyes. "I tried to explain to her that you're supposed to dress like someone from the game, some character."

Mrs. Olivia looked at Alice for a long time, the smile that touched her lips growing wider and wider. "Do you have plans for tonight, Alice?"

She shook her head. "I don't know. I want to— I'm not sure how—"

Taking her hand, Mrs. Olivier nodded. "I understand. Let's see what we can come up with together." And she led them down the sidewalk, joining the packed crowds that surrounded the store. Alice glimpsed Mayor Cointreau getting out of his car.

"Hi, Mrs. Olivier," a man said, standing at the end of the line, dressed in the black pants and ScreenStop T-shirt uniform of one of the security crew.

"Could you walk us inside?" She grabbed onto Charlie and Alice. "Hold on, girls. We're going around the line."

Charlie let out a squeal of glee and Alice glanced around. They were already attracting attention as they jumped forward, the security guard ushering them beyond the ropes. There was a bright red ribbon stretching across the front of the store, just waiting for Paul and Andy to cut it.

"Must be performing."

"Weirdest costume ever."

"Who *is* that?"

"I think it's Lady Gaga! She wears crazy stuff. Remember that meat dress?"

Alice tried to get Mrs. Olivier's attention. "I don't want special treatment. I just wanted..."

"To see Paul? We're going to have to come up with something to get his attention. These things are a real madhouse." Mrs. Olivier laughed over her shoulder as they moved to the side of the building. The security guard flashed a badge, and two men waved them through the open, double doors leading into the main area of the store.

"You don't mind missing the ribbon-cutting, right? We've got to get you set up somewhere." Mrs. Olivier glanced around.

"Set up?" Alice swallowed the lump in her throat. "I'm not trying to ambush him. I just thought it would be nice if I came to the party." She scanned the room, sure that Paul was going to be only a few feet away. The interior looked like something from a movie. The lights were dimmed, except for spotlights shining on stacks of equipment around the perimeter. There was a stage set up in the middle of the store. Glass and steel gleamed with the reflection of multi-colored laser beams roaming the space above the first floor. There were black-shirted workers standing at the ready, their stations marked by red and black balloons.

"Of course, dear." Mrs. Olivier squinted toward a counter. "I think you need to be a shopper who needs help. I'll tell him it's a friend of mine."

"Mrs. Olivier, please." Alice felt panic grip her. "I don't want to lie to him just to get him to talk to me."

She turned, reaching out for Alice's hand. "Honey, nothing I said there was a lie." She gave Alice a quick kiss and pointed her toward a display of electronics. "You stand right here until the hullabaloo dies down."

And then she was gone, leaving Alice and Charlie parked in the corner of the store. Alice felt sweat bead on her forehead and she swiped a sleeve over her face. This had been a really bad idea, and she'd only made it worse with her choice of outfit. Now that Paul's mother was involved, her fate was sealed.

"Miss Alice, I'm gonna go get a game and stand near the check out. I can't believe we got to pass all those people." Charlie was already skipping toward a tower of games.

"Sure," she said, her voice hardly more than a whisper.

There was a roar from outside and Alice jumped. The ribbon cutting had started. Any moment now, Paul would come inside and see her standing there, a nineteenth-century poet in the land of dragon-riding queens.

The front doors opened and a stream of people flooded in, the noise level rising to deafening levels. Alice didn't see Paul come in and soon she was surrounded by people, most of whom were wearing some sort of armor. She pressed back against the wall and tried to stay out of the way.

"Here he comes!"

"Wait, I have to get my phone."

"Can you sign my arm?"

Alice looked up to see Paul moving toward her, a group of people surrounding him like he was some kind of rock star. His expression was pleasant and he stopped for what seemed like an endless stream of selfies. Pretty girls wrapped their arms around his waist and beamed into the camera. Alice watched him, feeling as if she was observing someone she'd never met and certainly never considered a friend.

"Ok, guys. I've got to help someone so give me five minutes." He was moving away from the crowd. "I'll be right back."

They let out a collective sigh and dispersed, leaving Paul to finally reach the counter. The smile was gone from his face. His mouth looked tight, although his voice was cheerful enough. "Hey, Tina, my mother said there was a friend of hers here who needed some help?"

The dark-haired girl behind the counter shook her head. "She didn't tell me anything. I've been standing right here."

Paul frowned and patted his pocket. "I could try to call her but she almost never answers." He sighed. "Well, if you hear anything, will you—"

Alice stepped out from the shadows. For a moment, Paul's expression was blank as he took in her costume, from the black boots to the parted hair. One side of his mouth lifted.

She cleared her throat. "I was thinking of buying one of these." She pointed to an e-reader. "I hear there are some really good books you can only get in digital."

He didn't say anything for a moment, just looked her up and down. His smile stretched wider until he was grinning. "Miss Browning?"

Alice laughed, nodding. "Charlie tried to give me some kind of weapon but I told her if I got to dress up, I wanted to be someone I really admire." The smile faded from her face. "Paul, I know this isn't really the time or the place—"

He stepped closer and took her hands in his. "It's just the right time." He glanced around. "And a pretty nice place, if I say so myself."

She snorted. "Rub it in."

They smiled at each other for a moment and then Paul reached into his jacket pocket over his heart. "I was going to have Charlie bring this to you, but since you're here…." He held out a small envelope. "I put them on another chain."

Alice took it, opening the flap. She withdrew the necklace, feeling the warmth in the gold where they had rested against Paul's chest. Her parents' wedding rings sparkled in the light, a permanent reminder of the love they'd shared, the love that had brought her into being. But ever after, the rings would also be a sign of one man's generosity.

"Let me put it on you," he said, taking the necklace back. She turned, letting him fasten it around her neck. She put up a hand, her throat tight with the knowledge that something irreplaceable had been returned to her.

She turned back to him. "I don't know where to start."

"Skip to the end," he said, smiling. "We can talk about the middle parts later."

Alice swallowed hard. Words ran through her mind. Poems, quotes, famous lines. Nothing fit. Finally, she stepped forward and kissed him. It was a short kiss, just the barest touch. "I'm sorry," she whispered. "*Again.*"

"And I accept, again." He said, leaning his head down to hers. "I'm so far from perfect, Alice. The next time, I'll be the one apologizing. I can promise you that."

The next time. Alice closed her eyes against sudden tears. She felt his arm reach around her waist and pull her close. Their first kiss bore the freshness and innocence two people who had barely met. The second kiss bore the passion of two people who refusing to give an inch, not able to find that middle ground. This one carried the weight of the days that had passed. It spoke of misunderstandings and mistakes, of hard choices and bad decisions, of anger and heart ache and forgiveness. And most of all, it spoke of hope for all the days ahead.

Alice leaned against him, unable to believe that it had been that simple. The help of a few good friends, a simple apology, and he was there in her arms. She closed her eyes against the flashing strobe lights and the noise of the crowd. Even here, in this place, she felt at peace. Her heart had finally found a shelter 'out of the swing of the sea'.

Epilogue

Whoever says
To a loyal woman, "Love and work with me,"
Will get fair answers, if the work and love
Being good themselves, are good for her–the best
She was born for

I, too, have my vocation, –work to do,
The heavens and earth have set me, —
Most serious work, most necessary work,
As any of the economists'."
— Aurora Leigh, *Elizabeth Barrett Browning*

"I don't see why I have to dress up. I think a hat and a jacket are enough." Alice frowned at Charlie as the girl fussed with Alice's hair.

"I want to get some pictures and I want you to look cute," Charlie said. She caught Alice's look. "Cuter, I mean."

"You have tons of photos of me." Alice sighed. "I love the Christmas light festival, but I was really hoping Paul could be here." She held up a hand. "I know he's busy running a big company. That fact doesn't escape me."

"Well, there's always next year," Charlie said. "And doesn't New York have some great parades? You guys can go see something up there."

Alice nodded, unconvinced. It seemed everybody loved New York City but her. It was so crowded, so noisy. "It's the festival's eighty-seventh year, and I just thought it would be so romantic. It took Bix and me all day Friday to put up our lights. I think our building is the nicest."

Charlie finished Alice's French chignon and stepped back to admire her work. "You're ready." She put her hands together and Alice was alarmed to see tears in her eyes.

"Are you okay?" She stood up from the chair. "Did something happen? I know I've been preoccupied with Paul and then I left for that week last month. Is it school? Are you worried about starting college?"

"No, no!" Charlie shook her head. "None of that. And we're going to be late. Bix and Ruby are holding our seats for the parade."

Alice frowned as Charlie bolted from the bathroom. She'd been acting strange all week and Alice was worried. Maybe she should reach out to Charlie's parents and see if they knew anything.

A few minutes later they were headed down the boardwalk. The river reflected the bright colors that draped the buildings all along the waterfront. Long boats floated lazily up and down, their sides and beams strung with twinkle lights. Alice inhaled the chill air of a December in Cane River and she smiled. It was almost perfect. If only Paul— No. She was going to enjoy this night and focus on the people here with her at the moment. She put a hand to her necklace, feeling the warmth of the rings against her palm.

"There they are," Charlie said, pointing out a familiar straw hat and army-green coat. Bix waved from a chair near the end of the block. Ruby beamed beside him.

"*Donne moi un p'tit bec.*" Ruby stood up and planted a kiss on her cheek.

Alice started to reply but Charlie stepped in and wiped the lipstick from her cheek. Alice shot her a confused look.

"Pictures," Charlie said, waving her camera.

"How's your new grandbaby doing, Ruby? How old is he now?" Alice asked.

"Oh, he's real fine. And let's see. He's not old enough to eat Popeye's but he can suck on a biscuit."

She grinned. She could see why Bix got such a kick out of Ruby. They were one of those couples that reminded you true love existed. Her mind went back to Paul and she tried not to sigh. She was as bad as Charlie had been the year she'd been struck with unrequited love for the school quarterback. Paul certainly loved her back, but he wasn't here. Christmas was a time for family, and she missed him so much she ached with it.

"*Bonswe*, Alice."

For a moment, she thought she'd imagined that voice. She turned, eyes opening wide. The next moment she'd launched herself into Paul's arms.

He hugged her tight, laughing into her hair. "Surprise!"

She leaned back and socked him a few times in the shoulder. "I hate surprises."

"Even this one?" he asked, and knelt down.

Alice felt the world stop around her. Charlie had her camera up, trying to take shots while wiping her eyes.

"I love you, Alice, probably from the moment you asked me about the books on my shelf. Definitely from the moment you refused to sell me a book even though you had a whole store of them." His voice was rough. He held out a small box, a ring glinted in the darkness. "Love and work with me, Alice?"

She looked from him to the ring and back. His words slowly filtered through the shock and she laughed out loud. "Oh, you couldn't just ask me to marry you the normal way, could you? And Aurora Leigh turns Romney down in that poem, you know."

"Elizabeth Barrett Browning always says it better. And I figured I'd take my chances." He was grinning. He knew her answer before she spoke.

"Yes," she whispered, trying hard to make herself heard. "I'll love and work with you."

Bix and Ruby let out a cheer, and Charlie almost dropped her camera as she clapped. The tourists around them turned to look and soon they were surrounded by a crowd of well-wishers. Alice didn't recognize a single face, but they were all celebrating with the two of them as they stepped out in faith.

He stood up, gathering her close. She felt her parents' rings against her chest, warmed between them, a connection that was broken and then repaired by grace and generosity.

Paul leaned back, took the ring from the box and reached for her hand. "The heavens and the earth have set you a most serious work, a most necessary work," he said, quoting another line of the poem. Alice nodded, her throat tightening with the words. Aurora Leigh believed she had work to do and Alice believed it, too. Keeping By the Book open to the people of Cane River was important and Paul saw it as clearly as Alice did.

"But the real question is whether you're willing to share shelf space. You know our books might not get along," he said, his mouthing tilting up.

Alice looked down at the round ruby inset into gold, and smiled as he slid it onto her finger. "I think the answer might be separate book cases." She leaned back, looking him in the eye. "Paul, are you really sure? We've had such a rocky start."

"You put the pepper in the gumbo, Alice. I wouldn't give you up for anything in the world," he said, laughing. He kissed her cheeks, her eyes, her hair.

She closed her eyes, reveling in that perfect moment. Paul whispered something in her ear, familiar words from the language of her childhood, words that she didn't quite catch but that her heart understood all the same. It seemed impossible that his love had been waiting for her all those years, and one day she'd woken up, and he was there, the way it was always meant to be.

Acknowledgements
I'd like to give special thanks to people who generously offered their expertise in several areas. All errors are my own, especially any confusion caused by Paul's grand prize that I created just for the story line. To John Abramowitz for gaming terminology and etiquette, and legal terminology. To Janelle Leonard for reading the first chapter when it was just a dim idea of a plot. To Michael J. Frazier for gaming and technology information. To Dennis Carmichael for insight into business and programming, including the dynamic of boards and appointed officers. To Jessica L. Baldwin for cosplay terminology. To Christalee Scott May for her advice on Southern food and culture, for helping me decide whether Converse was ever plural, for pointing out that my heroine's eyes changed color every few chapters and for cheerfully suffering through several very rough drafts of this book. To Sandra Bell Calhoune for her constant encouragement in all things book related and her fabulous sense of humor. To my daughters Isabel and Ana for being the beta readers who never gave up, helping me bring this book to completion. And to all my children, for reminding me that moments spent running around the park or watching a few episodes of *Arrow* are good for the writerly brain.

Dear Reader,

Thank you for reading the first book in my new series, *Cane River Romance*. I hope you enjoyed reading it as much as I enjoyed writing it!

Every writer finds herself penning a story that involves a bit of wish fulfillment and this is that book for me. I've always wanted to run a rare book store, have a whole herd of cats, and live without technology interfering in my daily life. I also adore anything from the nineteen-forties and fifties, wish I had the tiny waist to wear those shirtdresses and the ankles to walk in high heels. It was pure fun to write this character.

If you enjoyed this story, be sure to leave a review on Amazon or Goodreads. I love visiting with readers on my author page of *Pride, Prejudice and Cheese Grits*, or on my blog at The Things That Last!

BIOGRAPHY

Mary Jane Hathaway is an award-nominated writer of Christian fiction and a home schooling mom of six young children who rarely wear shoes. She holds degrees in Linguistics and Religious Studies from the University of Oregon and lives with her habanero-eating husband, Crusberto, who is her polar opposite in all things except faith. They've learned to speak in short-hand code and look forward to the day they can actually finish a sentence. In the meantime, she thanks God for the laughter and abundance of hugs that fill her day as she plots her next book. She also writes under the pen name of Virginia Carmichael.

OTHER TITLES by Mary Jane Hathaway

Pride, Prejudice and Cheese Grits
Emma, Mr. Knightley and Chili-Slaw Dogs
Persuasion, Captain Wentworth and Cracklin' Cornbread

OTHER TITLES by Virginia Carmichael

All The Blue of Heaven
Purple Like the West
Leaving Liberty
Season of Joy
Season of Hope
A Home for her Family

Novels, illustrators, poetry, and poets which play a role in this story:

Indeed, there is an Arthur Rackham illustrated portfolio of *Peter Pan in Kensington Gardens* that can be had for the low, low sum of sixty thousand dollars. Most of the books mentioned(*Mother Carey's Chickens, The Dukes' Secret, Tom the Telephone Boy, Beau Geste, Pride and Prejudice, North and South*, and *Jane Eyre*) are books I read in childhood and which occupy a spot on my shelf today. The poets (George MacDonald, Alexander Pope, Elizabeth Barrett Browning, Gerard Manley Hopkins, Sara Teasdale, Christina Rossetti, and Percy Bysshe Shelley) are some of my favorites. I return to them again and again throughout the year, marking the seasons with treasured lines.

Sometimes Paul and Alice refer to their favorite poets by their initials and EBB in the story is Elizabeth Barrett Browning.

Movie references

You've Got Mail, with Meg Ryan and Tom Hanks
Casablanca
Breakfast at Tiffany's
Parfumerie
Twelve Years a Slave

Louisiana Creole glossary

According to the last census, a quarter of a million people speak French in the home in Louisiana. Most of these speakers use Cajun French, Louisiana Creole, or Creole French. These dialects are similar, but distinct. The Creole people of the Natchitoches region speak Louisiana Creole and that is the dialect that appears in the story.
Sha = dear, sweetie
Merci (spelled a variety of ways) = thank you
Misye = monsieur, sir

Manzelle = mademoiselle, miss
Bonswe = good evening
Donne moi un p'tit bec = give me a kiss
Mais = well

Recipes

Natchitoches Meat Pies

I know this recipe has about a gazillion steps but it's worth the time and effort! It's a long list of ingredients, but they're ones you probably already have and you need every one, so don't skip any. (Except maybe the jalapeño. People argue about that one. I included it here because more people say it should be in there, than it should be out. I personally don't care for jalapeños, so I leave them out. If you need it a little hotter, adjust the Louisiana hot sauce to maybe 2 tsp instead of just the one.)

Ingredients

- 1 tablespoon vegetable oil
- 1 pound ground beef
- 1 tablespoon salt
- 1 teaspoon paprika
- 1/2 teaspoon cayenne pepper
- 1/2 teaspoon chili powder
- 1/2 teaspoon ground cumin
- 1/2 teaspoon black pepper
- 4 small tomatoes, diced
- 1 green bell pepper, finely chopped
- 1 medium jalapeño pepper, finely chopped (optional)
- 1 small yellow onion, finely chopped
- 5 bay leaves
- 1 teaspoon thyme
- 1/2 teaspoon Worcestershire sauce
- 1 teaspoon Louisiana hot sauce or similar
- 2 tablespoons all-purpose flour

- 2 tablespoons water
- ½ cup sliced green onions
- Pie dough, chilled (You can make it from a mix, or use the frozen pie dough, but store-bought pie crust doesn't fry as well as the home made. Just a heads up!)
- 1 large egg, lightly beaten
- Vegetable oil, for frying

1. Combine the meat, salt, paprika, cayenne, chili powder, cumin, and black pepper in a large skillet (even better if it's cast iron!). Cook the meat over medium-high heat until it is lightly browned and all the ingredients are combined.
2. Throw in the chopped tomatoes, onion, bell pepper, jalapeño. Stir well. Add in the bay leaves, thyme, and Worcestershire sauce. Cook for an additional 10 minutes or so, until the veggies have gone soft and the liquid starts to evaporate. Take out the bay leaves and throw them away. Sprinkle the flour over the meat and add the water. Stir it all together. Adding the flour keeps the mix from getting too runny while it cooks in the pie dough. Add in the green onions and hot sauce, mix well. (Nobody wants all the hot sauce in one pie.) Pour the meat mixture into a bowl or pan to cool on the counter for about 20 minutes. (Make sure you cover it if you have cats like I do. My first batch went to the kitties. Apparently, they don't mind Louisiana hot sauce at all.) Then put it in the fridge until completely cooled. This will make it easier to work with and you can store it covered, up to a day.
3. Roll out the dough to about 1/8 of an inch thick. Then, using a 4-inch biscuit cutter, cut the

dough into circles. Beat the large egg. Brush the outer edges of each circle with beaten egg. Place 2 1/2 tablespoons of filling into the center. Fold the circle over the filling to make a half circle. Press the edges closed with a fork and place onto a baking sheet.

The pies fry up better if you keep the dough nice and chilled, so when a sheet is filled, pop it into the fridge to keep it firm. When you're ready to fry, you can bring them out one sheet at a time.

I love using a Fry Daddy or Fry Baby, but you can always fry the meat pies in a cast iron skillet or Dutch oven. Use a candy thermometer to check when about 2- 3 inches of vegetable oil reaches 350° F. Fry them four or five at a time, until golden brown. Remove from the oil and set on a plate covered with several paper towels, to soak up the excess oil. Let them cool for several minutes and enjoy!

Gumbo

This recipe takes a lot of time, stirring, and watching the pot. But it's absolutely worth it. If you've never had home-made gumbo, you've just never had gumbo!

Ingredients

- 1 cup all-purpose flour
- 3/4 cup bacon drippings
- 1 large green bell pepper, chopped
- 1 cup chopped celery, about three stalks
- 1 large onion, chopped
- 2 cloves garlic, minced
- 1 pound good sausage, like Andouille sausage, sliced
- 3 quarts beef stock
- 1 tablespoon white sugar
- salt to taste

- 2 tablespoons Louisiana hot sauce or to taste (I usually cut this to one tablespoon, because I'm a weenie)
- 1/2 teaspoon Cajun seasoning blend (see below for a homemade blend)
- 5 bay leaves
- 1/2 teaspoon dried thyme
- 1 (14.5 ounce) can whole stewed tomatoes
- 1 (6 ounce) can tomato sauce
- 2 teaspoons gumbo file powder (you can order this online)
- 2 tablespoons bacon drippings (I know we already have bacon drippings, but this is for another step. Yay for lard! Seriously, you can substitute olive oil.)
- 2 (10 ounce) packages frozen cut okra, thawed
- 2 1/2 tablespoons distilled white vinegar
- 1 pound crabmeat
- 3 pounds uncooked medium shrimp, peeled and deveined
- 2 tablespoons Worcestershire sauce
- 2 teaspoons gumbo file powder

Creole seasoning

There are lots of recipes for Creole seasoning but I like this one from Emeril Lagasse. I adjusted it a little because I like more garlic powder!

- 2 tablespoons paprika
- 2 tablespoons salt
- 2 1/2 tablespoons garlic powder
- 1 tablespoon black pepper
- 1 tablespoon onion powder
- 1 tablespoon cayenne pepper
- 1 tablespoon dried oregano
- 1 tablespoon dried thyme

Directions

1. Whisk the flour and 3/4 cup bacon drippings together in a large, heavy saucepan (like cast iron) over medium-low heat until it's smooth. This is your roux and it's the basis of much of Creole cooking. Whisk constantly, until it turns to a rich, mahogany brown color. This takes about twenty minutes and if you don't watch, it will burn. I always set one of my kids on this step so I can keep chopping ingredients. After it browns, take it from the heat and keep whisking until it's cooled or it will burn even after you've removed it from the stove. The joy of cast iron pans!
2. Finely chop the celery, onion, green bell pepper, and garlic. Stir the vegetables and sausage into the roux. Bring the mixture to a simmer, and cook until vegetables are translucent and tender, about 10 to 15 minutes. Set to the side.
3. Bring the beef stock to a boil in a large soup pot. Make sure you have enough room for what you're going to add in, so a nice tall pot will do. Slowly whisk the roux mixture into the boiling water. Mix in the sugar, salt, hot pepper sauce, Cajun seasoning, bay leaves, thyme, tomatoes, and tomato sauce. Lower the heat to a simmer. Let it simmer for one hour. Mix in 2 teaspoons of file gumbo powder about half way through that hour.
4. Melt the 2 tablespoons of bacon drippings (or olive oil) in your pan. Cook the okra with vinegar over medium heat for about 15 minutes. Add the okra to the gumbo, leaving the drippings in the pan. Mix in the crabmeat, shrimp, and Worcestershire sauce. Simmer until flavors have blended, about another hour. Stir in 2 more teaspoons of file gumbo powder about ten minutes before serving. Enjoy!